*Praise for Kevin Kwan's*

# CHINA RICH GIRLFRIEND

"As frothy as the egg whites on the sort of cocktail you should drink while reading Kwan's books. . . . Highly entertaining."
—*The Washington Post*

"A crazy parade through the lives of the aspirational elite."
—*Los Angeles Times*

"The equivalent of a Bubble Tea concoction laced with Henry James extracts and Jackie Collins sprinkles. . . . In the same way that Edith Wharton catalogued the Gilded Age via novels like *The Age of Innocence*, Kwan—in his novels—is doing his bit for a China that now has the second-highest number of millionaires in the world."
—*The Daily Beast*

"A taste of Asian opulence served with skewering humor."
—*Daily News*

"Kwan's characters are powerful and attractive, living in the lap of luxury."
—*All Things Considered*, NPR

"Very enjoyable. . . . Just as funny as *Crazy Rich Asians*, this globe-spanning tale of excess includes enough snootiness and class snobbery to fill a multitude of designer handbags."
—*Star Tribune* (Minneapolis)

"An equally good-natured, catty-as-hell sequel. . . . Part Oscar Wilde, part Judith Krantz, part Arthur Frommer. . . . Hilarious. . . . Over-the-top and hard to stop."
—*Kirkus Reviews*

"*China Rich Girlfriend* is the most fun I've had reading a book in quite some time. . . . A jam-packed, lively story."
—Amy Scribner, *BookPage*

"A heady taste of vicarious escapism. . . . Read *China Rich Girlfriend* for the exuberant spectacle of zippy vintage cars, gossipy matriarchs-who-lunch and reckless profligacy but read it also for its very engaging narrative about people like us."
—Thuy On, *The Sydney Morning Herald*

"[An] amusing, whirlwind novel."　　　　—*The Miami Herald*

"Like *Gossip Girl* and *Dynasty* and the royal family of England all at the same time. Kwan's characters behave hideously—and it's hilarious."　　　　—Elaine "Lainey" Lui, *Flare*

"Will have readers clamoring for more."
—*Library Journal* (starred review)

"An engaging page-turner with a multi-layered, inventive narrative. Kwan has clearly taken a few lessons from one of America's great social satirists—think Tom Wolfe set loose on the wealthiest enclaves of Confucian Asia."
—*South China Morning Post*

KEVIN KWAN

# CHINA RICH GIRLFRIEND

Kevin Kwan is the author of *Crazy Rich Asians*, the international bestseller now being adapted as a major motion picture. Born and raised in Singapore, Kwan has called Manhattan home for the past two decades but still craves pineapple tarts and a decent plate of Hokkien mee.

www.kevinkwanbooks.com

# CHINA RICH GIRLFRIEND

# CHINA RICH
# GIRLFRIEND

A NOVEL

# KEVIN KWAN

ANCHOR BOOKS

A DIVISION OF PENGUIN RANDOM HOUSE LLC

NEW YORK

FIRST ANCHOR BOOKS EDITION, MAY 2016

*Copyright © 2015 by Kevin Kwan*

All rights reserved. Published in the United States by Anchor Books,
a division of Penguin Random House LLC, New York. Originally
published in hardcover by Doubleday, a division of Penguin Random
House LLC, New York, in 2015.

Anchor Books and colophon are registered trademarks of
Penguin Random House LLC.

The Library of Congress has cataloged the Doubleday edition as follows:
Kwan, Kevin.
China rich girlfriend : a novel / Kevin Kwan.—First edition.
pages ; cm
1. Fiancées—Fiction.    2. Rich people—China—Shanghai—Fiction.
3. Socialites—Singapore—Fiction.    I. Title.
PS3611.W36 C48 2015    813'.6—DC23    2015003996

**Anchor Books Trade Paperback ISBN: 978-0-8041-7206-6**
**eBook ISBN: 978-0-385-53909-8**

www.anchorbooks.com

Printed in the United States of America
20 19 18 17 16

*For my brothers and my cousins*

# EVERYBODY WHO'S ANYBODY IN
## CRAZY RICH ASIANS

NICHOLAS YOUNG—NYU history professor and heir to one of the largest fortunes in Asia. He innocently took his girlfriend to Singapore for his best friend's wedding, not realizing how it was going to ruin her life. Now they live together in Manhattan, despite the wishes of his mother and grandmother.

RACHEL CHU—An American-born-Chinese ("ABC") economics professor who is now the envy of every eligible woman in Singapore because of her relationship with Nicholas.

ELEANOR YOUNG—Nicholas's estranged mother, who could devour Tiger Moms for lunch. She divides her time between Sydney and Singapore.

SHANG SU YI—Nicholas's imperious grandmother. The matriarch of the Shang and Young clans, she lives at her palatial Singapore estate, Tyersall Park, and refuses to forgive Nicholas for defying her wishes about whom he should marry.

**ASTRID LEONG**—Nicholas's ravishingly beautiful and faultlessly elegant cousin. A "double heiress" destined to inherit from both sides of her aristocratic family, she lives in Singapore with her tech-titan husband, Michael Teo, and son, Cassian.

**EDISON CHENG**—The maniacally snobbish Hong Kong cousin of Nicholas Young and Astrid Leong. With a personality not even a mother could love, Eddie works in private banking but really spends more time getting fitted for custom suits at his tailor's.

**OLIVER T'SIEN**—An art and antiquities historian whose real expertise is knowing all the gossip on Asia's most important families. Naturally, he's also Nicholas's cousin.

**KITTY PONG**—The former Hong Kong soap-opera star who broke up with Alistair Cheng and took off to Las Vegas to get married to Bernard Tai, the boorish playboy son of tycoon *Dato'* Tai Toh Lui.

**CHARLIE WU**—Astrid Leong's first love and ex-fiancé, a Hong Kong–based tech billionaire.

**GOH PEIK LIN**—Rachel Chu's best friend from college. Daughter of a very wealthy Singapore real estate family, she had no idea there were families even richer than hers.

LONDON, 8 SEPTEMBER 2012, 9:00 A.M. GMT

*A red Ferrari 458 Italia crashed through the window of the Jimmy Choo shoe boutique on Sloane Street sometime between 4:00 a.m. and 4:30 a.m. last night. No one witnessed the accident. Metropolitan Police reported that two passengers were taken to St Mary's Paddington, where they are being treated for serious but noncritical injuries. The vehicle owner's name was not released pending further investigation.*

—SARAH LYRE, *The London Chronicle*

CHINA RICH GIRLFRIEND

# BEIJING CAPITAL INTERNATIONAL AIRPORT

SEPTEMBER 9, 2012, 7:45 P.M.

"Wait a minute—I'm in first class. Take me to first class," Edison Cheng said contemptuously to the flight attendant escorting him to his seat.

"This *is* first class, Mr. Cheng," the man in the crisp navy uniform informed him.

"But where are the cabins?" Eddie asked, still confused.

"Mr. Cheng, I'm afraid British Airways does not have private cabins in first class.* But if you'd allow me to show you some of the special features of your seat—"

"No, no, that's fine." Eddie tossed his ostrich leather briefcase onto the seat like a petulant schoolboy. *Fucky fuck—the sacrifices I have to make for the bank today!* Edison Cheng, the pampered "Prince of Private Bankers"—famous in Hong Kong society pages for his bon vivant lifestyle, his dapper wardrobe, his elegant wife (Fiona), his photogenic children, and his superb lineage (his mother is Alexandra Young, of

---

* Unfortunately for Eddie, only Emirates, Etihad Airways, and Singapore Airlines have private cabins aboard their Airbus A380s. Emirates even has two Shower Spa bathrooms with sumptuous shower stalls for first-class travelers. (Mile High Club members take note.)

the Singapore Youngs)—was unaccustomed to such inconveniences. Five hours ago he had been interrupted during a luncheon at the Hong Kong Club, rushed aboard the company jet bound for Beijing, and then hustled onto this flight to London. It had been years since he had suffered the indignity of flying *commercial*, but Mrs. Bao was on this godforsaken plane, and Mrs. Bao needed to be accommodated.

But where exactly was the lady? Eddie expected to find her seated nearby, but the chief purser informed him that there was no such person by that name in the cabin.

"No, no, she's supposed to be here. Can you check the flight manifest or something?" Eddie demanded.

Minutes later, Eddie found himself being led to row 37, seat E of the aircraft—economy class—where a petite woman in a white vicuña turtleneck and gray flannel slacks sat sandwiched between two passengers.

"Mrs. Bao? Bao Shaoyen?" Eddie inquired in Mandarin.

The woman looked up and smiled wanly. "Are you Mr. Cheng?"

"Yes. So glad to meet you, but I'm sorry we had to meet like this." Eddie smiled in relief. He had spent the past eight years managing the Bao family's offshore accounts, but they were such a secretive lot, he had never met any of them until today. Even though she looked rather tired at the moment, Bao Shaoyen was much prettier than he had imagined. With alabaster skin, large eyes that slanted upward at the edges, and high cheekbones accentuated by the way she wore her jet-black hair—pulled into a tight, low ponytail—she did not look old enough to have a son in grad school.

"Why are you seated here? Was there some mix-up?" Eddie asked urgently.

"No, I always fly economy class," Mrs. Bao replied.

Eddie couldn't hide his look of surprise. Mrs. Bao's husband, Bao Gaoliang, was one of Beijing's top politicians, and

what's more, he had inherited one of China's biggest pharmaceutical firms. The Baos weren't just one of his regular clients;
they were his ultra-high-net-worth clients.

"Only my son flies first class," Bao Shaoyen explained,
catching Eddie's look. "Carlton can eat all the fancy Western food and, being a student under so much pressure, he
needs all the rest he can get. But for me, it's not worth it. I
don't touch airplane food, and I can never sleep on these long
flights anyway."

Eddie had to resist the urge to roll his eyes. *Typical Mainlanders!* They lavished every penny on their Little Emperor
and suffered in silence. Well, look where that got them.
Twenty-three-year-old Carlton Bao was supposed to be at
Cambridge finishing his master's dissertation, but had instead
spent the previous evening doing his best Prince Harry
impersonation—running up a £38,000 bar tab at half a dozen
London nightspots, wrecking his brand-new Ferrari, destroying public property, and almost getting himself killed. And
that wasn't even the worst of it. The worst of it Eddie had
been explicitly instructed not to reveal to Bao Shaoyen.

Eddie faced a conundrum. He urgently needed to go
over the plans with Mrs. Bao, but he would sooner endure
a colonoscopy than spend the next eleven hours slumming
it in *coach*. God in heaven, what if someone recognized him?
A picture of Edison Cheng crammed into an economy-class
seat would go viral within seconds. Yet Eddie grudgingly realized that it would be unseemly for one of his bank's most
important clients to remain here in steerage while he was up
front, stretched out on a flatbed recliner, sipping twenty-year-
old cognac. He eyed the spiky-haired youth slouching dangerously close to Mrs. Bao on one side, and the elderly woman
clipping her nails into the air sickness bag on her other side, a
solution springing to mind.

Lowering his voice, Eddie said, "Mrs. Bao, I would of

course be happy to join you in this cabin, but as there are some *highly confidential* matters we need to discuss, would you allow me to arrange a seat for you up front? I'm certain the bank would insist that I upgrade you to first class—at our expense, of course—and we will be able to talk much more *privately* there."

"Well, I suppose—if the bank insists," Bao Shaoyen replied a little hesitantly.

After takeoff, when aperitifs had been served and they were both comfortably ensconced in the sumptuous, pod-like seats facing each other, Eddie wasted no time updating his client.

"Mrs. Bao, I was in contact with London just before boarding. Your son has been stabilized. The surgery to repair his punctured spleen was completely successful, and now the orthopedic team can take over."

"Oh thank all the gods." Bao Shaoyen sighed, easing back in her seat for the first time.

"We've already lined up the top reconstructive plastic surgeon in London—Dr. Peter Ashley—and he will be in the operating room alongside the orthopedic team attending to your son."

"My poor boy," Bao Shaoyen said, her eyes getting moist.

"Your son was very lucky."

"And the British girl?"

"The girl is still in surgery. But I'm sure she will pull through just fine," Eddie said, putting on his peppiest smile.

· · ·

Barely thirty minutes earlier, Eddie had been on another plane parked in a private hangar at Beijing Capital International Airport, taking in the grim details during a hastily arranged crisis-management meeting with Mr. Tin, the gray-haired head of security for the Bao family, and Nigel Tomlinson, his bank's Asia chief. The two men had climbed aboard the Learjet as soon as it landed, huddling over Nigel's laptop while an associate in London gave the latest update via secure-feed videoconference.

"Carlton is out of surgery now. He was quite a bit banged up, but being in the driver's seat with his airbag and everything, he actually suffered the least injuries. But with the English girl, it's touch and go—she's still in a coma, and they've relieved the swelling in the brain, but that's all they can do for now."

"And the *other* girl?" Mr. Tin asked, squinting at the small pixilated pop-up window.

"We're told she died on impact."

Nigel sighed. "And she was Chinese?"

"We believe so, sir."

Eddie shook his head. "What a fucky, fucky mess. We need to track down the next of kin immediately, before they are contacted by the authorities."

"How do you even fit three people into a Ferrari?" Nigel asked.

Mr. Tin twirled his phone nervously on the lacquered walnut console. "Carlton Bao's father is on a state visit to Canada with the premier of China, and nothing must interrupt him. My orders from Mrs. Bao are that no hint of any scandal must ever reach his ears. He must never know about the dead girl. Do you understand? There is too much at stake—given his political position—and it is an especially sensitive time with the big once-in-a-decade changeover in party leadership happening right now."

"Of course, of course," Nigel assured him. "We will say that the *white* girl was his girlfriend. As far as the father is concerned, there was only *one* girl in the car."

"Why does Mr. Bao even need to know about the white girl? Don't worry, Mr. Tin. I have handled much worse dealing with some of those sheikhs' children," Eddie boasted.

Nigel shot Eddie a warning glare. The bank prided itself on the utmost discretion, and here was his associate blabbing away about other clients.

"We have a tactical response team in place in London that I am personally directing, and I can assure you we will do everything to contain this," Nigel said, before turning to Eddie. "How much do you think it will take to keep Fleet Street quiet?"

Eddie inhaled deeply, trying to do some quick calculations. "It's not just the press. The policemen, the ambulance drivers, the hospital staff, the families. There's going to be an assload of people to shut up. I would suggest ten million pounds for starters."

"Well, the minute you land in London, you need to take Mrs. Bao straight to the office. We need her to sign off on the withdrawal before you take her to the hospital to see her son. I'm just wondering what we should say if Mr. Bao asks us why we needed so much," Nigel pondered.

"Just say the girl needed some new organs," Mr. Tin suggested.

"We can also say we needed to pay the boutique," Eddie added. "Those Jimmy Choos are bloody pricey, you know."

## 2 HYDE PARK

LONDON, SEPTEMBER 10, 2012

Eleanor Young sipped on her morning tea, crafting her little white lie. She was holidaying in London with three of her closest friends—Lorena Lim, Nadine Shaw, and Daisy Foo—

and after two days of being with the ladies nonstop, she desperately needed a few hours on her own. The trip was a much-needed distraction for all of them—Lorena was recovering from a Botox allergy scare, Daisy had gotten into yet another fight with her daughter-in-law over the choice of kindergartens for her grandchildren, and Eleanor herself was depressed that her son, Nicky, had not spoken to her for more than two years. And Nadine—well, Nadine was appalled by the state of her daughter's brand-new apartment.

"*Alamaaaaaaak!* Fifty million dollars and I can't even flush the toilet!" Nadine screeched as she entered the breakfast room.

"What do you expect, when everything is so bloody high-tech?" Lorena laughed. "Did the toilet at least help you *suay kah-cherng?*"*

"No, *lah!* I waved and waved at all the stupid sensors but nothing happened!" Feeling defeated, Nadine plopped down into an ultramodern chair that appeared to be constructed out of a tangled pile of red velvet ropes.

"I don't want to criticize, but I think this apartment of your daughter's is not only hideously modern, it's hideously overpriced," Daisy commented between bites of toast topped with pork floss.

"*Aiyah,* she's paying for the name and the location, nothing more," Eleanor sniffed. "Personally, I would have chosen a unit with a nice view of Hyde Park, rather than the view facing Harvey Nichols."

"You know my Francesca, *lah!* She could care less about the park—she wants to fall asleep staring at her favorite department store! Thank God she finally married someone who can pay her overdraft." Nadine sighed.

The ladies kept quiet. Things hadn't been easy for Nadine

---

*   Hokkien for "wash your bottom."

ever since her father-in-law, Sir Ronald Shaw, woke up from a six-year coma and turned off the money spigot on his family's free spending. Her profligate daughter, Francesca (once voted one of the Fifty Best Dressed Women by *Singapore Tattle*), did not respond well to being put on a clothing budget, and decided that her best solution was to embark on a brazen affair with Roderick Liang (of the Liang Finance Group Liangs), who had only just married Lauren Lee. Singapore's social set was scandalized, and Lauren's grandmother, the formidable Mrs. Lee Yong Chien, retaliated by making sure every old-guard family in Southeast Asia shut their doors firmly on the Shaws and the Liangs. In the end, a severely chastened Roderick chose to crawl back to his wife rather than run off with Francesca.

Finding herself a social pariah, Francesca fled to England and quickly landed on her feet by marrying "some Iranian Jew with half a billion dollars."* Since moving into 2 Hyde Park, the obscenely expensive luxury condominium backed by the Qatari royal family, she was finally on speaking terms with her mother again. Naturally, this gave the ladies an excuse to visit the newlyweds, but of course they just wanted to check out the much-publicized apartment and, more important, have a free place to stay.†

As the women discussed the day's shopping agenda, Eleanor launched into her white lie. "I can't go shopping this morning—I'm meeting those boooring Shangs for breakfast. I need to see them at least once while I am here, or else they will be terribly insulted."

---

* According to Cassandra Shang aka "Radio One Asia."
† Women of Eleanor's background would rather camp out six to a room or sleep on the floor of anyone they remotely know than spend money on hotels. These are the same women who wouldn't blink at shelling out $90,000 on a South Sea pearl "trinket" while on holiday.

"You shouldn't have told them you were coming," Daisy chided.

"*Alamak*, you know that Cassandra Shang will find out sooner or later! It's like she has some special radar, and if she knew I was in England and didn't pay my respects to her parents, I would never hear the end of it. What to do, *lah*? This is the curse of being married to the Youngs," Eleanor said, pretending to bemoan her situation. In reality, even though she had been married to Philip Young for more than three decades, his cousins—"the Imperial Shangs," as they were known to all—had never extended her any courtesies. If Philip had come with her, they would surely have been invited to the Shangs' palatial estate in Surrey, or at the very least to dinner in town, but whenever Eleanor came to England on her own, the Shangs remained as silent as tombs.

Of course, Eleanor had long since given up trying to fit in with her husband's snobbish, insular clan, but lying about the Shangs was the only way to stop her girlfriends from prying too much. If she was seeing anyone else, her *kay poh** friends might surely want to tag along, but the mere mention of the Shangs intimidated them from asking too many questions.

While the ladies decided to spend the morning sampling all the free gourmet delicacies at Harrods' famed Food Halls, Eleanor, discreetly dressed in a chic camel-colored Akris pantsuit, racing green MaxMara swing coat, and her signature gold-rimmed Cutler and Gross sunglasses,[†] left the swanky building on Knightsbridge and walked two blocks east to the Berkeley hotel, where a silver Jaguar XJL parked in front of a row of perfectly round topiaries awaited her. Still paranoid that

---

\* Hokkien for "nosy" or "meddlesome."
† Eleanor, who normally didn't wear pricey designer clothes and made a point of bragging that she "started getting brand-name fatigue back in the seventies," kept a few choice pieces reserved specifically for special occasions like today.

her friends might have followed her, Eleanor glanced around quickly before getting into the sedan and being whisked off.

At Connaught Street in Mayfair, Eleanor emerged in front of a smart row of townhouses. Nothing about the red-and-white-brick Georgian façade or the glossy black door hinted at what awaited beyond. She pressed the intercom button, and a voice responded almost immediately: "May I help you?"

"It's Eleanor Young. I have a ten o'clock appointment," she said in an accent that was suddenly much more British. Even before she had finished speaking, several bolts clicked open, and an intimidatingly thickset man in a pinstripe suit opened the door. Eleanor entered a bright, stark antechamber, where an attractive young woman sat behind a cobalt blue Maison Jansen desk. The woman smiled sweetly and said, "Good morning, Mrs. Young. It won't be a minute—we're just calling up."

Eleanor nodded. She knew the procedure well. The entire back wall of the antechamber consisted of steel-framed glass doors leading into a private garden courtyard, and she could already see a bald man in a black suit crossing the garden toward her. The pinstripe-suited doorman ushered her toward the bald man, saying simply, "Mrs. Young for Mr. D'Abo." Eleanor noticed that both of them sported barely visible earpieces. The bald fellow escorted her along the glass-canopied walkway that bisected the courtyard, past some neatly trimmed shrubbery, and into the adjoining building, this one an ultramodern bunker clad in black titanium and tinted glass.

"Mrs. Young for Mr. D'Abo," the man repeated into his earpiece, and another set of security locks clicked open smoothly. After a short ride in the elevator, Eleanor felt a sense of relief for the first time that morning as she at last stepped into the richly appointed reception room of the Liechtenburg Group, one of the world's most exclusive private banks.

Like many high-net-worth Asians, Eleanor maintained accounts with many different financial institutions. Her parents, who had lost much of their first fortune when they were forced into the Endau concentration camp during the Japanese occupation of Singapore in World War II, had instilled in their children a key mantra: *Never put all of your eggs in one basket.* Eleanor remembered the lesson over the next few decades as she amassed her own fortune. It didn't matter that her hometown of Singapore had become one of the world's most secure financial hubs; Eleanor—like many of her friends—still kept money distributed among various banks around the globe, in safe havens that would prefer to remain unnamed.

The Liechtenburg Group account, however, was the jewel in her crown. They managed the biggest chunk of her assets, and Peter D'Abo, her private banker, consistently provided her with the highest rate of return. At least once a year, Eleanor would find some excuse to come to London, where she relished her portfolio reviews with Peter. (It did not hurt that he resembled her favorite actor, Richard Chamberlain—around the time he was in *The Thorn Birds*—and on many an occasion Eleanor would sit across Peter's highly polished macassar ebony desk and imagine him in a priest's collar while he explained what ingenious new scheme he had put her money in.)

Eleanor checked her lipstick one last time in the tiny mirror of her Jim Thompson silk lipstick case as she waited in the reception lounge. She admired the huge glass vase filled with purple calla lilies, their bright green stems twisted into a tight spiral formation, and thought about how many British pounds to withdraw from her account on this trip. The Singapore dollar was on a weakening trend this week, so it would be better to spend more in pounds at the moment. Daisy had paid for lunch yesterday, and Lorena covered dinner, so it was her turn to treat today. The three of them had made a pact to take turns paying for everything on this trip, knowing how tight things were for poor Nadine.

The silver-edged double doors began to open, and Eleanor rose in anticipation. Instead of Peter D'Abo, however, a Chinese lady came walking out, accompanied by Eddie Cheng.

"My goodness, Auntie Elle! What are you doing here?" Eddie blurted out before he could stop himself.

Eleanor knew of course that her husband's nephew worked for the Liechtenburg Group, but Eddie was head of the Hong Kong office, and never would she imagine running into him here. She had specifically opened her account at the London office so that she would *never* run the risk of bumping into anyone she might know. Turning scarlet in the face, she stammered, "Oh . . . oh, hi. I'm just meeting a friend for breakfast." *Aiyoh aiyoh aiyoh I've been caught!*

"Ah, yes, breakfast," Eddie replied, realizing the awkwardness of the situation. *Well of course the crafty bitch would have an account with us.*

"I got here two days ago. I'm here with Nadine Shaw—you know, visiting Francesca." *Now the whole damn family will know I have money stashed away in England.*

"Ah yes, Francesca Shaw. Didn't I hear she married some Arab?" Eddie asked politely. *Ah Ma is always worried Uncle Philip doesn't have enough to live on. Wait till she hears THIS!*

"He's an Iranian Jew, very handsome. They just moved into a flat at 2 Hyde Park," Eleanor replied. *Thank goodness he can never know my sixteen-digit account number.*

"Wah—he must do very well," Eddie said in mock awe. *My God, I'm going to have to grill Peter D'Abo about her account, not that he'll tell me anything—that stuffed shirt.*

"I would imagine he does very well—he's a banker just like you," Eleanor retorted. She noticed that the Chinese woman looked rather anxious to leave and wondered who she might be. For a Mainlander, she was dressed in an elegant, understated manner. Must be one of his bigwig clients. Of course, Eddie was doing the proper thing by *not* introducing her. *What were the both of them doing in London?*

"Well, I hope you enjoy your *breakfast*," Eddie said with a smirk as he took off with the lady.

. . .

Later that day, after Eddie had taken Bao Shaoyen to the intensive care unit of St. Mary's Paddington to see Carlton, he brought her to dinner at Mandarin Kitchen on Queensway, thinking the lobster noodles* might cheer her up, but apparently women lost their appetites when they couldn't stop crying. Shaoyen had been utterly unprepared for the sight of her son. His head had swollen to the size of a watermelon, and there were tubes sticking out everywhere—from his nose, his mouth, his neck. Both of his legs were broken, there were second-degree burns on his arms, and the part that remained unbandaged looked as if it had been completely smashed in, like a plastic bottle that had been stepped on. She wanted to stay with him, but the doctors wouldn't let her. Visiting hours were over. No one told her it had been this bad. Why didn't someone tell her? Why didn't Mr. Tin? And where was her husband? She was furious with him. She was mad that she had to face this all alone, while he was off cutting ribbons and shaking hands with Canadians.

Eddie squirmed awkwardly in his seat as Shaoyen sobbed uncontrollably in front of him. Why couldn't she just get a

---

* Never mind that the restaurant inexplicably resembles a 1980s Greek taverna, with its whitewashed barrel vault ceilings, Asian foodies will fly to London just to savor Mandarin Kitchen's signature dish, because nowhere else in the world can one get Chinese hand-pulled egg noodles braised in an intoxicating ginger scallion sauce, served with giant lobsters caught daily from the Scottish Sea.

grip? Carlton had *survived*! A few rounds of plastic surgery and
he would be as good as new. Maybe even better. With Peter
Ashley, the Michelangelo of Harley Street working his magic,
her son would probably turn out looking like the Chinese
Ryan Gosling. Before arriving in London, Eddie assumed that
he could clean up this mess in a day or two and still have time
to get fitted for a new spring suit at Joe Morgan's and maybe a
couple new pairs of Cleverleys. But big cracks were beginning
to show in the dam. Someone had tipped off the Asian press,
and they were sniffing around furiously. He needed to meet
with his inside man at Scotland Yard. He needed to get to his
Fleet Street contacts. Things were in danger of bursting wide
open, and he did not have time for hysterical mothers.

Just when things couldn't get any worse, Eddie saw a
familiar flash out of the corner of his eye. It was damn Auntie Elle again, entering the restaurant with Mrs. Q. T. Foo, that
woman what's her name from the L'Orient Jewelry family,
and that tacky Nadine Shaw. *Fucky fuck, why must all the Chinese
visiting London dine at the same three restaurants?*[*] Just what he
needed—Asia's biggest gossip queens witnessing Bao Shaoyen having a meltdown. But wait—maybe this wasn't necessarily a bad thing. After this morning at the bank, Eddie knew
he had Eleanor by her proverbial balls. He could get her to
do almost anything. And right now, he needed someone he
could really trust to handle Bao Shaoyen while he handled the
cleanup. If the lady was seen having a marvelous dinner in
London with Asia's leading socialites, it could actually work
to her advantage and get the ravenous reporters off their trail.

Eddie got up and strutted over to the round table in
the middle of the dining room. Eleanor was the first to see
him approaching, and her jaw tightened in annoyance. *Of*

---

[*]   The Holy Trinity are Four Seasons for the roast duck, Mandarin Kitchen
for the aforementioned lobster noodles, and Royal China for the dim sum.

*course Eddie Cheng would come here. The idiot better not say anything about seeing me this morning or I will sue Liechtenburg Group till kingdom come!*

"Auntie Elle, is that you?"

"Oh my goodness, Eddie! What are you doing in London?" Eleanor gasped, giving a look of utter surprise.

Eddie grinned broadly, leaning over to give her a peck on the cheek. *My God, somebody hand her the Oscar now.* "I'm here on business. What a lovely surprise to see you here, of all places!"

Eleanor breathed a sigh of relief. *Thank God he's playing along.* "Ladies, you all know my nephew from Hong Kong? His mother is Philip's sister, Alix, and his father is the world-famous heart surgeon Malcolm Cheng."

"Of course, of course. Such a small world, *lah!*" the women chirped excitedly.

"How is your dear mother these days?" Nadine asked eagerly, even though she had never in her life met Alexandra Cheng.

"Very well, very well. Mum is in Bangkok at the moment visiting Auntie Cat."

"Yes, yes, your Thai auntie," Nadine answered in a slightly awed tone, knowing that Catherine Young had married into Thai aristocracy.

Eleanor had to resist the temptation to roll her eyes. That Eddie didn't waste any opportunity to do some name-dropping.

Switching to Mandarin, Eddie said, "May I introduce all you lovely ladies to Mrs. Bao Shaoyen?"

The women nodded politely at the newcomer. Nadine noted immediately that she was wearing a Loro Piana cashmere cardigan, a beautifully cut pencil skirt from Céline, sensible low-heel pumps from Robert Clergerie, and a pretty patent leather handbag of indistinguishable brand. Verdict: *Boring, but unexpectedly classy for a Mainlander.*

Lorena zeroed in on her diamond ring. That rock was between 8 and 8.5 carats, D color, VVS1 or VVS2 grade, radiant cut, flanked by two triangular yellow diamonds of 3 carats apiece, set in platinum. Only Ronald Abram in Hong Kong had that particular setting. Verdict: *Not too vulgar, but she could have gotten a better stone if she'd bought from L'Orient.*

Daisy, who didn't care one bit about how someone looked and was rather more interested in bloodlines, asked in Mandarin, "Bao? Might you be related to the Baos of Nanjing?"

"Yes, my husband is Bao Gaoliang," Mrs. Bao said with a smile. *At last, someone who speaks proper Mandarin! Someone who knows who we are.*

"*Aiyah*, what a small world—I met your husband the last time he was in Singapore with the Chinese delegation! Ladies, Bao Gaoliang is the former governor of Jiangsu Province. Come, come, you should both join us. We were just about to order dinner!" Daisy graciously offered.

Eddie beamed. "You're much too kind. Actually, we could use some company. You see, it's been quite a distressing time for Mrs. Bao. Her son was injured in a car accident two days ago in London—"

"Oh my GOD-ness!" Nadine cried.

Eddie continued, "I'm afraid I can't stay, as I have to take care of some pressing matters for the Bao family, but I am quite sure Mrs. Bao would enjoy your company. She doesn't know London well, so she's at quite a loss here."

"Don't worry, we'll take good care of her!" Lorena offered charitably.

"I'm so relieved. Now, Auntie Elle, can you point me to the best spot to catch a taxi?"

"Of course," Eleanor said, walking her nephew out of the restaurant.

While the ladies consoled Bao Shaoyen, Eddie stood outside the restaurant giving Eleanor the lowdown. "I know this is a big favor I'm asking of you. Can I count on you to keep Mrs. Bao occupied and entertained for a while? More important, can I count on your absolute discretion? We need to ensure that your friends do not ever discuss Mrs. Bao with the press, especially the Asian press. I will be in your debt."

"*Aiyah*, you can trust us one hundred percent. My friends would never gossip or anything," Eleanor insisted.

Eddie nodded solicitously, knowing full well that all the ladies would be texting the news back to Asia at warp speed the minute he was gone. Those pesky gossip columnists would be sure to mention it in their daily reports, and everyone would think Shaoyen was just in London to shop and eat.

"Now, can I count on *your* discretion?" Eleanor asked, looking him straight in the eye.

"I'm not sure I know what you're talking about, Auntie Elle," Eddie said with a smirk.

"I'm talking about my *breakfast* . . . this morning?"

"Oh, don't worry, I already forgot about that. I took an oath of secrecy when I joined the world of private banking, and I wouldn't *dream* of ever betraying it. At the Liechtenburg Group, what can we offer but discretion and trust?"

Eleanor returned to the restaurant, feeling rather relieved by this strange turn of events. She was getting to even the score with her nephew. A huge platter upon which lay the most enormous lobster over a bed of steaming hot noodles sat in the middle of the table, but no one was eating. The ladies all looked up at Eleanor with rather peculiar expressions on their faces. She figured they must be dying to know what Eddie had told her outside.

Daisy smiled brightly as Eleanor sat down and said, "Mrs. Bao was just showing us some pictures of her handsome son on her phone. She is so worried about his face, and I was just assuring her that the plastic surgeons in London are some of the best in the world."

Daisy handed over the phone, and Eleanor's eyes widened almost imperceptibly as she locked onto the image.

"Don't you think he's handsome?" Daisy asked in an almost too cheery tone.

Eleanor looked up from the phone and said, ever so nonchalantly, "Oh yes, very handsome."

None of the other ladies said anything else about Mrs. Bao's son for the rest of the dinner, but all of them were thinking the same thing. There was no way it could be a coincidence. Bao Shaoyen's injured son looked just like the woman who had caused the great estrangement between Eleanor and her son, Nicholas.

Yes, Carlton Bao was the spitting image of Rachel Chu.

# PART ONE

*Everyone claims to be a billionaire these days. But you're not really a billionaire until you spend your billions.*

—OVERHEARD AT THE HONG KONG JOCKEY CLUB

# THE MANDARIN

HONG KONG, JANUARY 25, 2013

In early 2012, a brother and sister clearing out their late mother's attic in the London neighborhood of Hampstead discovered what appeared to be a cluster of old Chinese scrolls at the bottom of a steamer trunk. By chance, the sister had a friend who worked at Christie's, so she dropped them off—in four Sainsbury's grocery sacks—at the auctioneer's salesroom on Old Brompton Road, hoping they might "take a look and tell us if they're worth anything."

When the senior specialist of Chinese Classical Paintings opened up one of the silk scrolls, he nearly went into cardiac arrest. Unfurled before him was an image so remarkably rendered, it immediately reminded him of a set of hanging scroll paintings long thought to be destroyed. Could this be *The Palace of Eighteen Perfections*? The artwork, created by the Qing dynasty artist Yuan Jiang in 1693, was believed to have been secretly removed from China during the Second Opium War in 1860, when many of the royal palaces were ransacked, and lost forever.

As staffers scurried around unrolling the scrolls, they discovered twenty-four pieces, each almost seven feet tall and in immaculate condition. Placed side by side, they spanned thirty-seven feet, almost filling the floor space of two work-rooms. At last, the senior specialist could confirm that this was undoubtedly the mythical work described in all the classical Chinese texts he had spent much of his career studying.

The Palace of Eighteen Perfections was an opulent eighth-century imperial retreat in the mountains north of modern-day Xi'an. It was said to be one of the most magnificent royal residences ever built, with grounds so vast that one had to travel between the halls on horseback. On these ancient silk scrolls, the intricate pavilions, courtyards, and gardens that meandered through a dreamlike blue-and-green mountain landscape were painted in colors so vibrantly preserved, they seemed almost electric in their iridescence.

The auction-house staff stood over the exquisite master-piece in awed silence. A find of this caliber was like discovering a long-hidden painting by da Vinci or Vermeer. When the inter-national director of Asian Art rushed in to see them, he began to feel faint and forced himself to take a few steps back for fear that he might fall onto the delicate artwork. Choking back his tears, the director finally said, "Call François in Hong Kong. Tell him to get Oliver T'sien on the next flight to London."*

The director then declared, "We need to give these beau-ties the grand tour. We're going to start out with an exhibi-tion in Geneva, then London, then at our Rockefeller Center showroom in New York. Let's give the world's top collectors a chance to see it. Only then will we take it to Hong Kong, and sell it right before the Chinese New Year. By then the Chinese should be frothing at the mouth in anticipation."

---

* Oliver T'sien—one of Christie's most highly valued deputy chairmen—has long-standing relationships with many of the world's top collectors. (Being related to practically every important family in Asia didn't hurt.)

Which is precisely how Corinna Ko-Tung came to be sitting in the Clipper Lounge of the Mandarin Hotel in Hong Kong a year later, impatiently awaiting the arrival of Lester and Valerie Liu. Her richly embossed business card listed her as an "art consultant," but for a few select clients, she was a great deal more than that. Corinna was born to one of Hong Kong's most pedigreed families, and she secretly parlayed her extensive connections into a very profitable sideline. For clients like the Lius, Corinna did everything from refining the art on their walls to the clothes on their back—all in service of getting them memberships at the most elite clubs, their names onto the right invitation lists, and their children into the city's top schools. In short, she was a special consultant for social climbers.

Corinna spotted the Lius as they ascended the short flight of stairs up to the mezzanine lounge overlooking the lobby. The couple cut quite a striking picture, and she had to pat herself on the back for this. The first time Corinna met the Lius, they were both in head-to-toe Prada. To these new arrivals from Guangdong, it was the height of sophistication, but to Corinna, it just screamed clueless Mainland money. Thanks to her handiwork, Lester entered the Clipper Lounge looking particularly dapper in a bespoke three-piece suit from Kilgour of Savile Row, and Valerie was chicly clad in a silvery Persian lamb parka from J. Mendel, appropriately sized black pearls, and dove-gray suede Lanvin ankle boots. But there was something a little off about her outfit—the handbag was a mistake. The glossy ombré-dyed reptile-skin bag obviously came from some nearly extinct species, but it reminded Corinna of the sort of handbag only a mistress would carry. She made a mental note to drop a hint at the appropriate moment.

Valerie arrived at the table apologizing profusely. "I'm sorry we're late. Our chauffeur mistakenly took us to the *Landmark* Mandarin Oriental instead of this one."

"Not a problem," Corinna replied graciously. Tardiness was one of her pet peeves, but with the kind of retainer the Lius were paying her, she wasn't about to complain.

"I'm surprised you wanted to meet here. Don't you think the tearoom at the Four Seasons is much nicer?" Valerie asked.

"Or even the Peninsula," Lester chimed in, casting a dismissive eye at the rectangular 1970s-era chandeliers cascading from the ceiling of the lobby.

"The Peninsula gets too many tourists, and the Four Seasons is where all the new people go. The Mandarin is where *proper* Hong Kong families have been coming to tea for generations. My grandmother Lady Ko-Tung used to bring me here at least once a month when I was a girl," Corinna patiently explained, adding, "You must also leave out the 'Oriental'—we locals simply call it 'the Mandarin.'"

"Oh," Valerie replied, feeling a little chastised. She glanced around, taking in the subdued oak-paneled walls and armchairs with just the perfect amount of sag in the seat cushions, her eyes suddenly widening. Leaning closer in, she whispered excitedly to Corinna, "Do you see who's over there? Isn't that Fiona Tung-Cheng with her mother-in-law, Alexandra Cheng, having tea with the Ladoories?"

"Who are they?" Lester asked, a little too loudly.

Valerie nervously shushed her husband in Mandarin. "Don't stare—I'll tell you later!"

Corinna smiled in approval. That Valerie was a quick study. The Lius were relatively new clients, but they were Corinna's favorite type of clients—*Red Royals*, she called them. Unlike fresh-off-the-boat Mainlander millionaires, these heirs of China's ruling class—known in China as *fuerdai*, or "second-generation-rich"—had good manners and good teeth, and had never known the deprivation of their parents' generation. The tragedies of the Great Leap Forward and the Cultural Revolution were ancient history as far as they were concerned.

Obscene gobs of money had come easily to them, so obscene gobs they were ready to part with.

Lester's family controlled one of China's largest insurance companies, and he met Valerie, the Shanghai-born daughter of an anesthesiologist, when they were both at the University of Sydney. With an ever-growing fortune and ever-refining taste, this thirtysomething couple was ambitiously striving to make their mark on the power scene in Asia. With homes in London, Shanghai, Sydney, and New York, and a newly constructed house that resembled a cruise liner in Hong Kong's Deep Water Bay, they were anxiously filling the walls with museum-quality art in the hopes that *Hong Kong Tattle* might soon do a feature.

Lester got right down to business. "So how much do you think these scrolls will end up going for?"

"Well, that's what I wanted to discuss with you. I know you said you were prepared to go up to fifty million, but I have a feeling we will break all records tonight. Would you be prepared to go up to seventy-five?" Corinna said carefully, testing the waters.

Lester didn't flinch. He reached for one of the sausage puffs on the silver cake stand and said, "Are you sure it's worth that much?"

"Mr. Liu, this is the single most important work of Chinese art to ever come on the market. It's a once-in-a-lifetime opportunity—"

"It's going to look so good in the rotunda!" Valerie couldn't help blurting out. "We're going to hang it so that the whole painting is panoramic, and I'm having the walls on the first and second floors repainted to exactly match the colors. I love those turquoise tones . . ."

Corinna ignored Valerie's chatter and continued. "Aside from the artwork itself, the value of owning it will be incalculable. Think how much it will raise your profile—your family's profile—once it's known that you acquired it. You will have beat out the top collectors in the world. I'm told that representatives for the Bins, the Wangs, and the Kuoks are bidding. And the Huangs just flew in from Taipei—interesting timing, isn't it? I also have it on good authority that Colin and Araminta Khoo sent a special team of curators from the National Palace Museum in Taipei to examine the piece last week."

"Ooh—Araminta Khoo. She's so beautiful and chic! I couldn't stop reading about that incredible wedding of hers. Do you know her?" Valerie asked.

"I was at the wedding," Corinna said simply.

Valerie shook her head in wonder. She tried to imagine the middle-aged, mousy-looking Corinna, who always wore the same three Giorgio Armani pantsuits, at the most glamorous event ever to hit Asia. Some people had all the luck, being born into the right family.

Corinna continued her lecture. "So let me give you the drill. The auction tonight begins at eight sharp, and I have secured us entry to the Christie's VVIP skybox. That is where you will be throughout the auction. I will be downstairs on the auction room floor, bidding exclusively for you."

"We won't be with you?" Valerie was confused.

"No, no. You'll be in this special lounge where you can look down onto all the action."

"But won't it be more exciting to be down on the floor itself?" Valerie pressed on.

Corinna shook her head. "Trust me, you don't want to be seen on the auction floor. The VVIP skybox is where you want to be. That's where all the top collectors will be, and I know you will enjoy that—"

"Wait a minute," Lester interrupted. "What's the point of buying the damn thing then? How will anyone know we made the winning bid?"

"First of all, you will be seen by everyone at the VVIP sky-box, so people will already suspect, and first thing tomorrow, I will have one of my sources at the *South China Morning Post* issue an unconfirmed report that Mr. and Mrs. Lester Liu of the Harmony Insurance family acquired the painting. Trust me, that's the classy way to do it. You want people to specu-late. You *want* to be that unconfirmed report."

"Ooh, you're so brilliant, Corinna!" Valerie squealed in excitement.

"But if it's 'unconfirmed,' how will people know?" Lester was still confused.

"Hiyah, slow tortoise, everyone will see the painting when we throw our housewarming party next month," Valerie chastised her husband, smacking him on the knee. "They will confirm it with their own envious eyes!"

. . .

The Hong Kong Convention and Exhibition Centre, situ-ated right on the harbor in Wan Chai, boasted overlapping curved roofs that resembled a gigantic manta ray gliding through the water. That same evening, a parade of starlets, boldface-name socialites, low-level billionaires, and the sort of people Corinna Ko-Tung deemed to be inconsequential paraded through the Grand Hall, vying for the most visible seats at the auction of the century, while the back of the room was packed to the rafters with the international press and onlookers. Upstairs in the plush VVIP skybox, Valerie and Lester were in seventh heaven as they rubbed elbows with the serious-money crowd over Laurent-Perrier champagne and canapés prepared by Café Gray.

When at last the auctioneer stepped up to the polished wood podium, the lights in the hall began to dim. A mas-sive gold latticework screen ran along the wall facing the stage, and at the appointed moment, the screen began to part, revealing the hanging scrolls in all their glory. Brilliantly enhanced by the state-of-the-art lighting system, they almost appeared to glow from within. The crowd gasped, and when the lights came up again, the auctioneer promptly began the session without any fuss: "An exceedingly rare set of twenty-four hanging scrolls from the Qing dynasty, ink and color on silk, depicting the Palace of Eighteen Perfections, by Yuan Jiang. Inscribed by the artist, and dated 1693. Shall we have an opening bid of—one million?"

Valerie could feel the adrenaline coursing through her veins as she saw Corinna raise her blue-numbered paddle to volley the first bid. A flurry of paddles began popping up around the room, and the price began its stratospheric climb. Five million. Ten million. Twelve million. Fifteen million. Twenty million. Within a matter of minutes, the bid was at forty million. Lester leaned forward in his chair, analyzing the action on the auction-room floor like some complex chess match, and Valerie clawed her nails into his shoulder repeatedly in high anticipation.

When the bidding hit sixty million, Lester's phone rang. It was Corinna sounding frantic. "*Suey doh sei*,* it's going up too fast! We're going to pass your seventy-five-million limit in no time. Do you want to keep bidding?"

Lester breathed in deeply. Any expenditure over fifty million would surely be noticed by his father's bean counters, and there would be some explaining to do. "Keep going till I stop you," he ordered.

Valerie's head was spinning in excitement. They were so close. Imagine, soon she would own something that even *Araminta Khoo* coveted! At eighty million, the bidding finally slowed down. No more paddles in the room were raised with

---

* Cantonese for "So rotten I could die!"

the exception of Corinna's, and it seemed like there were only two or three telephone buyers remaining to bid against the Lius. The price was going up only in increments of half a million, and Lester closed his eyes, praying he would get it for under ninety million. It was worth it. It was worth the scolding he would get from his father. He would make his plea that he had bought the family a billion dollars' worth of good publicity.

Suddenly there came a commotion from the back of the auction room. Murmurs could be heard as the standing-room-only crowd began to give way. Even in a room packed with celebrities dressed to the nines, a hush came over the space as a strikingly attractive Chinese woman with jet-black hair, powdered white skin, and crimson lips, dramatically dressed in a black velvet off-the-shoulder gown, emerged from the crowd. Flanked by two snow-white Russian wolfhounds on long diamond leashes, the lady began to walk slowly up the central aisle as every head swiveled toward the sensational sight.

Clearing his throat discreetly into the mic, the auctioneer tried to regain the attention of the room. "I have eighty-five point five million, who will say eighty-six?"

One of the associates manning a telephone nodded. Corinna immediately raised her paddle to challenge that bid. And then the lady in black velvet raised her paddle. Looking down from the skybox, the director of Christie's Asia turned to his associates in astonishment and said, "I thought she was just some publicity seeker." Straining to take a better look, the director observed, "Her paddle number is 269. Someone find out who she is. Is she even prequalified to bid?"

Oliver T'sien, who was in the lounge bidding on behalf of a private client, had been staring intently with his opera glasses at the lady with the silken-haired dogs ever since she entered. He let out a chuckle. "Don't worry, she's prequalified."

"Who is she?" the director demanded.

"Well, her nose and chin have been refined and it looks like she's also gotten cheek implants, but I'm quite certain bidder number 269 is none other than Mrs. Tai."

"Carol Tai, the widow of *Dato'* Tai Toh Lui, that tycoon who died last year?"

"No, no, she's the wife of Bernard, the *dato*'s son who inherited all of his father's billions. That lady in black is the soap-opera star formerly known as Kitty Pong."

WAN CHAI, HONG KONG, 8:25 P.M.

*This is special correspondent Sunny Choy reporting for CNN International. I'm live at the Hong Kong Convention and Exhibition Centre, where the world's top collectors are in a frenzied state of bidding for* The Palace of Eighteen Perfections. *The price has just hit $90 million. To put this into perspective, a Qianlong vase sold in London for a record-breaking US$85.9 million in 2010. But that's London. In Asia, the highest price ever achieved was US$65.4 million for an ink painting by Qi Baishi in 2011.* * *So this painting has already broken TWO world records. Now, about ten minutes ago, the former actress Kitty Pong—who is married to the billionaire Bernard Tai—brought the auction to a standstill when she made an entrance with two gigantic dogs on diamond leashes and began bidding. Right now, there are four others bidding against her. We're told that one is a representative for the Getty Museum in Los Angeles, another suspected bidder is the heiress Araminta Lee Khoo, and there are unconfirmed reports that the third bidder is a representative for the Liu insurance family. We don't know who the fourth mystery bidder is yet. Back to you, Christiane.*

---

* The authenticity of the painting was later questioned, and the buyer retracted the bid. (They probably realized it wouldn't match their sofa.)

UPPER GUDAURI, REPUBLIC OF GEORGIA, 12:30 A.M.

"There's some ridiculous woman in black with two friggin' dogs *who will not stop bidding!*" Araminta cursed into her laptop, not recognizing Kitty Pong in the live video feed of the auction. After a long day of heli-skiing in the Caucasus Mountains, her muscles ached and this auction was delaying her much-needed soak in the gigantic sunken tub of their winter chalet.

"What's the price up to now?" Colin asked drowsily as he lay stretched out on the black-and-white yak-skin rug by the fireplace.

"I'm not telling—I know you're not going to approve."

"No, really, Minty, how much is it?"

"Shhh! I'm bidding!" Araminta admonished her husband, resuming her dialogue with the Christie's associate on the line.

Colin pulled himself up from the cozy rug and padded over to the desk where his wife was set up with her computer and satellite phone. He blinked twice at the video feed, not sure if he believed what he was seeing. "*Lugh siow, ah!*" You're really going to pay ninety million for a bunch of old scrolls?"

Araminta gave him a look. "I don't say anything when you buy huge ugly canvases with elephant dung on them, so don't you start on me now."

"Wait a minute, my Chris Ofilis only cost about two, three million each. Think about how many elephant-dung paintings we could buy—"

Araminta cupped her hand over the mouthpiece. "Make yourself useful and get me another hot chocolate. With extra marshmallows, please. This auction isn't over until I say it's over!"

---

\* Hokkien for "Are you out of your mind?"

"Where are you even going to hang them? We have no more wall space left in the house," Colin continued.

"You know, I think they would go splendidly in the lobby of the new hotel my mother's building in Bhutan. BLOODY HELL! The bitch in black isn't giving up! Who the hell is she? She looks like a Chinese Dita Von Teese!"

Colin shook his head. "Minty, you're getting too emotional. Hand me the phone—I'll do the bidding if you really want it that bad. I have much more experience with this than you do. The most important thing is to set your limit. What's your top limit?"

COLD STORAGE JELITA, SINGAPORE, 8:35 P.M.

Astrid Leong was at the supermarket when her phone rang. She was trying to cobble together a meal for the cook's night off tomorrow, and her five-year-old son, Cassian, was standing in the front section of the cart, doing his best impression of Leonardo DiCaprio on the prow of the *Titanic*. As always, Astrid was a little mortified to use her phone in a public place, but seeing that it was her cousin Oliver T'sien calling from Hong Kong, it couldn't be helped. She steered the cart toward the frozen vegetables section and took the call.

"What's up?"

"You're missing all the fun at the auction of the year," Oliver reported gleefully.

"Oh, was that today? So tell me, what's the damage?"

"It's still going! You're not going to believe this, but Kitty Pong made quite the entrance and has been bidding up the painting like there's no tomorrow."

"*Kitty Pong?*"

"Yes, in a Madame X cocktail dress with two borzois on diamond leashes. It's quite the spectacle."

"When did *she* become an art collector? Is Bernard there? I didn't think he spent his money on anything but drugs and boats."

"Bernard is nowhere to be seen. But if Kitty succeeds in acquiring this painting, they will immediately be considered *the* top collectors of Asian art in the world."

"Hmm—I *am* missing out on all the fun."

"So it's down to Kitty, Araminta Lee, some Mainland couple that Corinna Ko-Tung is bidding for, and the Getty Museum. We're up to ninety-four million on the painting. I know you didn't set a limit, but I just want to be sure you want to keep going."

"Ninety-four? Keep going. Cassian, stop playing with those frozen peas!"

"It's ninety-six now. Oops. Holymarymotherofgod— we've just broken a hundred million! Bid?"

"Sure."

"The Mainlanders have finally dropped out —poor things, they look like they've just lost their firstborn child. We're at one hundred and five."

"Cassian, I don't care how much you beg, I'm not letting you eat microwavable mini sliders. Think of all the preservatives in that beef—put them back!"

"This is Guinness book territory here, Astrid. No one has ever paid this much for a Chinese painting. One ten. One fifteen. It's Araminta against Kitty. Keep going?"

Cassian was trapped inside the ice-cream freezer. Astrid stared at her child in exasperation. "I have to go. Just get it. As you said, this is something the museum ought to have, so I don't really care what I have to pay."

Ten minutes later, as Astrid stood in line at the checkout counter, her phone rang again. She smiled apologetically at the cashier as she took the call.

"Sorry to bother you again, but we're at a hundred and

ninety-five million now—your bid," Oliver said, sounding a bit frazzled.

"*Really?*" Astrid said, as she snatched away the Mars bar that Cassian was trying to hand to the cashier.

"Yes, the Getty dropped out at one fifty, and Araminta at one eighty. It's just you against Kitty, and it looks like she's hell-bent on having it. At this point, I can't in good conscience recommend it. I know Chor Ling at the museum would be horrified to find out you paid this much."

"She'll never know—I'm giving it anonymously."

"Even so. Astrid, I know it's not about the money, but at this price, we're in idiot territory."

"How annoying. You're right—one hundred and ninety-five million is just silly. Let Kitty Pong have it if she wants it that badly," Astrid said. She fished a stack of super-saver coupons out of her purse and presented them to the cashier.

Thirty seconds later, the gavel went down on *The Palace of Eighteen Perfections*. At one hundred and ninety-five million, it was the most expensive Chinese work of art ever sold at auction. The glittering crowd burst into deafening applause as Kitty Pong preened for the cameras, the flashes going off like IEDs in downtown Kabul. One of the Russian wolfhounds started to bark. Now the whole world would know that Kitty Pong—or Mrs. Bernard Tai, as she now insisted on being called—had indeed arrived.

# CUPERTINO, CALIFORNIA

FEBRUARY 9, 2013—CHINESE NEW YEAR'S EVE

"The boys are back from their football game. Steer clear of Jason—he's going to be one giant sweat rag," Samantha Chu warned her cousin Rachel as soon as she heard the boisterous echoes coming from the garage. The two of them were perched on wooden stools in the kitchen of Rachel's uncle Walt and auntie Jin, making dumplings for the Chinese New Year's Eve feast.

Samantha's twenty-one-year-old brother came bursting through the screen door ahead of Nicholas Young. "We made the Lin brothers eat dirt!" Jason triumphantly announced, grabbing two Gatorades from the fridge and tossing one to Nick. "Hey, where did the parentals go? I expected to find more hysterical aunties fighting over kitchen counter space."

"Dad's picking up Great-auntie Louise from the retirement home, and Mom, Auntie Flora, and Auntie Kerry went to 99 Ranch," Samantha reported.

"Again? Glad I didn't get roped into driving them this time—that place is always so packed with fobbies,[*] the park-

---

[*] A nickname for "fresh off the boat" Asian immigrants, used mainly by second-, third-, or fourth-generation Asian Americans to denote their superiority.

ing lot looks like a Toyota dealership! What did they run out of this time?" Jason asked.

"Everything. Uncle Ray called—he's bringing the whole family after all, and you know how much those boys can eat," Samantha said as she scooped some minced-pork-and-chive filling onto a dough wrapper and handed it off to Rachel.

"Get ready, Jase—I'm sure Auntie Belinda's going to say something about your new tattoo," Rachel teased as she folded little pleats on the top of the dumpling and molded it into a perfect crescent shape.

"Who's Auntie Belinda?" Nick inquired.

Jason made a face. "Dude! You haven't met her yet, have you? She's Uncle Ray's wife. Uncle Ray is this mega-bucks oral surgeon, and they have this huge McMansion in Menlo Park, so Auntie Belinda acts like she's the Queen of Downtown Abbey. She's insanely uptight, and every year she drives Mom nuts by waiting till the very last minute to decide whether she and her spoiled-rotten kids will grace us with their presence."

"It's Down*ton* Abbey, Jase," Samantha corrected. "And come on, she's not that bad. She's just from Vancouver, that's all."

"You mean Hongcouver," Jason retorted, tossing his empty bottle from across the kitchen into the oversized Bed Bath and Beyond plastic bag on the pantry door that served as the recycling bin. "Auntie Belinda's going to *love* you Nick, especially when she hears you speak like that dude from *Notting Hill*!"

By six thirty, twenty-two members of the extended Chu clan had arrived at the house. Most of the older uncles and aunties sat around the big rosewood dining table that was covered in thick protective plastic sheeting, while the younger adults sat with the children at three folding mah-jongg tables that spilled out into the living room. (The teens and college-age Chus were spread out in front of the big-screen television in the den watching basketball and gobbling down fried pot stickers by the dozen.)

As the aunties began bringing out the heaping platters of roast duck, jumbo shrimp deep fried in batter, steamed kai-lan with black mushrooms, and Chinese long-life noodles with barbecued pork and scallops, Auntie Jin looked around at the gathered crowd. "Ray is still not here? We're not waiting any longer or the food will get cold!"

"Auntie Belinda is probably still trying to decide which Chanel dress to wear," Samantha quipped.

Just then the doorbell rang, and Ray and Belinda Chu swept into the house with their four teenage sons, all sporting Ralph Lauren polo shirts in different hues. Belinda wore high-waisted cream silk trousers, an iridescent orange blouse with billowing organza sleeves, her trademark Chanel gold belt, and a pair of oversize champagne pearl earrings more appropriate for the opening night of the San Francisco Opera.

"Happy New Year, everyone!" Uncle Ray announced jovially as he presented his eldest brother, Walt, with a big box of Japanese pears, while his wife ceremoniously handed Auntie Jin a covered Le Creuset dish. "Would you mind warming this up for me in the oven? Just 115 degrees for twenty minutes."

"Hiyah, you didn't have to bring anything," Auntie Jin said.

"No, no, this is my dinner—I'm on a raw food diet now," Belinda announced.

When everyone had finally settled into their seats and begun attacking the dishes with gusto, Uncle Walt beamed across the table at Rachel. "I'm still not used to seeing you at this time of the year! You usually only come back for Thanksgiving."

"It worked out because Nick and I had to deal with some last-minute wedding stuff," Rachel explained.

Auntie Belinda suddenly exclaimed imperiously, "Rachel Chu! I can't believe I've been here ten minutes and you STILL

HAVEN'T SHOWN ME YOUR ENGAGEMENT RING!
Get over here right now!" Rachel got up from her seat and
walked toward her aunt dutifully, stretching out her hand for
inspection.

"My, it's so . . . *pretty!*" Auntie Belinda remarked in a shrill
voice, barely concealing her surprise. *Wasn't this Nick fellow supposed to come from money? How did poor Rachel get saddled with this
little pebble? It couldn't have been more than a carat and a half!*

"It's just a simple ring—exactly what I wanted," Rachel
said modestly, eyeing the huge marquis-cut rock on her aunt's
finger.

"Yes, it's very simple, but it suits you perfectly," Auntie
Belinda pronounced. "Wherever did you find a ring like this,
Nick? Is it from Singapore?"

"My cousin Astrid helped me. It's from her friend Joel in
Paris,"* Nick answered politely.

"Hmm. Imagine going all the way to Paris for this," Auntie
Belinda murmured.

"Hey, didn't you get engaged in Paris?" Rachel's older
cousin Vivian, who lived in Malibu, excitedly cut in. "I think
my mom told me something about a troupe of mimes performing at your proposal."

"*Mimes?*" Nick gave Vivian a look of horror. "I assure you,
no mimes were ever involved!"

"Hiyah, then tell us the whole story!" Auntie Jin cajoled.

Nick glanced over at Rachel. "Why don't you take this
one? You tell it much better."

Rachel took a deep breath as everyone around the table
looked at her expectantly. "Okay, here goes. On the last night

---

*    Joel Arthur Rosenthal, aka JAR of Paris, whose precious handmade jewels
are among the most coveted in the world. If Belinda had a more discerning eye,
she might have realized that Rachel's ring was a flawless oval-cut diamond held
in place by ribbons of white gold almost as thin as hairs, interwoven with tiny
blue sapphires. (Nick would not tell Rachel how much he paid for it.)

of our Paris trip, Nick arranged a surprise dinner. He wouldn't tell me where we were going, so I had a feeling something was up. We ended up at this beautiful historic residence on an island in the middle of the Seine—"

"The Hôtel Lambert, right at the tip of the Île Saint-Louis," Nick offered.

"Yes, and there was a candlelit table for two set up on the roof. The moonlight was reflecting off the river, a cellist sat in the corner playing Debussy, everything was just perfect. Nick had hired this French Vietnamese chef from one of Paris's top restaurants to prepare the most exquisite meal, but I was so nervous I completely lost my appetite."

"In retrospect, a six-course tasting menu was probably not the best idea," Nick mused.

Rachel nodded. "Every time the waiter lifted the silver dome from a dish, I thought I'd find a ring underneath. But nothing happened. By the time the dinner was over and the cellist began packing up her stuff, I thought, 'I guess tonight's not the night.' But then, as we were about to leave, we heard these horns coming from the river. It was one of those Bateaux Mouches tourist barges, and all these people were assembled on the top deck. As the barge passed below the building, music started blaring out of the loudspeakers and the people started leaping on the benches like gazelles. Turns out they were from the Paris Opera Ballet, and Nick had commissioned them to perform a special dance just for me."

"How lovely!" Auntie Belinda gasped, finally impressed. "And after that did Nick propose?"

"Noooo! The performance ended and we began to descend the staircase. I was still on a high from seeing this amazingly choreographed performance, but a bit disappointed that it didn't end in a proposal. So when we got downstairs, the street was deserted except for a guy standing under a tree overlooking the river. Then the guy started playing his

guitar, and I recognized it was the Talking Heads' 'This Must
Be the Place'—the song that we had heard a street musician
performing in Washington Square Park on the first night we
met. The guy began to sing, and I suddenly realized it was the
*very same guy from the park*!"

"Shut up!" Samantha clasped both hands to her mouth,
as everyone in the room continued to listen in rapt attention.

"Nick had somehow tracked the singer down all the way
in Austin and had flown him to Paris. He no longer had blond
dreads, but I could never forget that voice. Then before I
knew what was happening, Nick was down on one knee, staring up at me with a little velvet box in his hand. That's when I
completely lost it! I started bawling uncontrollably, and before
Nick could finish asking me to marry him, I said *yes, yes, yes* and
all the dancers on the barge began cheering like crazy."

"That's the coolest proposal I've ever heard!" Samantha gushed, wiping the tears from her eyes. When she had
first heard about what had happened to Rachel in Singapore,
Samantha had been furious with Nick. How could he not
have noticed how badly Rachel was being treated? Rachel had
moved out of Nick's place immediately after returning from
Asia, and Samantha was glad her cousin was rid of him. But
as the months passed and Rachel began to see Nick again,
Samantha found herself having a change of heart as well.
After all, he had come to Rachel's rescue and sacrificed his
relationship with his own family to be with her. He had waited
patiently in the wings, giving Rachel all the time she needed to
heal. And now they were getting married at long last.

"Well done, Nick! We're all looking forward to the big day
next month in Montecito!" Uncle Ray declared.

"We decided to spend a few extra nights at Ojai Valley Inn
and Spa," bragged Auntie Belinda, looking around the table
to make sure all the family had heard her.

Rachel chuckled to herself, knowing that her other relatives wouldn't even have a clue what Belinda was talking about. "That sounds wonderful. I wish we had the time to do something like that. We're going to have to wait till the semester ends in May before we go on our honeymoon."

"But weren't you and Nick just in China?" Uncle Ray inquired.

Rachel's auntie Jin tried to make eyes at Ray from across the table, warning him off the topic, while his wife pinched him hard on his left thigh. "Owww!" he let out before realizing his gaffe. Belinda had told him that Rachel and Nick had been to Fuzhou again, chasing yet another false lead in the search for her father, but this apparently was another in a long list of family secrets he wasn't supposed to talk about.

"Yes, we made a short trip," Nick answered quickly.

"Well, you two are brave souls. I for one cannot stomach any of the food over there. I don't care how 'gourmet' they say the food has gotten, all their animals are loaded with carcinogens. And look at this duck you're all eating! I bet it was fed with growth hormones too," Auntie Belinda scoffed as she gnawed on her turnip.

Rachel stared at the plump roast duck with its glossy amber sheen, suddenly losing her appetite.

"Yes, you can trust the food in Hong Kong, but not anywhere on the Mainland," Auntie Jin said, deftly removing every bit of fat from her roast duck with her chopsticks.

"That's just not true!" Samantha argued. "Why are you guys still so prejudiced against China? When I was there last year, I had some of the best meals of my life. You really haven't had good *xiao long bao*\* until you've eaten it in Shanghai."

At the end of the table, Great-auntie Louise, the oldest

---

\* Dumplings filled with meat and piping hot broth that—due to their increased popularity in recent years on the international food scene—have been scalding uninitiated mouths around the world.

member of the Chu clan, suddenly blurted out, "Rachel, what news of your father? Have you found him yet?"

Cousin Dave spat out a half-chewed piece of barbecued pork in surprise. The dining room fell silent, a few people exchanging furtive glances. Rachel's face clouded over a bit. She inhaled deeply before responding, "No, we haven't found him."

Nick grasped Rachel's hand and added encouragingly, "We thought we had a very interesting prospect last month, but that didn't pan out."

"Things can be very tricky over there," Uncle Ray mused, trying for one more jumbo shrimp fritter but finding his hand smacked away by his wife.

"At least we are certain now that Rachel's father changed his name. Because all official documentation of him stops in 1985, shortly before he graduated from Beijing University," Nick explained.

"Speaking of universities, does everyone know that Penny Shi's daughter, who was the class valedictorian at Los Gatos, didn't get into *any* of the Ivy League schools that she applied to?" Auntie Jin chirped, trying to change the subject. It was so dreadful to bring up Rachel's father in front of Kerry, Rachel's mother, who had already suffered enough over the past three decades as a single parent.

Cousin Henry, ignoring his auntie Jin's remark, chimed in, volunteering, "You know, my firm works with this amazing lawyer based out of Shanghai. Her father is very high up in the government and she's super-well-connected. Do you want me to see if she can help out?"

Kerry, who had been silent until now, suddenly slammed her chopsticks onto the table and said, "Hiyah, this is all such a waste of time. It's no use chasing ghosts!"

Rachel looked at her mother for a moment. Then she got up from the table and walked out of the room without a word.

Samantha spoke up, her voice cracking a little with emotion. "He's not a ghost, Auntie Kerry. He's her father, and she has a right to have some sort of relationship with him. I can't even imagine what my life would be like without my dad. Can you blame Rachel for wanting to find him?"

## SCOTTS ROAD

"When you get here, just drive straight up to the garage," Bao Shaoyen told Eleanor over the phone. Eleanor did as she was instructed, pulling up to the security booth and explaining that she was paying an after-dinner visit to the Baos, who had recently rented a unit in this brand-new condominium off Scotts Road.

"Ah yes, Mrs. Young. Please keep to the left and follow the arrows," the attendant in the dark gray uniform said. Eleanor drove down the ramp into a spotless underground parking garage that seemed curiously devoid of cars. *They must be one of the first tenants to move in,* she thought, veering to the left and approaching a white metallic garage door with a sign overhead that read UNIT 01 MECHANISED CAR PARK (FOR RESIDENTS ONLY). The door rose quickly and a green signal light began to flash. As she pulled forward into the brightly lit chamber, a digital sign in front of her flashed STOP. PARKING POSITION OK. *How strange . . . am I just supposed to park right here?*

Suddenly the ground began to move. Eleanor gasped and grabbed hold of the steering wheel reflexively. Only after a few seconds did she realize she had driven onto a rotating platform that was slowly pivoting her car ninety degrees. When the car stopped turning, the entire floor began to rise. *For heaven's sake, it's a drive-in elevator!* To her right was a wall of windows, and as the elevator continued to ascend, the full glory of Singapore's nighttime skyline unfurled below her.

*This high-tech apartment must be Carlton's idea*, Eleanor thought. Since meeting Bao Shaoyen in London last September, she had come to know the family well. Eleanor and her friends had lent their support to Shaoyen and her husband, Gaoliang, during those tense few weeks when Carlton was in and out of surgeries at St. Mary's Paddington, and as soon as he was out of danger, it was Eleanor who suggested that he complete his recuperation in Singapore rather than Beijing.

"The climate and air quality will be much better for him, and we have some of the best physical therapists in the world. I'm related to all the top doctors in Singapore, and I'll make sure Carlton gets the best treatment," she had urged, and the Baos thankfully concurred. Of course, Eleanor did not reveal the true motive behind her altruism—having them close by would allow her to find out everything she could about the family.

Eleanor knew plenty of overindulged sons, but never had she met one with a mother so wrapped around his finger. Shaoyen had flown three maids down from Beijing to assist in Carlton's care but still insisted on doing practically everything for Carlton herself. And since arriving in Singapore last November, they had inexplicably moved three times. Daisy Foo had done what she considered to be a special favor for the Baos, and using her family connections had secured them a Valley Wing suite at the Shangri-La at a very discounted rate—but Carlton had for some reason been dissatisfied with one of Singapore's top hotels. The Baos soon moved into a furnished apartment at Hilltops, the luxurious high-rise on Leonie Hill, and a month later they switched again to an even swankier pad off Grange Road. And now here they were in this building with the ridiculous car elevator.

Eleanor remembered reading about this place in the property section of *Business Times*—it was the first luxury condo in Asia to boast biometrically controlled car elevators and "en suite sky garages" in every apartment. Only expats on could-give-a-damn expense accounts or Mainlanders with too much money would want to live in a place like this. Carlton, obviously in the latter category, had gotten exactly what he wanted.

Fifty levels up, the ground finally came to a halt and Eleanor found herself peering into a sprawling living room. Shaoyen stood on the other side of a glass wall waving at her, with Carlton—in a wheelchair—by her side.

"Welcome, welcome!" Shaoyen said excitedly as Eleanor entered the apartment.

"*Alamak*, I got the fright of my life! I thought I was getting a vertigo attack when the floor started to turn!"

"Sorry, Mrs. Young, it was my idea—I thought you'd enjoy the novelty of the car lift," Carlton explained.

Shaoyen gave Eleanor a look of resignation. "I hope you see now why we had to move in here. The handicap van comes right up to this floor, and Carlton can just wheel himself right into the apartment with no fuss."

"Yes, very convenient," Eleanor said, not believing for one moment that handicap access played a role in the selection of this apartment. She turned around to look at the gimmicky garage again, but noticed that the wall of glass had turned an opaque shade of white. "Wah, how clever! I thought you'd have to sit in your living room and stare at your car all day. It would be so unfortunate if you drove an old Subaru."

"Well, you can stare at your car if you want to," Carlton said, touching the screen on his iPad mini. The wall instantly became transparent again, but this time, special spotlights and mood lighting in the garage made her twelve-year-old Jaguar look like it was a museum showpiece. Eleanor was secretly relieved that her driver, Ahmad, had polished the car the day before.

"Imagine how gorgeous a chrome-colored Lamborghini Aventador would look sitting in there," Carlton said, shooting his mother a hopeful look.

"You are not getting behind the wheel of another sports car," Shaoyen said in a huff.

"We'll see about that," Carlton muttered under his breath, shooting Eleanor a conspiratorial look. Eleanor smiled back at him, thinking how utterly transformed he seemed. For the first few weeks after he had been moved to Singapore for his rehabilitation, Carlton seemed totally catatonic, barely making eye contact or saying a word to her. But today, the young man in the wheelchair was talking, even joking with her. Maybe they had put him on Zoloft or something.

Shaoyen steered Eleanor into the formal sitting room, an aggressively modern space with floor-to-ceiling windows and backlit onyx walls. A Mainland Chinese maid entered carrying a tray groaning with an elaborate Flora Danica tea service that Eleanor privately judged incongruous with the rest of the decor.

"Come, come, have some tea. You are so nice to spend time with us on New Year's Eve when you should be with your husband," Shaoyen said graciously.

"Well, Philip doesn't arrive until late tonight. Our family doesn't celebrate New Year's until tomorrow. Speaking of husbands, is Gaoliang around?"

"You just missed him. He had to fly back to Beijing. There are so many official functions he has to attend over the next few days."

"How unfortunate. Well, you'll have to save some of these for him," Eleanor said as she handed Shaoyen a large plastic OG shopping bag.*

"Oh, you really shouldn't have!" Shaoyen reached into the bag and began to take out half a dozen different containers. "Now, what are all these delicious-looking confections?"

"Just some traditional New Year goodies made by my mother-in-law's cooks. Pineapple tarts, love letters, almond cookies, and assorted *nyonya* cakes."

"This is so nice of you. *Xiè xie!*† Wait a minute, I have something for you," Shaoyen said, scurrying off to another room.

Carlton eyed the desserts. "Awfully nice of you to bring all these treats, Mrs. Young. Which one should we try first?"

"I would start with something not too sweet, like the *kueh bangkit* almond cookies, and work your way up to the pineapple tarts," Eleanor advised. She studied Carlton's face for a moment. The scar on his left cheek was just a faint hairline now, and it actually added a dash of roguish charm to his boringly perfect cheekbones. He was a handsome young chap, and even after all the reconstructive surgery still resembled Rachel Chu so closely that it was rather disconcerting to look at him at times. Thankfully, his posh English accent, which reminded her so much of Nicky's, was much more attractive than Rachel's absurd American drawl.

"Mind if I share a secret with you, Mrs. Young?" Carlton suddenly whispered.

"Of course," Eleanor said.

---

* Oriental Garments, better known as OG, is a homegrown department store chain established in 1962. Offering value-for-money apparel, accessories, and household items, it's the go-to place for old-money Singaporean ladies of a certain generation who claim that they only wear Hanro underwear but secretly buy all their discount Triumph bras and panties there.
† Mandarin for "thank you."

Carlton peered over at the hallway for a moment to see if his mother was approaching, and then, slowly, he lifted himself up from the wheelchair and took a few tentative steps.

"You're walking now!" Eleanor exclaimed in astonishment.

"Shhhhh! Not so loud!" Carlton said, sitting down in his wheelchair again. "I don't want my mother to see this until I can walk clear across the room. My PT thinks I'll be walking normally again within a month, and running by this summer."

"Oh my goodness! I'm so happy for you," Eleanor said.

Shaoyen reentered the room. "What's all the excitement? Did Carlton tell you about his *mazi* coming to visit?"

"Noooo?" Eleanor replied, her interest piqued.

"She's not my girlfriend, Mother," Carlton said.

"Okay, Carlton's *friend* is coming to visit us next week," Shaoyen clarified.

Carlton let out an embarrassed groan.

"*Aiyah*, Carlton is so handsome and so smart, of course he would have a *friend*! Too bad, I had so many eligible pretty girls lined up to *gaai siu*,"* Eleanor said mischievously.

Carlton blushed a little. "Do you like the view, Mrs. Young?" he said, trying to change the subject.

"Yes, it's very nice. You know, you can see my apartment from here," Eleanor said.

"Really? Which one is it?" Shaoyen said with interest, going up to the window. They had been in Singapore for three months now, and she found it a bit curious that Eleanor had never once invited them over.

"It's the one on top of that hill over there. Do you see the tower that looks like it's built on top of that old mansion?"

"Yes, yes!"

"Which floor are you on?" Carlton asked.

---

* Cantonese for "introduce."

"I have the penthouse."

"Wicked! We tried to get the penthouse here but it was already taken," Carlton bragged.

"This is big enough, don't you think? Don't you have the whole floor?"

"Yes. It's three thousand five hundred square feet, with four bedrooms."

"My goodness, you must be paying an arm and a leg in rental fees."

"Well, we decided to buy the place rather than pay rent on it," Carlton said with a satisfied grin.

"Oh," Eleanor said, surprised.

"Yes, and now that we've moved in, we like it so much that we've decided to buy the floors above and below and create a triplex—"

"No, no, we're just thinking about it," Shaoyen cut in quickly.

"What do you mean, Mother? We signed the contract two days ago! There's no backing out now!"

Shaoyen pursed her lips tightly before catching herself and forcing a smile. She was obviously uncomfortable that her son had said so much.

Eleanor tried to put her at ease. "Shaoyen, I think you've made a very wise decision. Prices in this district will always go up. Singapore properties are becoming even more sought after than New York, London, or Hong Kong."

"That's exactly what I told Mother," Carlton said.

Shaoyen said nothing, but reached over to pour a cup of tea for Eleanor.

Eleanor smiled as she took the tea, while the adding machine in her brain began to do its work. In such a prime location, this flat must easily have cost the Baos $15 million—probably more with the sky garage—and now it turns out they bought *two* more floors. With Eddie Cheng as their private banker, Eleanor assumed the Baos had to be loaded, but apparently she had underestimated how loaded.

Daisy Foo had been right all along. Shortly after meeting Shaoyen in London, Daisy had theorized, "I bet these Baos are richer than God. You have no idea how wealthy all these Mainlanders have become—it seems like yesterday Peter and Annabel Lee were the first Mainland billionaires, and now there are hundreds. My son tells me that China will have more billionaires than America within five years." Mr. Wong, the trusty private investigator Lorena had connected her to, had been crisscrossing China for the last few months trying to dig up every piece of dirt on the Baos, and now Eleanor was even more anxious to read his dossier.

After Carlton and Shaoyen had made a respectable dent in the New Year desserts, Shaoyen handed a large red-and-gold shopping bag to Eleanor. "Here, just a small token for you to celebrate the holiday. *Xin nian kuai le.*"[*]

"*Aiyah*, no need *lah*! What's this?" Eleanor said, pulling out an instantly recognizable orange-and-brown-trimmed box from the shopping bag. Lifting the cover, she saw that the box contained an Hermès Birkin bag.

"Do you like it? I know you tend to wear neutral colors, so I got you the White Himalayan Nile Crocodile," Shaoyen explained.

Eleanor knew that this handbag, dyed in the chocolate, beige, and white tones of a Himalayan cat, had to cost at least a hundred thousand dollars. "*Alamak!* This is far too lavish! I can't accept this!"

"It's just a small token, really," Shaoyen said demurely.

"I appreciate the gesture, but I cannot accept it. I know

---

[*] "Happy New Year" in Mandarin.

how much these things cost. You should be saving this for
yourself."

"No, no, too late," Shaoyen said as she unfastened the
buckle and lifted up the front flap of the handbag. Embossed
on the leather were Eleanor's initials—E.Y.

Eleanor sighed. "This is too much. I must pay you for
this—"

"No, no. Do not insult us. This is nothing compared to all
the kindness you have shown us over the past few months."

*You don't know what I'm really up to*, Eleanor thought. She
turned to Carlton and said, "Help me out here. This is
outrageous!"

"It's really no big deal," Carlton said.

"It IS a big deal! You know I can't possibly accept such a
generous gift from your mother."

Carlton scoffed. "Come, Mrs. Young. Let me show you
something." He wheeled himself out of the sitting room,
beckoning Eleanor to follow. At the end of the hallway, he
opened the door to one of the guest bedrooms and turned
on the light. Eleanor peered into the room. It was sparsely
furnished but almost impossible to walk into.

Covering the entire floor were Hermès bags and matching
boxes, and displayed on top of each box was a Birkin or Kelly
handbag—in every color of the rainbow, in every possible
variation of exotic leather. Along every wall were custom-
built cabinets that displayed rows and rows of Hermès handbags, all illuminated by soft accent lights. There were more
than a hundred handbags in the room, and the calculator in
Eleanor's brain started going into overdrive.

"This is my mother's gift room. She's giving an Hermès to
every single doctor, nurse, and physical therapist at Camden
Medical Centre who's helped me over the past few months."

Eleanor stared at all the handbags crammed into the room,
her mouth agape.

"My mother has one weakness. And now you know what it is," Carlton said with a laugh.

Shaoyen proceeded to show Eleanor some of the most unique Hermès bags—customized just for her. Privately, Eleanor felt it was a gigantic waste of money. *Think how many Noble Group or CapitaLand shares she could buy instead!* But publicly, she made a show of oohing and aahing over the bags.

Eleanor thanked them again for the lavish gift and prepared to depart. Carlton rolled over to the entrance foyer and said, "Take the elevator this time, Mrs. Young. I'll send your car down by itself, and it will be waiting for you when you reach the lobby."

"Oh thank you so much, Carlton. I was thinking I might have a panic attack if I had to go in that car elevator again!"

Shaoyen and Carlton waved goodbye at the elevator vestibule. The doors closed, but instead of going down immediately, there was an unusual pause. On the other side of the door, Eleanor heard Carlton let out a sudden yell.

"Ow! Ooow! That one really hurt, Mother! What have I done?"

"*BAICHI!*\* How dare you tell Eleanor Young so much of our business? Have you learned nothing?" Shaoyen screamed in Mandarin.

Then the elevator began its rapid descent, and Eleanor could hear no more.

---

\*    Mandarin for "Idiot!"

# RIDOUT ROAD

SINGAPORE

---

**From: Astrid Teo<astridleongteo@gmail.com>**
**Date: February 9, 2013 at 10:42 PM**
**To: Charlie Wu<charles.wu@wumicrosystems.com>**
**Subject: HNY!**

Hey you,

Just wanted to wish you a Happy New Year! I got home
from the annual yee sang* dinner with my in-laws, and I
suddenly remembered the year I came over to your house
for the dish, and one of the ingredients was 24-carat gold-
leaf shavings. I remember telling my mum about it, knowing
it would scandalize her. ("Goodness gracious, those Wus

---

\* Eaten during Chinese New Year in Singapore, *yee sang*, or "raw fish," consists of a huge plate piled with raw fish, shredded pickled vegetables, and a
variety of spices and sauces. On cue, the diners at the table stand and toss the
ingredients in the air with their chopsticks while wishing each other prosperity
and abundance. Known as the "prosperity toss," the belief is that the higher
you toss, the higher your fortunes will grow.

have run out of ways to spend their money, so now they are literally eating it!" was what she had to say.)

Apologies for not writing in a while but these past few months have been rather insane. I've become a working girl of sorts . . . I'm now involved with the Fine Arts Museum, helping behind the scenes with some strategic next-phase acquisitions as the museum expands. (Please keep all this to yourself. They wanted to officially make me a trustee or name a wing for me but I declined both. No desire to see my name carved into a wall—I actually think it's kind of morbid.)

Speaking of acquisitions, Michael's new company has been on a tear! He bought two U.S.-based tech start-ups last year, giving me an excuse to accompany him on a couple of trips to California to visit my brother. Alex and Salimah now have three kids and live in a lovely home in Brentwood. This year my mum finally agreed to come with me to LA to meet her grandchildren (Dad still refuses to acknowledge Salimah and "those" kids). Of course Mum fell in love with them—they are adorable.

The same cannot be said for Cassian, who's been more than a handful. I made it through the terrible twos but no one told me about the terrible fives! You ought to count your lucky stars that you have girls. We are now trying to decide whether to hold him back another year before he starts primary school at ACS. (Of course, Michael doesn't think he should go to ACS at all and wants him to go to an international school. What do you think of that?)

Also, in October we moved to a new house on Ridout Road. Yes, finally! Although it didn't take much to convince Michael to leave our little flat now that he could buy a house with his own money. It's one of those lovely Kerry Hill–designed bungalows from the 1990s—classic tropical modern built around three courtyards with reflecting pools, etc. We hired a young local architect who had apprenticed with Peter Zumthor to do some updating, and a fantastic Italian landscape designer to make the grounds less Bali and more Sardinia. (Yes, I'm still inspired by our trip to Cala di Volpe all those years ago!)

So of course moving and setting up the new house became a full-time job, even though I supposedly had a whole design team at my disposal. But guess what? We're already outgrowing 9,000 sq. ft. as Michael has become addicted to collecting historical artifacts and vintage Porsches. What was supposed to be our downstairs living room is now practically a car showroom. Can you believe it? Two years ago, I couldn't even convince my husband to buy a new suit!

Anyway, how are you? I saw you on the cover of Wired last month—so proud of you! How are the girls? How's Isabel? From your last e-mail it sounded like the two of you are in a really great place. What did I tell you? A week in the Maldives with no phones or Wi-Fi will reinvigorate any marriage!

If you're coming to S'pore this year please let me know—I'll give you a tour of my new car dealership!

xo,
A

---

**From: Charlie Wu<charles.wu@wumicrosystems.com>**
**Date: February 10, 2013 at 1:29 AM**
**To: Astrid Teo<astridleongteo@gmail.com>**
**Subject: Re: HNY!**

Hi Astrid,

The museum work is perfect for you—I've always thought
you'd make a great force in the cultural scene. Glad you
finally have a home with enough room to swing a cat. Not
sure if you'd consider me lucky these days: my younger
one, Delphine (4), has become an exhibitionist (the other
day she stripped off all her clothes and ran around Lane
Crawford for ten minutes before the nannies caught her—
I suspect they were too busy shopping the pre–New Year
sale to notice), and her older sister, Chloe (7), is going
through a major tomboy phase. She found my old Northern
Exposure DVDs and for some reason has fallen in love with
the show (even though I think she's too young to get any
of it). She now wants to be either a bush pilot or a sheriff.
Isabel is not at all happy about this, but at least she's much
happier with me these days.
     Happy Year of the Snake to you and your family!

Regards,
Charlie

---

**From: Astrid Teo<astridleongteo@gmail.com>**
**Date: February 10, 2013 at 7:35 AM**
**To: Charlie Wu<charles.wu@wumicrosystems.com>**
**Subject: Re: Re: HNY!**

God, I remember how we used to binge on Northern
Exposure back in our London days! I was totally obsessed
with John Corbett. Wonder what he's up to these days?
Remember that idea you had, inspired by Adam the chef's
stint at the Brick? You wanted to find an old truck-stop diner
in the middle of nowhere—on some desolate road in the
Orkney Islands or Canada's Northwest Territories—and hire
a genius chef who'd apprenticed in the best restaurants in
Paris to work there. We'd serve the most exquisite, innova-
tive food, but we would not redecorate the place one bit
and still serve on the old plastic diner plates and charge
diner prices. I would be the waitress and wear only Ann
Demeulemeester. And you would be the bartender and
serve only the finest single malt scotches and the rarest
wines, but we'd scrape off all the labels so no one would
know. People would just stumble in every once in a while
by accident and be treated to the best food in the world.
I still think it's a brilliant idea! Don't worry too much
about your daughters. I think nudism is a beautiful thing
in children (but maybe you ought to send her to Sweden
for the summer), and my cousin Sophie went through
a tomboy phase too. (Oh wait a minute, she's over thirty
now and I've still never seen her in makeup or a skirt.
Oops.)

xo,
A

p.s. What's up with your increasingly minimalist responses? Your last few e-mails have been painfully short compared to my tomes. If I didn't know how busy and important you are taking over the world, I would start to get offended!

---

**From: Charlie Wu<charles.wu@wumicrosystems.com>**
**Date: February 10, 2013 at 9:04 AM**
**To: Astrid Teo<astridleongteo@gmail.com>**
**Subject: Re: Re: Re: HNY!**

John Corbett has been living with Bo Derek since 2002.
I think he's doing just fine.
Regards, C

p.s. I'm not taking over the world—your husband is. I've been busy on a hunt to find a genius chef who is willing to live in Patagonia and cook for six customers a month.

*This message and any attached documents contain information from Wu Microsystems or its subsidiaries and may be confidential and/or privileged. If you are not the intended recipient, you may not read, copy, distribute, or use this information. If you have received this transmission in error, please notify the sender immediately by reply e-mail and then delete this message.*

# TYERSALL PARK

SINGAPORE, CHINESE NEW YEAR, MORNING

Three Mercedes S-Class sedans in the identical shade of iridium silver bearing license plate numbers TAN01, TAN02, and TAN03 idled in the morning traffic on their way to Tyersall Park. In the lead car, Lillian May Tan, matriarch of the family with the surname so unabashedly flaunted on its vehicles, peered out at the red-and-gold Chinese New Year decorations that assaulted every façade along Orchard Road. Every year, the decorations seemed to get more and more elaborate and less and less tasteful. "What in God's name is that?"

Seated in the front passenger seat, Eric Tan studied the ten-story LED billboard flashing an epileptic-seizure-inducing animation and let out a chuckle. "Grandma, I think it's supposed to be a red snake . . . entering some . . . um, golden tunnel."

"It's a curious-looking snake," Eric's new wife, Evie, commented in her high-pitched voice.

Lillian May refrained from mentioning what she thought the engorged creature with the flared head resembled, but it reminded her of something she had seen a long time ago when her late husband—bless his soul—took her to a most peculiar live show in Amsterdam. "We should have taken Clemenceau Avenue! Now we're stuck in all this Orchard Road traffic," Lillian May said, fretting.

"*Aiyah*, no matter which way we go, it's going to be jammed up," her daughter Geraldine said.

Beginning on the first day of the Chinese New Year, Singaporeans participate in a most unique ritual. All over the island, people frantically dash around to the homes of family and friends to offer New Year greetings, exchange *ang pows*,* and gobble down food. The first two days of the New Year are most crucial, and a strict protocol is observed as people arrange their visits in specific order of seniority— paying respects to the oldest, most esteemed (and usually richest) relatives first. Adult children not living at home are expected to visit their parents, younger siblings have to visit each of their older siblings in descending order of age, second cousins twice removed visit first cousins once removed, and after spending all day driving around the city paying tribute to the paternal side, they have to repeat the whole process the next day on the maternal side.† In large families the whole affair would often involve complicated Excel flow charts, *ang*

---

* Hokkien for "red packet," these red envelopes embossed in gold are stuffed with cold hard cash and are given out during Chinese New Year by married couples to single people, especially children, for good luck. Amounts vary according to the giver's income bracket, but it is safe to say that the minimum amount in more affluent households is a hundred dollars. By the end of the week, most kids make out with thousands of dollars, and for some, their entire allowances for the year depend on this ritual. In another departure from tradition, the *ang pows* at Tyersall Park were made of a pale pink vellum, and always contained a nominal but symbolic amount. This explains the generations of children taken to Tyersall Park every New Year who would blurt out in disappointment, "*Kan ni nah*—only two dollars inside!"

† If your parents were divorced and remarried or you came from one of those families where Grandpa had taken multiple wives and sired multiple families, you were totally fucked.

*pow* tracking apps, and plenty of Russian vodka to dull the migraine-inducing confusion of it all.

The Tans prided themselves on always being the first to arrive at Tyersall Park on New Year's Day. Even though these descendants of the nineteenth-century rubber tycoon Tan Wah Wee were third cousins to the Youngs and technically not supposed to be the first visitors, they had established a tradition of showing up promptly at 10:00 a.m. since the 1960s (mainly because Lillian May's late husband did not want to miss out on rubbing shoulders with all the VVIPs who tended to show up early).

As the convoy of vehicles finally reached Tyersall Avenue and made its way up the private gravel road of the sprawling estate, Geraldine gave Evie a last-minute crash course on her new relatives. "Now, Evie, be sure to greet Su Yi in Hokkien like I instructed you, and don't address her unless you are spoken to first."

"Okay." Evie nodded, gaping at the elegant colonnade of palm trees leading to the most majestic house she had ever seen, getting more nervous by the second.

"And just avoid making any eye contact with her Thai ladies-in-waiting. Great-auntie Su Yi always has these two maids standing by her side who will give you the evil eye," Eric remarked.

"Oh God—"

"*Aiyah*, stop scaring the poor girl," Lillian May scoffed. As the family emerged from their cars and prepared to enter the house, Geraldine whispered a final warning to her mother. "Remember . . . DO NOT bring up Nicky again. You almost caused Auntie Su Yi to have a stroke last year when you asked where he was."

"What makes you think Nicky won't be here this year?" Lillian May asked as she crouched down by the Mercedes's side mirror to rearrange the elaborate wisps of hair cascading down her neck.

Geraldine glanced around quickly before continuing. "*Aiyah*, you don't even know the latest! Monica Lee told me that her niece Parker Yeo heard the most sensational tidbit from Teddy Lim: Apparently, Nicky's all set to marry that girl next month. Instead of a grand wedding here they are getting married in California *on a beach*! Can you imagine?"

"Hiyah—what a disgrace! Poor Su Yi. And poor Eleanor. What a loss of face—all her efforts to position Nicky as the most favored grandson have been dashed."

"Remember, Mummy, *um ngoi hoi seh, ah.*[*] Don't say anything!"

"Don't worry, I won't say a thing to Su Yi," Lillian May promised. She was glad to be here at Tyersall Park at last, in this oasis of splendor far removed from the garish New Year kitsch that adorned the rest of the island. To Lillian, there was this sense of being in an enchanted time warp the moment she passed through the front door. It was a house that adhered only to the traditions decreed by its exacting chatelaine, transforming for the festive season in its own subtle ways. The white phalaenopsis orchids that usually greeted visitors on the ancient stone table in the foyer were replaced by a towering arrangement of pink peonies. Upstairs in the drawing room, a twenty-foot-long calligraphy scroll bearing a New Year poem by Xu Zhimo—composed in tribute to Su Yi's late husband, Sir James Young—would be unfurled against the silver- and lapis-inlaid wall, and the white voile curtains that usually flapped against the veranda doors would be swapped for watered-silk panels in the palest shimmering rose.

---

[*]   Cantonese for "don't put a curse of death," meaning "don't sabotage the situation."

In the sun-soaked conservatory, the New Year tea ritual was just beginning. Su Yi, resplendent in a high-necked turquoise silk charmeuse dress and a single opera-length strand of cultured pearls, sat on a cushioned wicker chair by the French doors with her trusty Thai lady's maids standing solemnly behind her, while three of her middle-aged children stood in a row before her like school kids waiting to turn in their homework. Felicity and Victoria watched as their brother, Philip, ceremoniously offered the little teacup to his mother with both hands and formally offered wishes of good health and prosperity. After Su Yi took a sip of the oolong tea infused with dried red dates, it was Eleanor's turn. As Eleanor began pouring the steaming liquid from the ornately carved Qing dragon teapot, the first guests of the morning could be heard arriving.

"Hiyah, those Tans come earlier and earlier every year!" Felicity said irritatedly.

Victoria shook her head in disapproval. "That Geraldine is always worried that she'll miss out on the food. She gets fatter and fatter every year—I'm scared to imagine what her triglyceride level must be."

"Now, didn't that good-for-nothing Eric Tan just marry some Indonesian girl? I wonder how dark she is going to be," Felicity said.

"She's Indonesian Chinese—her mother is one of the Liem sisters, so I bet you she will be fairer than all of us put together. Now don't say a thing, but Cassandra warned me that Auntie Lillian May just got back from America and is sporting a new wig. She thinks it makes her look younger, but Cassandra thinks she looks like a *pontianak*,"* Victoria muttered.

---

* A female ghost with long, rat-nest-like hair that lives in a banana tree. From Indonesian and Malay mythology, *pontianak*s are said to be spirits of women who died while giving birth. A *pontianak* kills her victims by digging into their stomachs with her sharp dirty fingernails and devouring their organs. Yum.

"Goodness gracious!" Felicity giggled.

Just then, Lillian May breezed into the room, followed by a retinue of sons and daughters, assorted spouses, and grandchildren. The matriarch of the Tan family approached Su Yi, bowed ever so slightly, and offered the traditional New Year greeting: "*Gong hei fat choy!*"[*]

"*Gong hei fat choy.* And who are you?" Su Yi asked, peering at her through her trademark tinted bifocals.

Lillian May looked taken aback. "Su Yi, it's *me*. Lillian May Tan!"

Su Yi paused for a moment before saying, completely deadpan, "Oh, I didn't recognize you with your new hairstyle. I thought that wicked English woman from *Dynasty* had come to visit me."

Lillian didn't know whether to be pleased or offended, but everyone else in the room broke out in laughter.

Soon, more members of the extended Young–T'sien–Shang clan began to arrive, and everyone rushed around *gongheisatchoy*ing the hell out of each other, handing *ang pows* to the kids, complimenting one another's outfits, commenting on who had put on weight or looked too skinny, trading reports on whose house just sold for how much, showing off pictures of their most recent holiday/grandchild/medical procedure, and stuffing their faces with pineapple tarts.

As guests began dispersing toward the grand staircase and the upstairs drawing room, Lillian May took the opportunity to greet Eleanor. "I didn't want to compliment you in front of Felicity and Victoria, who are always so jealous of you, but I must say your purple wrap dress is a winner! You are by far the most elegant woman in the room!"

---

[*] "Congratulations and wishing you prosperity," the proper greeting in Cantonese. Naughtier children prefer to say "Happy New Year—I pull your ear!" or "*Gong hei fat choy—ang pow tae lai!*" (Now gimme that *ang pow*!)

Eleanor smiled graciously. "You look lovely too. That's *quite* an outfit . . . is the caftan detachable?"

"I got this when I was visiting my sister in San Francisco. It's this marvelous new designer I discovered. What was the name? Let me think . . . Eddie Fisher. No, no, that's not right . . . Eileen Fisher! Now, the West Coast has really had an unseasonably cold winter. You really must pack some extra-warm clothing for your trip."

"My trip?" Eleanor furrowed her brow.

"To California?"

"I'm not going to California."

"But surely you and Philip are going to—" Lillian began, before suddenly breaking off.

"To what?"

"Dear me, I'm such a fool . . . I'm sorry, I confused you with someone else for a moment," Lillian sputtered. "*Geik toh sei!**  I am getting so senile. Oh look, Astrid and Michael are here! Doesn't Astrid look divine? And little Cassian looks so adorable in that bow tie. I must go and pinch that cutie pie's cheeks!"

Eleanor's jaw tightened. This Lillian May was such a bad liar. Something was up in California, and Eleanor's mind reeled at all the possibilities. Why would she and Philip ever go to godforsaken California together? Unless there was some big event involving Nicky. Was he finally getting married? Yes, yes, that must be what was happening. Of course, the one person who would know the truth was Astrid, who at this very minute was standing at the staircase landing while Lillian May rather bizarrely stroked her dress. From afar, Astrid appeared to be wearing a rather simple white shift with blue detailing on the sleeves and hemline, but as Eleanor got closer, she realized that the blue detailing was actually silk embroidery that mimicked Delft china patterns.

---

*    Cantonese for "This irritates me to death!"

"*Aiyah*, Astrid, every year I come here just to see what couture dress you'll be wearing! And you certainly didn't disappoint—you are by far the most elegant woman in the room. Who are you wearing? Is it Balmain? Chanel? Dior?" Lillian May gushed.

"Oh, this is just a little experiment that my friend Jun* whipped up for me," Astrid said.

"It's absolutely divine! And Michael—from Toa Payoh to tycoon! My son tells me you have become the Steve Gates of Singapore!"

"Ha, ha. No *lah*, Auntie," Michael responded, too polite to correct the old lady.

"It's true. Every time I open *Business Times* I see your face. Do you have a hot tip for me?" Eleanor asked as she joined the group.

"Auntie Elle, from what my friends at G. K. Goh tell me, *you're* the one who could give me a few stock tips!" Michael laughed, clearly enjoying this new adoration from his wife's relatives.

"Rubbish, *lah*! I am just a small fry compared to you. Excuse me, but I need to borrow your wife for a minute," Eleanor said, grabbing hold of Astrid's elbow and steering her down the long gallerylike drawing room to the corner by the grand piano. The young pianist, who looked like he was barely out of his first year at the Raffles Music College as he sweated profusely in his suit, was playing some innocuous Chopin étude.

Astrid knew from the force of her grip that Eleanor meant business. Talking over the music, Eleanor said, "I want you to tell me the truth. Is Nicky getting married in California?"

---

* Jun Takahashi, the creative force behind the cult fashion label Undercover. The prototype of Astrid's dress was quite possibly the inspiration for his autumn–winter 2014 collection.

Astrid took a deep breath. "Yes."

"And when is this happening?"

"I don't want to lie to you, but I specifically promised Nicky I would not give out any details, so you'll have to ask him yourself."

"You know as well as I do that my son has refused to take my calls for over two years!"

"Well, that's between you and him. Please don't put me in the middle of this."

"You are in the middle of this whether you like it or not, because you two have been keeping secrets!" Eleanor was fuming.

Astrid sighed. She hated confrontations like this. "Given the circumstances, I think you know exactly why I can't tell you."

"Come on, I have a right to know!"

"Yes, but you have no right to sabotage his wedding."

"I'm not going to sabotage anything! You *have* to tell me! I'M HIS MOTHER, DAMN IT!" Eleanor exploded, forgetting where she was. The shocked pianist stopped playing, and suddenly all eyes in the room were on them. Astrid could see that even her grandmother was peering over in their direction with displeasure.

Astrid pursed her lips, refusing to say anything.

Eleanor looked at her sharply. "This is unbelievable!"

"No, what's unbelievable is how you can expect Nicky to want you anywhere near his wedding," Astrid said, her voice shaking, before she stalked off.

. . .

Three weeks before the New Year, the chefs from the Young, Shang, and T'sien households would gather at Tyersall Park's cavernous kitchen to begin the marathon production of New

Year delicacies. Marcus Sim, the Shang family's acclaimed pastry chef based at their estate in England, would fly in to prepare all manner of *nyonya* desserts—rainbow-hued *kueh lapis*, delicately sculpted *ang koo kueh*, and of course, his famous *kueh bangkit* cookies with Marcona almonds. Ah Lian, the T'siens' longtime cook, would supervise the team responsible for the labor-intensive preparation of pineapple tarts, sinfully sweet *nien gao*, and savory *tsai tao kueh* radish cakes. And Ah Ching, the chef at Tyersall Park, would oversee the New Year's Day luncheon where a gigantic baked ham (with her famous pineapple brandy sauce) would make its annual appearance.

But for the first time in as many years as she could remember, Eleanor did not enjoy her lunch. She hardly touched any of the ham that Geraldine Tan proclaimed to be "even juicier than last year's," and she couldn't even face her favorite *neen gao*. She loved the way the sticky-rice-flour dessert cake was prepared here—cut into half-moon slices, dipped in egg batter, and fried to a golden brown so that the outer layer of the cake was light and crisp, yet sweet and gooey the minute you bit into it. But today, she just didn't have the appetite for anything. Following strict seating protocol, she was trapped next to Bishop See Bei Sien, and she glared at her husband on the other side of the table, who was tucking into another helping of ham as he chatted with the bishop's wife. *How could he eat at a time like this?* An hour ago, she had asked Philip whether he had heard anything regarding Nicky and a wedding, and he had shocked her by saying, "Of course."

"WHAAAT? Why didn't you tell me, *lah*?"

"There was nothing to tell. I knew we weren't going to go."

"What do you mean? TELL ME EVERYTHING!" Eleanor demanded.

"Nicky called me in Sydney and asked me if I wanted to come to his wedding. I asked if you were invited, and he said no. So I told him, Good luck chap, but I won't be coming if your mother doesn't," Philip calmly explained.

"Where is the wedding? When is it?"

"I don't know."

"*Alamak!* How can you not know when he invited you?"

Philip sighed. "I didn't think to ask. It wasn't relevant since we weren't going."

"Why didn't you tell me about the conversation in the first place?"

"Because I knew you were going to be unreasonable about it."

"You are a moron! An absolute moron!" Eleanor screeched.

"See, I knew you were going to be unreasonable."

Eleanor played with her braised noodles, seething on the inside as she pretended to listen to the bishop complain about some pastor's wife who was spending millions trying to become a famous pop star. At the children's table, Cassian's au pair was trying to coax him into finishing his lunch. "I don't want noodles! I want ice cream!" the boy fussed.

"It's Chinese New Year. No ice cream for you today," his au pair said firmly.

Suddenly, an idea came to Eleanor. She whispered to one of the serving maids, "Can you please tell Ah Ching that I have a sore throat from all this heaty food and I'm desperately craving some ice cream?"

"Ice cream, ma'am?"

"Yes, any flavor. Anything you might have in the kitchen. But don't bring it to me here—I'll meet you in the library."

. . .

Fifteen minutes later, after having paid off Cassian's au pair with five crisp hundred-dollar bills, Eleanor was sitting at the black lacquered scholar's table in the library, watching the little boy devour an ice-cream sundae out of a large silver bowl.

"Cassian, when your mummy is away, you just tell Ludivine to call me, and my driver will come and pick you up and take you for ice cream anytime you like," Eleanor said.

"Really?" Cassian said, wide-eyed.

"Absolutely. It will be our little secret. When is your mother going away? Did she tell you she is getting on an aeroplane and going to America soon?"

"Uh-huh. In March."

"Did she tell you where she was going? Is she going to Cupertino? Or San Francisco? Los Angeles? Disneyland?"

"LA," Cassian said while gulping down another spoonful.

Eleanor breathed a sigh of relief. March gave her enough time. She patted the boy on the head and smiled as he stained the entire front of his Bonpoint dress shirt with hot fudge. *Serves Astrid right for trying to keep things from me!*

# MORTON STREET

FEBRUARY 10, 2013 6:38 PM PST

*Text messages to Nicholas Young's private cell phone (the one his parents don't have the number for)*

ASTRID: Yr mum found out about the wedding. Happy New Year.

NICK: WTF! How did she find out?

ASTRID: Not sure who leaked. She confronted me @Ah Ma's. Things got ugly.

NICK: Really?!?

ASTRID: Yes. She went nuts and made a scene when I wouldn't give her any details.

NICK: So she doesn't know when, where, etc.?

ASTRID: No, but I'm sure she'll find out eventually. Get ready.

NICK: I'll double down on security at the venue. Will hire ex-Mossad.

ASTRID: Make sure they are all from Tel Aviv. With good tans, lots of stubble, and great abs.

NICK: No, we need really sinister guards. Maybe I should call Putin and see whom he can recommend.

ASTRID: Miss u. Gotta run. Ling Cheh's ringing the lunch gong.

NICK: Please wish Ling Cheh gong hei fat choy, and save me some tsai tao kueh.

ASTRID: I'll save you all the crispy bits.

NICK: My favorite!

FEBRUARY 10, 2013 9:47 AM EST

*Message left on Nicholas Young's voice mail in New York*

Nicky, ah? Are you there? Happy New Year. Are you celebrating in New York? I hope you are going to do something. If you cannot find *yee sang* in Chinatown, at least have a plate of noodles. We have been at Ah Ma's all day. Everyone was there. All your cousins. Eric Tan's new Indonesian wife is very pretty and has very white skin. I think she must bleach it. I heard they had a ridiculously lavish wedding like Colin and Araminta's, but in Jakarta. Her side paid for most of it of course. I'm sure her side will pay for all of Eric's money-losing films from now on. Nicky, please call me when you get this message. There's something I need to discuss with you.

FEBRUARY 11, 2013 8:02 AM EST

*Message left on Nicholas Young's voice mail in New York*

Nicky, are you there? *Alamak*, this is getting ridiculous.
You cannot keep ignoring me like this. Please call me
back. I have something very important to tell you. Something you will want to know, I promise. Please call me as
soon as possible.

FEBRUARY 12, 2013 11:02 AM EST

*Message left on Nicholas Young's voice mail in New York*

Nicky, is that you? Nicky? He's not in . . . Dad here. Please
call your mother. She needs to speak to you urgently. I
want you to put aside your feelings and just call her. It's
Chinese New Year. Please be a good son and call home.

· · ·

It was Rachel who heard the messages first. They had just
arrived home from California, and after setting the luggage
down, Nick had run out to grab some sandwiches at La
Panineria while Rachel unpacked and checked the voice mails
on the home line.

"They were out of mortadella so I got a prosciutto and
fontina with fig mustard and a mozzarella, tomato, and pesto
panini—I thought we could share both," Nick announced
upon returning to the apartment. Handing the paper sack to
Rachel, he sensed that something was off. "You okay?"

"Um, you need to listen to the voice mails," Rachel said,
handing him the cordless phone. While Nick listened, Rachel

went into the kitchen and began unwrapping the sandwiches. She noticed that her fingers were trembling, and she found herself unable to decide whether to leave the sandwiches on the wax paper or put them on plates. For a moment, she became angry with herself. She hadn't thought that hearing Eleanor Young's voice again after all this time would have this effect on her. What was it she was feeling? Anxiety? Dread? She wasn't quite sure.

Entering the kitchen, Nick said, "You know, I think that's the first time in my life my dad's *ever* left me a voice mail. I'm always the one who calls him. My mum must be giving him hell."

"Looks like the cat's out of the bag." Rachel forced a smile, trying to mask her nerves.

Nick grimaced. "Astrid sent a text warning me while we were at your uncle's, but I didn't want to mention anything while we were all celebrating New Year's. Things were tense enough with all the talk about your father. I should have known this was coming."

"What do you think you'll do?"

"Absolutely nothing."

"You're really going to ignore her calls?"

"Of course. I'm not going to play her game."

Rachel felt relieved at first, but then a little conflicted about whether this was the right way for Nick to handle things. Ignoring his mother had gotten them into all that trouble the first time around. Was he making a big mistake again? "Are you sure you don't want to at least speak to your father . . . maybe try to clear the air before the wedding?"

Nick thought about it for a moment. "You know, there's really nothing to clear. My dad already gave us his blessing when I spoke to him last month. *He's* happy for us, at least."

"But what if the messages have nothing to do with our wedding?"

"Listen, if there was anything truly important my parents needed to tell me, they would have just told me on the voice mail. Or Astrid would have told me. This is just some new scheme my mother has cooked up in her last-ditch effort to prevent us from marrying. I gotta hand it to her—she's like a rabid dog that just won't let go of your leg," Nick said, fuming.

Rachel walked into the living room and sank down onto the sofa. Here she was, a girl who had grown up never knowing her father. As much as she detested Eleanor Young, she couldn't help but feel sad that Nick had become so estranged from his mother. She knew it wasn't her fault, but she hated that she was part of why it happened. She gathered her thoughts for a few minutes before finally speaking. "I wish things didn't have to be this way. I never thought I'd ever put you in a position like this."

"You didn't put me in any position. This was my mother's own doing. She only has herself to blame."

"I just never imagined I'd be at a place where my future husband's parents weren't invited to our wedding, and most of his family won't be there . . ."

Nick took a seat beside Rachel. "We talked about this already. It's going to be fine. Astrid and Alistair will be there, and they are my closest cousins. You know I've always hated those traditional Chinese weddings where everyone and their cat is invited. We're going to have an intimate ceremony surrounded by your family and our closest friends. Just you, me, and our chosen family. No one else matters."

"Are you sure?"

"I'm more than sure," Nick said as he began to kiss the tender spot at the nape of her neck.

Sighing softly, Rachel closed her eyes and hoped he really meant what he said.

. . .

A couple of weeks later, the students enrolled at New York University in the course Britain Between the Wars: The Lost Generation Rediscovered, Deconstructed, and Restored were treated to the most curious spectacle. In the middle of Professor Young's lecture, two extremely tan, extremely blond women of Amazonian proportions entered the classroom. Dressed in identical outfits of figure-hugging navy-blue cashmere sweaters, immaculately pressed white linen slacks, and white nautical caps with gold piping on the brims, the pair sauntered up to the front of the classroom and addressed the professor.

"Mr. Young? The favor of your presence has been requested. If you would please come with us," one of the blondes said in a thick Norwegian accent.

Not sure what to make of this, Nick replied, "My class isn't over for another twenty-five minutes. If you'd care to wait outside, we can speak when it's over."

"I'm afraid that's not possible, Mr. Young. The matter is extremely urgent and we've been requested to collect you immediately."

"Immediately?"

"Yes, immediately," the other blonde replied. This one had an Afrikaans accent that made her sound much sterner than the Norwegian. "Please come with us now."

Nick was starting to get a little annoyed by the disruption when suddenly it hit him—this had to be some pre-wedding prank, most likely courtesy of his best friend, Colin Khoo. He had assured Colin that he didn't care for a bachelor party or any sort of fuss, but it sure looked like these two leggy blondes were part of some elaborate ploy.

"And what if I don't go with you?" he said with a playful grin.

"Then you will give us no choice but to resort to extreme measures," the Norwegian replied.

Nick found himself fighting to keep a straight face. He hoped these women were not about to bust out a boom box and start stripping. His classroom would descend into total chaos and he would lose control of these already attention-deficient kids. Not to mention all his hard-earned credibility, since he hardly looked older than most of his students.

"Give me a few minutes to wrap things up," Nick finally said.

"Very well." The women nodded in unison.

Ten minutes later, Nick exited the classroom as his students excitedly whipped out their phones and began texting, tweeting, and instagramming pictures of their instructor being led away by two statuesque blondes in nautical-inspired outfits. Waiting in front of the building on University Place was a silver BMW SUV with tinted windows. Nick got in a little reluctantly, and as the sedan began speeding across Houston Street and onto the West Side Highway, he wondered where in the world he was being taken.

At Fifty-second Street, the car merged into one of the exit lanes leading toward the Manhattan Cruise Terminal, where the cruise ships that visited New York all docked. Moored at Pier 88 was a superyacht that looked like it had at least five levels of decks. *The Odin*, it was called. *Good God, Colin has way too much time and money on his hands!* Nick thought, staring up at the gargantuan vessel, which seemed to sparkle as shards of sunlight reflecting off the water danced across its midnight-blue hull. He climbed up the gangway and entered the grand foyer of the yacht, a soaring atrium with a circular glass elevator in the middle that looked like it could have been stolen from an Apple store. The blondes escorted Nick into the lift, which rose just one floor before opening up again.

"We could have taken the stairs," Nick remarked wryly to the ladies. He stepped out of the elevator, half expecting to find the room filled with friends like Colin Khoo, Mehmet

Sabançi, and some of his cousins, but instead found himself alone on what seemed to be the main deck of the yacht. The ladies led him through a series of sumptuous spaces, past sleek lounges paneled in golden sycamore, barstools upholstered in whale foreskin, and a salon with a ceiling that glowed like a James Turrell installation.

Nick began to have the sinking feeling that none of this had anything to do with a bachelor party. Just as he was beginning to consider his options for a hasty exit, they arrived at a pair of sliding doors guarded by two tall, strapping deckhands.* The men slid the doors apart, revealing a skylit dining deck. At the end of the deck, lounging on a dining settee in a white pique blazer, white jodhpurs, and camel-colored F.lli Fabbri riding boots, was none other than Jacqueline Ling.

"Ah, Nicky, just in time for the soufflé!" she said.

Nick approached his old family friend, feeling equally amused and exasperated. He should have clued in earlier that all this Scandinavian silliness had something to do with Jacqueline, whose longtime partner was the Norwegian billionaire Victor Normann.

"What kind of soufflé is it?" Nick asked nonchalantly, taking a seat across from the legendary beauty dubbed "the Chinese Catherine Deneuve" by the society pages.

"I believe it's kale and Emmentaler. Don't you think all the sudden hype about kale is getting a bit much? I want to know who's been doing all the PR for the kale industry—they should really get an award. Now, aren't you the least bit surprised to see me?"

"Actually, I'm rather disappointed. For a while I thought I'd been kidnapped and forced to be an extra in a James Bond movie."

"Didn't you enjoy meeting Alannah and Mette Marit? I

---

* Also blond, most likely Swedish.

knew you wouldn't come if I had just called up and invited you to lunch."

"Of course I would have, but at a more normal time—I hope you're going to find me a new job when NYU fires me for abandoning my class in the middle of a lecture."

"Hiyah, don't be such a spoilsport! You have no idea how hard it was to find a place to dock this beast. Now, I thought New York was supposed to be such a world-class city, but do you know your biggest marina can only hold up to a hundred and eighty feet? Where is *anyone* supposed to park their yacht?"

"Well, this is quite a beast. Lürssen, I presume?"

"Fincantieri, actually. Victor did not want his baby built anywhere near Norway, with those pesky journalists always scrutinizing his every move, so he chose an Italian shipyard instead. Of course, Espen[*] designed this one, like he has all our boats."

"Auntie Jacqueline, I don't think you summoned me here to talk about shipbuilding. Why don't you say what you really came to say?" Nick said, breaking off a corner of a still-warm baguette and dipping it into his soufflé.

"Nicky, I told you never to call me 'Auntie.' You make me feel like I'm past my sell date!" Jacqueline said in mock horror as she flicked a lustrous lock of black hair behind her shoulders.

"Jacqueline—you don't need me to tell you that you don't look a day over forty," Nick said.

"Thirty-nine, Nicky."

"Okay, thirty-nine." Nick laughed. He had to admit that

---

[*]   She's naturally referring to Espen Oeino, one of the world's leading naval architects, who has designed superyachts for the likes of Paul Allen, the Emir of Qatar, and the Sultan of Oman.

even as she sat across from him in the bright sunlight with only a touch of makeup on, she was still one of the most stunningly attractive women he had ever known.

"There's that handsome smile of yours! For a while I was afraid you were beginning to get surly. Don't ever get surly, Nicky, it's most unbecoming. My son, Teddy, always has the most surly, supercilious look about him—I should never have sent him to Eton."

"I don't think Eton had anything to do with it," Nick offered.

"You're probably right. He has those snobby recessive Lim genes from my late husband's side. Now, you should know that all of Singapore was talking about you over the Chinese New Year."

"I highly doubt that *all* of Singapore was talking about me, Jacqueline. I haven't lived there in over a decade and I really don't know many people."

"You know what I mean. I hope you don't mind my being frank. I've always been very fond of you, so I don't want to see you do the wrong thing."

"And what's the 'wrong thing'?"

"Marrying Rachel Chu."

Nick rolled his eyes in frustration. "I really don't want to be drawn into a discussion about this with you. It would be a waste of your time."

Ignoring him, Jacqueline continued. "I saw your Ah Ma last week. She summoned me to visit her, and we had tea on her veranda. She is very distressed by your estrangement from her, but at this point she is still willing to forgive you."

"Forgive *me*? Oh, that's rich."

"I see you are still reluctant to see her side of things."

"I'm not reluctant at all. I can't even *begin* to see her side of things. I don't know why my grandmother can't be happy for me, why she cannot trust me to make a decision about who I want to spend the rest of my life with."

"It has nothing to do with trust."

"Then what is it about?"

"It's a matter of respect, Nicky. Your Ah Ma cares for you dearly, and she has always had your best interests at heart. She knows what is best for you, and only asks that you respect her wishes."

"I used to respect my grandmother, but I'm sorry, I can't respect her snobbery. I'm not going to roll over and marry into one of the five families in Asia deemed acceptable by her."

Jacqueline sighed and shook her head slowly. "There is so much you don't know about your grandmother, about your own family."

"Well, why don't you tell me? Let's not keep it a mystery."

"Listen, there is only so much I can say. But I will tell you this: If you choose to go through with your wedding next month, I can assure you that your grandmother will take necessary measures."

"Meaning what? Meaning she's going to cut me out of her will? I thought she did that already," Nick said mockingly.

"Forgive me if I sound patronizing, but the arrogance of youth has led you astray. I don't think you truly realize what it means for the gates of Tyersall Park to be closed to you forever."

Nick laughed. "Jacqueline, you sound like some character out of a Trollope novel!"

"Laugh all you want, but you're being rather foolhardy about this. There is this sense of entitlement that was bred into you, and you are letting that affect your decisions. Do you really know what it means to be cut off from your fortune?"

"I'm doing just fine."

Jacqueline gave Nick a patronizing smile. "I'm not talking about the twenty or thirty million your grandfather left you.

That's just *teet toh lui*.* You can't even buy a proper house in Singapore with that these days. I'm talking about your real legacy. Tyersall Park. Are you prepared to lose it?"

"Tyersall Park is going to be left to my father, and one day it will pass to me," Nick said matter-of-factly.

"Let me give you some news—your father long ago gave up any hope of inheriting Tyersall Park."

"That's just idle gossip."

"No it's not, Nicky. It's a fact, and aside from your grandmother's lawyers and your great-uncle Alfred, I am probably the only person on the planet who knows this."

Nicky shook his head in disbelief.

Jacqueline sighed. "You think you know everything. Do you know I was with your grandmother the day your father announced that he was going to immigrate to Australia? No, because you were away at boarding school during that time. Your grandmother was furious at your father, and then she was brokenhearted. Imagine, a woman of her generation, a widow, having to suffer the indignity of this. I remember she cried to me, 'What's the use of having this house and all these things, when my only son is abandoning me?' That's when she decided to change her will and leave the house to you. She skipped over your father and put all her hopes in you."

Nick couldn't mask his look of surprise. For years, his busybody relatives had engaged in covert speculation over the contents of his grandmother's will, but this was one twist he hadn't imagined.

"Of course, your recent actions have sabotaged those plans. I have it on good authority that your grandmother is preparing to change her will again. How will you feel if Tyersall Park goes to one of your cousins?"

"If Astrid gets it, I'd be happy for her."

---

* Hokkien for "play money."

"You know how your grandmother is—she will want the house to go to one of the boys. It won't go to any of the Leongs, because she knows that they already have too many properties, but it could very well go to one of your Thai cousins. Or one of the Chengs. How would you feel if Eddie Cheng became lord and master of Tyersall Park?"

Nick looked at Jacqueline in alarm.

Jacqueline paused for a moment, carefully considering what she wanted to say next. "Do you know anything about my family, Nicky?"

"What do you mean? I know your grandfather was Ling Yin Chao."

"In the 1900s my grandfather was the richest man in Southeast Asia, revered by all. His house on Mount Sophia was bigger than Tyersall Park, and I was born in that house. I grew up much like your family did, in a kind of luxury that hardly exists today."

"Wait a minute . . . you're not going to tell me that your family lost all their money?"

"Of course not. But my grandfather had too many damn wives and too many children, so the fortune's been dispersed. Collectively, we'd still rank high on the Forbes list, but not when there are so many of us feeding from the pot these days. But look at me, *I'm a girl*. My grandfather was an old-fashioned man from Amoy, and for people like him, girls weren't supposed to inherit—they were just married off. Before he died, he put all his holdings in a labyrinthine family trust, stipulating that only males born with the Ling surname could benefit. I was expected to marry well, and I did, but then my husband died much too young, and I was left with two small children and some *teet toh lui*. Do you know how it feels to live among some of the richest people in the world and feel like you have nothing compared to them? Take it from me, Nicky—you have no idea what it's like to come from everything and then lose it all."

"You're not exactly hurting." Nick gestured at their surroundings.

"True, I've managed to maintain certain standards, but it has not happened with the sort of ease that you might imagine."

"I appreciate your story, but the difference between you and me is that I don't require all that much. I don't need a yacht or a plane or a huge estate. I spent half my life in houses that were far too big, and it's such a relief to live the way I do in New York. I'm perfectly content with my life just the way it is."

"I think you misunderstand me. How can I put it to you more clearly?" Jacqueline pursed her lips for a moment and considered her finely painted manicure, as if she wasn't quite sure what she wanted to say. "You know, I grew up thinking that I was born into a certain world. My whole identity was wrapped up in the notion that I belonged to this family—that I was a *Ling*. But the moment I got married, I found out that I was not considered a Ling anymore. Not in the truest sense. All my brothers, half brothers, and idiot male cousins would inherit hundreds of millions each from the Ling Trust, but I wouldn't be entitled to a cent. But then I realized it wasn't really the loss of money that was affecting me the most. It was the loss of the privilege. To suddenly realize that you are inconsequential even within your own family. If you go through with this marriage, I promise you will feel a seismic shift. You can act self-righteous in front of me right now, but believe me, when it is all taken away, you won't know what hit you. Doors that have been open to you all your life will suddenly be closed, because in everyone's eyes, you are nothing without Tyersall Park. And I would hate to see that happen.

You are the rightful heir. How much is that land worth today? Sixty of the most prime acres in the heart of Singapore . . . it's like owning Central Park in New York. I can't even begin to fathom the value. If Rachel only knew what you were giving up."

"Well, I'm certainly not interested in having any of it if I can't share my life with her," Nick said adamantly.

"Who said you couldn't be with Rachel? Why don't you live with her as you have been? Just don't get married now. Don't rub it in your grandma's face. Go home and make peace with her. She is in her nineties, how many years does she have left? After she goes, you can do anything you want."

Nick considered her words in silence. There was a gentle knock on the door, and a steward bearing a tray of coffee and desserts entered.

"Thank you, Sven. Now try some of this chocolate cake. I think you'll find it to be quite interesting."

Nick took a bite, recognizing immediately that it tasted exactly like the airy yet rich chocolate chiffon cake made by the cook at his grandmother's house. "How did you manage to pry the recipe out of Ah Ching?" he asked in surprise.

"I didn't. I smuggled a slice into my handbag when I had lunch with your grandmother last week and had it flown straight to Marius, the genius chef we have aboard. He spent three days doing his own forensics on the cake, and after about twenty attempts, we got it just right, don't you think?"

"It's perfect."

"Now, how would you feel if you could never have this chocolate cake again?"

"I'll just have to be invited back to your yacht."

"This isn't my yacht, Nicky. None of this is mine. And don't think I'm not reminded of this every day of my life."

# BELMONT ROAD

SINGAPORE, MARCH I, 2OI3

The man with the machine gun tapped on the tinted glass of Carol Tai's Bentley Arnage. "Lower your window, please," he said gruffly.

As the window came down, the man peered in, carefully scrutinizing Carol and Eleanor Young in the backseats.

"Your invitations, please," he said, extending a Kevlar-gloved hand. Carol handed over the engraved metal cards.

"Please have your handbags open and ready for inspection when you get to the entrance," the man instructed, gesturing for Carol's chauffeur to drive on. They passed through the security roadblock, only to find themselves bumper-to-bumper with other fancy sedans trying to make their way toward the house with the red lacquered front door on Belmont Road.

"*Aiyah*, if I knew it was going to be this *lay chay*,* I wouldn't have come," Carol complained.

"I told you it wouldn't be worth the headache. It never

---

* Hokkien for "troublesome."

used to be like this," Eleanor said, glaring at the traffic jam and thinking back to the earlier days of Mrs. Singh's jewelry tea party. Gayatri Singh, the youngest daughter of a maharaja, possessed one of Singapore's legendary jewelry collections, said to rival that of Mrs. Lee Yong Chien or Shang Su Yi. Every year, she would return from her annual trip to India with another stash of heirlooms spirited away from her increasingly senile mother, and starting in the early 1960s, she had begun inviting her dearest friends—women hailing from Singapore's elite families—to come over for tea to "celebrate" her latest baubles.

"Back when Mrs. Singh was running the show, it was such a relaxed affair. It was just a bunch of nice ladies in beautiful saris sitting around the living room. Everyone took turns fondling Mrs. Singh's jewels while gossiping and gobbling down Indian sweets," Eleanor recalled.

Carol scrutinized the long queue trying to get through the front door. "This looks anything but relaxed. *Alamak*, who are all these women all dressed up like they are going to a cocktail party?"

"It's all the *new people*. The whoest-who of Singapore society that no one has ever heard of—mainly Chindos,"* Eleanor sniffed.

Ever since Mrs. Singh lost interest in counting her carats and began spending more time in India studying Vedic scriptures, her daughter-in-law Sarita—a former minor Bollywood actress—had taken over the affair, and the homey ladies' tea party evolved into a high-profile charity exhibition to raise money for whatever happened to be Sarita's cause du jour. The event was breathlessly chronicled by all the glossy magazines, and anyone who could pay the exorbitant entry fee had the privilege of traipsing through the Singhs' elegant modernist

---

\*    Crazy Rich Chinese + Indonesia = Chindos

bungalow and gawking at the jewelry, which nowadays consisted of some specially themed exhibition.

This year's show was devoted to the works of the acclaimed Norwegian silversmith Tone Vigeland, and as Lorena Lim, Nadine Shaw, and Daisy Foo peered into the glass vitrines in what was now the "gallery," converted from the former table-tennis room, Nadine could not help but register her dismay. "*Alamak*, who wants to see all this Scandinavian *gow sai*\*? I thought we would get to see some of Mrs. Singh's jewels."

"Keep your voice down! That *ang moh*† over there is the curator. Apparently she is some hotshot from the Austin Cooper Design Museum in New York," Lorena warned.

"*Aiyah*, I don't care if she's Anderson Cooper! Who wants to pay five hundred dollars a ticket to see jewelry made of rusty nails? I came to see rubies the size of rambutans!"

"Nadine has a point. This is such a waste of money, even though we got these free tickets from my banker at OCBC," Daisy said.

Just then, Eleanor entered the gallery, squinting at the bright lights. She immediately put her sunglasses back on.

"Eleanor!" Lorena said in surprise. "I didn't know you were coming to this!"

"I wasn't planning to, but Carol was given tickets by her banker at UOB, and she convinced me to come. She needs cheering up."

"Where is she?"

"In the toilet, of course. You know her weak bladder."

"Well, there's nothing here that will cheer her up, unless she wants to see jewelry that will give her tetanus," Daisy reported.

"I told Carol this would be a waste of time! Sarita Singh

---

\*   Hokkien for "dog shit."

†   "Red hair" in Hokkien, this is a slang term used to refer to Caucasians of all stripes, even though the majority of Caucasians don't have red hair (or stripes).

only wants to impress her arty-farty international friends these days. Three years ago she invited me, Felicity, and Astrid, and it was all this Victorian mourning jewelry. Nothing but black jet and brooches made from the hair of dead people. *Hak sei yen!*[*] Only Astrid could appreciate it."

"Let me tell you what I'm appreciating right now—your new Birkin bag! I never thought you'd be caught dead with one of these. Didn't you once say that only tacky Mainlanders carried such bags?" Nadine asked.

"Funny you should say that—this was a gift from Bao Shaoyen."

"*Wah, ah nee ho miah!*[†] I told you the Baos were loaded," Daisy said.

"Well, you were right—the Baos are loaded beyond belief. My God, the way I've seen them spend in just the few months they've been here! Nadine, if you thought your Francesca was a spendthrift, you should see how that Carlton spends. I have never seen a boy more obsessed with cars in my life! At first his mother swore she would never let him set foot in another sports car, but every time I go over there, there's some exotic new car in their sky garage. Apparently he's been buying cars and shipping them back to China. He claims he'll make a fat profit reselling them to his friends."

"Well, it sounds like Carlton has made quite a recovery!" Lorena said.

"Yes, he hardly even needs his crutches anymore. Oh, in case you were still thinking of him for your Tiffany, you should stop. Apparently he's already got a girlfriend. A fashion model or something like that—she lives in Shanghai but flies down to see him every weekend."

---

[*] Although this Cantonese phrase means "Scares people to death," it is used to describe anything that's gross or creepy.
[†] Hokkien for "You have such a good life."

"Carlton is so handsome and charming, of course there must be a long line of girls trying to catch him," Nadine said.

"He may be all that, but I can see now why Shaoyen loses sleep over her son. She told me that the past few months have been the most relaxed time she's had in years. She's afraid that once Carlton is fully back on his feet again and they return to China, he will be impossible to manage."

Lowering her voice, Lorena asked, "Speaking of China, did you meet with Mr. Wong?"

"Of course. *Aiyah*, that Mr. Wong has put on so much weight—I think the private investigating business must be *zheen ho seng lee*."*

"So, everything is good? Did you read the dossier?"

"Did I ever. You won't *believe* what I found out about the Baos," Eleanor said with a little smile.

"What? What?" Lorena asked, leaning in closer.

Just then, Carol entered the gallery and made a beeline for Lorena and Eleanor. "*Alamak*, there was such a long line for the bathroom! How's the show?"

Daisy took her by the arm and said, "I think there were more interesting things to see in the *jambun*† than in this show. Come, let's see if the food is any better. I hope they have some spicy samosas."

As the ladies made their way down the passageway toward the dining room, an Indian woman with snow-white hair wearing a simple bone-colored sari emerged from one of the rooms and caught sight of them. "Eleanor Young, is that you looking so mysterious behind those sunglasses?" the woman asked in an elegant, lilting voice.

Eleanor took off her sunglasses. "Ah, Mrs. Singh! I didn't realize you were back in town."

---

*  Hokkien for "a very profitable business."
†  Malay for "toilet."

"Yes, yes. I'm just hiding from the crowd. Tell me, how is Su Yi? I missed her *Chap Goh Meh*\* party the other night."

"She's very well."

"Good, good. I've been meaning to pay her a visit since I got back from Cooch Behar, but I've been so jet-lagged this time. And how is Nicky? Did he return for New Year's?"

"Not this year, no," Eleanor said, forcing a smile.

Mrs. Singh gave her a knowing look. "Well, I'm sure he'll be back next year."

"Yes of course," Eleanor said, as she proceeded to introduce the ladies. Mrs. Singh nodded graciously at everyone. "Tell me, are you all enjoying my daughter-in-law's exhibition?"

"It's very *interesting*," Daisy offered.

"To be honest, I much preferred when you used to show your own jewelry," Eleanor ventured.

"Come with me," Mrs. Singh said with a mischievous smile. She led the women up a back staircase and down another passageway lined with Mughal-era portraits of various Indian royals in antique gilt frames. Soon they came upon an ornate doorway inlaid with turquoise and mother-of-pearl, guarded by a pair of Indian police officers. "Don't tell Sarita, but I decided to have a little party of my own," she said, flinging the door open.

Inside was Mrs. Singh's private sitting room, an airy space opening onto a luxuriant veranda lined with lime trees. A butler was handing out steaming cups of chai, while a sitar player plucked a soft, entrancing melody in a corner. Several ladies in iridescent saris sprawled on the deep purple divans, nibbling on sweet *ladoos*, while others sat cross-legged on the Kashmir

---

\*    Hokkien for "Fifteenth Night," a celebration held on the fifteenth day of the first lunar month to mark the official end of New Year celebrations. On this evening, single ladies will cast oranges in the river under the full moon in the hopes of finding good husbands, while everyone else in Singapore starts planning their diets.

silk carpet, admiring the rows upon rows of jewels blindingly arrayed on large forest green velvet trays in the middle of the floor. It felt like being at a pajama party inside the vault of Harry Winston.

Daisy's and Nadine's jaws dropped, and even Lorena—whose family owned an international chain of jewelers—couldn't help but be impressed by the sheer variety and magnificence of the pieces. There were easily hundreds of millions' worth of jewels just lying on the ground in front of them.

Mrs. Singh breezed into the room, a swish of chiffon trailing behind her. "Come in, ladies. Don't be shy, and please feel free to try anything on."

"Are you serious?" Nadine asked, her pulse beginning to race.

"Yes, yes. When it comes to jewels, I ascribe to the Elizabeth Taylor school of thought—jewels should be worn and enjoyed, not stared at from behind a glass case."

Before Mrs. Singh could even finish her sentence, Nadine had instinctively grabbed one of the biggest pieces on display—a necklace composed of twelve strands of ridiculously oversize pearls and diamonds. "Oh my GOD-ness, it's all one necklace!"

"Yes, it's such a silly thing. Believe it or not, Garrard made it for my grandfather for Queen Victoria's Jubilee, and since he weighed over three hundred pounds, it draped nicely across his entire belly. But how can you even wear such a thing in public these days?" Mrs. Singh said as she struggled to fasten the enormous baroque pearl clasp behind Nadine's neck.

"Now that's what I'm talking about!" Nadine said excitedly, a little bubble of spit forming at the corner of her mouth as she gazed at her reflection in the full-length mirror. Her entire torso was smothered in diamonds and pearls.

"You'll get a backache if you have it on for more than fifteen minutes," Mrs. Singh warned.

"Oh, it's worth it! It's worth it!" Nadine panted as she began to try on a cuff bracelet made entirely of cabochon rubies.

"Now this I like," Daisy said, picking out an exquisite brooch in the shape of a peacock feather inlaid with lapis, emeralds, and sapphires that perfectly matched a peacock's natural hues.

Mrs. Singh smiled. "That was my dear mama's. Cartier designed it for her in the early 1920s. I remember she used to wear it in her hair!"

Two maids entered bearing bowls of freshly made *gulab jamun*,* and the ladies began enjoying the sinfully sweet treat in one of the corners of the room. Carol finished her dessert in two bites and looked into her silver dessert bowl rather wistfully. "I thought all this would make me happier, but I probably should have just gone to church instead."

"*Aiyah*, what's the matter, Carol?" Lorena asked.

"Take a guess, *lor*. It's that son of mine. Ever since *Dato'* died, I've hardly seen or heard from Bernard. It's as if I don't exist anymore. I've only met my granddaughter twice since she was born—first time at Gleneagles Hospital, and then when they came back for *Dato'*s funeral. Now Bernard doesn't even return my calls. The maids tell me that he is still in Macau, but that wife of his is flying off somewhere else every day. Her baby is not even three and she is neglecting her already! Every week I open the paper and see some news about her at this party or that party, or buying something new. Did you hear about that painting she bought for almost two hundred million?"

Daisy looked at her sympathetically. "*Aiyah*, Carol, I've learned over the years to stop listening to all the stories about my children's spending. *Wah mai chup.*† At a certain point, you

---

\* Deep-fried milk dumplings soaked in a sweet rose syrup.
† Hokkien for "I couldn't give a damn."

have to let them make their own choices. After all, they can afford it."

"But that's precisely my worry—they *can't* afford it. Where are they getting all this money from?"

"Didn't Bernard gain control of all the businesses when *Dato'* died?" Nadine asked, suddenly more interested in Carol's story than in the gold-and-cognac diamond sautoir she was holding up to the sunlight.

"Of course not. Do you think my husband would be foolish enough to put Bernard in control while I'm still alive? He knows that boy would sell my own house from under me and leave me on the roadside if he could! After Bernard ran off with Kitty to Las Vegas to get married, *Dato'* was furious. He forbid anyone in the family office from giving Bernard access to any money and totally locked up his trust fund. He cannot touch the principal—only the annual income."

"So how did they afford to buy that painting?" Lorena asked.

"They must be spending on overdraft. The banks all know how much he'll be worth one day, so they are only too happy to lend to him now," Eleanor conjectured as she fiddled with a bejeweled Indian dagger.

"*Aiyoh*, so shameful! I can't imagine my son ever having to borrow money from a bank!" Carol moaned.

"Well, if you say he doesn't have any money right now, I can assure you that is what he must be doing. That's what one of Philip's cousins did. He was living like the Sultan of Brunei, and only when his father died did they realize he had mortgaged the house, mortgaged everything, to support his lifestyle and his two mistresses—one in Hong Kong and one in Taipei!" Eleanor said.

"Bernard has no money. He only gets about ten million a year to live on," Carol confirmed.

"Well, definitely they must be borrowing heavily, because

that Kitty seems to be spending like a *siow tsah bor*,"* Daisy said. "What's that you're playing with, Elle?"

"It's some unusual Indian dagger," Eleanor replied. It was actually two daggers that went into opposite ends of a scabbard encrusted in cloudy, colorful gems, and she had flicked the latch open on one end and was absentmindedly sliding the small sharp knife in and out. Looking around for her hostess, she said, "Mrs. Singh, tell me about this lovely little weapon."

Mrs. Singh, who was seated on the corner of a nearby divan chatting with another guest, glanced over for a moment.

"Oh that's not a weapon. It's a very ancient Hindu relic. Be careful not to open it, Eleanor, it's very bad luck! In fact, you shouldn't even be touching it. There is an evil spirit that's being held captive in there by the two knives, and a great misfortune will befall your firstborn if you unleash it. Now, we don't want anything to happen to dear Nicky, do we? So please leave that alone."

The ladies looked at her in horror, and for one of the few times in her life, Eleanor was absolutely speechless.

---

* Hokkien for "insane woman."

# DIAMOND BALLROOM, RITZ-CARLTON HOTEL

HONG KONG, MARCH 7, 2013

**PINNACLE MAGAZINE'S "SOCIAL SWELLS" COLUMN**
*by Leonardo Lai*

Last night, a star-studded crowd lit up the Fifteenth Annual Ming Foundation Pinnacle Ball. The event is a labor of love for **Connie Ming**, the first wife of Hong Kong's second richest man, **Ming Ka-Ching**, and the HK$25,000-per-seat tickets to this year's soiree sold fast when word got out that the **Duchess of Oxbridge**, a cousin of **H.M. Queen Elizabeth II**, would attend, and that the **Four Heavenly Kings**[*] would reunite to perform a tribute to legendary songstress **Tracy Kuan**, the recipient of this year's Lifetime Pinnacle Award.

The theme was "Nicholas and Alexandra," the romantic yet ill-fated imperial couple of Russia, and there was no more perfect setting than the Ritz-Carlton

---

[*]  Four male Cantopop stars in the 1990s—Jacky Cheung, Aaron Kwok, Leon Lai, and Andy Lau—who dominated the Asian music charts, packed stadiums, and made it acceptable for macho Asian men to frost their hair and wear sequined blazers.

Diamond Ballroom on the third floor of Hong Kong's tallest building. Guests arrived to find the space transformed into "St. Petersburg in Winter," with an ocean of Swarovski crystal icicles dangling from the ceiling, birch trees covered in "snow," and towering Fabergé egg centerpieces on every table. **Oscar Liang**, the enfant terrible of Cantonese fusion cuisine, outdid himself with his succulent and inventive Ekaterinburg Pork—suckling pig riddled with truffle-infused gold-leaf "bullets" and thrown down a cellar chute before being flame-roasted over Russian coffee grounds.

In this fabulous setting, Hong Kong's most royal brought out all the big stones from their vaults. Hostess supreme Connie Ming wore a czar's ransom worth of canary diamonds with her custom strapless black-and-white beaded Oscar de la Renta gown, **Ada Poon** wore the famous Poon rubies against her rose chiffon couture Elie Saab, and China's biggest star, **Pan TingTing**, drew gasps of delight in the gossamer white Empire waist gown once worn by Audrey Hepburn in the film *War and Peace*. The **Kai brothers** got into a fistfight (again), and a crisis was narrowly averted when **Mrs. Y. K. Loong** was shown to the wrong table, where the children from her late husband's second family were seated (the lawsuit to settle the estate resumes later this month). But all was forgotten by the time Tracy Kuan made her entrance on a reindeer sleigh pulled by eight six-pack-popping shirtless male models in Cossack uniforms. Tracy, in a white-fur-and-leather corset dress by Alexander McQueen enchanted the audience by singing three encores accompanied by the Four Heavenly Kings, who really sang live this time.

Also honored was Business Pinnacle of the Year

**Michael Teo**, the ridiculously photogenic tech titan whose meteoric rise has been much talked about. After the stock price of his tiny software firm shot up higher than Mount Fuji two years ago, Michael took the proceeds and opened his own venture capital firm, which made gazillions more launching some of Asia's most winning digital start-ups, like Gong Simi?, the Singlish messaging app. The big question I have is where has Michael been hiding his beautiful Singaporean wife all this time? The doe-eyed **Astor Teo** looked absolutely ravishing in a wispy black lace number (vintage Fontana), though I wished there was more bling to her diamond-and-aquamarine earrings. (With all the money her husband has made lately, it's high time he upgraded her jewels!)

**Sir Francis Poon**, who was awarded the Philanthropic Pinnacle Award, got the biggest surprise of the evening when **Mrs. Bernard Tai** (aka the former soap star Kitty Pong), overcome with emotion from Sir Francis's touching slide show about his medical rescue missions, rushed onstage and shocked the crowd by spontaneously announcing a $20 million gift to his foundation! Mrs. Tai wore a scene-stealing scarlet Guo Pei gown with what looked like a billion dollars' worth of emeralds and a six-foot-long train made out of peacock feathers. But it sure looks like she won't need any feathers to soar to new social heights.

· · ·

Astrid settled into a club chair at the SilverKris Lounge at Hong Kong International Airport, waiting for her flight to Los Angeles to begin boarding. She got out her iPad to do a final check of e-mails, and an instant message popped up.

CHARLIE WU: Good seeing you last night.

ASTRID LEONG TEO: Likewise.

CW: What are you up to today? Lunch possible?

ALT: Sorry, I'm already at the airport.

CW: Such a short trip!

ALT: Yes, that's why I didn't call you beforehand. This was a one-nighter on my way to LA.

CW: Your hubby buying up another Silicon Valley company this week?

ALT: No, hubby's already back in S'pore. I'm going to California for Nicky's wedding in Montecito. (Shh! It's a secret, and no one in my family knows I'm going except my cousin Alistair, who's traveling with me.)

CW: So Nicky's finally marrying that girl everyone couldn't stop talking about a couple of years ago?

ALT: Yes, Rachel. She's great.

CW: Please give him my congratulations. Michael's not going to the wedding?

ALT: It would have looked too suspicious if both of us ran off to the U.S. so soon after our last trip. BTW, he was thrilled to meet you last night. Apparently he's a huge fan of yours and couldn't believe I was the one making the introductions.

CW: Did he not know we were once engaged?!?

ALT: Of course, but I don't think it really clicked in his mind until last night. He associates you with his tech crowd, so he couldn't really conceive of the two of us actually knowing each other. You really boosted my street cred!

CW: He's a nice chap. And congrats again on his award. He's really made some smart moves.

ALT: You should have told him that! Why were you being so quiet last night?

cw: Was I?

alt: You hardly said a thing and looked like you couldn't wait to run off.

cw: I was trying to avoid Connie Ming, who's already trying to commit me to underwriting next year's ball! And I guess I wasn't expecting to see you there.

alt: Of course I would be there to support Michael!

cw: Yes, but I thought you didn't do charity galas, especially in Hong Kong. Wasn't it the rule in your family never to attend these big to-dos?

alt: The rule is more relaxed now that I'm a boring housewife. When I was younger, my parents didn't want pictures of me appearing everywhere for their paranoid security reasons, and they didn't want me to associate with the fast party crowd—the "International Chinese Trash" as Mum called it.

cw: People like me.

alt: LOL!

cw: Last night was especially bad. Lots of people your mum wouldn't approve of.

alt: It wasn't so bad.

cw: Really? I saw you were seated at Ada Poon's table.

alt: Okay, I confess—THAT was awful.

cw: Hahaha!

alt: Ada and her tai tai* friends totally froze me out for the first hour.

---

\* A Cantonese term that means "supreme wife" (implying a situation where a man has several wives) but no longer strictly interpreted, since polygamy has been banned in Hong Kong since 1971. Nowadays *tai tai* refers to a privileged lady of means, usually of high standing within Hong Kong society. A prerequisite of being a *tai tai* is being married to a wealthy man, thus allowing the *tai tai* a tremendous amount of leisure time to lunch, shop, visit the beauty parlor, decorate, gossip, establish a pet charity, enjoy afternoon tea, take tennis lessons, schedule tutors for her children, and terrorize her maids, not necessarily in that order.

cw: Did you tell them you were from Singapore?

alt: Michael's bio was in the programme, and everyone knew I was his wife. I know Hong Kongers have become a bit touchy ever since Singapore's airport was voted the world's best.

cw: Well, in my opinion we still have better shopping at our airport. Who needs a free cinema or an orchid garden when you can go from Loewe to Longchamp in less than ten steps? Anyway, the real reason the ladies gave you the cold shoulder was because you didn't go to St. Paul's, St. Stephen's, or Diocesan's. They didn't know where to rank you in their hierarchy.

alt: But there is such a thing as common courtesy. We're at an event for charity, for chrissake. All the ladies could not stop trying to outdo each other bragging about the huge fines they all had to pay on their illegal basements. It was such a bore. But then after the duchess made her speech, she came right up to my table and said, "Astrid! I thought that was you! What are you doing here? I'm seeing your parents for lunch next week at Stoker and Amanda's. Will you be at Chatsworth too?" And that's all it took. Suddenly the tai tais could not leave me alone.

cw: I bet they couldn't!

alt: Hong Kong women fascinate me. The style here really is so different than in Singapore. It's a studied opulence that's just breathtaking to behold. I don't think I've seen SO MUCH jewelry in one room at one time. Truly felt like the Russian Revolution, when all the aristocrats were fleeing the country with every piece of jewelry they had, some sewn into their clothing.

cw: They really piled it on, didn't they? What did you think of all those tiaras?

ALT: I don't think a woman should wear a tiara unless it's been in her family for several generations.

CW: Not sure if you look at our gossip columns, but there is this fool named Leonardo Lai . . .

ALT: Haha, yes! My cousin Cecilia just sent me the article.

CW: Leonardo obviously had NO CLUE who you were and couldn't even get your name right, but he's apparently concerned that you don't have enough jewelry. LOL!

ALT: I'm so glad he misspelled my name! Mum would be furious to see me in the gossip columns. I guess Leonardo wasn't impressed by pieces from the actual Imperial collection—my earrings used to belong to Dowager Empress Maria Feodorovna.

CW: Of course they did. I noticed them immediately— they looked like something I would have bought you back in our London days, from that little vintage jewelry shop in the Burlington Arcade that you loved poking around in. You were the best-dressed woman at the ball, no contest.

ALT: You're too sweet. But come on, I did not go all out like some of those Hong Kong fashionistas who wore specially commissioned gowns in the style of Catherine the Great or whomever.

CW: You've always dressed to please yourself—that's precisely why you looked great. You and Kitty Pong, of course.

ALT: You're funny. I actually thought she looked fantas-tic! Her dress was very Josephine Baker.

CW: She was naked except for all those feathers and emeralds.

ALT: The dress worked. But stealing the spotlight from Francis Poon was rather shameless. I was afraid poor old Francis was going to have a heart attack when she rushed onstage and grabbed the microphone from him while he was trying to make his speech!

cw: Ada Poon should have jumped up and slapped Kitty Pong just like any good third wife would.

alt: She was too weighed down by all that jewelry to do any jumping.

cw: I really do wonder what's happened to Bernard Tai. Why is Kitty everywhere but he's not? Is he even still alive?

alt: She's probably got him chained up in a dungeon somewhere with a ball gag in his mouth!

cw: Astrid Leong! You shock me!

alt: Sorry, I've been reading too much Marquis de Sade lately. Dare I ask where YOUR wife was? Am I ever going to meet the legendary Isabel Wu?

cw: Isabel is too snotty to go to events like these. She only goes to two or three of the old-guard balls every year.

alt: LOL! Old-guard balls. I don't even want to tell you what just came into my head!

cw: Sir Francis Poon?

alt: You're terrible! Oh—my cousin's waving me over. It's boarding time.

cw: Why you still fly commercial I'll never understand.

alt: We're Leongs, that's why. My dad thinks it would be shameful if the family is seen flying private since he is a "public servant." And he claims it's far safer in a big commercial airliner than in a small one.

cw: I think it's much safer on your own plane, with a dedicated ground crew. You get there in half the time and feel less jet lag.

alt: I don't ever get jet lag, remember? Also, we don't have Charlie Wu $$$.

cw: That's a funny one! You Leongs could buy me for
   breakfast any day. Anyway, have a good flight.
alt: Nice chatting. Next time we're in HK, I promise
   I'll give you more notice.
cw: Okay.
alt: Michael and I will take you to dinner. There's this
   great Teochew place in Hutchison House that my
   cousin keeps telling me about.
cw: No, no, no—my town, my treat.
alt: We'll fight about it later. xo.

Charlie logged off his computer and swiveled his chair
around to face the window. From his office on the fifty-fifth
floor of *Wuthering* Towers he had a sweeping view of the
harbor and could see every eastbound flight that departed out
of Hong Kong International Airport. He stared into the hori-
zon, scanning each plane that was taking off, searching for
Astrid's. *I should never have IM'd her today,* he told himself. *Why
in the world do I keep doing this to myself? Every time I hear her voice,
every time I read an e-mail or even exchange a text with her, it's pure
torture. I tried to stop. I tried to leave her alone. But seeing her again
for the first time in so long, entering the room in nothing but black lace
against glowing bare skin, I was just hit so hard by her beauty.*
    When at last Charlie saw the double-story Airbus A380
gliding through the sky with its telltale navy-and-gold mark-
ings, he found himself inexplicably picking up the phone and
calling his private hangar. "Johnny, ah? Could you please have
the plane ready within an hour? I need to go to Los Angeles."
*I'll surprise Astrid at the arrival lounge with red roses, just like I did
back in our university days in London. This time there will be five hundred red roses awaiting her when she gets off the plane. I'll take her to
Gjelina for lunch, and then maybe we can rent a car and drive to some
amazing spa up the coast for a few days. It will be just like the old days,
when we used to take the Volante over to France and drive all over the*

*Loire Valley exploring ancient castles together, going to wine tastings. Oh what the hell am I thinking? I'm married to Isabel and Astrid is married to Michael. I am the biggest idiot in the whole world. For one moment, one brief moment, I had a chance to win her back, when her insecure husband was feeling too poor to afford her, but instead I made him a fortune. Christ, what was I thinking when I did that? And now they are back together, so damn happy and perfectly in love. And here I am, with a wife who hates me, miserable as fuck.*

# THE LOCKE CLUB

HONG KONG, MARCH 9, 2013

Kitty Pong was brimming over with anticipation as she stood in the crowded elevator. For years she had heard about this place, and at long last she was about to have lunch here. Located on the fifth floor of a nondescript office building on Wyndham Street, the Locke Club was Hong Kong's most exclusive dining club—the holy of holies—and its members consisted of the crème de la crème of Hong Kong society and the international jet set. Unlike other private dining clubs,* where fame or a fat checkbook would gain you instant membership, the Locke played by its own rules. The place didn't even have a membership waiting list—you had to be invited to join by its strict and secretive board, and even feign-

---

* In a city where people are almost as obsessed with food as they are with status, perhaps the best-kept secret of the dining scene is that the finest cuisine arguably isn't found at the Michelin-starred restaurants in five-star hotels but rather at private dining clubs. These members-only establishments are sanctuaries of luxury hidden away on upper floors of office buildings, where the famous and well-heeled gather to enjoy their meals far from the prying eyes of paparazzi. These clubs often have years-long waiting lists for membership, and only the best concierges at the top hotels can be bribed into getting you a special "guest membership," provided you are fabulous enough.

ing a passing interest in belonging could mean that you would never, ever be asked.

Back in the days when she had a minor role on the soap opera *Many Splendid Things*, Kitty often overheard Sammi Hui—the show's biggest star—brag about her lunches at the Locke, and how she was seated in the same room as the Queen of Bhutan or Leo Ming's latest mistress. Kitty couldn't wait to see which sumptuous room she would be seated in today, and which important personages would be dining at the tables around her. Would they all be savoring the specialty of the house—turtle soup served in camphor-wood cups?

It was such a stroke of luck that she had been seated at Evangeline de Ayala's table at the Pinnacle Ball. Evangeline was the glamorous young wife of Pedro Paulo de Ayala, a scion of one of the oldest real estate families in the Philippines, and though the couple were fairly recent transplants to Hong Kong (via London, where Pedro Paulo had worked at Rothschild's), their aristocratic connections—not to mention aristocratic-sounding surname—had made them popular new members at the club. Evangeline appeared to be wowed by Kitty's big donation to Sir Francis Poon's foundation, and when she suggested meeting for lunch at the Locke, Kitty wondered if she was finally going to be invited to join. After all, she had in two short months transformed herself into Hong Kong's leading art collector and philanthropist.

The elevator door finally opened, and Kitty pranced into the front foyer of the club, with its glossy ebony-paneled walls and dramatic black-marble-and-steel staircase leading up to the fabled dining room. One of the hosts at the reception desk smiled at her.

"Good afternoon. May I help you?"

"Yes, I am meeting Miss de Ayala for lunch."

"*Missus* de Ayala?" the host officiously corrected.

"Yes, I meant missus," Kitty replied nervously.

"I'm afraid she isn't here yet. Please have a seat in our parlor, and we'll show you to the dining room as soon as she arrives."

Kitty walked into a room with silk-covered walls and took a seat in the middle of the red Le Corbusier sofa so that she could show herself off to best advantage. A few of the ladies coming off the elevator stared at her intently as they passed by, and she felt certain it was because of the outfit she had taken such care in choosing. She had opted for a sleeveless Giambattista Valli black-and-red floral-print dress, a red Céline knotted lambskin clutch, and Charlotte Olympia red flats with a gold buckle. Her only jewelry was a pair of cabochon ruby earrings from Solange Azagury-Partridge. Even with a peekaboo slit on the side of her dress, the look bordered on demure, and she dared any uppity *tai tai* to criticize her today.

Unbeknownst to Kitty, one of the ladies in the elevator had been Rosie Ho, who was on her way to join Ada Poon and a few of their former Maryknoll classmates for lunch. Rosie made a mad dash to the dining room and breathlessly announced, "Girls, you're never going to believe who is sitting in the parlor right now. Three guesses. Quick, quick!"

"Give us some sort of clue," Lainey Lui said.

"She's wearing a floral-print dress, and she definitely had breast reduction surgery."

"Oh my God, is it that lesbian girlfriend of Bebe Chow's?" Tessa Chen cackled.

"No, even better—"

"Hiyah, tell us!" the ladies implored.

"It's *Kitty Pong*!" Rosie triumphantly announced.

Ada's face went white with contempt.

Lainey seethed, "*Mut laan yeah?** How dare she show up here after the stunt she pulled the other night!"

---

* Cantonese for "What the fuck?"

"Who was stupid enough to bring her?" Tessa asked.

Ada rose slowly from the table and smiled tightly at her lunch companions. "Will you excuse me for just one minute? Please keep eating—don't let the delicious turtle soup get cold."

Evangeline de Ayala entered the parlor in a pretty black-and-white Lanvin shift dress and gave Kitty a double-cheek kiss. "So sorry to be late—I have no good excuse, except that I am always on Manila time."

"Don't worry—I was just admiring the art," Kitty graciously responded.

"Quite cool, isn't it? Do you collect?"

"I'm just beginning to, so I am trying to educate myself," Kitty said modestly, wondering whether Evangeline was just pretending not to know that she had recently bought the most expensive painting in all of Asia.

The ladies approached the reception desk together, and the same host greeted them warmly. "Good afternoon, Mrs. de Ayala. Joining us for lunch today?"

"Yes, just the two of us," Evangeline replied.

"Wonderful. Please come with me," the host said, escorting the ladies up the curved marble staircase. When they entered the dining room, Kitty noticed quite a few people gawking at them. The manager of the club came rushing toward them with a look of importance.

*Goody, he's coming to welcome me personally to the club,* Kitty thought.

"Mrs. de Ayala, I do apologize, but there seems to have been a huge mix-up with our computerized reservation system. I'm afraid we are completely overbooked today and will not be able to accommodate you for lunch."

The host looked taken aback by his manager's declaration, but said nothing.

Evangeline looked puzzled. "But I made the booking two days ago, and no one called to inform me."

"Yes, I am aware of that. We're truly sorry—but if you'll allow me, I have made a booking for you right around the corner at Yung Kee on Wellington Street. They have a lovely table awaiting you, and I hope you will allow us to treat you to lunch, to make up for the inconvenience."

"Surely you can seat us for a quick lunch here? We're just two, and I see a few empty tables along the window," Evangeline said hopefully.

"Unfortunately those tables have already been spoken for. Once again, please accept my apologies, and I do hope you enjoy Yung Kee—be sure to order their fabulous roast goose," the manager said as he authoritatively steered Kitty and Evangeline toward the staircase.

As they left the club, Evangeline was still perplexed. "How bizarre! I'm so sorry—nothing like that has ever happened before. But the Locke does have rather strange rules. Now, let me just text my driver about our change of plans." As Evangeline got out her phone, she saw that her husband was trying to call.

"Hey *swithart*,[*] how are you? The strangest thing just happened," Evangeline cooed into the phone. Then she jumped at the torrent of cursing that came from the other end.

"Nothing! We did nothing!" she said in a defensive tone.

Kitty could hear Evangeline's husband continue to rant.

"I can't explain . . . I don't know what happened," Evangeline kept sputtering into the phone, her face getting paler and paler. Finally she put her phone down and gave Kitty a rather dazed look.

"I'm sorry, but I'm suddenly not feeling too well. Do you mind if we take a rain check on lunch?"

"Of course. Is everything okay?" Kitty asked, rather concerned for her new friend.

---

[*]  Filipino slang for "sweetheart."

"That was my husband. Our membership at the Locke Club has just been revoked."

After Evangeline's driver had picked her up, Kitty stood at the curb, trying to process what had just happened. She had woken up this morning feeling so happy and excited, and now she was rather crestfallen that her lunch plans had gone so awry. Poor Evangeline. What an awful thing to happen to her. Just as she was about to call for her driver, Kitty noticed a gray-haired woman in a dowdy-looking pantsuit smiling at her.

"Are you okay?" the woman asked.

"Yes," Kitty responded, a little confused. Did she know her from somewhere?

"I was just at lunch at the Locke, and I couldn't help but notice what happened in the dining room," the woman said by way of introduction.

"Yes, it's quite strange, isn't it? I feel so bad for my friend."

"How so?"

"She didn't realize that she had lost her membership at the club, and she was trying to take me to lunch there. I think she must feel very embarrassed right now."

"*Evangeline de Ayala* was kicked out of the club?" the woman said incredulously.

"Oh—you know her? Yes, right after we left the club, her husband called with the news. He must have done something terribly wrong for them to be kicked out without any notice like that."

The woman paused for a few moments, as if she was trying to ascertain whether Kitty was being serious. "My poor dear, you are completely out to sea. You really have no clue what actually happened, do you? In the history of the club, they've only ever revoked a membership three times. Today was the fourth. The de Ayalas obviously were kicked out because Evangeline tried to bring *you* to the club."

Kitty looked incredulous. "*Me?* What a silly idea! That was my first time setting foot in the club—what did I have to do with it?"

The woman shook her head pitifully. "The fact that you don't even realize this makes me extremely sad. But I think I can help you."

"What do you mean help me? Who are you?"

"I'm Corinna Ko-Tung."

"As in Ko-Tung Park?"

"Yes, and Ko-Tung Road and the Ko-Tung wing at Queen Mary Hospital. Now, come with me. I know you must be starving. I'll explain everything over *yum cha*."*

Corinna led Kitty down On Lan Street and into an alley behind New World Tower. Taking the service elevator up three floors, they were deposited at the back entrance of Tsui Hang Village restaurant, where VIPs could pass through unnoticed.

The manager recognized Corinna at once and rushed up to her, bowing deeply. "Ms. Ko-Tung, such an honor to have you dining with us today."

"Thank you, Mr. Tong. Can we have a private room, please?"

"Certainly. Please come with me. How is your mother these days? Please send my best wishes to her," the manager said effusively as he escorted them down a hallway.

The ladies were shown to a private dining room done up in subtle shades of beige, with a large round table and a flat-screen television along the back wall set on CNBC with the volume on mute.

"I will let the chef know that you are here—I'm sure he will want to send out all his special dishes."

---

* The Cantonese phrase literally means "drink tea," but in Hong Kong it usually connotes a lunchtime meal of tea and dim sum.

"Please thank him for me in advance. Now, could you please turn off the television?" Corinna instructed.

"Oh I'm so sorry, of course," the manager said, lunging for the remote control as if it were the most offensive thing in the world.

After hot towels were ceremoniously distributed, two cups of tea had been poured, and the waitstaff had finally left the room, Kitty said, "You must be a regular here."

"I haven't been here in a while. But I thought it would be a convenient place for us to speak freely."

"Do they always treat you this well?"

"Generally. It also helps that my family owns the land this tower is built on."

Kitty was quietly impressed. Even after becoming Mrs. Bernard Tai, she had never been treated with such reverence anywhere. "Now, do you really think the de Ayalas got thrown out of the club because of me?"

"I don't think—I *know*," Corinna answered. "Ada Poon is on the membership committee."

"But what does she have against me? I just made a huge donation to her husband's foundation."

Corinna sighed. This was going to be harder than she thought. "I wasn't at the Pinnacle Ball, since I don't attend such affairs, but the very next morning my phone was ringing off the hook. *Everyone* was talking about what you did."

"What did I do?"

"You gravely insulted the Poons."

"But I was just trying to be generous—"

"You may see it that way, but everyone there saw it differently. Sir Francis Poon is eighty-six years old, and he is revered by all. That award was his big moment, the culmination of decades of humanitarian work, but when you barged onstage and announced your big donation right in the middle of his speech, it was seen as a huge affront to him. You offended his family, his friends, and perhaps most important, his wife. It was supposed to be Ada's night too, and you stole the limelight from her."

"It was never my intention to do that," Kitty shot back.

"Be honest with yourself, Kitty. *Of course it was.* You wanted all the attention on yourself, just like you did when you bought *The Palace of Eighteen Perfections.* But while the crowd at Christie's might appreciate a good floor show, Hong Kong society does not. Your actions over the past few months are seen as nothing but blatant attempts to buy your way into the right crowd. Now, many people have done just that, but there's a right way to do it, and there's a wrong way."

Kitty was indignant. "Ms. Ko-Tung, I know exactly what I'm doing. Just do a Baidu search under my name. Look at all the magazines and newspapers. The bloggers and gossip columnists can't stop writing about me. My pictures are in all the magazines every month. I've totally changed my style over the past year, and in last week's *Orange Daily,* they ran three pages on my red-carpet looks."

Corinna shook her head dismissively. "Don't you see that those magazines are just exploiting you? Sure, the average reader of *Orange Daily* living in Yau Ma Tei must think your life is a dream come true, but at a certain level of Hong Kong society, it doesn't matter if you wear the finest couture and millions of dollars' worth of diamonds. At this level, anyone can do that. Everyone is rich. Anyone can make a twenty-million-dollar donation if they really want to. To these people, having your picture in the party pages all the time actually does more damage than good—it is seen as desperate. Trust me, being in *Tattle* is not going to help your image. It won't get you a membership at the Locke Club, or an invitation to Mrs. Ladoorie's annual garden party at her villa in Repulse Bay."

Kitty didn't know whether or not to believe her. How could this woman who looked like her hair had been cut by some cheap hairdresser in Mong Kok dare to give her advice on her image?

"Mrs. Tai, let me tell you a bit about what I do. I advise people who want to secure a place among Asia's elite, among the real people of influence."

"With all due respect, I'm married to Bernard Tai. My husband is one of the richest men in the world. He's already influential."

"Oh *really*? Well where is Bernard these days, then? Why is he not at all the functions I go to? Why wasn't he at the Chief Executive's* lunch honoring the Fifty Most Influential Leaders in Asia last Thursday? Or at the party that my mother threw for the Duchess of Oxbridge last night? Why weren't you there?"

Kitty didn't know how to respond. She felt a wave of humiliation sweep over her.

"Mrs. Tai, if I may be very frank, the Tais have never had the best reputation. *Dato'* Tai Toh Lui was a corporate raider from some Malay backwater. The other tycoons despised him. And now his son is seen as a ne'er-do-well party boy who inherited a fortune but hasn't worked a day in his life. Everyone knows Carol Tai still controls the purse strings. No one takes Bernard seriously, especially after he married a former porn star turned soap-opera actress from Mainland China."

Kitty looked like she had been slapped in the face. She opened her mouth to protest, but Corinna pressed on. "I don't care what the truth is—I'm not here to judge you. But I feel that you need to know this is what everyone in Hong Kong has been saying about you. Everyone except Evangeline de Ayala, who we both know is very new in town."

"She was the first person who has been nice to me since I

---

* Refers to the Chief Executive of Hong Kong, who is supposedly the head of the government.

got married," Kitty said sadly. She looked down at her napkin for a moment before continuing. "I'm not as stupid as you think. I know what people are saying. I've been treated horribly by everyone, and it started long before the Pinnacle Ball. I was seated next to Araminta Lee at the Viktor & Rolf show in Paris last year, and she pretended like I didn't even exist. What have I done to deserve this? There are so many other socialites with murky pasts, much worse than mine. Why am I being singled out?"

Corinna assessed Kitty for a few moments. She had expected her to be far more mercenary, and she was unprepared to discover the naïveté of the girl sitting in front of her. "Do you really want me to tell you?"

"Yes, please."

"First of all, you are Mainland Chinese. You know how most Hong Kongers feel about Mainlanders. Like it or not, you have to work extra hard right out of the gate to overcome all the prejudices. But you handicapped yourself early on in the race. There's a whole crowd who will never forgive you for what you did to Alistair Cheng."

"Alistair?"

"Yes. Alistair Cheng is immensely popular. When you broke his heart, you made enemies out of all the girls who have adored him and all the people who respect his family."

"I didn't think Alistair's family was *that* special."

Corinna snorted. "Didn't Alistair take you to Tyersall Park?"

"Tire-what?"

"My God, you never even got near the palace gates, did you?"

"What are you talking about? What palace?"

"Never mind. The point is, Alistair's mother is Alix Young—because of her, Alistair is related to almost every important family in Asia. The Leongs of Malaysia, the aristocratic T'siens, the Shangs—who own practically everything. I'm sorry to have to break this to you, but you placed your bet on the wrong horse."

"I had no idea," Kitty said in a whisper.

"How could you? You didn't grow up among these people. You've never been properly schooled in the ways of the manor-born. Let me assure you, if we choose to work together, you will get the insider's view on everything. I will teach you the ins and outs of this world. I will share with you all the secrets of these families."

"And how much is all this going to cost me?"

Corinna took a leather folio out of her battered Furla tote bag and presented it to Kitty. "I charge an annual retainer, and you are contractually obligated to sign on for a minimum of two years."

Kitty looked over the schedule of fees and burst out laughing. "You've got to be joking!"

Corinna's expression turned grave. She knew the moment had arrived for the hard sell. "Mrs. Tai, let me ask you something. What do you really want out of life? Because this is where I see your life heading: You'll keep flying around Asia for the next few years, going to galas and benefits and whatnot, getting your picture in the magazines. Over time, you might strike up friendships with other rich Mainlanders or the *gweilo*[*] wives of men stationed here with three-year contracts at some foreign bank or private equity firm. You might even be invited to join the boards of inconsequential charities started by these bored expat wives. Your in-box will be filled with invitations for cocktails at the Chopard boutique

---

[*] This is a common Cantonese derogatory term usually applied to Caucasian foreigners, which literally translates as "foreign devil." These days, many Hong Kongers frequently use the term to refer to foreigners in general and don't consider it derogatory.

or art openings in Sheung Wan. Sure, you may occasionally be invited to one of Pascal Pang's parties, but the real Hong Kong will always be closed to you. You will never be asked to join the best clubs or attend the most exclusive parties in the best houses—and I'm not talking about Sonny Chin's mansion on Bowen Road. Your children will never get into the best schools and have playdates with children from the top families. You will never get to know any of the people who move the economy, who have the ear of the top politicians in Beijing, who affect culture. People who truly matter in Asia. How much is that worth to you?"

Kitty remained silent.

"Here, let me show you a few pictures," Corinna said, placing an iPad on the table. As she began to scroll through an album of images, Kitty recognized a few of the city's top social figures posing casually with Corinna in private settings. Here was Corinna at breakfast on board the plane of a certain Mainland tycoon who now lived in Singapore, at the graduation of Leo Ming's son from St. George's School in Vancouver, in the delivery room at Matilda Hospital holding a famous Hong Kong socialite's newborn baby.

"These are people you can introduce me to?"

"These are my clients."

Kitty's perfectly mascaraed eyes suddenly widened. "Ada Poon? *She's* one of your clients?"

Corinna smiled. "Let me show you a picture of what she looked like before I began working with her. For your eyes only."

"Oh my God—look at that outfit! And those teeth!" Kitty cackled.

"Yes, Dr. Chan did some of his best work ever on her teeth, didn't he? Did you know that before she became the third Mrs. Francis Poon, she worked in the Chanel boutique on Canton Road in Kowloon? That's how she met Francis—he came in looking for a little something for his wife, but left with a little something for himself."

"How interesting. I thought she came from a good Hong Kong family."

Corinna chose her words carefully. "I can tell you about Ada's past because it's a well-known fact. But you see, practically anyone can rise up in Hong Kong society. It's all about perception, really. And the careful reinvention of personal history. We will refocus your image. Anyone can be forgiven. *Anything* can be forgotten."

"So you will improve my image? You are going to help change Hong Kong's perception of me?"

"Mrs. Tai, I am going to change your life."

# ARCADIA

MONTECITO, CALIFORNIA, MARCH 9, 2013

Rachel led her friends down the long hallway and opened a door. "Here it is," she said in a hushed tone, gesturing for Goh Peik Lin and Sylvia Wong-Swartz to look in.

Peik Lin squealed as she caught her first glimpse of Rachel's wedding gown hanging on a vintage mannequin in the middle of the dressing room. "Ooooh! *It's gorgeous! Absolutely gorrrgeous!*"

Sylvia walked around it, inspecting the dress from every angle. "It's nothing like what I was expecting, but it's beautiful. So *you*. I still can't believe Nick took you to Paris to shop for your dress and you ended up finding this at the Temperley sample sale in SoHo!"

"I just didn't fall in love with anything in Paris. Every dress I saw this season was so over-the-top, and I really didn't want to deal with the fuss of a couture gown—you know, having to fly back and forth to Paris for all those fittings," Rachel said a little bashfully.

"Oh you poor thing, what torture, having to go to Paris for your fittings!" Sylvia teased.

Peik Lin patted Sylvia on the arm. "*Aiyah*, I've known

Rachel since she was eighteen. She's much too practical—we'll never change her. At least this dress looks like it could be haute couture."

"Wait till you see it on. It's all about the way it drapes," Rachel said excitedly.

Sylvia narrowed her eyes. "Hmm . . . that's not a typical Rachel Chu statement. We just might make a fashionista out of you yet!"

Rachel's cousin Samantha, looking rather authoritative with a headset on, entered the room all flustered. "There you are! I've been searching everywhere for you. Everyone's arrived, and we're all waiting to start the rehearsal."

"Sorry, I didn't know you guys were waiting," Rachel replied.

"Found the bride! We're on our way back!" Samantha barked into the headset as she shepherded the girls out of the main house and across the great lawn toward the Palladian-style music pavilion where the ceremony was to be held. Sylvia marveled at the mountains in the distance on one side of the lawn and the views of the Pacific Ocean on the other. "Tell me again how you guys found this amazing property."

"We got really lucky. Nick's friend Mehmet told us about Arcadia—the owners are friends of his family. They only come here once a year for a few weeks in the summer, and never lend the place out for events, but they made a special exception for us."

"Is Mehmet the hunk with the stubble and those incredible hazel eyes?" Samantha asked.

"You got it. The Turkish Casanova, we call him," Rachel said.

"Imagine how rich you have to be to maintain this huge estate all year to use it for just a few weeks," Sylvia said in astonishment.

"Speaking of rich, some of the women who just got here

look like they stepped out of the pages of *Vogue China*. There's a tall, leggy, supermodel type wearing boots that clearly cost more than my Prius, and there's another stunning girl in the most to-die-for linen shirtdress with such a posh English accent—Aunt Belinda already has her nose halfway up her hoo-ha," Samantha reported.

Rachel laughed. "I'm guessing that Araminta Lee and Astrid Leong have arrived."

"She goes by Araminta Khoo these day," Peik Lin corrected.

"Ooh, I can't wait to meet all these women I've been hearing so much about—it's gonna be like an issue of *Vanity Fair* magazine come to life!" Sylvia said gleefully.

The ladies entered the Tuscan-stone portico in front of the pavilion, where everyone involved in the wedding ceremony had assembled. The decorating crew was still putting the finishing touches to an intricate bamboo trellis entwined with wisteria and jasmine that led up the aisle to an arch where the couple would exchange their vows.

Belinda Chu rushed up to Rachel, looking rather distressed. "Your floral designer promises that the wisteria will be at its peak tomorrow, just in time for the ceremony, but I'm not convinced. Look at how small some of these buds are. They won't be blooming for days! You'll need to put hair dryers on them! Tsk, tsk, tsk, you really should have used my guy, who does the flowers for all the best homes in Palo Alto."

"I'm sure it will be just fine," Rachel said calmly as she winked at Nick, who was standing in front of the arch talking to Mehmet, Astrid, and one of the crewmen.

Astrid greeted Rachel warmly with a hug. "Everything looks so beautiful, it makes me want to get married all over again!"

Nick's phone began to ring. Not recognizing the number, he ignored the call and put the phone on vibrate. The crewman standing next to Nick waved at Rachel shyly, and she realized with a start that it was Colin Khoo. With his shock of dark hair grown out to his shoulders, she hadn't recognized him.

"Look at you! Now you *really* look like a Polynesian surfer!" Rachel exclaimed.

"That's rad!" Colin replied as he gave the bride-to-be a kiss on the cheek. Araminta, who stood out from the crowd in her vintage Yves Saint Laurent safari jacket and gold leather caged thigh-high Gianvito Rossi sandals, was next to greet Rachel with a double-cheek kiss.

"That's the heiress whose wedding Rachel went to where all the trouble started," Auntie Jin murmured under her breath to Ray Chu.

"Who's the fellow beside her in the torn jeans and flip-flops?"

"That's her husband. I heard he's a billionaire too," Kerry Chu whispered back.

"It's like all my patients these days—I never know whether the kid in my dental chair is homeless or owns Google," Ray said gruffly.

After everyone in the wedding party had been introduced to one another and Jason Chu had snapped enough pictures of himself with the supermodel and Nick's hottie cousin Astrid—who he swore had to be that babe from *House of Flying Daggers*—Samantha began corralling everyone into position for the procession up the aisle.

"Okay, after Mehmet has made sure all the guests have taken their seats, the procession can begin. Jase—you need to escort Aunt Kerry up the aisle first, before you come back for Mom. Once you get Mom to her seat, you're done and you can take the seat next to her. Now, I need Alistair Cheng. Where are you?" Alistair identified himself as Samantha checked the chart on her iPad. "Okay, you'll be escorting Astrid Leong up the aisle, since she is representing Nick's family. That's Astrid over there. Will you remember her tomorrow?"

"I think so. She's my cousin," Alistair said in his usual laconic manner.

"My bad—I didn't realize you were a cousin too!" Samantha giggled.

Nick's phone started buzzing again, and he dug into his jeans pocket in annoyance. It was from the same number, but this time it was a text message. Nick scrolled to the text, which read:

Sorry—tried everything I could to stop Mum. Love, Dad.

Nick stared at the text again. What on earth could his father mean?

Samantha began barking out new orders. "Okay, now it's time for the groom and his best man to enter. Nick and Colin—both of you will be at the staging area to the left of the pavilion while all the guests are being seated. When you hear the cello solo begin, that's your cue to walk down the path toward—"

"'Scuse me for one sec," Nick said, dashing away from the arch. He stood at the back corner of the forecourt, frantically trying to call his father. This time, it went straight to voice mail: "I'm sorry, but the person you called has a voice-mail box that has not been set up yet. Please try your call again later."

*Damn.* Nick tried calling his father's regular Sydney number, an avalanche of dread suddenly beginning to engulf him.

Colin came up to check on him. "Everything okay?"

"Um, I don't know. Hey, don't you have security wherever you travel?"

Colin rolled his eyes. "Yes. It's a big nuisance, but Araminta's father insists on it."

"Where's your security detail now?"

"There's a team posted outside the gates, and that woman over there is Araminta's personal bodyguard," Colin replied, indicating a woman with a frizzy spiral perm seated inconspicuously among Rachel's relatives. "I know she looks like a bank teller, but let me tell you, she's former Chinese Special Forces and can disembowel a man in under ten seconds."

Nick showed Colin the text message from his father. "Can you please call your security people and request extra backup for tomorrow? I'll pay whatever it takes. We need to go into full lockdown and make sure that only the people on the guest list are allowed onto the property."

Colin grimaced. "Um, I think it's a little too late for that."

"What do you mean?"

"Look dead ahead. Twelve o'clock."

Nick stared for a second. "No, that's not my mum. That's a cousin of Rachel's from New Jersey."

"I mean look up. In the sky . . ."

Nick squinted into the bright blue sky. "*Oh. My. Fucking. Hell.*"

· · ·

"Viv, is Ollie ready?" Samantha said, bending down to give Rachel's little toddler cousin the blue velvet pillow for the wedding rings. The boy took hold of the pillow for two seconds before it suddenly blew out of his hands. The branches on the towering oak trees began to tremble, and a deafening hum filled the air. From out of nowhere, a large black-and-white helicopter zoomed over the portico and hovered above the great lawn as it slowly began to land. Samantha and Rachel stared in horror as the wind gusts from the giant propellers began to tear apart everything on the portico like a tornado that had just touched down.

"Get away from the trellis! It's coming down!" a workman screamed as everyone began running for cover. The arch toppled over just as the trellis began to collapse. Parts of bamboo began blowing off the structure at high speed, and the wisteria buds were blown clear off their stems. Aunt Belinda screamed as a big clump of jasmine hit her in the face.

"Hiyah, everything is ruined!" Kerry Chu cried.

When the propellers of the AgustaWestland AW109 finally ground to a halt, the forward door opened and a burly man in dark sunglasses jumped out to open the main cabin door. A Chinese woman clad in a chic saffron-colored pantsuit stepped out.

"Jesus, *of course* it's Auntie Eleanor!" Astrid groaned.

Rachel went absolutely numb as she watched Nick sprint across the lawn toward his mother. Colin and Araminta rushed up behind her, followed by a Chinese lady with a bad perm, who was for some reason brandishing a gun.

"Let's get you back to the house," Colin said.

"No, no, I'll be fine," Rachel replied. Witnessing the sheer absurdity of the situation, a sudden realization had come over her. She had absolutely nothing to fear. Nick's mother was the one who was filled with fear. She was so afraid of this marriage actually taking place that she would go to all the trouble of chartering a helicopter and landing right in the friggin' middle of their wedding site! Rachel found herself involuntarily walking onto the lawn toward Nick. She wanted to be by his side.

Nick stormed up to his mother in fury. "What the hell are you doing here?"

Eleanor looked at her son calmly and said, "I knew you were going to be mad. But there was no other way to reach you since you refused to return any of my calls!"

"So you think you could stop my wedding by launching this . . . this invasion? You're out of your fucking mind!"

"Nicky, stop using that kind of language! I did not come here to stop your wedding. I have no intention of doing that. In fact, I *want* you to marry Rachel—"

"We're calling security—you need to get off the premises right now!"

By this point, Rachel was beside him. Nick glanced at her quickly in concern, and Rachel smiled at him reassuringly. "Hello, Mrs. Young," she said, finding a renewed confidence in her voice.

"Hello, Rachel. Can we please speak somewhere private?" Eleanor asked.

"No, Rachel is not speaking to you in private! Haven't you already done enough?" Nick interjected.

"*Alamak*, I'll pay to have everything fixed. Actually, you should be thanking me that rickety bamboo thing came down—that was a lawsuit waiting to happen. Listen to me, I'm really not here to ruin your wedding. I came here to ask for your forgiveness. I want to give you my blessing."

"It's a bit late for that. Please just LEAVE US ALONE!"

"Trust me, I know where I'm not wanted, and I will gladly leave. But I felt that I needed to make things right for Rachel before she walks down the aisle. Do you really want to deprive her of meeting her father before her wedding?"

Nick stared at his mother as if she was deranged. "What are you talking about?"

Eleanor ignored her son and looked Rachel straight in the eyes. "I'm talking about your *real* father, Rachel. I found him for you! That's what I've been trying to tell the both of you for the past month!"

"I don't believe you!" Nick said defiantly.

"I don't care if you believe me. I met Rachel's father's wife through your cousin Eddie when I was in London last year—you can ask him yourself. It was all a complete coincidence, but I managed to put two and two together and confirmed that he really is her father. Rachel, your father's name is Bao Gaoliang, and he's one of the top politicians in Beijing."

"Bao Gaoliang . . ." Rachel said the name slowly, in utter disbelief.

"And right now, he's at the Four Seasons Biltmore in Santa Barbara, and he's hoping to see your mother, Kerry, again. And he's dying to meet you. Come with me, Rachel, and I'll take all of you to him."

"This is another bullshit scheme of yours. You're not taking Rachel anywhere." Nick was seething.

Rachel put her hand on Nick's arm. "It's fine. I want to meet this guy. Let's see if he's really my father."

. . .

Rachel did not speak during the short helicopter ride to the hotel. She clutched Nick's hand tightly and looked pensively at her mother sitting across from her. She realized from her mother's expression that all this was much more difficult for her, since it was the first time in more than three decades that Kerry would be seeing the man she had been in love with, the man who had rescued her from her abusive husband and the terror of his family.

As they disembarked from the helicopter, Rachel had to pause for a moment before continuing into the hotel.

"Are you going to be okay?" Nick asked.

"I think so . . . it's all happening too fast," Rachel said. This was not how she had imagined it would happen. She didn't really have a set vision of how things might unfold, but after the disappointment of her last two trips to China, she had begun to lose hope that she would ever find her father. Or else, it would happen years from now, after making a long, arduous journey to some far outpost. She never thought that she would meet him for the first time at a resort in Santa Barbara on the day before her wedding.

Rachel and her mother were led through the mimosa-scented lobby, then down a long Mediterranean-tiled corridor, and outside again. As they walked through the lush gardens toward one of the private cottage suites, Rachel felt as though she were floating through some strange, nebulous dream. Time seemed to have sped up, and everything seemed so unreal. It was all too bright, too tropical for such a momentous occasion. Before she could fully collect herself, they were at the front of the cottage, and Nick's mother was giving the Mission-style wooden door a few rapid knocks.

Rachel took a deep breath.

"I'm right here with you," Nick whispered from behind, giving her shoulder an affectionate squeeze.

The door was opened by a man with an earpiece who Rachel assumed was some sort of bodyguard. Inside the room was another man in an open-collared shirt and a pale yellow sweater vest, sitting in front of the fireplace. His rimless glasses framed a vibrant, fair-complexioned face, and his jet-black hair, meticulously combed with a part on the left, had a few graying streaks at the temples. Could this really be her father?

Kerry stood at the doorway hesitantly, but as the man got up and came toward the light, she suddenly put her hands to her mouth and let out a small gasp. "Kao Wei!"

The man came up to Rachel's mother and stared into her face searchingly for a split second, before scooping her into a tight embrace.

"Kerry Ching. You are even prettier than I remember," he said in Mandarin.

Kerry broke out in loud, violent sobs, and Rachel found her eyes flooding uncontrollably with tears as she watched her mother crying against the man's chest. Managing to collect herself after a few moments, Kerry turned to her daughter and said, "Rachel, this is your father."

Rachel couldn't believe she was hearing those words. She stood by the doorway, suddenly feeling as if she were five years old again.

Standing outside the cottage, Eleanor turned to her son and said in a rather choked-up voice, "Come on, let's give them some privacy."

Nick, a little misty-eyed himself, answered, "That's the best thing I've heard you say in a long time, Mum."

# FOUR SEASONS BILTMORE

## SANTA BARBARA, CALIFORNIA

Comfortably ensconced in the hotel lounge with her requisite cup of hot water and lemon, Eleanor proceeded to recount to Nick the full story of how she came to discover Rachel's real father.

"Bao Shaoyen was so grateful to all of us in London. Your hopeless cousin Eddie left after a few days, after getting fitted for his new suits, and Shaoyen didn't know a soul in London. So we took care of her. We took her to visit Carlton every day in the hospital while he was recovering from his surgeries, we took her to eat at the halfway decent Chinese restaurants, and Francesca even drove all of us to the Bicester Village outlets one day. Shaoyen was in seventh heaven when she discovered that they had a Loro Piana outlet store there. My God, you should have seen how much cashmere that woman bought! I think she had to buy three big suitcases at the Tumi outlet just to fit everything.

"As soon as Carlton was out of intensive care, I encouraged Shaoyen to let him do his rehabilitation in Singapore. I even called up Dr. Chia at NUH to pull strings and get Carlton into the best physical therapy program. So of course Carlton's father came down to visit from Beijing, and I got to know the family well over the next few months. Meanwhile, Auntie Lorena's private investigator in China went to dig up everything he could on the family."

"Auntie Lorena and her shady investigators!" Nick scoffed, taking a sip of his coffee.

"*Alamak*, you should be grateful Lorena hired Mr. Wong! Without his snooping around and paying off the right people, we would never have been able to get to the truth. It turned out that Bao Gaoliang had changed his name right after he graduated from university. Kao Wei was always a boyhood nickname—his actual name was Sun Gaoliang. He grew up in Fujian, but his parents made him take the surname of his godfather, who was a well-respected party official in Jiangsu Province, because then he could move there and get a better start to his career."

"So how did you break the news to the Baos?"

"At one point, Shaoyen had to go back to China to attend to some business, and Gaoliang was alone in Singapore visiting Carlton. One night, I took him to have *kai fun* at Wee Nam Kee,[*] and I asked him about his younger days. He started to tell me about his college days in Fujian, so at one point I just blurted out, 'Did you ever know a woman by the name of Kerry Ching?' Gaoliang's face went white as a ghost. He said,

---

[*]  Hainanese chicken rice, which could arguably be considered the national dish of Singapore. (And yes, Eleanor is ready for foodie bloggers to start attacking her restaurant choice. She chose Wee Nam Kee specifically because the United Square location is only five minutes from the Bao condo, and parking there is $2.00 after 6:00 p.m. If she took him to Chatterbox, which she personally prefers, parking at Mandarin Hotel would have been a nightmare and she would have had to valet her Jaguar for $15. Which she would RATHER DIE than do.)

'I don't know anyone by that name.' Then he suddenly wanted to finish his dinner quickly and leave. That's when I finally confronted him with the truth. I said, 'Gaoliang, please don't be alarmed. You can leave if you want, but before you do, please hear me out. I feel that fate has brought us together. My son is engaged to a woman by the name of Rachel Chu. Please let me show you her picture, and I think you will understand that something remarkable has happened.'"

"What photo of Rachel do you have?" Nick asked.

Eleanor blushed. "It's the one from her California driver's license that I got from the first detective I hired in Beverly Hills. Anyway, Gaoliang took one look at the photo and went into complete shock. He immediately asked, 'Who is this girl?' It's just so obvious—the girl in the picture looks *exactly* like Carlton, but with long hair and makeup, of course. So I said, 'That girl is the daughter of a woman who goes by the name of Kerry Chu. She now lives in California, but she used to live in Xiamen when she was married to a man by the name of Zhou Fang Min.' And that's when Gaoliang finally cracked."

"Wow. You should do this professionally," Nick said with a raised eyebrow.

"You can make fun of me all you want, but Rachel wouldn't be meeting her father today if it wasn't for my interfering."

"No, no, I wasn't being sarcastic, I meant it as a compliment."

"I know you are still angry with me for all that's happened, but I want you to know that everything I did, I did for your sake."

Nick shook his head indignantly. "How do you expect me to react? You almost ruined the love of my life. You didn't trust my judgment, and you just assumed the worst of Rachel from the beginning. You thought she was a gold digger even before you met her."

"Hiyah, how many times can I say I'm sorry? I misjudged her. I misjudged you. Gold digger or not, I didn't want you to marry Rachel because I knew that it would lead to heartache for you as soon as your grandmother became involved. I knew Ah Ma would never approve, and I wanted to spare you her wrath. Because once upon a time, I was that unacceptable daughter-in-law. And I was not even the daughter of a single mother from Mainland China! Believe me, I know what it feels like to suffer under her disapproval. But you never saw that side of her. I protected you from that. She adored you from the day you were born, and I never wanted that to change."

Nick noticed the tears brimming in his mother's eyes, and he softened his stance. A waiter walked by, and Nick gestured to him. "Excuse me, could we please have another cup of hot water with lemon slices on the side? Thank you."

"Very hot, please," Eleanor added, as she dabbed away her tears with the crumpled pieces of Kleenex she always seemed to have in her purse.

"Well, I'm sure you know that Ah Ma plans to disinherit me now. Jacqueline Ling told me just as much a few weeks ago."

"That Jacqueline always does your Ah Ma's dirty work! But you can never be sure what Ah Ma is going to do. Anyway, it doesn't matter as much, because you have Rachel. I truly mean it now when I say I am very glad she is going to be your wife."

"My, how your tone has changed! I guess you don't disapprove of Rachel now that you know her real father is some bigwig politician in China."

"He's not just some politician. He is much more than that."

"What do you mean?"

Eleanor did a quick scan of the room to make sure no

one could overhear her. "Bao Gaoliang's father started Millennium Pharmaceuticals, one of the largest medical companies in China. The stock is a blue chip on the Shanghai Stock Exchange."

"So? I don't understand how that impresses you. Everyone you know is rich."

Eleanor leaned in closer and lowered her voice. "*Aiyah*, these people aren't just everyday rich with a few hundred million. They are *China* rich! We're talking billions and billions. More important, they only have one son . . . and now one daughter."

"So *that's* why you're suddenly so keen on us getting married!" Nick groaned as his mother's true motives finally dawned on him.

"Of course! If Rachel plays her cards right, she will be a great heiress and you will benefit too!"

"I'm so glad I can always count on you to have some sort of ulterior motive that involves money."

"I'm just looking out for you! Now that your inheritance from Ah Ma is so uncertain, you can't blame me for wanting the best for you."

"No, I don't suppose I can," Nick said quietly. As frustrated as he was, he realized that he was never going to change his mother. Like so many of her generation, her entire existence revolved around the acquisition and preservation of fortune. It seemed like all her friends were in the same contest to see who could leave the most houses, the biggest conglomerates, and the fattest stock portfolios to their children after they died.

Eleanor leaned in closer. "Now, here are some things you need to know about the Baos."

"I don't need to hear any idle gossip."

"*Aiyah*, it's not idle gossip! These are important details

I've learned just from being around them, and from what Mr. Wong found out—"

"Stop right there! I don't want to know," Nick said emphatically.

"*Aiyah*, I need to tell you for your own good!"

"Give it a rest, Mum! Rachel just met her dad twenty minutes ago and now you want to spill all the secrets of his family? Your digging around and secrets are what almost ruined my relationship in the first place. It's not fair to Rachel, and it's not the way I want to begin my marriage."

Eleanor sighed. This son of hers was impossible. He was too stubborn and too self-righteous and couldn't even see that she was trying to help him. Well, she would have to wait for another opportunity. Squeezing more lemon into her water and not making direct eye contact with her son, she asked, "So, is there a chance you'll let your poor lonely mother come to her only child's wedding tomorrow?"

Nick was silent for a moment. "Let me talk to Rachel. I'm not sure whether she's ready to roll out the red carpet after you just destroyed her wedding site, but I'll ask."

Eleanor got up from the table in excitement. "I'm going to talk to the concierge right now. We'll fix it. We'll fly in all the wisteria in the world if we have to. I'll make sure her wedding is back to perfection."

"I'm sure Rachel will appreciate that."

"And let me go call Dad. He should get on a plane right now. It's still not too late for him to make it here by tomorrow afternoon."

"You know, I said I'd talk to Rachel. I didn't promise anything," Nick cautioned.

"*Aiyah*, of course she will let me come! I can tell she is the forgiving type just by looking at her face. That's the one good thing about her—she doesn't have high cheekbones. Women with high cheekbones are very *gow tzay*.* Now, will you please do one thing for me?"

"What?"

"Pleeeease go to the barber shop and get your hair cut before tomorrow! It's far too long and I can't stand to see you on your wedding day looking like some *chao ah beng*."†

---

* No English words can properly do justice to this charming Hokkien term, which is used to describe people who are equal parts bitchy, unreasonable, stuck up, and impossible to deal with.

† Hokkien for "stinky low-class gangster."

# 12

ARCADIA

The late-afternoon sun hovered over the crest of the Santa Ynez Mountains, suffusing everything in a golden haze. The bamboo trellis had been fully restored to its former glory, creating a luxuriant canopy of hanging wisteria and jasmine over the central aisle, its delicately sweet scent wafting across the guests as they took their seats on the portico. With a neoclassical music pavilion carved from Tuscan stone as a backdrop and towering two-hundred-year-old oaks framing the gardens, the scene looked like something straight out of a Maxfield Parrish painting.

At the appointed moment, Nick emerged from the pavilion with his best man, Colin, and took his place beside an arch majestically radiating with white dendrobium orchids. He surveyed the hundred or so guests, noticing that his father—just arrived from Sydney and wearing an extremely rumpled gray suit—was seated next to Astrid, while his mother was a row behind gossiping with Araminta, who had minutes ago caused a stir when she entered the portico in a show-stopping emerald green Giambattista Valli gown with a deconstructed-ruffle neckline that plunged all the way down to her navel.

"Don't fidget!" Astrid mouthed from the front row as Nick fussed nervously with his cuff links. She couldn't help but recall the skinny boy in soccer shorts who used to run around with her in the gardens of Tyersall Park, scaling trees and jumping into ponds. They were forever inventing games and getting lost in fantasy worlds, Nicky always the Peter Pan to her Wendy, but now here he was, all grown up and looking utterly dashing in his celestial blue Henry Poole tuxedo, ready to create his own new world with Rachel. There would be great trouble to come once their grandmother found out about the wedding, but at least for tonight, Nicky was getting to marry the girl of his dreams.

The wall of French doors at the front of the pavilion opened, and from inside a musician on a grand piano began to play a vaguely familiar melody as Rachel's bridesmaids— Peik Lin, Samantha, and Sylvia, in pearl gray bias-cut silk dresses—began the procession up the aisle. Auntie Belinda, in a gold lamé St. John gown with matching bolero top, suddenly recognized that the pianist was playing Fleetwood Mac's "Landslide" and began to sob uncontrollably into her Chanel handkerchief. Uncle Ray, mystified by his wife's behavior, pretended not to notice and stared straight ahead, while Auntie Jin turned around and glared at her. "Sorry . . . sorry . . . Stevie just gets me every time," Belinda whispered, trying to collect herself.

After the pianist had finished, another surprise awaited the crowd as the lights inside the pavilion dimmed and a scrim hanging above the building came down, revealing a full ensemble of musicians from the San Francisco Symphony on the roof. The conductor raised his baton, and as the delicate opening strains of Aaron Copland's "Appalachian Spring" began to fill the air, Rachel appeared at the steps of the portico on the arm of her uncle Walt.

The wedding guests murmured in approval at the bride,

who looked stunning in a figure-hugging gown of silk crepe de chine with delicate knife pleats that fanned out over the fitted bodice and a column skirt that draped across the front in romantic cascading folds. With her long, luxuriant hair worn down in loose curls and pinned on the sides with a pair of feather-shaped art deco diamond clips, she was the epitome of a relaxed, modern bride with just a touch of 1930s Hollywood glamour.

Rachel clutched her bouquet of long-stemmed white tulips and calla lilies, smiling at all the people she knew. Then she caught sight of her mother seated in the front row next to Bao Gaoliang. She had of course insisted that Uncle Walt, who had always been the closest thing to a paternal figure, walk her down the aisle, but seeing her mother and father together like this stirred up a whole new set of emotions.

Her parents were here. *Her parents.* She realized that this was the first time in her life that she could actually use that term properly, and her eyes began to well up. *There goes that hour spent in the makeup chair.* Just yesterday morning, she had almost given up hope of ever meeting her real father, but by the end of the day, she discovered that not only was her father alive and very much real but she also had a half brother. It was more than she could have ever hoped for, and in a strange roundabout way, she had Nick to thank for all of this.

Bao Gaoliang couldn't help but feel a peculiar sense of pride as he watched his daughter glide gracefully down the aisle. Here was a woman he had not met until yesterday, but already he could feel an undeniable connection with her, something he couldn't seem to forge with his own son. Carlton and Shaoyen had a special bond that he was never able to penetrate, and he suddenly began to dread the conversation that he knew would take place when he returned to China. He had yet to discuss any of Eleanor Young's revelations with Shaoyen, who thought he was on a diplomatic mission in Australia. *How in the world was he ever going to explain all this to his wife and son?*

"I can't believe how beautiful you look," Nick whispered when Rachel reached his side.

Rachel, too moved to say anything, simply nodded. She looked into the kind, beautiful, sexy eyes of the man she was about to marry and wondered whether this was all a dream.

. . .

After the ceremony, as the wedding guests adjourned to a reception inside the music pavilion, Eleanor sidled up to Astrid and began her commentary. "The only thing missing from that service was a good Methodist pastor. Where is Tony Chi when you need him? I didn't really care for that we-are-all-nature Unitarian minister. Did you see he was wearing an earring? What sort of *kopi*-license* minister is he?"

Astrid, who hadn't spoken to Eleanor since her *Apocalypse Now*–style arrival the day before, gave her a sharp look. "Next time you plan on plying my child with a gallon of ice cream, you have to take him for the rest of the day. You have no idea how long it took us to pry him off the ceiling."

"Sorry, *lah*. But you knew I *had* to find out about the wedding. See? It all worked out in the end, didn't it?"

"I suppose so. But you could have spared everyone so much heartache."

---

* *Kopi* is Singlish slang for coffee. "*Kopi* license" refers to any sort of license or certificate that was obtained not by true merit but by paying a small bribe to an official—enough for him or her to buy a coffee with. Though the term is used to insult doctors, lawyers, or some other qualified individual, it is most often used while swearing at bad drivers, who surely must have bribed the examiner in order to pass their driving test. (Believe it or not, Asians can sometimes be bad drivers too.)

Refusing to be any more contrite, Eleanor tried changing the subject. "Hey, did you help Rachel choose her dress?"

"No, but doesn't she look lovely?"

"I find it a bit plain."

"I think it's exquisitely simple. It looks like something Carole Lombard would have worn to a dinner party on the French Riviera."

"I find your dress much more striking," Eleanor said, admiring Astrid's cobalt blue halter-neck Gaultier outfit.

"*Aiyah*, you've seen me in this a dozen times."

"I thought I recognized it! Didn't you wear it to Araminta's wedding?"

"I wear it to every wedding."

"Why on earth do you do that?"

"Don't you remember Cecilia Cheng's wedding years ago, when people couldn't stop talking about my dress in front of her? I felt so bad, I decided from that day on to always wear the same dress to every wedding."

"You're a funny one. No wonder you get along with my son, with all his funny ideas."

"I'll take that as a compliment, Auntie Elle."

. . .

The sunken garden behind the music pavilion had been transformed into an al fresco ballroom. Hundreds of candles in antique crystal orbs sparkled in the eucalyptus trees surrounding the garden, while old-fashioned klieg lights cast a silver-screen glow onto the dance floor.

Astrid leaned on the stone balustrade overlooking the garden, wishing her husband could have been here to dance with her under the moonlight. The phone inside her minaudière gave a quick buzz, and she smiled, thinking Michael must have just read her mind and pinged her. She got out her phone eagerly and found a text message:

> Hope you're enjoying the wedding. Guess what? Had to come to San Jose on business. If you're staying in CA for a few days, let's meet up. Maybe San Francisco? I can send my plane to pick you up. There's an Italian place in Sausalito I know you'd love.
> CHARLES WU
> +852 6775 9999

The guests began gathering on the terrace to watch the newlyweds have their first dance, but before the music started up, Colin suddenly began clinking loudly on his champagne glass to get everybody's attention.

"Hello everyone, I'm Nicky's best man, Colin. Don't worry, I'm not going to bore anyone with a long-winded toast. I just felt that on this most special of occasions, the happy couple needed a little surprise."

Nick shot Colin a look that said, *What the hell are you doing?*

Grinning from ear to ear, Colin continued, "A few months ago, my wife and I ran into a friend of Rachel's at the Churchill Club." He looked over at Peik Lin, who raised her champagne glass conspiratorially. "It turns out that all through college, Rachel would play a *certain song* over and over until it drove Peik Lin up the wall. And guess what? I just happen to know it was one of Nick's favorite songs too. So Nick and Rachel thought they would be dancing to some romantic waltz by the San Francisco Symphony right now, but they're not. Ladies and gentlemen, please help me welcome Mr. and Mrs. Young to the dance floor for the very first time, accompanied by one of the world's greatest singers."

With those words, a band of musicians entered the small stage at the edge of the garden, followed by a petite woman with a shock of platinum blond hair. The crowd began to scream in excitement, while many of the older folks looked utterly baffled by all the excitement.

Nick and Rachel stared first at Colin and then at Peik Lin, their mouths agape.

"I can't believe it! Did you know anything about this?" Rachel exclaimed.

"No! Sneaky bastards!" Nick said as he led Rachel onto the dance floor. The first chords of a familiar hit song began to fill the air, and the crowd roared in approval.

Philip and Eleanor Young stood on the steps leading down to the garden, watching as their son twirled his bride around with debonair ease. Philip glanced over at his wife. "Your son is happy at last. It wouldn't hurt for you to smile a little too."

"I'm smiling, *lah*, I'm smiling. I've been smiling till my face hurts at all those annoyingly friendly relatives of Rachel's. Why do all these ABCs talk to you as if they think you are their best friend? It's so presumptuous. I was all prepared for them to hate me."

"Why would they hate you? You ended up doing a very good deed for Rachel."

Eleanor began to say something, but then changed her mind.

"Just say it, darling, you know you want to. You've been wanting to tell me something all night," Philip egged her on.

"I'm not so sure Rachel will think I did such a good deed once she really gets to know her new family."

"What do you mean by that?"

"Mr. Wong e-mailed me a new report late last night. I need to show it to you. Frankly, I think I might have made a mistake getting mixed up with the Baos in the first place." Eleanor sighed.

"Well, it's a little too late, darling. We're related to them now."

Eleanor gave her husband a look of abject horror. It was the first time this had occurred to her.

. . .

Nick and Rachel swayed together to the rhythm of the song, feeling almost delirious with happiness. "Can you believe we really pulled this off?" Nick asked.

"Not really. I'm waiting for the next helicopter to land."

"No more helicopters, and no more surprises ever, I promise," Nick said as he twirled her around. "From now on we're just going to be a boring married couple."

"Oh, please! When I decided to walk down the aisle with you, Nicholas Young, I knew I'd be signing up for a lifetime of surprises. I wouldn't want it any other way. But you have to at least give me a clue where we're going on our honeymoon this summer."

"Well, I had all these grand plans that involved the midnight sun and a few fjords, but then your father just asked if we would visit him in Shanghai as soon as summer break starts. He's eager for you to meet your brother, and he swears he'll hook us up at the most romantic spots in all of China. So what do you think of that?"

"I think it's the best idea I've ever heard," Rachel said, her eyes lighting up with excitement.

Nick pulled her into an embrace. "I love you, Mrs. Young."

"And I love you. But who says I'm going to take your name?"

Nick frowned like a hurt child, and then broke out into a grin. "You don't have to take my name, hon. You can be Rachel Rodham Chu for all I care."

"You know what I realized today? Rachel Chu was the name my mother gave me, but it turned out not to be my name. And even though my father's last name is Bao, that really wasn't his name either. The only name that's truly all mine is Rachel Young, and that's a choice *I'm* making."

Nick gave Rachel a long tender kiss as the wedding guests broke out into applause. Then he waved for everybody to join them on the dance floor, and as Cyndi Lauper continued her song, the newlyweds began to sing along:

*If you're lost, you can look and you will find me,*
*time after time.*

# PART TWO

*If you want to know what God thinks of money, just look at the people he gave it to.*

—DOROTHY PARKER

**KO-TUNG CONSULTING GROUP**
**SOCIAL IMPACT ASSESSMENT**

*Prepared for Mrs. Bernard Tai by Corinna Ko-Tung*
*April 2013*

Let us be completely frank and start with the obvious:
Your former name was Kitty Pong, and you were not
born on Hong Kong Island, Kowloon, or any of the surrounding islands that make up the former British Crown
Colony of Hong Kong. Remember, for the crowd you
seek to impress, your money means nothing. Especially
these days, when twentysomething Mainlanders have
burst onto the scene with billions apiece, the old guard
have resorted to new ways of stratifying themselves.
What matters more than ever now are bloodlines and
when your family first made its money. Which province
of China did your family originate from? Which dialect
group? Were they part of the tightly knit Chiu-Chow
clans, or the Shanghai émigré class? Are you second-,

third-, or fourth-generation rich? And how was the fortune made? Was it in textiles or property (pre–Li Ka-Shing or post-1997)? Every minute detail matters. For instance, you can have ten billion dollars but still be considered nothing more than a speck of dirt by the Keungs, who are down to their last hundred million but can trace their lineage to the Duke of Yansheng.* Over the next few months, I intend to change the narrative about you. We will take your most embarrassing biographical details and turn them into assets. We will do this in a variety of ways. Let us begin.

## APPEARANCE

*Physique and Features*
First of all, the breast reduction was one of the most astute moves you could have made, and your physique is now optimal. Before your surgery, your hourglass figure only served to fuel the rumors of your cinematic extra-curricular activities, but now you have the body shape considered ideal to the women you seek to cultivate— delicately emaciated, with just a hint of a well-managed eating disorder. <u>Please do not lose any more weight.</u>

I must also commend your surgeon on a remarkable job on your face (remind me to get his name from you—for some of my other clients, of course). The rounder curves of your cheeks have been sculpted down and your nose has been exquisitely reshaped. (Admit it: You copied Cecilia Cheng Moncur's nose, didn't you? I would recognize that patrician bump anywhere.) But now you run the risk of looking too perfect, and this will

---

* A direct descendant of Confucius who was also rather fabulously known as the "Holy Duke of Yen."

only incite jealousy from your social competitors. So
please refrain from any further procedures in the immediate future. No more fillers for now, and the Botox
injections to your forehead are also no longer necessary,
as I would like to see a few fine lines develop in the area
between your eyebrows. We can always erase them in
the future, but for the time being, possessing the ability
to make tiny frowns will allow you to convey empathy.

*Hair*
Your long jet-black hair is one of your best features, but
the high ponytails and dramatic updos you currently favor
convey a look of aggression. When you enter a room,
the ladies immediately think, "This woman is either
going to steal my husband, my baby, or my yoga mat." I
recommend wearing your hair down in a more layered
look for most occasions, and swept into a relaxed low
chignon for formal occasions. Your hair also needs to be
colored to add some brown lowlights, as this will soften
your features overall. I will refer you to Ricky Tseung at
ModaBeauty on Seymour Terrace in Mid-Levels. You are
no doubt accustomed to some overpriced salon located in
one of the fancier hotels, but trust me, Ricky is someone
you must cultivate. Not only is he a bargain, he is *the*
hairdresser of choice to ladies from the best families—
Fiona Tung-Cheng, Mrs. Francis Liu, Marion Hsu. When
you first meet Ricky, tell him absolutely **nothing** about
yourself (he will already know far too much). Over time,
I will craft anecdotes that you can share with him (i.e.,
your daughter's ability to sing "Wouldn't It Be Loverly"
in a perfect Cockney accent, the injured Siamese cat that
you rescued, anonymously paying for a former teacher's
chemotherapy bills, etc.). These tales will make their
way into the ears of all the right ladies. *Note: You do not*

*need to tip Ricky, since he is the owner of the salon. But
occasionally, you can feed him some Cadbury chocolate.
He loves expensive chocolates!*

*Makeup*
Your makeup, unfortunately, requires a complete
overhaul. The tofu-milk skin and cherry-red lips no
longer suit you—now that you are a respectable wife
and mother, it is essential that you no longer appear like
the unattainable object of fantasy for pubescent boys.
We need to create a visage that is pleasing and non-
threatening to well-bred women of all age groups. You
want your color and complexion to look as if you only
spent fifty seconds on it because you were too busy
repotting tulips in your garden. I will accompany you to
Germaine, my beauty consultant at the Elizabeth Arden
counter at Sogo Causeway Bay. (You need not actually
buy all your new products at Arden—they are far too
overpriced. We can pick up new cosmetics at Mannings
Pharmacy, but you will buy one or two lipsticks at
Arden in order to qualify for the free consultation and
makeover. I may also have an additional coupon for a
free gift with purchase—please remind me.)

*Other Grooming Suggestions*
Discontinue the use of nail polish in red or any
shades of red. (Yes, pink is a shade of red.) This is
nonnegotiable—you must remember that we have the
Herculean task of removing any connotations of talons,
claws, or grasping hands from your person. If I could
get you to wear white gloves or wrap your fingers in
rosary beads all the time, I would. From now on, get
used to nude nails or monochromatic tones of beige.

For special occasions, Jin Soon's "Nostalgia" is a shade of pink beige polish that I will allow.

In order to further avoid being mistaken for one of those girls who have been set up with a driver and a one-bedroom flat in Braemar Hill, you will also discontinue use of any perfumes or scented products. I will provide you with an essential oil made from ylang-ylang, sage, and other secret ingredients that will make you smell like you have been baking apple tarts all morning.

**WARDROBE**

I know you have been working with a top Hollywood fashion stylist who introduced you to couture and gave you an avant-garde look. Well, that look achieved its goals—you were noticed. But one of my most urgent goals is to purge you from the photo sections of all the magazines. As I have mentioned to you more than once, the sort of people you are now striving to cultivate prize <u>invisibility</u> more than anything. When was the last time you saw Jeannette Sang or Helen Hou-Tin in the party pages? I'll tell you the answer: ONCE OR TWICE A YEAR AT MOST. There has been far too much conversation about and coverage on your clothes, and you are more overexposed than the Venus de Milo. It's now time to evolve into your next persona: *Mrs. Bernard Tai—dedicated mother and humanitarian on the rise.*

(Please do not ever refer to yourself as a "philanthropist" again. It is the height of pretension. If anyone asks you what you do, say: "I am a full-time mother, and I do some part-time charity work.")

My assistants and I have done a full assessment and audit of your closet, and you will find that all apparel and

accessories deemed appropriate remain as they are, while
inappropriate clothing and accessories have been relo-
cated into the second, third, and fourth guest bedrooms
(with some additional overflow in the Karaoke room).
I hope you are not too alarmed by the rigorous edit we
have done. I know the average outfit in your wardrobe
costs more than a semester of tuition at Princeton, but it
makes you look like a community college during sum-
mertime: NO CLASS. From my tally, there are twelve
pieces remaining in your closet that are still fit to be seen
in public, and three handbags. (Four, actually—I will
allow you to carry the Olympia Le Tan "To Kill a Mock-
ingbird" book clutch on special occasions, only because
it has such noble connotations.) Please see APPENDIX
A, which lists all approved designers and brands for your
new wardrobe. Any designers **not** listed there are off-
limits for the next year, with one exception: <u>You should
under no circumstances wear Roberto Cavalli ever again.</u>
Please do not think me brutal: I have specially curated
this list in order for you to be dressed elegantly—but
*forgettably*—in daily life. As Coco Chanel said, "Dress
impeccably and they notice the woman."

For big functions (and you will only be attending a
few in the next year), we will choose an elegant gown
that exudes a quiet luxury. (Please google "Queen
Rania of Jordan" for some examples.)

**JEWELRY**

The vast majority of your jewelry is of such a size and
flamboyance that it crosses the point of vulgarity and
enters into a territory that can only be described as
obscene. Don't you realize that at your age, big gemstones only serve to make you seem older? As they say,

"The larger the diamonds, the older the wife, the more the mistresses." You do not need to look like a sixty-something matron who has been placated with jewels by a husband who is keeping girlfriends in every province of China. All the pieces <u>not listed</u> below—especially the 55-carat diamond ring given to you by Her Majesty the Sultana of Borneo—should be stored in your vault for the foreseeable future. Evening jewelry for official functions will be negotiated on a case-by-case basis, but your daytime jewelry will now be restricted to the following:

· Wedding band (not your Tiffany one but your original wedding ring from the Little Chapel of the West in Las Vegas)
· Graff 4.5-carat diamond solitaire ring
· Mikimoto pearl stud earrings
· Lynn Nakamura Tahitian black pearl drop earrings
· K. S. Sze single-strand champagne pearl necklace
· 3-carat pear-shaped diamond earrings (to be worn only with extremely casual sportswear—which creates a refreshingly unexpected juxtaposition and makes the size of the gemstones acceptable)
· L'Orient ruby ring on tension mounting
· Carnet orchid brooch
· Pomellato Madera quartz ring
· Edward Chiu diamond-and-jade tennis bracelet
· Vintage Cartier Tank Américaine wristwatch

*To this collection, you should add a few fun, cheap trinkets to wear—like some Tibetan prayer beads, a Jawbone UP band, a child's toy necklace, or a rubber wristband supporting some charitable cause. This will further solidify the notion that you are Mrs. Bernard Tai, and you no longer have anything to prove to anyone!*

## LIFESTYLE

*Interior Design and Decoration*
Kaspar von Morgenlatte did an admirable job with your
apartment, but the look is somewhat outdated and more
than a little disturbing. (If I recall, the design concept
was commissioned by your husband in the early 2000s
to evoke the Miami Beach bachelor pad of a Bolivian
drug cartel kingpin. This was done extremely success-
fully. I particularly admired the "chalk body outline"
mother-of-pearl inlay on the ebony wood floor and the
trompe l'oeil "bullet marks" on your master bedroom
headboard, but I think that it would be inadvisable to
host a children's birthday party here, especially while
those Lisa Yuskavage paintings are still hanging.)

Rather than attempt a decor overhaul, which would take
far too long anyway, I think you should instead be on the
hunt for a new property. Living in a penthouse at Optus
Towers sends the wrong message at this stage in your
life—you are neither the second son of a tycoon nor the
managing director of some third-tier Swiss bank. It may
have been designed by that famous American architect
(overrated, in my opinion), but it is not considered one
of the "good family" buildings. I would like to see you
relocate to a house in one of the neighborhoods on the
south side of the island—Repulse Bay, Deep Water Bay,
or even Stanley. This will send the message that you are a
seriously committed wife and mother (never mind all the
French expats in Stanley that ought to be committed).

*Art Collection*
I was expecting to see *The Palace of Eighteen Perfections* in the pride of place at your apartment. Where is
it? I would suggest integrating a few important works

of art into your collection. The contemporary Chinese artists are completely overbought at the moment, and don't even get me started on the Americans. But German photography might be an interesting option for you—I think it would give your collection some sorely needed gravitas and gain you notice in serious collector circles if you were to possess one of Thomas Struth's epic images of pharmaceutical plants, Candida Höfer's riveting studies of municipal libraries in Lower Saxony, or a delightful grouping of rusting water towers by Bernd und Hilla Becher.

*Household*

I am very pleased to observe that your domestic help are well treated and have actual bedrooms. (You wouldn't believe how many people I personally know who force their helpers* to sleep in spaces no larger than closets or pantry rooms, and yet have spare bedrooms filled with clothes, shoes, or Lladro figurines.) Instead of making them wear those French maid uniforms, might I suggest a smart modern uniform of navy blouses and white cotton slacks from J.Crew? Remember—your domestic helpers will talk with other domestic helpers on their days off, and having a reputation as a benevolent mistress will only further your cause.

**TRANSPORT**

*Automobiles*

You should no longer be chauffeured around in that Rolls-Royce. I have always felt that unless one is either

---

* In Asia, the new generation of ruling class are using the term "helper" to refer to the people their parents call "maids" and their grandparents call "servants."

over sixty years of age or in possession of a silver helmet of hair that resembles Her Majesty Queen Elizabeth II's, being seen in a Rolls is completely ridiculous. Instead, please purchase a Mercedes S-Class, Audi A8, or BMW 7 Series like everyone else. (Or if you are feeling particularly brave, a Volkswagen Phaeton.) We can discuss the possibility of a Jaguar after one year, depending on your social standing then.

*Aircraft*
Your Gulfstream V is perfectly acceptable. (Please do not upgrade to the GVI yet, at least until Yolanda Kwok takes delivery of hers. She will be furious if you get one before she does and will block your Chinese Athletic Association membership application.)

**DINING**

The restaurants that you customarily patronize are deplorable. They are filled with nothing but expats, soap opera stars, social climbers, and—most disagreeable of all—foodies. As part of my new campaign to associate you only with establishment circles, you can no longer risk being seen at any trendy "culinary destinations." If a restaurant is less than two years old or has been featured in *Hong Kong Tattle* or *Pinnacle Magazine* in the past eighteen months, I consider it trendy. Please see APPENDIX B for a list of approved dining clubs and restaurants with private dining rooms. Six months from now, if I feel that you have reached a certain threshold of social acceptability, I will arrange for you to be snapped by paparazzi eating a bowl of wonton noodles at a *dai pai dong*.* This will do wonders for your image, and I can already picture the headline: "Social Goddess Unafraid to Dine with the Masses."

## SOCIAL LIFE

Your social resurrection will first begin with social death. For the next three months, you will completely disappear from the scene. (Take a trip, spend time with your child, or why not both?) You will therefore refrain from attending social functions held at any retail establishment or designer boutique—until the right people begin inviting you. (An invitation from the PR firm is not acceptable; a handwritten note from Mr. Dries Van Noten requesting the honor of your presence is.) You will also refrain from all random receptions, gala dinners, annual balls, fund-raising benefits, charity auctions, "cocktail parties in aid of" anything, polo matches, tastings, or any other events that you would instinctually feel compelled to attend. After your three-month purgatory, we will slowly reintroduce you to the world in a series of carefully choreographed appearances. Depending on how well you perform, I may orchestrate further invitations to select events in London, Paris, Jakarta, and Singapore. Dipping your toes in the international scene will further enhance your reputation as "one to watch." (Note: Ada Poon didn't begin to receive invitations to Lady Ladoorie's annual garden party until she was seen attending Colin Khoo and Araminta Lee's wedding in Singapore.)

---

* An open-air roadside food stall. The *dai pai dong* where Corinna stages all her paparazzi shots is a particularly picturesque one located on St. Francis Yard, opposite the Club Monaco men's concept shop.

## TRAVEL

I know you've been going to Dubai, Paris, and London
for your holidays, but that's what every common jet-
setter in Hong Kong does these days. To stand out from
the crowd, you need to begin traveling to new locales
to demonstrate that you are someone of originality and
interest. This year, I suggest that you plan a tour of
famous religious pilgrimage sites such as the Shrine
of Our Lady of Fatima in Portugal, the Sanctuary of
Lourdes in France, and Santiago de Compostela in
Spain. Be sure to post pictures of these places on your
Facebook. In this way, even if you are photographed
biting into a Galician ham croquette, people will
still associate you with the Blessed Virgin Mother. If
this trip goes well, we can organize a visit to Oprah's
schools in South Africa next year.

## PHILANTHROPIC AFFILIATIONS

In order to truly ascend to a higher social stratosphere,
it is important for you to become affiliated with one
charitable cause. My mother of course has long been
associated with the Hong Kong Horticultural Society,
Connie Ming has a lock on all the art museums, Ada
Poon owns cancer, and in a brilliant maneuver, Jordana
Chiu was able to wrestle control of irritable bowel syndrome from Unity Ho last year at the Serenity Colon
Ball. We can discuss some of your personal interests
and decide if there is anything suitable that dovetails
with our goals. Otherwise, I will select a cause from
whatever available options remain so that we can send a
unified message about what you stand for.

## SPIRITUAL LIFE

When I feel you are ready, I will introduce you to Hong Kong's most exclusive church, which you are to begin attending on a regular basis. <u>Before you protest, please note that this is one of the cornerstones to my methodology of social rehabilitation.</u> Your true spiritual affiliations do not concern me—it does not matter to me if you are Taoist, Daoist, Buddhist, or worship Meryl Streep—but it is absolutely essential that you become a regular praying, tithing, communion-taking, hands-in-the-air-waving, Bible-study-fellowship-attending member of this church. (This has the added bonus of ensuring that you will be qualified for burial at the most coveted Christian cemetery on Hong Kong Island, rather than having to suffer the eternal humiliation of being interred at one of those lesser cemeteries on the Kowloon side.)

## CULTURE AND CONVERSATION

Your chief handicap to social success will always be the fact that you did not attend the right kindergarten with any of the right crowd. This eliminates you from participating in seventy percent of the conversations that occur during dinner parties at the best houses. You do not know the gossip that goes back to these people's childhoods. And this is the secret: They are all still completely obsessed with what happened when they were five. Who was fat or thin? Who wet her pants during choir practice? Whose father shut down Ocean Park for the day so that he could have a huge birthday party? Who spilled red bean soup all over whose party dress when they were six years old and still has not been forgiven? Twenty percent of the other conversations at parties consist of complaining about Mainlanders, so by default you will not be able to join in that discussion. Another five percent is earmarked for complaining about the Chief Executive, so in order to distinguish yourself in the remaining meager five percent conversational window, you must either have one hell of a good stock tip or learn to become a scintillating conversationalist. Beauty fades, but wit will keep you on the invitation lists to all the most exclusive parties. To that end, you will embark on a reading program that I have designed specifically for you. You will also attend one cultural event per week. This can include but is not restricted to plays, opera, classical music concerts, ballet, modern dance, performance art, literary festivals, poetry readings, museum exhibitions, foreign-language or independent films, and art openings. (Hollywood movies, Cirque du Soleil, and Cantopop concerts do not count as culture.)

## READING LIST

I noticed many magazines but not a single book in your entire house, with the exception of a Chinese-language translation of Sheryl Sandberg's *Lean In* found in one of the maid's bedrooms. You will therefore complete one book per fortnight, with the exception of Trollope, where you will be allowed three weeks per book. As you read these books, you will hopefully come to understand and appreciate why I am making you read them. The books are to be read in the following order:

*Snobs* by Julian Fellowes
*The Piano Teacher* by Janice Y. K. Lee
*People Like Us* by Dominick Dunne

*The Power of Style* by Annette Tapert and Diana
   Edkins (this is out of print; I will lend you my copy)
*Pride and Avarice* by Nicholas Coleridge
*The Soong Dynasty* by Sterling Seagrave
~~*Freedom* by Jonathan Franzen~~
*D.V.* by Diana Vreeland
*A Princess Remembers: The Memoirs of the Maharani
   of Jaipur* by Gayatri Devi
Jane Austen—complete works beginning with *Pride
   and Prejudice*
Edith Wharton—*The Custom of the Country*, *The Age
   of Innocence*, *The Buccaneers*, *The House of Mirth*
   (must be read in strict order—you will understand
   why when you finish the last one)
*Vanity Fair* by William Makepeace Thackeray
*Anna Karenina* by Leo Tolstoy
*Brideshead Revisited* by Evelyn Waugh
Anthony Trollope—all the books in the Palliser
   series, beginning with *Can You Forgive Her?*

   I shall do an assessment when you have completed
these books to see whether you are ready to attempt
some light Proust.

## FINAL NOTE

There's no easy way to put this: We need to talk about
Bernard. None of our goals will be effective if people
are under the impression that your husband is somehow
incapacitated, in a coma, or has become your sex slave
in a dungeon. (That is the latest rumor going around.)
We need to orchestrate a very public appearance with
your husband and daughter very soon. Let's discuss the
options tomorrow at the Mandarin over tea and scones.

# RACHEL AND NICK

SHANGHAI, JUNE 2013

"And *this*," the general manager said with a flourish, "is your living room." Rachel and Nick walked through the foyer and into a room with double-height ceilings and a grand art deco–style fireplace. One of the associates in the general manager's entourage pushed a button, and the sheer curtains in front of the tall picture window parted silently to reveal a breathtaking view of the Shanghai skyline.

"No wonder you call this the Majestic suite," Nick said. Another associate popped open a bottle of Deutz champagne and began pouring the bubbly into a pair of tall flutes. To Rachel, the sprawling hotel suite felt like a decadent box of chocolates—from the black marble bathroom with its oval soaking tub to the ridiculously plush pillows on the bed, every corner was just waiting to be savored.

"Our yacht is at your disposal, and I would highly recommend a late-afternoon cruise so that you can see the city transition from day to night."

"We'll definitely keep that in mind," Nick said, eyeing the plush sofa longingly. *Could these lovely people please just leave so I can kick off my shoes and crash for a bit?*

"Please let us know if there is anything else we can do to make your stay more enjoyable," the manager said, placing his hand on his chest and making an almost imperceptible bow before discreetly exiting the room.

Nick plopped down on the sofa lengthwise, grateful to be able to stretch out after their fifteen-hour flight from New York. "Well this is a surprise."

"I know! Can you believe this place? I'm pretty sure the bathroom alone is larger than our whole apartment! I thought our hotel in Paris was something else, but this is on a whole other level," Rachel gushed as she returned to the living room.

They were supposed to be staying with her father for the first couple of weeks of their vacation in China, but upon landing at Pudong International Airport, they were greeted at the gate by a man in a gray three-piece suit who had a note from Bao Gaoliang. Rachel took the piece of paper out of her purse and read it again. Written in Mandarin script in bold black ink, the note translated to:

*Dear Rachel and Nick,*

*I trust you had a good flight. My apologies that I am unable to greet you at the airport myself, but I had to be in Hong Kong at the last minute and will only be returning later today. Since you are now officially on your honeymoon, I felt it would be much more fitting for you to spend your first days at the Peninsula Hotel as my guest. It will certainly be far more romantic than my house. Mr. Tin will speed your way through passport control and the Peninsula has sent a car to take you to the hotel. Have a relaxing afternoon, and I look forward to introducing you to your family at a celebratory dinner tonight. I will contact you*

*with more details before the evening, but let's plan on meet-
ing at 7:00 p.m.*

*Yours truly,*
*Bao Gaoliang*

Nick noticed Rachel's face light up as she reread the letter, her eyes skimming over the words "your family" for the
umpteenth time. Taking another sip of the champagne, he
said, "It was so cool of your father to arrange all this for us.
Very thoughtful."

"Wasn't it? It's all a bit over the top—from this ginormous
suite to the Rolls that picked us up at the airport. I felt a little
embarrassed to be riding in it, didn't you?"

"Nah, the new Phantoms are perfectly discreet. Colin's
grandmother had a vintage Silver Cloud from the 1950s that
looked like it came straight from Buckingham Palace. Now
*that* was embarrassing to ride in."

"Well, I'm still not used to all this, but I guess this is how
the Baos live."

As if reading her mind, Nick asked, "How are you feeling
about tonight?"

"I'm excited to meet everyone."

Nick remembered the hints his mother had made about
the Baos back in Santa Barbara, and he had shared all the
details of that conversation with Rachel a few days after their
wedding. At that time, Rachel had said, "I'm happy that my
father and his family have done well, but it really makes no
difference to me whether they are rich or poor."

"I just wanted you to know what I know. It's part of my
new 'full disclosure policy,'" Nick had said with a smile.

"Ha—thanks! Well, I'm a lot more comfortable navigat-
ing around the Richie Rich crowd, thanks to you. I've already

gone through a baptism of fire with *your* family. Don't you think I'm ready for anything now?"

"You survived my mother—I think everything else from here on out is a piece of cake," Nick had laughed. "I just want you to be fully aware of what you're getting yourself into this time."

Rachel had given him a thoughtful look. "You know, I'm really going to try to approach this with no illusions—I know it'll take a while to get to know my new family. I imagine it's just as much of a shock for my brother and my stepmother as it is for me. They probably have issues out the wazoo about all this, and I'm not expecting to bond with them overnight. It's enough for me to know they exist and to meet them."

Now that they were actually on Chinese soil, Nick could sense that Rachel wasn't feeling as laid-back as she had been in Santa Barbara. He could feel her nervous energy even as she lay nestled against him on the sofa, both of them trying to battle through their jet lag. Even though she tried to play it cool, Nick knew how much she longed to be accepted by this newfound family of hers. He had grown up rooted in a long-established lineage: The hallways of Tyersall Park had always been hung with ancestral portraits in ancient rosewood frames, and in the library, Nick had spent many a rainy after-noon paging through volumes of hand-bound books con-taining intricate family trees. The Youngs had documented their ancestors going all the way back to AD 432, and it was all there in the brittle, brown pages of these ancient tomes. He wondered what it was like for Rachel to grow up not knowing a thing about her father, about the other half of her family. A soft buzz interrupted his thoughts.

"I think someone's at the door," Rachel said with a yawn, as Nick got up reluctantly to open it.

"Delivery for Ms. Chu," the green-uniformed bellman said

cheerily. He entered the suite pulling a luggage cart groaning with stacks of immaculately wrapped boxes. Behind him was another bellboy with a second luggage cart packed full of cartons.

"What's all this?" Nick asked. The bellboy smiled and handed over an envelope. Scrawled on a plush creamy note card was: "Welcome to Shanghai! Thought you could use some essentials. Cheers, C."

"It's from Carlton!" Rachel exclaimed in surprise. She opened the first box and found four different jams nestled against the packing hay: Seville Orange Marmalade, Redcurrant Jelly, Nectarine Compote, Lemon and Ginger Curd. Stamped on the minimalist glass jars in elegant white type were the words DAYLESFORD ORGANIC.

"Oh! Daylesford is an organic farm in Gloucestershire owned by my friends the Bamfords. They make the most glorious foods. Are all the boxes from them?" Nick asked, duly impressed.

Rachel opened another carton and found it full of bottles of Sparkling Apple and Bilberry Juice. "Who's even *heard* of bilberries?" she remarked. As the two of them dove into the boxes, they discovered that Carlton had for all intents and purposes supplied them with Daylesford's entire product line. There were crackers with sea salt, shortbreads, and biscuits of dizzying variety to go along with the fine cheeses, farmed Shetland Isles Smoked Salmon, and exotic chutneys. And there were sparkling wines, cabernet francs, and bottles of whole milk to wash it all down.

Rachel stood amid the open boxes in astonishment. "Can you believe all this? There's enough stuff here to last us for a year."

"Whatever we can't eat we'll save for the zombie apocalypse. I must say Carlton seems to be a rather generous fellow."

"That's putting it mildly! What a sweet welcome gift—I can't wait to meet him!" Rachel said excitedly.

"Judging by his taste, I think I'm going to like him. Now, what should we try first? The white-chocolate-dipped lemon biscuits or the chocolate-dipped ginger biscuits?"

## Bao Residence, Shanghai

### EARLIER THAT MORNING

Gaoliang was on his way upstairs to shower after his morning jog when he encountered two maids coming down with several pieces of black-and-tan Tramontano luggage.

"Whose bags are those?" he asked one of the maids.

"Mrs. Bao's, sir," the girl replied, not daring to make eye contact with him.

"Where are you taking them?"

"Just out to the car, sir. They are for Mrs. Bao's trip."

Gaoliang headed into his bedroom, where he found his wife seated at her dressing table putting on a pair of opal-and-diamond earrings.

"Where are you off to?" he asked.

"Hong Kong."

"I didn't know you had a trip planned today."

"It's a last-minute thing—there are some problems at the Tsuen Wan factories I need to sort out," Shaoyen replied.

"But Rachel and her husband are arriving today."

"Oh, was that today?" Shaoyen said.

"Yes. We have a private room booked at the Whampoa Club tonight."

"I'm sure dinner will be very good. Be sure to order the drunken chicken."

"You won't be back in time?" Gaoliang said, a little surprised.

"I'm afraid not."

Gaoliang sat down on the chaise lounge beside his wife, knowing full well why she was making this sudden trip. "I thought you said you were okay with all this."

"For a while, I thought I was . . ." Shaoyen said slowly, letting her voice trail off as she methodically wiped one of the earring posts with a cotton ball soaked in disinfectant. "But now that it's really happening I've realized I'm not comfortable with any of it."

Gaoliang sighed. Since his reunion with Kerry and Rachel back in March, he had spent many a long night trying to placate his wife. Shaoyen had been shocked, of course, by the bombshell he had dropped after returning from California, but over the past two months, he thought he had succeeded in reassuring her. Kerry Chu was a woman he had loved, ever so briefly, when he was only eighteen. He was a boy. It was a lifetime ago. When he brought up the idea of inviting Rachel to visit, thinking it would actually help her see that everything would be fine, Shaoyen raised no objections. He should have known it wouldn't be that easy.

"I know how difficult this must be for you," Gaoliang ventured to say.

"Do you? I'm not so certain you do," Shaoyen said, spritzing her neck with Lumière Noire.

"Surely you can imagine that this isn't easy for Rachel either . . ." Gaoliang began.

Shaoyen glared into her husband's eyes in the mirror for a few seconds, and then she smashed the perfume bottle against the table. Gaoliang jumped out of his seat in shock.

"Rachel, Rachel, all you've talked about for weeks is Rachel! But you haven't really listened to a word I've said! You haven't thought about my feelings," Shaoyen screamed.

"All I have been trying to do is be considerate of your feelings," he said, trying to remain calm.

Shaoyen glowered at her husband. "Huh! If you were truly being considerate, you wouldn't expect me to sit there and smile through dinner while you parade your bastard daughter around to a room full of our family and friends. You give me no face!"

Gaoliang winced at her words, but he tried to defend himself. "I've only invited our closest relatives—people who need to know about her."

"Still, for her to meet our family—your parents, Uncle Koo, your sister and her husband and his big mouth—the word will get out in no time and you will have no more face in Beijing. You can kiss any hope of becoming the vice-premier goodbye."

"It's *precisely* to avoid any scandal that I wanted to be open about all this from the very beginning. I didn't want to have any secrets. You're the one who's stopped me from telling anyone. Don't you think people will see that I'm only doing the right thing, the honorable thing, for my daughter?"

"If you think that's what people will see, you're more naïve than I thought. Enjoy your dinner. I'm going to Hong Kong, and Carlton is coming with me."

"What? But Carlton's been looking forward to meeting his sister!"

"He's only been saying that to keep you happy. You have no idea the hell he's been going through—his mood swings, his despair. You only see what you want to see."

"I see a great deal more than you think!" Gaoliang said, raising his voice for the first time. "Carlton's depression has more to do with his reckless ways that led to almost being killed in a car wreck. Please don't drag him into the middle of your issues with Rachel."

"Don't you see? He is in the very middle of this whether

you like it or not! By accepting your illegitimate daughter, you bring nothing but shame upon him! You do what you want to ruin your own future, but I'm not going to let you ruin our son's!"

"You realize that Rachel and Nick are going to be staying with us for two months? I don't know what you think you'll accomplish by avoiding them now."

Shaoyen said through gritted teeth, "I've decided that I cannot—will not—sleep under the same roof as Rachel Chu or Nicholas Young."

"Now what could you possibly have against Nicholas Young?"

"He is the son of that two-faced schemer who wormed her way into our lives."

"Come on, Eleanor Young was such a great help to us when Carlton was in the hospital."

"That's only because she knew who he was from the very beginning."

Gaoliang shook his head in frustration. "I'm not going to continue arguing with you when you are being this unreasonable."

"I'm done arguing too. I have a plane to catch. But mark my words: I will not allow Rachel or Nicholas into this house, or any of my houses."

"Stop being unreasonable!" Gaoliang exploded. "Where are they supposed to stay?"

"There are a thousand hotels in this city."

"You're insane. They are landing in a few hours! How can I suddenly tell my daughter she isn't welcome in my house after she's just spent twenty hours on a plane?"

"You figure it out. But this is my house too, and either you choose them, or you choose your wife and son!" Shaoyen stormed out, leaving her husband alone in a room that reeked of spiced rose and narcissus.

## ASTRID

"Ludivine, I'm not sure if you can hear me, but you're breaking up. I'm on a gondola in the middle of a canal right now,
and the connection is very weak. Please text me and I'll call
you back as soon as I get off this boat." Astrid put her phone
away and smiled apologetically at her friend, Contessa Domiella Finzi-Contini. She was there for the Venice Biennale, and
they were being rowed to the Palazzo Brandolini for a dinner
party honoring Anish Kapoor.

"This is Venezia—there is never a signal anywhere, much
less in the middle of Canal Grande." Domiella laughed as
she tried to stop her pashmina from flapping away in the evening breeze. "Now, finish telling me the story of your amazing find."

"Well, I always thought Fortuny only worked with heavier
silks and velvets, so when I came across this voile dress in an
antique shop in Jakarta, of all places, I didn't know what to
think. I thought at first it was some kind of Peranakan wedding gown from the 1920s, but the distinctive pleating caught
my eye. And the pattern—"

"It's his classic Delphos pattern, of course, but this fabric—

my God, so light!" Domiella said as she fondled the hem of Astrid's long diaphanous skirt. "And the color—I've never seen this shade of violet before. Obviously hand-painted, probably by Fortuny himself or his wife, Henriette. How is it that you are always finding these remarkable treasures?"

"Domiella, I swear to God, they just find me. I paid about three hundred thousand rupiahs for it—that's about twenty-five U.S. dollars."

"*Cazzo!* I am going to vomit with jealousy! I'm sure any museum would love to have it. Be careful, Dodie will probably want to buy it off your body the minute she sees you tonight!"

The grand entrance of the Palazzo Brandolini was jammed oar to oar with guests arriving in gondolas, launches, and vaporettos, allowing Astrid to check her phone again. This time, there was an e-mail that read:

Madame,

I write to you with grave concerns about recent actions taken in regards to Cassian while you are away. I arrived home after my day off and found that Cassian was locked up in the upstairs hall closet, and Padma was sitting on a stool outside looking at her iPad. I asked her what was happening, and she said, "Sir told me not to let Cassian out." I asked her how long Cassian had been inside the closet and she said four hours. Your husband was out at a business dinner. When I let Cassian out, the boy was very distressed.

Apparently Michael was punishing Cassian for his latest infraction—the boy was playing with his lightsaber this afternoon and accidentally made a small scratch on the door of the vintage Porsche 550 Spyder in the great hall. Two nights ago, Michael sent Cassian to bed without any supper because the boy used a Chinese swear term. Apparently it is the bad word of the week at Far Eastern Kindergarten, and every boy has been using it, even though they have no idea what they are saying. Ah Lian explained to me what it meant. I assure you a five-year-old cannot even begin to comprehend such an act between a father and a daughter.

In my view, such disciplinary measures toward Cassian are counterproductive. They do not address the underlying issues and will only cause him to develop new phobias and resentment toward his father. It is past 1:00 a.m. now and Cassian still cannot sleep. For the first time since he was three, he is afraid of the dark again.

Ludivine

Astrid read the e-mail with increasing frustration and sadness. She sent a quick text message to her husband, and then allowed herself to be helped out of the gondola after the contessa. They entered the front hall of the palazzo, which was dominated by an enormous metallic-gold concave sculpture suspended from the ceiling.

"*Bellissima!* I wonder, is it one of Anish's new installations?" Domiella turned to gauge Astrid's reaction, and found that she hadn't even noticed the sculpture hovering above her. "Is everything okay?"

Astrid sighed. "Every time I go away, there seems to be a new problem with Cassian."

"He misses his mama."

"No, that's not it. I mean, I'm sure he misses me, but I intentionally make these short trips so that Cassian might bond with his father. He's too much of a mama's boy, and I'm trying to change that—I see what that's done to my brother.

But every time I go away, there's always a problem. Michael and he just seem to always be at loggerheads."

"What is loggerheads?"

"They fight. Michael doesn't have any tolerance for anything other than perfect behavior from his son. He treats him as if he were in the military. Tell me, when Luchino and Pier Paolo were Cassian's age, if they broke something valuable, what would you do to them?"

"My God, my sons tore up everything in the house! Furniture, rugs, everything! They put an elbow through a Bronzino one day when they were fighting with each other. Thankfully, it was a portrait of a very ugly woman. Some inbred ancestor of my husband's."

"And what did you do? Did you punish them?"

"For what? They are boys."

"Exactly!" Astrid sighed.

"Oh dear, here comes that odious art dealer who keeps trying to sell me a Gursky. I keep telling him that if I had to look at a huge photo of Amsterdam's Schiphol Airport all day, I'd hang myself. Let's go upstairs."

Despite their best efforts, the dealer caught up to them in the Grand Ballroom on the second floor. "Contessa—how good to see you," he said in an extremely affected accent, attempting to give her a double-cheek kiss. She only allowed one cheek. "How are your parents these days?"

"Still alive," Domiella said wistfully.

The man paused for a split second, before letting out a guffaw. "Oh, har har!"

"This is my friend Astrid Leong Teo."

"Howdoyoudo," he said, pushing up his obnoxiously thick horn-rimmed spectacles. He had memorized dossiers on every high-net-worth Asian collector who might attend the Biennale this year, but as he did not recognize Astrid, he continued to zero in on the contessa. "Contessa, I do hope you will give me a chance to walk you through the German Pavilion sometime."

"Excuse me, I have to make a brief phone call," Astrid said, as she moved toward the outdoor balcony.

Domiella looked at the art dealer and shook her head pitifully. "You just missed the chance of a lifetime. Do you know who my friend was? Her family are the Medicis of Asia, and she's on a buying binge for a museum in Singapore."

"I assumed she was just some model," the dealer sputtered.

"Oh look—Larry's talking to her. *He's* obviously done his homework. Too late for you now," Domiella tut-tutted.

· · ·

After assuring the art dealer who cornered her on the terrace that she truly had no interest in seeing his big shiny Koons, Astrid placed a call to her husband.

Michael picked up his cell phone after four rings, sounding sleepy. "Hey. Is everything okay?"

"Yes."

"You know it's one thirty in the morning here, right?"

"I do. But I think you're the only one in the house who's able to sleep. Ludivine just texted me that Cassian is still up. He's terrified of the dark now. Locking him in the closet . . . *really?*"

Michael let out a sigh of frustration. "You don't understand. He's been a little pest all week. Whenever I come home, he goes berserk."

"He's acting out to get your attention. He wants to play."

"The great hall is not a playroom. My cars are not toys. He has to learn to control himself—at his age, I was not jumping around like an orangutan all day."

"He is an active, high-spirited kid. Like his father was."

"Hnnh!" Michael snorted. "If I had acted the way he does,

I would have been whipped by my pa. Ten strokes on my ass with his *rotan*."*

"Well, thank God you're not your father then."

"Cassian is a wild child, and this is the time for him to learn some discipline."

"He is disciplined. Do you see how much calmer he is when I am there? I think you would get much farther if you would give him more of your attention. And I don't mean sitting by the pool with your laptop while he plays. Take him to the zoo, take him to Gardens by the Bay. He just wants to be with his father."

"So now you're trying to make me feel guilty."

"Darling, I'm not trying to make you feel anything. But don't you see? My being away is a special opportunity for you to spend more quality time with him. He'll be in Primary One next year, and then the whole academic race begins. He's growing up so fast—this is a time in his life you'll never get back."

"Okay, *lah*, okay *lah*, you win. I'm a bad father."

Astrid balled up some of the fabric of her skirt in frustration. "This is not about winning, and you're not a bad father. It's just—" Astrid began, before Michael interrupted her.

"I'll try to do better tomorrow while you're having fun in Venice. Have a Bellini on me."

"You're not being fair. You know I promised to take this trip for the museum. We are trying to make some important things happen here for the good of Singapore. I spend most of my waking hours with Cassian all year and you are the one who travels eighty percent of the year."

"Excuse me for working my ass off to ensure a future for

---

* A rattan cane popularly used by generations of Singaporean fathers, school principals, and after-school Chinese tutors for corporal punishment. (Mrs. Chan, I still hate you.)

my family. While you're working 'for the good of Singapore,' everything I'm doing is for Cassian and you!"

"Michael, we're not going to go hungry anytime soon, and you know that."

Michael was silent for a long moment. "You know what the real problem is, Astrid? The problem is that you've never had to worry about money a single day in your life. You don't realize how hard it is to make money—you blow your nose and money comes out! You've never understood the fear that normal people have. Well, I was motivated by that fear. And I built my own fortune out of it. I want to instill in my son that same fear. He is going to inherit a great deal of money one day, and he needs to know that he has to earn it. He has to have boundaries. Otherwise—he's just going to end up like your brother Henry, or any one of your pompous, entitled cousins who haven't worked a day in their lives but feel like they own the world."

"Now you're just being mean, Michael. That's an extremely unfair generalization."

"You know I speak the truth. At the end of the day, your son made a decision to damage my car. Your son made the decision to use filthy language. And you just continue making excuses for him."

"He's only FIVE!" Astrid said, raising her voice.

"AND THAT'S MY POINT, HONEY! If we don't correct his problems now, we're never going to."

Astrid sighed deeply. "Michael, I really don't want to get into a big fight with you over this right now."

"I don't either. I want to get some sleep. Some of us have to work in the morning."

With that, Michael hung up on her. Astrid put her phone back into her purse and leaned against the balustrade, feeling frustrated. The blue hour was upon the city, and the water began to shimmer in the reflection of the lights coming on in all the palazzos across the Grand Canal. *This is ridiculous. I've just been standing at one of the most beautiful spots on the planet, getting into a long-distance argument over my son.*

Domiella led a group of people out onto the terrace, and Astrid recognized her friend Grégoire L'Herme-Pierre among them.

"Astrid! I couldn't believe it when Domiella told me you were here too! What are you doing in Venice? I didn't know this art crowd was your thing," Grégoire said, giving Astrid his usual Parisian quadruple kiss.

"I'm just soaking in the sights," Astrid said distractedly, still trying to collect herself after the call.

"Of course. Now, surely you know my friends here—Pascal Pang and Isabel Wu of Hong Kong?"

Astrid greeted the chic couple. Pascal wore an immaculately tailored suit that had a slight iridescence, while Isabel was elegantly clad in a strapless black Christian Dior dress with a flared, knee-length skirt. Her hair was swept up into a Grecian chignon, and around her neck was a striking Michele Oka Doner gold necklace in the shape of palm fronds. Suddenly Astrid had a realization that the two of them weren't a couple. *Could this Isabel Wu standing in front of her be Charlie's wife?*

The lady caught Astrid's flash of recognition, and said simply, "I know who you are."

Grégoire chuckled. "See, it's always such a small world when you're around!"

"It's a pleasure to meet you at last," Astrid said to Isabel, adding, "Charlie told me all about your fund-raising efforts for M+ museum. I think it's terrific what you're doing. It's high time Hong Kong has a world-class contemporary art space."

"Thank you. Yes, I believe you saw Charlie recently, didn't you?" Isabel asked.

"Yes. I am sorry you weren't able to join us on our California road trip."

Isabel paused, taken aback. *California?* She knew that Charlie had bumped into Astrid at the Pinnacle Ball, but she knew nothing about a road trip. "So, you had a nice time then?"

"Oh yes. We were planning on going to Sausalito, but then we decided on the spur of the moment to drive down the coast to Monterey and Big Sur."

"Let me guess . . . did he take you to Post Ranch Inn for dinner?" she continued breezily.

"We went for lunch, actually. Heavenly there, isn't it?"

"Yes, you could say that. Well, it was good to meet you at last, Astrid Leong." Isabel turned to reenter the ballroom with Pascal, while Astrid remained on the balcony with Domiella and Grégoire. The summer heat still lingered in the soft evening breeze, and in the distance, the bells of the Basilica di San Marco began to peal.

Pascal suddenly reappeared on the balcony and said hurriedly to Grégoire, "Isabel needs to leave this instant. Are you staying or coming?"

"Is everything okay?" Astrid asked.

Pascal gave Astrid a glacial stare. "So nice of you to rub it in Isabel's face like that."

"I'm sorry?" Astrid said, confused.

Pascal inhaled deeply, trying to contain his rage. "I don't know who you think you are, but I've never seen anyone as brazen as you. Did you have to make it so apparent to Isabel that you've been fucking her husband up and down the California coast?"

Domiella gasped and gripped Astrid's shoulder.

Astrid shook her head wildly. "No, no, there's been a big misunderstanding. Charlie and I are just old friends—"

"Old friends? Ha! Until tonight, Isabel wasn't even sure you were still alive."

# THE BAOS

## THREE ON THE BUND, SHANGHAI

The hotel's Brewster green Rolls-Royce was waiting in the driveway to ferry Nick and Rachel to dinner, but with their destination just six blocks away, they decided to walk. It was an unseasonably cool evening for early June, and as they strolled along the legendary riverfront boulevard known as the Bund, Nick could still remember a morning in Hong Kong when he was around six years old.

His parents took him on a drive far out into the country-side of Kowloon's New Territories, up a winding mountain road. At the top of the mountain was a lookout point crowded with tourists, snapping away at the view and lining up to use the swiveling metal binoculars that had been mounted on a rusty metal railing. Nick's father lifted him up so that he could see through the viewfinder. "Can you see it? That's the border of China. That's where your great-great-grandparents came from," Philip Young told his son. "Take a good look, because we aren't able to go past that border."

"Why not?" Nick had asked.

"It's a Communist country, and our Singapore passports

are stamped 'No Entry into the People's Republic of China.' But one day, hopefully, you will be able to go."

Nick squinted at the almost barren, muddy brown landscape. He could discern some roughly plowed fields and irrigation ditches, but not much else. Where was the border? He was trying to find a great wall, a moat, or any sort of proper demarcation to indicate where the British Crown Colony of Hong Kong ended and the People's Republic of China began, but there was nothing. The viewfinder lenses were grimy, and his armpits hurt from the grip of his father's large hands. Nick asked to be put down and made a beeline for the lady selling snacks in the concrete hut nearby. A Cornetto ice-cream cone was far more interesting than the view of China. China was boring.

But the China of Nick's childhood bore no resemblance to the incredible sights that surrounded him in every direction now. Shanghai was a vast, sprawling megalopolis on the banks of the Huangpu River, the "Paris of the East," where hyperbole-defying skyscrapers vied for attention with stately early-twentieth-century European façades.

Nick began pointing out some of his favorite buildings to Rachel. "That's the Broadway Mansions Hotel right across the bridge. I love its hulking, Gothic silhouette—so classic art deco. Did you know Shanghai has the largest concentration of art deco architecture in the world?"

"I had no idea! All the buildings around us are just jaw-dropping—I mean, look at that crazy skyline!" Rachel gestured excitedly to the intimidating expanse of skyscrapers on the other side of the river.

"And that's just Pudong—it was all pretty much farmland, and none of those buildings even existed ten years ago. Now it's a financial district that makes Wall Street look like a fishing village. That structure with the two huge round orbs is the

Oriental Pearl Radio and TV Tower. Doesn't it look like something out of *Buck Rogers in the 25th Century*?" Nick remarked.

"Buck Rogers?" Rachel gave him a blank look.

"It was a 1980s TV show set in the future, and all the
buildings looked like some ten-year-old's fantasy of another
galaxy. You probably didn't watch any of the bad eighties
shows that came to Singapore years after they bombed in the
U.S. Like *Manimal*. Do you remember that one? It was about
this guy who could change into different types of animals.
Like an eagle, a snake, or a jaguar."

"And what was the point of that?"

"He was fighting the bad guys, of course. What else would
he be doing?"

Rachel smiled, but Nick could tell that underneath their
banter, she was getting more and more nervous as they got
closer to their destination. Nick stared up at the moon for a
moment and made a wish to the universe. He wished for the
dinner to go smoothly. Rachel had waited all these years and
come all this way to meet her family, and he hoped her dreams
would be fulfilled tonight.

They soon reached Three on the Bund, an elegant post-
Renaissance-style building crowned by a majestic cupola. Nick
and Rachel took the elevator up to the fifth floor and found
themselves in a dramatic crimson-walled foyer. A hostess
stood in front of a gold inlaid fresco that depicted a beautiful
maiden in flowing robes flanked by two gigantic prostrating
warriors.

"Welcome to the Whampoa Club," the woman said in
English.

"Thank you. We are here for the Bao party," Nick said.

"Of course. Please follow me." The hostess, dressed in
an impossibly tight yellow cheongsam, walked them past the
main dining room packed with chic Shanghai families enjoying their meals and down a hallway lined with art deco club

chairs and green glass lamps. Along one side of the hallway was another gold-and-silver carved fresco, and the hostess pushed open one of the wall panels to reveal a private dining room.

"Please make yourselves comfortable. You are the first ones to arrive," she said.

"Oh, okay," Rachel said. Nick wasn't sure whether she sounded more surprised or relieved. The private room was luxuriously appointed with a grouping of armchairs upholstered in raw silk on one end and a large round table with lacquered rosewood chairs by the window. Rachel noted that the table was set for twelve. She wondered whom she would be meeting tonight. Aside from her father, his wife, Shaoyen, and her half brother, Carlton, what other relatives would be joining them?

"Isn't it interesting that since we've arrived, practically everyone has addressed us in English instead of Mandarin?" Rachel commented.

"Not really. They can tell from the minute we walk in that we're not native Chinese. You're an Amazon compared to most of the women here, and everything else about us is different—we don't dress like the locals, and we carry ourselves in a completely different way."

"When I was teaching in Chengdu nine years ago, my students all knew I was an American, but they still spoke to me in Mandarin."

"That was Chengdu. Shanghai has always been a sophisticated, international city, so they are much more used to seeing pseudo-Chinese like us here."

"Well, we're certainly not as dressed up as many of the locals I've seen today."

"Yeah, these days *we're* the bumpkins," Nick joked.

As the minutes ticked by, Rachel sat on one of the sofas and began to flip through the tea menu. "It says here they have over fifty premium teas from across China, served in traditional ceremonies in their private tearooms."

"Maybe we'll get to sample some tonight," Nick replied as he paced around the room, pretending to admire the contemporary Chinese art.

"Can you just sit down and chill? Your pacing is making me nervous."

"Sorry," Nick said. He took a seat across from her and started flipping through the tea menu too.

They sat in silence for another ten minutes, until Rachel could take it no more. "Something's gone wrong. Do you think we've been stood up?"

"I'm sure they're just stuck in traffic." Nick tried to sound calm, although he was secretly fretting as well.

"I don't know . . . I have a strange feeling about this. Why would my father book a room so early when no one's showed up for more than half an hour?"

"In Hong Kong, people are notoriously late to everything. I'm thinking Shanghai must be the same. It's a matter of face—no one wants to be the first to show up, in case they look too eager, so they try to outdo one another in lateness. The last one to arrive is deemed the most important."

"That's totally ridiculous!" Rachel snorted.

"You think? I feel a similar thing happens in New York, though it's not quite as overt. At your department meetings, isn't the dean or some star professor always the last to show up? Or the chancellor just 'drops in' at the tail end, because he's too important to sit through the whole meeting?"

"That's not the same."

"It isn't? Posturing is posturing. Hong Kongers have just elevated it to an art form," Nick opined.

"Well, I can see that happening for a business lunch, but this is a family dinner. They are really quite late."

"I was once at a dinner in Hong Kong with my relatives, and I ended up waiting over an hour before everyone else got there. Eddie was the last to arrive, of course. I think you're getting paranoid a little too quickly. Don't worry—they'll be here."

A few minutes later, the door slid open, and a man in a dark navy suit entered the room. "Mr. and Mrs. Young? I'm the manager. I have a message for you from Mr. Bao."

Nick's heart sank. *What now?*

Rachel looked at the manager anxiously, but before he had a chance to say anything, they were distracted by a commotion in the hallway. They poked their heads out of the doorway and saw someone surrounded by a crowd of gawkers. It was a girl in her early twenties, strikingly attired in a figure-hugging strapless white dress with an ornately sequined red matador cape flung casually over her milk-white shoulders. Two burly security guards and a woman with a faux-hawk hairstyle wearing a pinstriped suit attempted to clear the way, while proper teenage girls who had minutes before been enjoying polite, posh dinners with their families had suddenly transformed into shrieking fans taking pictures with their camera phones.

"Is she a movie star?" Nick asked the manager, staring at the girl as she posed glamorously with her fans. With long, voluminous raven hair piled up into a loose beehive, a perfectly sculpted ski-jump nose, and bee-stung lips, she seemed larger than life—like a Chinese Ava Gardner.

"No, that's Colette Bing. She is famous for her clothes," the manager explained.

Colette finished autographing some dinner napkins and headed straight toward them. "Ah, I'm glad I found you!" she said to Rachel as if she were greeting an old friend.

"Are you talking to me?" Rachel stared at her, utterly stunned.

"Of course! Come on, let's get out of here."

"Um, I think you've mistaken me for someone else. We're meeting some people for dinner here—" Rachel began.

"You're Rachel, right? The Baos sent me—the plans have changed. Come with me and I'll explain everything," Colette said. She took Rachel by the arm and began walking her out of the room. The girls in the hallway started squealing again and taking more pictures.

"Where is your service elevator?" the woman with the faux-hawk demanded of the manager. Nick followed along, baffled by everything that was happening. They were shuffled into an elevator and then down another service corridor on the ground floor. But as soon as the doors opened onto Guangdong Road, they were met by the blinding flashbulbs from a pack of paparazzi.

Colette's security guards tried to clear a path through the phalanx of photographers. "Back off! Back the fuck off!" they yelled at the jostling pack.

"This is nuts!" Nick said, almost colliding with an over-zealous photographer who had jumped right in front of him.

The woman in the faux-hawk turned to him and said, "You must be Nick. I'm Roxanne Ma—Colette's personal assistant."

"Hi, Roxanne. Does this happen everywhere Colette goes?"

"Yes. But this is nothing—these were only photographers. You should see what happens when she walks down Nanjing West Road."

"Why is she so famous?"

"Colette is one of China's foremost fashion icons. Between Weibo and WeChat, she has more than thirty-five million followers."

"Did you say thirty-five *million*?" Nick was incredulous.

"Yes. I'm afraid your picture is going to be everywhere tomorrow. Just look straight ahead and keep smiling."

Two large Audi SUVs suddenly pulled up, almost running into one of the photographers. The bodyguards quickly hustled Colette, Rachel, and Nick toward the first car, shutting the door firmly behind them before the swarming photographers could take any more shots.

"Are you okay?" Colette asked.

"Besides my barbecued retinas, I think I'm fine," Nick said from the front passenger seat.

"That was intense!" Rachel said, trying to catch her breath.

"Things have really gotten out of control in Shanghai. It all started after my *Elle China* cover," Colette explained in a carefully modulated British accent tinged with the staccato tones of a native Mandarin speaker.

Still on high alert, Nick asked, "Where are you taking us?"

Before Colette could answer, the car came to a sudden halt a few blocks away from the restaurant. The car door opened and a young man jumped in beside Rachel. She let out a quick gasp.

"Sorry—didn't mean to scare you," the man said in an accent that sounded just like Nick's, before giving her a disarming smile. "Hi—I'm Carlton."

"Oh, hi." It was all Rachel could say as they gazed at each other, both momentarily transfixed. Rachel studied her brother for the first time. Carlton had the same perpetual nut-brown tan that she did, and hair cropped closely on the sides but thicker and fashionably mussed on top. Nattily dressed in tan corduroys, a faded orange polo shirt, and a Harris Tweed blazer with elbow patches, he looked like he had jumped right out of a fashion shoot for *The Rake*.

"My God, the two of you look so much alike!" Nick exclaimed.

"I know! The minute I saw Rachel I thought I was meeting Carlton's long-lost twin!" Colette said breathlessly.

Rachel found herself at a loss for words, but it had nothing to do with her brother's resemblance to her. She felt an instant, innate connection with him—something that she hadn't even experienced when she first met her father. She closed her eyes for a moment, overcome with emotion.

"Are you okay?" Nick asked.

"Yes. Never been better, actually," Rachel said in a slightly choked voice.

Colette placed a hand on Rachel's arm. "I'm sorry for this madness—it's all my fault. When we arrived at Three on the Bund, I got recognized immediately and a mob started to follow us up to the restaurant. It was so annoying! And things only got worse at the Whampoa Club, as you could see. Carlton didn't want to meet you for the first time in front of three million people, so I told him to wait for us a few blocks away."

"It's totally fine. But where is everyone else?" Rachel asked.

Carlton began to explain. "My father sends his profuse apologies. The family dinner had to be called off because my parents had to fly to Hong Kong to deal with an emergency. Dad thought he could make it back in time for dinner, but he miscalculated. So I flew back on my own."

"Wait a minute, you just came from Hong Kong?" Rachel was confused.

"Yes. That's why we were late."

Colette jumped in. "When everything went wonky with the dinner plans, I suggested that Carlton and I fly up to meet you."

"We couldn't possibly leave you two alone on your first night in Shanghai, could we?" Colette said.

"That's so nice of you. But Carlton, are your parents okay?" Rachel inquired.

"Yes, yes. It was just a business emergency . . . at their factories in Hong Kong. My father should be back in a few days," Carlton said a little haltingly.

"I'm glad to hear it's nothing too serious," Rachel said.

"Anyway, I'm so thrilled that you and your girlfriend could be here."

Colette burst out laughing. "Oh how *cute*! Am I your girlfriend, Carlton?"

"Er, Colette's just a good friend." Carlton smiled in embarrassment.

"Sorry, I shouldn't have assumed—" Rachel began.

"That's quite all right. You're not the first to make that assumption. I'm twenty-three, and unlike most girls my age, I don't believe in tying myself down to anyone right now. Carlton's one of many suitors and perhaps someday—if he behaves himself—he will receive the final rose."

Rachel caught Nick's eye in the rearview mirror. He shot her a look that said, *Did she* REALLY *just say that?* Rachel bit into her lip and looked away, knowing that if she saw his expression again she would burst into laughter. After an awkward pause, she said, "Yes, when I was your age, getting married wasn't really a priority of mine either."

Carlton looked over at Colette. "So, Miss Bachelorette, what's the plan now?"

"Well, we can go anywhere. Do you want to go to a club, a lounge, a restaurant? Do you want to go to a deserted beach off the coast of Thailand?" Colette offered.

"You should know she's being totally serious," Carlton added.

"Er, beach later. I think some dinner might be nice," Nick said.

"What do you feel like eating?" Colette asked.

Rachel was still too frazzled to make any decision. "I'm up for anything. How about you, Nick?"

"Well, we're in Shanghai—where can we find the best *xiao long bao*?"

Carlton and Colette glanced at each other for less than a second before chanting in unison, "Din Tai Fung!"

"Wait a minute, is it the same as the Din Tai Fung in LA and Taipei?" Nick asked.

"Yes, it's the same Taiwanese chain. But believe it or not, it's better here. Ever since they opened, it's become wildly popular even with locals. There's always quite a queue, but thankfully, we're in special company tonight," Carlton said, winking at Colette.

"Let me text Roxanne—she'll arrange for us to get in through the back door. I'm done meeting my public for today," Colette declared.

. . .

Fifteen minutes later, Rachel and Nick found themselves comfortably ensconced in a private dining room with windows overlooking the skyline.

"Does everyone always dine in private rooms in China?" Rachel asked as she stared out at the nighttime view. Almost every building seemed to be putting on some kind of light show. A few towers looked like they were edged in Day-Glo, while others pulsated neon lights like giant boom boxes.

"Is there any other way? I can't imagine dining with the masses—all those people staring at you and taking pictures while you eat," Colette said, giving Rachel a look of horror.

Soon stacks of bamboo steamers containing Shanghai's most famous delicacy were paraded into the room. There were juicy *xiao long bao* dumplings of every imaginable variety along with other crowd-pleasing dishes—hand-pulled noodles with minced pork, chicken and golden egg fried rice, sautéed string beans with garlic, vegetable and pork wontons in a spicy sauce, Shanghai rice cake with shrimp, sweet taro buns. Before they began to eat, Roxanne rushed into the room and took a few pictures of Colette smiling over the food.

"Sorry to keep everyone from eating—I just have to throw

my fans a bone every hour!" Colette explained. She quickly perused the selection of images with Roxanne and instructed, "Just tweet the one of the black truffle dumplings."

Nick tried not to laugh. This Colette was a trip. He realized that she wasn't intentionally trying to sound pretentious—she was just perfectly blunt. Like someone who was born famous or royal, Colette seemed genuinely oblivious to how the rest of the world lived. Carlton, on the other hand, was down-to-earth compared to Colette. Nick had been forewarned by his mother that Carlton was "terribly spoiled," but he was nothing if not impressed by his impeccable manners. He expertly picked out all the dishes, ordered a round of beers, and made sure everyone—especially the ladies—had plenty of food on their plates before placing any on his own.

"You must have the first pork and crabmeat dumpling," Carlton said as he deftly placed one onto Rachel's porcelain spoon. Rachel nibbled carefully on the side of her dumpling, slurping most of the flavorful broth inside before downing the rest of the succulent meat.

"Did you see that? Rachel eats her soup dumplings exactly like Carlton does!" Colette said excitedly.

"Score one for genetics!" Nick quipped. "Well, Rachel, what's the verdict?"

"Oh my God, that's the best *xiao long bao* I've ever had! The broth is so light and yet so intense. I can probably eat about a dozen of these—they're like crack cocaine," Rachel said.

"You must be famished," Colette said.

"Actually we snacked a little earlier—which reminds me, Carlton, thank you so much for all the gifts!"

"Gifts? Not sure I know what you mean," Carlton said.

"The boxes of food from Daylesford Organic?"

"Oh, that was from *me*!" Colette interjected.

"Really? Wow, thank you!" Rachel replied in surprise.

"Yes—when I heard that Carlton's father had arranged for you to stay at a hotel at the very last minute, I thought, 'Poor things! They'll starve at the Peninsula! They are going to need provisions.'"

"So the hotel was a last-minute thing?" Nick inquired.

Colette pursed her lips, realizing she had made a slipup.

Carlton quickly came to the rescue. "Er . . . no . . . I mean, my father likes to plan things very far in advance, so this was rather last-minute by comparison. He wanted the two of you to have a special honeymoon treat."

"So did you like the goodies I sent up?" Colette asked.

"Oh, very much. I especially love Daylesford's marmalade," Nick said.

"Me too—I've been addicted ever since my days at Heathfield," Colette said.

"You were at Heathfield? I was at Stowe," Nick said.

"*Phwoar!* I'm an Old Stoic too!" Carlton pounded the table excitedly.

"I guessed as much. Your blazer was a dead giveaway," Nick said with a laugh.

"Which house were you in?" Carlton asked.

"Grenville."

"This is too much of a coincidence! Who was the housemaster? Was it Fletcher?"

"Chitty. You can imagine our nickname for him."

"Haha—brilliant! Did you play rugby or cricket?"

Colette rolled her eyes at Rachel. "I think we've lost the boys for the rest of the night."

"Clearly. Nick's like this when he gets together with his Singapore classmates too. A few more drinks and they'll start singing that song about Old Man whatshisname."*

---

* ACS Old Boys, all together now: "In days of yore from western shores, Oldham dauntless hero came . . ."

Carlton shifted his attention back to Rachel. "I'm being a terrible bore, aren't I? I take it you went to school in the States?"

"Monta Vista High in Cupertino."

"You're so lucky!" Colette said. "I was shipped away to school in England by my parents, but I always dreamed of going to high school in America. I wanted to be just like Marissa Cooper."

"Minus the car wreck, of course," Carlton chimed in.*

"Speaking of which, I'm glad to see how well you are after your accident," Nick said.

Carlton's face clouded over for a split second. "Thanks. You know, I must tell you how grateful I am to your mother. I don't think I would have made such a quick recovery if I hadn't done my rehab in Singapore, and of course, if it hadn't been for your mum, none of us would have ever met."

"Things have a strange way of working out, don't they?" Nick said.

As if on cue, Colette's personal assistant entered the room and announced, "Baptiste is here."

"At last! Send him in," Colette said excitedly.

"Baptiste is one of the top sommeliers in the world—he used to work at the Crillon in Paris," Carlton whispered to Rachel, as a man with a handlebar mustache entered the dining room bearing a wine satchel with such ceremony, one might have thought he was carrying a royal baby to its baptismal font.

"Baptiste! Did you find the right bottle?" Colette asked.

"Yes, Château Lafite Rothschild from the Shanghai private reserve," Baptiste replied, presenting the bottle to Colette for inspection.

---

* See *The O.C.*, season three. If you ask me, the show jumped the shark after its heroine, Marissa Cooper, played by the incomparable Mischa Barton, was (spoiler alert!) misguidedly killed off in a car accident.

"I usually prefer the even years for Bordeaux, but you'll notice that I chose a very special year—1981. Isn't that the year you were born, Rachel?"

"It sure is," Rachel said, touched by Colette's thoughtfulness.

"Allow me to make the first toast," Colette said, raising her glass. "Here in China, it's so rare for kids of our generation to have siblings. I have always dreamed of having a sibling, but I've never been so lucky. I've known Carlton for several years now, but I've never seen him more excited than the day he discovered he had a sister. So here's to the both of you—Carlton and Rachel. Brother and sister!"

"Here, here!" Nick cheered.

Carlton stood up next and declared, "First, I want to make a toast to Rachel. I'm glad you made it here safely, and I look forward to getting to know you and catching up on all the lost years. And to Colette—thank you for making this wonderful evening possible. I'm so glad you kicked my arse in gear and made me do this. Tonight I feel like I've gained not just a sister but a brother too. So here's to Rachel *and* Nick! Welcome to China! We're going to have a brilliant summer, aren't we?"

Nick wondered what Carlton had meant by Colette "kicking his arse in gear," but he said nothing for the moment. He looked over tenderly at Rachel, whose eyes brimmed with tears. This evening had turned out far better than he ever dared to dream.

# CHARLIE

*WUTHERING* TOWERS, HONG KONG

"Mr. Wu? It's 9:00 a.m. in Italy now," Charlie's executive assistant said, poking her head into his office.

"Thanks, Alice." Charlie reached for his ultra-private phone line and called Astrid's cell phone. She picked up after three rings.

"Charlie! Oh my God—thanks for calling me back."

"Am I calling too early?"

"No, I've been up for hours. I guess you heard about last night?"

"Yes—I am *so* sorry—" Charlie began.

"No, *I'm* sorry. I shouldn't have said a thing to Isabel."

"Nonsense—I'm the one who screwed up. I should have communicated better with my wife."

"So you talked to her? Did you explain that my cousin Alistair was with us the whole time in California?"

Charlie paused for a few seconds. "I did. Don't worry about it anymore."

"Are you sure? I couldn't sleep at all last night—I kept imagining that I had gotten you into trouble and that Isabel thought I was some philandering home wrecker. I was trying to find ways to contact her myself."

"Everything's fine. Once I explained how our California road trip was last-minute—that we all just happened to be there at the same time—she was fine." He wondered how convincing he sounded.

"I hope you told her that the most romantic thing that happened was watching Alistair projectile vomit out the car window after stuffing down too many In-N-Out burgers."

"I left that part out, but don't worry—it's all good," Charlie said, trying to add a little laugh.

Astrid let out a deep sigh of relief. "I'm so glad. You know, I should have been more circumspect. After all, she was meeting me for the first time, and I am the woman who—" She paused, suddenly unsure of how to put it.

"You're the woman who dumped her husband," Charlie said matter-of-factly.

"Yes, that's right. I hope she knows that we're much better friends now than we ever could have been before. My God, we were a terrible couple," Astrid said with a laugh.

"I think she realizes that now," Charlie said cautiously. He desperately wanted to change the subject. "So how's Venice? Where are you staying?"

"I'm staying with Domiella Finzi-Contini. Her family has the most spectacular palazzo near Santa Croce—I walked onto my balcony this morning and thought I had stepped into a Caravaggio. Do you remember Domiella from our London days? She was at LSE, but part of that whole crazy set that ran around with Freddie and Xan."

"Ah yes—messy blond hair, right?"

"It was platinum blond then, but she's back to her natural chestnut now. Anyway, we were having the most marvelous time together until last night."

Charlie groaned audibly. "I'm sorry again."

"No, no, it's nothing to do with Isabel. There's another drama brewing back home—I have two stubborn boys who are refusing to behave."

"They probably miss Mommy."

"Now, don't you start on me too! I feel bad enough as it is that Cassian's getting locked up in a closet."

"Who locked him in a closet?"

"His father."

"*What?*" Charlie said incredulously.

"For four hours yesterday, apparently. And he's only five."

"Astrid, I would *never* lock my child in a closet, no matter what age."

"Thank you. My feelings exactly. I think I need to cut this trip short."

"Um, sure sounds like it!"

Astrid sighed. "When is Isabel coming home?"

"Friday, I think."

"She's incredibly beautiful. She looked so elegant last night—I adored the necklace she was wearing. And she was perfectly civil to me even after I must have given her quite a shock. I'm so glad everything's okay now."

"I am too," Charlie said, forcing himself to smile. He heard somewhere that people could sense the smile in your voice, even over the phone.

Astrid paused. She felt she needed to make one more gesture to make up for her faux pas. "The next time Michael and I are in Hong Kong, we should go on a double date. I want to get to know Isabel under better circumstances."

"Yes, we should do that. A double date."

Charlie ended the conversation and got up laboriously from his desk. He was light-headed, and his stomach suddenly felt like someone had poured a gallon of bacon grease into it.

"Alice, I'm just going to pop downstairs for some fresh air," Charlie said into the intercom. He took his private express elevator to the lower street level and walked through the parking garage toward a side exit door. The moment he was outside, he leaned against the concrete wall and began inhaling and exhaling deeply. After a few minutes, he lumbered toward his favorite spot.

Sandwiched between *Wu*thering Towers and its neighboring skyscraper on Chater Road was a pedestrian alleyway where there was a small makeshift drink stand. A blue-and-white-striped plastic tarp stretched over the stall, anchored by two refrigerator units filled with soft drinks, packet juices, and fresh fruit. Under the single tube of fluorescent lighting was the owner, a middle-aged woman who stood all day preparing fresh soybean milk and juicing oranges, pineapples, and watermelons. There was always a queue during lunchtime and in the evenings when people left work, but in midafternoon, it was quiet.

"Playing hooky again?" the woman asked, teasing Charlie in Cantonese. She knew him as the office worker who always came down from one of the buildings for a drink at odd hours.

"Every chance I get, auntie."

"I worry for you, son—you take too many breaks. One day your boss is going to find you here and fire your ass."

Charlie cracked a smile. She was the one person in the vicinity that had no idea who he was, let alone that he owned the fifty-five-story tower that shaded her all day long. "Can I get a cold soybean milk, please?"

"Your color is no good today. Why are you as pale as a ghost? You shouldn't be drinking anything cold—you need something hot to help awaken your chi."

"I get like this sometimes, when I'm feeling a bit overworked," Charlie explained rather unconvincingly.

"You spend all day in air-conditioning. Bad recycled air. That's no good for you too," the woman continued. Her cell phone rang, and she began jabbering for a few minutes. While she spoke, she poured some hot water into a FIFA World Cup mug and filled it with a few slices of ginseng root. Then she stirred a few spoonfuls of grass jelly and sugar syrup into the concoction. "Drink this!" she ordered.

"Thanks, auntie," Charlie said, sitting on the plastic milk crate by a little folding Formica table. He took a few measured sips, too polite to tell her he didn't care much for grass jelly.

The woman finished her call and said excitedly, "That was my stockbroker. Here, let me give you a hot tip. You must start shorting TTL Holdings. You know TTL? Owned by Tai Toh Lui, that fellow who dropped dead of a heart attack two years ago in a brothel in Suzhou? My stockbroker knows for a fact that his good-for-nothing son who inherited the empire has been kidnapped by the Eleven Finger Triad. Once everyone finds out, the shares will collapse. You should start shorting it now."

"You should let me check on that rumor before you start shorting," Charlie advised.

"Hiyah, I already told my broker to start shorting. If I don't jump on it, I won't make any money."

Charlie took out his cell phone and called his chief financial officer, Aaron Shek. "Hey, Aaron—I know you're golfing buddies with the CEO of TTL. There's some rumor going around that Bernard has been kidnapped by the Eleven Finger Triad. Can you please check on that for me? What do you mean there's no need?" Charlie paused for a moment to listen to Aaron, and then burst into laughter. "Are you sure? Man, that's *way* better than the kidnapping rumor, but if that's what you're telling me, I believe you."

He ended the call and looked at the woman. "I just spoke to my friend who knows Tai Toh Lui's son very well. He has not been kidnapped. He is very much alive and free."

"Really?" the woman said in disbelief.

"Cover your shorts before the end of the day and you'll

make a good profit. It's just a vicious rumor, I promise. You may trust your stockbroker, but I'm sure you know there are others out there who are not so honest. They spread rumors just to move the price of the share a few points to make a quick profit."

"Hiyah, all these people and their rumors! I tell you, this is what's wrong with the world. People lying about everything."

Charlie nodded. Suddenly his father's words from a long time ago echoed in his head. It was one of the many occasions when Wu Hao Lian was in the hospital and thought his time was almost up. Charlie would stand at the foot of the bed while his father issued his final dictums, which went on for hours. Among the various exhortations about making sure his mother never had to move out of the big house in Singapore and that all his younger brother's Thai ladyboys needed to be paid off was this constant refrain: *I worry that when you're in charge, you'll run everything I've built over the last thirty years into the ground. Stick to the innovation side, because you're never going to manage on the finance side. You need to make sure management is always stocked with the biggest motherfucking assholes—only hire Harvard or Wharton MBAs—and then get out of the way. Because you're too damn honest—you're just not a good enough liar.*

Charlie had proved his father wrong when it came to running the business, but what he'd said was true. He hated being dishonest, and his stomach would feel like it was being put through a vise whenever he was forced to tell an untruth. He knew he was still feeling sick because of the lies he had told Astrid.

"Finish your drink—it's expensive ginseng I gave you, you know!" the woman admonished.

"Yes, auntie."

After braving the rest of his medicinal drink and paying the stall owner, Charlie returned to his office and sat down to compose an e-mail:

**From: Charlie Wu<charles.wu@wumicrosystems.com>**
**Date: June 10, 2013 at 5:26 PM**
**To: Astrid Teo<astridleongteo@gmail.com>**
**Subject: confession**

Hi Astrid,

I don't quite know how to begin this, so I'll just go for it. I haven't been completely honest with you. Isabel is furious at me. She called me up in the middle of the night screaming bloody murder, and then she had our daughters taken over to her parents' house. She refused to listen to my explanations, and now she won't return my calls. Grégoire told me that she's conveniently sailed away on Pascal Pang's yacht this morning. I think they are heading for Sicily.

The truth is, Isabel and I were not able to patch things up even after that Maldives second honeymoon. Things between us have been worse than ever, and I've been back at my Mid-Levels flat for a while now. The only agreement we've had is that I not do anything that would publicly embarrass her, anything that would give her a loss of face. Unfortunately, that happened last night. Her image of being happily married was shattered in front of Pascal Pang, and you know whatever he knows the rest of Hong Kong will soon know. I'm not sure I even care anymore.

You have to understand something, Astrid. My marriage to Isabel was a mistake even before it began. Everyone thinks I was sent to Hong Kong to take over my family's operations there, but the truth is I fled. I was devastated after our breakup and depressed for months. I was a complete failure at business, and my father ended up shoving me into a role in our R&D department just to get me out of the way, but that's where I began to thrive. I got lost in developing new product lines rather than just being a copycat contractor that steals from the best Silicon Valley tech firms. As a result, our business grew exponentially. I have you to thank for that.

I met Isabel at a party on a yacht that was thrown, coincidentally, by your cousin Eddie Cheng and his best friend Leo Ming. Eddie was one of the few people who actually took pity on me. I have to confess—I initially stayed far away from Isabel because she reminded me of you. Like you, she was constantly being underestimated because of her looks. Turns out she was an intensely smart lawyer, University of Birmingham Law School grad, and fast becoming one of Hong Kong's top litigators. And she had a sense of style and breeding that set her apart. Her father was Jeremy Lai, the distinguished barrister. The Lais are an old-money family from Kowloon Tong, and her mother is from a rich Indonesian Chinese family. I did not want to fall for another unattainable princess who was chained to the rules of her family.

But then as I got to know her, I found that she was nothing like you. No offense, but she was your polar opposite—wild and uninhibited, completely carefree. I found it exhilarating. She didn't give a damn what her family thought, and as it turns out, they thought the sun and moon orbited around her and she could do no wrong. And to top it off, her parents liked me. (I think it was partly because her last three boyfriends had been Scottish, Aussie, and African American, respectively, and they were just so relieved when she brought home a Chinese boy.) They welcomed me into the family even during the early days of our dating, and it was such a refreshing change to be accepted and even liked by my girlfriend's family. After six months of our whirlwind romance, we got married, and you know the rest.

But actually, you don't.

Everyone thinks that we got married so fast because I got her pregnant. Yes, she was pregnant, but it wasn't with my child. The thing I initially loved about Isabel—her unpredictability—was also her curse. Three months after we started dating, she suddenly disappeared. Things had been going so well, I was actually beginning to heal from our breakup. Then one day Isabel was gone. Turns out she had met up with one of her Indonesian cousins for a drink at Florida (you remember that ghastly bar in Lan Kwai Fong), and he had another friend tagging along. Some Indonesian chap who was a model. Before her cousin even knew what was happening, Isabel had disappeared with the guy. After a few days, I found out they had gone to Maui and were holed up in some private villa having a torrid romance. She wouldn't come back to Hong Kong, and she broke off contact with all of us. I couldn't understand what was happening. I was distraught, as were her parents.

Then it came out that something like this had happened before. Not once, but several times. The year before, she had met this African American guy on a plane on the way to London, and suddenly she quit her job and moved to New Orleans with him. Two years before that, it was the Aussie surfer and a condo on the Gold Coast. I soon realized that the problem was bigger than any of us could have fathomed—my sister was studying psychopharmacology at the time, and she thought Isabel might have borderline personality disorder. I tried to talk to her parents about it, but they seemed to be in denial. They could not face up to the fact that their darling daughter might have any sort of mental illness—albeit one that can be managed with proper treatment. Through all her episodes, they never made her see a psychologist or get a proper evaluation.

They just put up with her "dragon phases," as they called it. She was born in the year of the dragon, and that was always the excuse they had for her behavior. They implored me to go to Hawaii and "rescue her."

So I went. I flew to Maui, and it turns out the male model was long gone but Isabel was now living in some sort of commune with a bunch of Radical Faeries. And she was pregnant. Four months pregnant, no longer manic, but too embarrassed to come home. It was too late to have an abortion, she didn't want to give up her child, but she couldn't go back to Hong Kong like that. She told me no one ever loved her like I did, and she begged me to marry her. Her parents begged me to marry her quickly in Hawaii. And so I did. We had one of those "intimate weddings with only close family" at the Halekulani in Waikiki.

I want you to know that I went into this marriage with my eyes wide open. I saw the good in Isabel underneath her illness, and I desperately wanted to help her. When things were great, and when the full sunlight of her being shined on you, there was nothing like it. She was a magnetic, beautiful soul, and I was in love with that part of her. Or at least that's what I told myself. I thought that if she had a stable husband by her side, a husband who could help her properly manage her mental health issues, everything would be okay.

But things were not okay. After Chloe was born, the hormones really messed with Isabel, and she struggled with horrendous postpartum depression. She started hating me and blaming me for all her problems, and we stopped sleeping together. (I mean in the same bedroom, because we hadn't been physically intimate since before she took off for Maui.) She only wanted the baby in the bedroom with her. And the nanny. It was an unusual arrangement, to say the least.

One day she woke up and it was as if nothing had happened. I moved back into the bedroom, the nanny and Chloe went into their own room. Isabel was a loving wife for the first time in over a year. She went back to work, and we went back to being the social couple about town. I could focus a little more on my work again, and Wu Microsystems went through another terrific growth phase. Isabel became pregnant with Delphine, and I thought the worst was behind us.

Then suddenly, things turned on a dime again. This time it was less dramatic—there was no sudden whirlwind romance with a mysterious stranger, no fleeing to Istanbul or the Isle of Skye. Instead, Isabel's new behavior turned out to be more insidious and destructive. She claimed she was having secret affairs with married men. Three of them at her law firm—as you can imagine it made for insane office politics. She was also involved with a high-profile judge, whose wife found out about the affair and threatened to go public with everything. I will spare you the rest of this story, but by this point, Isabel and I were for all intents and purposes living totally separate lives. I was at the flat in the Mid-Levels, and she was at the house on The Peak with our daughters.

When you came back into my life, I realized two things: First, that I never stopped loving you. You were my first love, and I have loved you since the day I met you at Fort Canning Church when we were fifteen. And second, I also realized that, unlike me, you had moved on. I saw how much you loved Michael, and how you wouldn't give up on your marriage. I knew that I had been unfair to Isabel from the start—since I wasn't truly over you, I had never given all of myself to her. But I was determined to change things. I was ready to let go of you at last, and that would be the key to saving my marriage, to saving Isabel. I wanted to be able to love her free and clear, and to love my daughters as much as you love Cassian.

And so I redoubled my efforts, and you became my de facto marriage counselor. All those e-mails we've exchanged over the past two years were a beacon in the night for me as I tried to rebuild my marriage. But as you can clearly see, nothing has worked. The mistakes are all mine. Isabel and I might finally be heading to the bottom of the ocean once and for all, but it has been a long time coming.

This is my rambling way of trying to explain to you that you should not feel a single ounce of regret about what happened between you and Isabel in Venice. And more important, I want you to know the real story, because I can no longer live with any dishonesty between us. I hope that you'll be able to forgive me for not being truthful with you from the start. You are one of the few bright spots in my otherwise fucked-up life, and now more than ever, I count on our friendship.

With all my heart,
Charlie

Charlie sat in front of his computer, reading over his e-mail again and again. It was almost 7:00 p.m. in Hong Kong. It would be high noon in Venice. Astrid would probably be having lunch poolside at the Cipriani. He took a deep breath, and then he hit the delete button.

## CARLTON AND COLETTE

"You have broken my heart. And I don't know how it will ever heal," she said in a pained voice.

"I don't understand why you are being like this," Carlton groaned in Mandarin.

"You don't understand? You don't realize how much you have hurt me? How can you be so cruel?"

"Explain exactly how I am being cruel. Because I really don't get it. I'm just trying to do the right thing."

"You have betrayed me. You have taken his side. And by doing this you have destroyed me."

"Oh Mother, don't be so dramatic!" Carlton huffed into his phone.

"I took you to Hong Kong to protect you. Don't you see that? And you did the worst thing ever—you defied me and went back to Shanghai to meet that girl! That bastard girl!"

Lying on his king-size bed in Shanghai, Carlton could practically feel the volcanic seething of his mother at the other end of the line in Hong Kong. He tried shifting to a calmer tone. "Her name is Rachel, and you are really over-reacting. I actually think you'd like her a lot. And I'm not just saying that. She's intelligent—far more intelligent than me—but she doesn't put on any airs. She's one hundred percent authentic."

Shaoyen snorted in derision. "You stupid, stupid boy. How did I ever raise a son who is that stupid? Don't you see that the more you accept her, the more you stand to lose?"

"Just what am I losing, Mother?"

"Do I really have to spell it out for you? The very existence of this girl brings shame to our family. It tarnishes our name. *Your name.* Don't you realize how people will see us when they discover that your father had an illegitimate daughter with some country girl who kidnapped her own baby and took it to America? Bao Gaoliang, the new hope of the party? All his enemies are just waiting to tear him down. Don't you know how hard I have worked all my life to get our family to this position? *Aiyah*, God must be punishing me. I should never have sent you to England, where you got into so much trouble. That car accident knocked out every bit of sense from your brain!"

Colette, who until this moment had been lying quietly beside Carlton, started giggling when she saw his look of exasperation. Carlton quickly put a pillow over her face.

"I promise you, Mother, Rachel is not going to bring any shame to our . . . ouch . . . family." He coughed, as Colette began jabbing him playfully in the ribs.

"She already is! You are destroying your reputation by parading around Shanghai with that girl!"

"I assure you, Mother, I haven't done any parading," Carlton said as he tickled Colette.

"Fang Ai Lan's son saw you at the Kee Club last night. How foolish of you to be seen with her at such a visible place!"

"All types of people go to the Kee Club! That's why we went there—she could be anyone there. Don't worry, I'm tell-

ing everyone she's the wife of my friend Nick. Nick went to
Stowe too, so it's a very convenient story."

Shaoyen wouldn't let it go. "Fang Ai Lan told me she heard
from her son that you were making a fool of yourself with a
woman on each arm—Colette Bing and some girl he didn't
recognize. I didn't dare say a thing!"

"Ryan Fang is jealous because I was in the company of two
beautiful women. He's just bitter because his parents forced
him to marry Bonnie Hui, who on a good day resembles a
naked mole rat."

"Ryan Fang is a good son. He listened to his parents
and did what was best for his family. And now he's going to
become the youngest party secretary in—"

"I don't really care if he's the youngest man to rule
Westeros and sit on the Iron Throne,"* Carlton said, cutting
her off.

"That Colette put you up to this, didn't she? She's the insti-
gator! Colette knew I didn't want you anywhere near Shanghai
this week."

"Please leave Colette out of this. This has nothing to do
with her."

Hearing her name, Colette climbed onto Carlton, strad-
dled him, and peeled her top off. Carlton eyed her hungrily.
God, he never tired of her miraculously sculpted breasts.

"Ride 'em, cowboy!" she whispered. Carlton put his hand
over her mouth, and she began biting into the flesh of his palm.

"I know Colette has been influencing you. Ever since
she became your girlfriend, you've been nothing but heartache to me."

"How many times do I have to tell you: She's not my girl-

_____

* Actually, everyone knows that Tommen Baratheon, age seven, is the youngest man to sit on the Iron Throne. (See George R. R. Martin's *A Storm of Swords*.)

friend. We're just friends," Carlton droned as Colette began grinding herself slowly against him.

"That's what you say. So where did you spend the night last night? Ai-Mei told me you haven't been home in days."

"I have been spending time with my sister, and since you will not allow her to set foot in your house, I've had no choice but to stay with them at their hotel." Carlton was actually holed up in the enormous Presidential suite at the Portman Ritz-Carlton, where he knew his mother's spies would never look for him.

"Oh my God, you are calling her your *sister* now!"

"Mother, whether you like it or not, she *is* my sister."

"You are killing me slowly, son. You are killing me from the inside out."

"Yes, Mother, I know. I've heard it many times before: I'm such a disappointment, I have betrayed all my ancestors, you don't know why you ever bore the pain of giving birth to me," Carlton said, hanging up the phone.

"My God, your mother really laid it on thick this time, didn't she?" Colette said in English. (Of all her boyfriends, Carlton was the only one with a perfect posh British accent, and she found it so alluring to hear him use it.)

Carlton groaned. "She had a huge row with my father last night and kicked him out of the flat—he ended up checking in to the Upper House at two in the morning. I guess she wanted to make me feel just as bad."

"Why should you feel bad? It's not like you're responsible for any of this."

"Precisely—my mother's completely lost the plot! She's so worried that Rachel is somehow going to ruin our family's reputation, but her strange behavior is ruining her own reputation."

"She *has* been acting rather strange lately, hasn't she? She used to like me."

"She still likes you," Carlton said rather unconvincingly.

"Uh-huh. I'm really buying that."

"Trust me, the only person she's mad at right now is my father. She refused to leave Hong Kong, so when he said he was going back to Shanghai on his own, she told him that she would divorce him if he tried to see Rachel. She's afraid they'll be seen together in public and some scandal will erupt."

"Wow. It's gotten that bad?"

"It's an empty threat. She's just caught up in her anger."

"Why don't I arrange a dinner for Rachel to secretly meet your father at my house? That's not a public place."

"You just like causing trouble, don't you?"

"Am I the one causing trouble? I'm just being hospitable to your sister. It's rather ridiculous that she's been in Shanghai for over a week now and your father still hasn't seen her. He was the one who invited her in the first place!"

Carlton considered it for a moment. "We could try to arrange something. I'm not sure my father will come, though. He kicks and screams but he always ends up obeying every command of my mother's."

"Leave it to me. I'll call your father and tell him it's an invitation from *my* dad. That way he won't refuse, and he won't be expecting Rachel to be there."

"You're being awfully nice to Rachel and Nick."

"Why wouldn't I be? She's your sister, and I'm enjoying them very much. They are such a different species. Rachel is cool, there's no bullshit with her. And she's a total banana,* isn't she? Just look at how she dresses in those no-name brands, her painful lack of jewelry—she's not like any Chinese girl I've ever met. Nick I'm still trying to figure out. Didn't you say his parents were rich?"

"I think they do okay, but I don't get the impression they

---

* Yellow on the outside, white on the inside.

are *that* rich. The father used to be an engineer, and now he's a sports fisherman. And Mrs. Young does day-trading, I think."

"Well, he's been very well brought up. He has this very particular sort of relaxed charisma, and his manners are impeccable. Have you noticed that whenever we've been in an elevator, he always lets all the women exit first?"

"So?"

"That's the mark of a true gentleman. And I know he didn't get that from Stowe, since your manners are barbaric!"

"Fuck you! You just like him because you think he looks like that Korean heartthrob you like."

"How cute—are you jealous? Don't worry, I have no interest in stealing Nick from your sister. What is he, a university professor?"

"He teaches history."

Colette giggled. "A history professor and an economics professor. Can you imagine what their children will be like? I don't know why your mother would *ever* feel threatened by these people."

Carlton sighed. Deep down, he knew exactly why his mother was behaving the way she was. It really had nothing to do with Rachel and everything to do with his accident. She had never spoken to him about what he had done, but he knew that the stress of that tragedy had changed his mother irretrievably. She had always been short-tempered, but ever since London, she had become more irrational than he had ever known her to be. If he could just turn back the clock on that night. That fucking night that had ruined his life. He rolled over onto his side, facing away from Colette.

Colette could see that the black cloud had descended over Carlton again. It was happening so quickly these days. One minute they would be having the most brilliant time, and then suddenly he would just disappear into a pit of despair. Trying to snap him out of his funk, she unbuttoned the last few buttons of his shirt and began to trace circles around his navel. "I love it when you get all pouty and smoldering on me," she whispered in his ear.

"I don't know what you're talking about."

"Yes you do." Colette positioned her feet on both sides of Carlton's torso and stood up over him. "Now, do you really think it's true that President Obama was the last person to sleep in this bed?"

"This place is built like a fortress—all the presidents stay here," Carlton said flatly.

"I bet Mr. Obama never had *this* view," Colette said, sliding off her Kiki de Montparnasse panties in one slow, seductive motion.

Carlton stared up at her. "No, I don't believe so."

## NICK AND RACHEL

SHANGHAI, CHINA

Nick awoke to the vision of Rachel luxuriating in a patch of sunlight by the window, sipping her coffee. "What time is it?" he asked.

"It's about a quarter to one."

Nick bolted up reflexively as if an alarm bell had gone off. "Bloody hell! Why didn't you wake me?"

"You were sleeping so sweetly, and we're on vacation, remember?"

Nick stretched his arms and let out a groan. "Ugh. It doesn't feel much like a vacation."

"You just need some coffee."

"And aspirin. Lots of it."

Rachel laughed. Since their arrival last week, the two of them had been swept up in the tornado that was Carlton's social life. Actually, it was more like Colette's social life, since they had attended a mind-blowing number of fashion boutique parties, twelve-course banquets, art openings, restaurant soft openings, a recital at the French Consulate, VIP after-parties (followed by several VVIP *after*-after-parties), and something billed as a "site-specific transmedia performance piece"—all at Colette's invitation. And this was *before* hitting the clubs every night till dawn.

"Who knew that Shanghai's nightlife scene would put New York to shame? I'm ready for a quiet night in. Do you think your brother will be offended?" Nick asked.

"We'll just tell Carlton we're too old for his crowd," Rachel said, blowing on her coffee.

"Says the girl who was hit on about a dozen times last night! I thought I was really going to have to bust out some of my ninja moves to get those French guys to leave you alone at M1NT."*

Rachel laughed. "You're such a dork!"

"I'm the dork? I'm not the tech geek. Was it just me, or has every European fellow in Shanghai invented some app that's going to revolutionize the world? And do they all need to have that much stubble? I can't imagine what it would be like kissing them."

"Actually, that would be kinda hot—watching you and that cute Polytechnique grad make out! What was his name? Loïc?" Rachel cracked.

"Thanks, but I'd prefer Claryssa or Chlamydia or whatever that friend of Colette's name was."

"Haha—Chlamydia is exactly what you'll get if you kiss her! You're talking about that girl with the fake eyelashes who asked you point-blank if you had an American passport?"

"Her eyelashes were fake?"

"Honey, *everything* on her was fake! Did you see how crushed she looked when Colette broke it to her that we were

---

* Among the 220,000-plus foreigners living and working in Shanghai, there are now more than 20,000 French nationals, an alarming number of them INSEAD or École Polytechnique graduates. With Europe still stuck in an economic coma, graduates from Europe's top universities have been moving to Shanghai in droves. None of them speak a word of Mandarin, but who needs to when the bartenders at M1NT, Mr. & Mrs. Bund, or Bar Rouge don't either?

married? I don't understand how all these people missed the wedding bands on our fingers."

"You think a little piece of gold is going to stop them? Women here just don't understand your social cues. You confuse them—you look Chinese, but they don't get your body language. You don't behave like a typical wife, so they don't even realize we're together."

"Okay, from now on I'll be sure to drape myself over you and gaze adoringly into your face at all times. You're my one and only *gaofushuai*,"* Rachel cooed, fluttering her eyelashes facetiously.

"That's the spirit! Now where's my coffee?"

"It's in the coffeemaker at the bar, and you can refresh my cup too while you're at it!"

"What happened to my subservient little wife?" Nick padded languidly to the bar as Rachel called out from the other room, "Oh, my father called this morning."

"What did he have to say?" Nick asked, groggily trying to figure out which button to push on the unnecessarily high-tech espresso machine.

"He apologized again for not being here."

"Still sorting out problems in Hong Kong?"

"Well today he had to rush to Beijing. Some government emergency this time."

"Hmmm," Nick said as he scooped some coffee into the French press. He wondered what was really behind Bao Gaoliang's Houdini act. He was about to bring it up when Rachel continued, "He wanted us to meet him in Beijing this weekend, but apparently the smog is going to be terrible over the next few days. So he suggested we fly to Beijing next week if things clear up."

---

* Mandarin for "tall, rich, and handsome," the minimum requirements every Mainland Chinese girl looks for in a husband.

Nick returned to the bedroom and handed Rachel her refilled cup. She looked him in the eye and said, "I don't know about you, but I'm getting a strange feeling about all this."

"You're not the only one," Nick said, sitting down on the floor against the window. The sunlight pouring onto his back felt more invigorating than the smell of the coffee.

"I'm so glad to hear you say that! I'm not being totally paranoid, am I? I mean, his excuses are beginning to sound pretty lame. Smog in Beijing? Isn't it always smoggy there? I flew three thousand miles to get to know him—I'm not going to let some pollution get in the way. I kinda thought I'd be seeing a lot more of my dad, and I feel like he's avoiding us."

"I'm not disagreeing with you."

"Do you think Shaoyen has something to do with all this? I mean, we haven't heard a peep from her."

"It's possible. Has Carlton said anything to you?"

"Carlton doesn't say a thing! You know, we've seen him every night since we got here, but I don't feel like I've really got a read on him yet. I mean, he's very sweet, and a great conversationalist like all you British-public-school-educated boys, but he doesn't reveal much about himself. And he can be rather moody sometimes, don't you think?"

"Yeah, I've definitely noticed that. There are moments when he just seems to check out, like the other night when we were at that bar on top of the Ritz Pudong, having drinks with that woman with the big hair."

"Chinese Afro girl? Yeah, what was her name again?"

"No idea, but *she* was giving off strange vibes, and for a while Carlton went absolutely quiet and just stared at the view. I thought maybe he didn't like her or something, but then he snapped out of it and was back to his normal self again."

Rachel gave Nick a worried look. "You think maybe it's his drinking? I mean, the way he's been putting it away this week alone makes my liver ache."

"Well, it seems like everyone here takes drinking to a whole other level! But let's not forget his accident not too long ago—he did suffer major head trauma."

"You know, he seems so fit, I keep forgetting he even had that accident."

Rachel got up from her armchair and sat down next to Nick on the floor. She stared out the window at the twisting skeletal form of Shanghai Tower, a new skyscraper being built across the river that would one day be the tallest structure in the world. "It's so strange. I had this idea that we'd be spending all our time getting to know my dad, meeting other relatives over meals, that sort of thing, but it feels like all we've been doing day after day is partying with Shanghai's *Gossip Girl* crowd."

Nick nodded in agreement, but he didn't want to sound discouraging. "At some point, your dad has to show up. And you know, it's entirely possible we are being paranoid, and things haven't worked out because they haven't. Your father is a very important man and there's a lot cooking on the political front with the changeover in leadership that just happened. Maybe there's some other drama playing out that has nothing to do with you."

Rachel gave him a dubious look. "Do you think I should try to bring it up casually with Carlton?"

"If there really is something going on with the family, that might put him in an awkward position. Technically speaking, we have been very well looked after by the Baos, haven't we? I mean, we've been enjoying this fabulous suite, and Carlton's been entertaining us every day. Let's see how it plays out. In the meantime, I think it may finally be time for me to try that juice cleanse."

"Before you do—we have dinner tonight with Colette's parents."

"Oh—I'd forgotten about that. Do you know where? I

wonder if it's going to be yet another bacchanalian twenty-course feast."

"Carlton said something about going to a resort."

"Maybe they'll have cheeseburgers. I would kill for a burger and fries tonight."

"Me too! But I don't think that's in the cards. Something tells me Colette's not a burger-and-fries kind of gal."

"What gave that away? I bet you anything her monthly clothing budget exceeds our combined annual incomes."

"Monthly? Her *weekly* clothing budget is probably more accurate. Did you see those carved-dragon-heel shoes she was wearing last night? I swear to God I think they were made of ivory. She's basically Araminta 2.0."

Nick chortled. "Colette is *not* Araminta 2.0. Araminta is essentially a Singapore girl—she can glam it up when she wants to, but she's equally comfortable hanging out in yoga sweats and eating fresh coconut on the beach. Colette's a whole other advanced species yet to be classified. I think she'll either be running China or Hollywood in a few years."

"And yet she's grown on me. She's been the nicest surprise so far, hasn't she? When I first met her, I was like, *This girl cannot be for real.* But she's so sweet and so generous—she hasn't let us pick up a single tab since we got here."

"I hate to burst your bubble, but I think we've been comped at every restaurant or club we've been to. Do you notice how Colette gets Roxanne to take pictures of her everywhere we go? She just tweets or blogs about every place, and the rest of us eat for free. It's quite a racket."

"Still, I think she's good for Carlton."

"Yeah, but don't you think she's toying with him? She's clearly into him, and yet she's still chanting this 'He's just one of my many suitors' BS."

Rachel gave Nick a teasing look. "You just don't like it when the tables are turned! Colette's got her own career and her own goals and she's in no rush to get married. I think it's so refreshing. Most Chinese girls are under such enormous pressure to get married and have kids by their early twenties. I mean, how many Chinese girls do we get every semester that are really just at NYU to find the perfect husband?"

Nick cocked his head and thought about it for a moment. "I can't think of any besides you."

"Oh, har har. Jerk!" Rachel said, smacking him with a tasseled pillow.

. . .

At five that afternoon, as Nick and Rachel stood outside their hotel waiting for Carlton to pick them up, a thunderous roar could be heard coming from the Bund. Nick was dressed casually in jeans, a light blue oxford shirt, and his fawn-colored Huntsman summer blazer, while Rachel opted for an Erica Tanov summer linen smock dress. Moments later, a burned-apricot McLaren F1 pulled into the driveway of the Peninsula, its engines making a low, deliriously expensive rumble that sent the valet attendants scurrying around excitedly, each hoping for the chance to park this exotic driving machine. Their hopes were dashed when Carlton poked his head out the window and beckoned Nick and Rachel to get in.

"You take the front seat," Nick gallantly offered his wife.

"Don't be ridiculous—my legs are much shorter than yours," Rachel said. Their argument ended up being completely moot, because as the wing doors rose, they saw that the driver's seat was in the center of the car, with a passenger seat flanking either side.

"How cool! I've never seen anything like this!" Rachel said.

Nick peered in. "This is one sexy car you have here—is it street legal?"

"Hell if I know," Carlton said with a smirk.

"And here I thought you people went around in nothing but Audis," Rachel said as she climbed in on the right side.

"Oh, the Audis belong to Colette's family. You know why everyone drives Audis, don't you? It's the car most high-level politicians drive, so many people drive them because they think that other cars will give way and the police are more likely to leave them alone."

"How interesting," Rachel said as she settled into her surprisingly comfortable bucket seat. "I love this new-car smell."

"Actually, this car isn't new at all—it's from 1998," Carlton said.

"Really?" Rachel said in surprise.

"It's considered a classic—I only drive it on sunny, cloudless days like today. You're smelling the hand-stitched Connolly leather hides—made from cows even more pampered than the ones in Kobe."

"Looks like we've discovered another of Carlton's passions," Nick commented.

"Oh yeah! I've been importing cars for several years now and selling them to friends. I started during my Cambridge days, whenever I came up to London on weekends," Carlton explained as he sped onto Yan'an Elevated Road.

"You must have witnessed the Arab sports-car parade around Knightsbridge every year," Nick said.

"You bet! My friends and I would grab a table outside the Ladurée and watch them roll by!"

"What are you guys talking about?" Rachel asked.

Nick proceeded to explain. "Every June, all these young Arab squillionaires descend on London, bringing with them the most stupendous sports cars in the world. And they race them around Knightsbridge as if the streets are their private Formula One track. On Saturday afternoons, the cars converge behind Harrods at the corner of Basil Street like some swap meet. All these kids—some not more than eighteen, dressed in expensive tattered denim, and their girlfriends, covered up in their hijabs but wearing blinged-out sunglasses sitting in these million-dollar automobiles. It's an incredible sight."

Carlton nodded, his eyes flashing with excitement. "The same thing is happening here! This is now the number-one market for luxury cars in the world—especially exotic sports cars. The demand is unquenchable, and all my friends know I'm the best at finding the rarest of the rare. This McLaren we're sitting in—only sixty-four were ever built. So before a car even arrives on the dock in Shanghai, I have a waiting list of buyers."

"Sounds like a fun way to make a living," Nick commented.

"Tell that to my parents when you see them. They think I'm wasting my life."

"I'm sure they are just concerned for your safety," Rachel said, holding her breath as Carlton suddenly cut across three lanes at ninety miles per hour.

"Sorry, I just need to get around those trucks. Don't worry—I'm a very safe driver."

Nick and Rachel exchanged dubious looks, knowing Carlton's recent history. Rachel checked that her seat belt was securely fastened and tried not to look at the zigzagging cars in front of them.

"Everyone on the highway seems totally schizo—they're changing lanes constantly," Nick quipped.

"Listen, if you try to drive in an orderly fashion here and stay in your lane all the time, you'll just get killed," Carlton said, accelerating again to overtake a truck full of pigs. "The rational rules of driving do not apply in this country. I learned to drive in the UK, and when I came back to Shanghai the first time after getting my license, I got pulled over on my first day driving. The police officer screamed at me, 'You bloody fool! Why did you stop at that red light?'"

"Oh yeah, Rachel and I have almost gotten killed trying to cross the road several times. Traffic signals mean nothing to Shanghai drivers," Nick said.

"They are merely suggestions," Carlton agreed, suddenly slamming on the brakes and veering sharply to the right, narrowly avoiding a van in the far left lane.

"SWEET JESUS! WAS THAT VAN ACTUALLY BACKING UP IN THE FAST LANE?" Rachel screamed.

"Welcome to China," Carlton said nonchalantly.

Twenty minutes outside of downtown Shanghai, they finally exited the highway, much to Rachel's relief, and turned onto what appeared to be a recently paved boulevard.

"Where are we?" Rachel asked.

"This is a new development called Porto Fino Elite," Carlton explained. "It's modeled after those fancy neighborhoods in Newport Beach."

"Clearly," Nick commented as they passed a Mediterranean-style strip mall painted in shades of ochre, complete with a Starbucks. They turned off the main street and drove down a long avenue flanked by high stucco walls, at the end of which stood a cascading sculptural waterfall next to a gatehouse. Carlton pulled up in front of a massive gate with decorative steelwork panels, and three uniformed guards emerged from the gatehouse. One of the guards walked around the car warily, as if he was looking for hidden explosives, while another used an inspection mirror to peer under the car. The guard in charge recognized Carlton and checked him off a list. He gave Nick and Rachel a careful once-over, before nodding and waving the car through.

"That's pretty serious security," Nick commented.

"Yep—it's very private here," Carlton said.

The heavy gates clanked open, and the McLaren sped down a pristine white gravel road lined with Italian cypresses. Between the trees, Rachel and Nick could make out several small artificial lakes, from the middle of which sprouted fountains; sleek glass-and-steel buildings here and there; and the undulating mounds of a golf course. Finally, as they passed a pair of weathered obelisks, they came upon the main reception building—a majestic yet minimalist stone-and-glass structure surrounded by artfully planted pagoda trees.

"I had no idea they were building resorts like this in the suburbs outside Shanghai. What's this place called?" Nick asked Carlton.

"This isn't actually a resort. This is Colette's weekend retreat."

"Excuse me? This whole property is hers?" Rachel sputtered.

"Yes, all thirty acres of it. Her parents built it for her."

"And where do they live?"

"They have houses in many cities—Hong Kong, Shanghai, Beijing—but they spend most of their time in Hawaii these days," Carlton explained.

"They must have done rather well," Rachel commented.

Carlton gave her a look of amusement. "I guess I never mentioned—Colette's father is one of the five richest men in China."

# COLETTE

SHANGHAI, CHINA

Carlton's car pulled up to the front entrance of the house, and two attendants in matching James Perse black T-shirts and trousers appeared from out of nowhere. One of them helped Rachel out of the car, while the other informed Carlton, "Sorry, you can't leave your car here like you normally do. We are expecting Mr. Bing's arrival. You can either move it around into the car porch, or I can park it for you."

"I'll move it—thanks," Carlton replied. He zoomed off and returned shortly to join Rachel and Nick at the entrance. The imposing oxidized maple-wood doors opened, and they found themselves in a serene inner courtyard almost entirely composed of a dark, shallow reflecting pool. A travertine walkway ran down the middle of the pool toward tall lacquered doors the color of espresso, and bamboo block plantings ran along the walls of the courtyard. The lacquered doors parted silently as the three of them approached, revealing the inner sanctum.

Before them was an immense, eighty-foot-long living room decorated entirely in tones of black and white. Maids in long, black silk *qipaos** stood in a silent line by gray *shiku-men* brick pillars hung with black-ink calligraphy scrolls, while polished black-tile floors and low-slung white sofas suffused the space with a tranquil, seductive vibe. The glass wall at the end of the room revealed an outdoor lounge filled with sleek sofas and dark-wood coffee tables, beyond which one could see more reflecting pools and pavilions.

Even Nick, who had grown up among the splendors of Tyersall Park, was momentarily taken aback. "Wow—is this a house or a Four Seasons resort?"

Carlton laughed. "Actually, Colette fell in love with the Puli Hotel in Shanghai and tried to get her father to buy it. When they found it wasn't for sale no matter the price, he commissioned his architect to build her this place. This grand salon is inspired by the Puli's lobby."

An Englishman in a dapper black suit approached them. "Good afternoon, I'm Wolseley, the butler. May I offer you something to drink?"

Before anyone could respond, Colette made her entrance through another door in an oleander pink tea-length dress. "Rachel, Nick, so glad you could make it!" With her hair swept up into a high bun and her ruffled gazar skirt billowing about her as she walked into the room, Colette looked like she had just stepped off the cover of a 1960s issue of *Vogue*.

Rachel greeted her with a hug. "Colette, you look like you should be having breakfast at Tiffany's or something! And my God, your house is just incredible!"

Colette gave a modest giggle. "Here, let me give you a proper tour. But first, drinks! What libation can we tempt you with? I'm sure Carlton will have his usual tumbler of vodka,

---

* A body-hugging one-piece Chinese dress for women, created in the 1920s in Shanghai and perennially fashionable since Suzie Wong famously seduced Robert Lomax in one. In Singapore and Hong Kong, it is known by its Cantonese name—the *cheongsam*.

and I think I'll have a Campari and soda to match my dress. Rachel, do you feel like a Bellini?"

"Um, sure, only if it's not too much trouble," Rachel said.

"Not at all! We always have fresh white peaches for our Bellinis, don't we, Wolseley? Nick, what will it be?"

"I'll have a gin and tonic."

"Ugh, the boys are so boring." Colette rolled her eyes at Wolseley. "Come, follow me. Did Carlton explain to you my whole concept for this house?"

"We heard that you liked some hotel in Shanghai—" Rachel began.

"Yes, the Puli—but I've made this house even more luxurious. We used precious materials that you just wouldn't want to use in a public space like a hotel. I know many people have this impression that everyone in China lives in tacky Louis XIV mansions where everything is dipped in gold and it looks like a tassel factory exploded, so I wanted this house to be a showplace for the best of *contemporary* China. Every piece of furniture you see in this grand salon was custom-designed and handcrafted here by our finest designers, in the rarest materials. And of course, all the antiques are museum quality. The scrolls on the walls are by Wu Boli, from the fourteenth century, and that Ming dynasty wine cup over there? I bought it from a dealer in Xi'an two years ago for six hundred thousand—the curator from the St. Louis Museum just offered me fifteen million for it. As if I would ever sell!" Rachel stared at the small porcelain bowl painted with chickens, trying to believe it was worth a hundred times her annual salary.

The group stepped out into the back courtyard, which was dominated by another vast reflecting pool. Colette led them along a covered walkway as a haunting New Agey song played softly on hidden outdoor speakers. "The pride of this estate is my greenhouse—the most important thing you should know is that this whole property is one hundred percent certified green—all the roofs have solar paneling, and all the reflecting pools actually flow into a state-of-the-art aquaponics system."

The four of them entered a futuristic glass-roofed structure that was blindingly lit and lined with alternating rows of fish tanks and vegetable patches. "All the water gets channeled into the tanks, where we farm fish for eating, and then the nutrient-rich water fertilizes the organic vegetables grown here. See, I'm not just green—I'm emerald green!" Colette proudly informed them.

"Okay, I'm officially impressed!" Nick said.

Crossing the central courtyard again, Colette continued to explain. "Even though the buildings are modern in style, there are eight interconnected pavilions arranged in an Emperor's Throne formation to ensure proper feng shui. Everybody STOP!"

They stopped dead in their tracks.

"Now breathe in the air. Can't you just feel the good chi flowing everywhere?"

Nick could only detect a faint scent that reminded him of Febreze, but he nodded along with Rachel and Carlton.

Colette put her hands in the *namaskara* position and beamed. "Here we come to the entertainment pavilion. The wine cellar takes up the entire lower level—it was specially designed for us by the Taittinger people, and this is the screening room." Rachel and Nick poked their heads into a cinema where there were fifty ergonomic Swedish recliners arranged in stadium-style seating.

"Do you see what's hiding at the back?" Carlton asked.

Rachel and Nick stepped into the room and discovered that the entire back area of the screening room under the projector booth contained a slick sushi bar that looked like it had been transplanted straight from Tokyo's Roppongi district. A sushi chef in a black kimono bowed at them while his young apprentice sat at the bar carving radishes into cute little kitten faces.

"Get. Out. Of. Town!" Rachel exclaimed.

"And we thought we were being extravagant ordering in from Blue Ribbon Sushi on *Survivor* Wednesdays," Nick quipped.

"Did you see the documentary about the greatest sushi master in the world—*Jiro Dreams of Sushi*?" Colette asked.

"Oh my God—don't tell me that guy is one of his sons!" Rachel gaped in awe at the sushi chef as he stood behind the blond-wood counter massaging an octopus.

"No, that's Jiro's second cousin!" Colette said excitedly.

From there, the tour continued to the guest wing, where Colette showed off bedroom suites more sumptuous than any five-star hotel ("We only allow our guests to sleep on Hästens* mattresses stuffed with the finest Swedish horsehair"), and then into her bedroom pavilion, which had wraparound glass walls and a sunken circular lotus pond at one end of the room. The only other objects in the lusciously minimalist space were a cloud-like king-size bed in the middle of the room and bees-wax pillar candles flanking one wall ("I like my bedroom to be very Zen. When I sleep, I detach from all my worldly posses-sions"). Adjoining the bedroom pavilion was a structure four times its size—Colette's bathroom and closet.

Rachel stepped into the bathroom, which was a sprawl-ing daylight-flooded space entirely clad in glacier-white Cala-catta marble. Indentations were carved into the giant slab of unpolished marble to create organic-shaped sinks that looked like watering holes for chic hobbits, and beyond was a private circular courtyard with a dark blue malachite reflecting pool.

---

* Mattress makers to the Swedish royal family since 1852; the basic Hästens mattress starts at $15,000, and their top-of-the-line 2000T will set you back $120,000. But how much is it worth to you to sleep on a mattress that aficiona-dos claim can actually prevent cancer?

Growing out of the center of the pool was a perfectly manicured willow tree, and nestled under it was an egg-shaped
bathtub that appeared to have been sculpted from a single
piece of white onyx. Round stepping stones led across the
water to the tub.

"Oh my God, Colette—I'm just going to come right out
and say it: I am insanely jealous! This bathroom is just *beyond*—
it's straight out of my dreams!" Rachel exclaimed.

"Thank you for appreciating my vision," Colette said, her
eyes getting a little moist.

Nick looked at Carlton. "Why are women so obsessed with
their bathrooms? Rachel was obsessed with the bathroom in
our hotel, the bathroom at the Annabel Lee Boutique, and
now it looks like she's found bathroom nirvana."

Colette stared at Nick with contempt. "Rachel, this man
doesn't understand women AT ALL. You should get rid of
him!"

"Trust me, I'm beginning to think about it," Rachel said,
sticking her tongue out at Nick.

"All right, all right—when we get back to New York I'll
call the contractor and you can retile the bathroom like you
wanted." Nick sighed.

"I don't want it retiled, Nick, I want this!" Rachel declared,
stretching her arms out and caressing the lip of the onyx tub
as if it were a baby's bottom.

Colette grinned. "Okay, we better skip the tour of my
closets—I don't actually want to be blamed for your breakup.
Why don't I show you the spa?" The party walked through a
deep crimson passageway and were shown dimly lit treatment
rooms decorated with Balinese furniture, and then they came
to a stunning underground space with pillars like a Turkish
seraglio surrounding a massive indoor saltwater pool that
glowed an arresting shade of cerulean blue. "The entire floor
of the pool is inlaid with turquoise," Colette announced.

"You've got your own private spa right here!" Rachel said in disbelief.

"Rachel, we're good friends now—I have a confession to make. I used to have a terrible addiction . . . I was addicted to spa resorts. Before I found myself, I used to spend the whole year aimlessly flying from resort to resort. But I was never satisfied, because something was never quite right everywhere I went. I would find a dirty mop left in the corner of the steam room at the Amanjena in Marrakech, or I would have to put up with some creepy potbellied guy staring at me sunbathing in the infinity pool at One and Only Reethi Rah. So I decided I could only be happy if I could create my personal spa resort right here."

"Well, you're very fortunate that you have the resources to make this happen," Rachel said.

"Yes, but I'm also saving so much money by doing this! This whole development used to be farmland, and now that there are no more farms, I employ all the displaced locals to work on the estate, so it's really been good for the economy. And think of all the carbon offset points I'm racking up by not having to fly all over the world every weekend trying out new spas," Colette said earnestly.

Nick and Rachel nodded their heads diplomatically.

"I also hold many charitable events here. Next week, I'm planning a summer garden party with the actress Pan TingTing. It's going to be an ultra-exclusive fashion show with the latest collections from Paris—Rachel, tell me you'll come."

"Of course I will," Rachel politely replied, before wondering why she had agreed so quickly. The words "ultra-exclusive fashion show" filled her with dread, and she suddenly got flashbacks to Araminta's private-island bachelorette party.

Just then, a few thin barks could be heard coming down the stairs. "My babies are back!" Colette shrieked. The group turned to see Colette's personal assistant, Roxanne, entering with two Italian greyhounds straining excitedly against their ostrich-leather leashes.

"Kate, Pippa, I've missed you so much. Poor little things—are you jet-lagged?" Colette cooed as she bent down and cuddled her emaciated dogs.

"Did she *really* name her dogs . . ." Rachel began to whisper in Carlton's ear.

"Yes, she did. Colette adores the royals—at her parents' house in Ningbo, she has a pair of Tibetan mastiffs named Wills and Harry," Carlton explained.

"How were my darlings? Did everything go okay?" Colette asked Roxanne with a worried expression.

"Roxanne just flew Kate and Pippa on Colette's plane to see a famous dog psychic in California," Carlton informed Rachel and Nick.

"They were very good. You know, at first I had my doubts about that pet psychic in Ojai, but wait till you read her report. Pippa is still traumatized by the time she almost got blown out of the Bentley convertible. That's why she tries to burrow under the backseat and poo-poos every time she rides in it. I told the woman *nothing*—how did she know you had that kind of car? I am a total believer in pet psychics now," Roxanne reported earnestly.

Colette petted her dog with tears in her eyes. "I am so sorry, Pippa. I'll make it up to you. Roxanne, please take a picture of us and post on WeChat: 'Reunited with my girls.'" Colette posed expertly for the picture and stood up, smoothing away the wrinkles on her skirt. She then said to Roxanne in a blood-chilling tone, "I never want to see that Bentley again."

The group approached the final pavilion, the largest building of all and the only one that did not have any exterior windows. "Roxanne—code!" Colette ordered, and her headset-wearing assistant dutifully punched in an eight-digit code that unlocked the door. "Welcome to my family's private museum," Colette said.

They stepped into a gallery the size of a basketball arena, and the first thing that caught Rachel's eye was a large silk-screen canvas of Chairman Mao. "Is that a Warhol?" she asked.

"Yes. Do you like my Mao? My father gave that to me for my sixteenth birthday."

"What a cool birthday present," Rachel remarked.

"Yes, it was the favorite out of all my presents that year. I wish I had a time machine so I could go back and Andy could do my portrait." Colette sighed. Nick stood in front of the painting, staring with amusement at the Communist leader's receding hairline, alternately wondering what the dictator or the artist might have made of a girl like Colette Bing.

Nick and Rachel began heading toward the right, but Colette said, "Oh, you can skip that gallery over there, that's just filled with boring junk my father had to have when he first started collecting—Picassos, Gauguins, that sort of thing. Come see what I've been buying lately." They were steered into a gallery where the walls were a veritable checklist of the artists du jour from all the international art fairs—a mouthwatering Vik Muniz chocolate syrup painting, Bridget Riley's migraine-inducing canvas of overlapping tiny squares, a heroin-fueled scrawl by Jean-Michel Basquiat, and, of course, an immense Mona Kuhn image of two preposterously photogenic Nordic youths posing nude on a dewy doorstep.

Rounding the corner, they came into an even larger gallery that contained only one enormous piece of art—twenty-four scrolls that were hung together to form a vast, intricate landscape.

Nick was taken aback. "Hey, isn't that *The Palace of Eighteen Perfections*? I thought Kitty—"

At that moment, Roxanne gasped in alarm and put her

hand over her earpiece. "Are you sure?" she said into her headset, before grabbing Colette's arm. "Your parents just checked in at the guardhouse."

Colette looked panic-stricken for a split second. "Already? They're much too early! Nothing's ready!" Turning to Rachel and Nick, she said, "I'm sorry to end the tour now, but my parents have arrived."

The group rushed back toward the grand salon, as Colette barked out orders to Roxanne. "Alert all staff! Where's that damn Wolseley? Tell Ping Gao to start cooking the parchment chicken now! And tell Baptiste to decant the whiskey! And why aren't the bamboo groves around the central pool lit?"

"They are on a timer. They don't come on until seven o'clock along with the lights," Roxanne responded.

"Turn everything on now! And turn off this silly whimpering man—you know my father only likes listening to Chinese folk songs! And get Kate and Pippa into their cages—you know how allergic my mother is!"

Hearing their names, the dogs started yapping excitedly.

"Kill the Bon Iver and put on the Peng Liyuan!"* Roxanne rasped into her headset as she ran toward the service wing with the dogs, almost tripping on their leashes.

By the time Carlton, Colette, Nick, and Rachel reached the front door of the main pavilion, the entire staff was already assembled at the foot of the steps. Rachel attempted to count the number of people but stopped at thirty. The maids stood elegantly in their black silk *qipaos* on the left and the men in their black James Perse uniforms on the right, creating two diagonal lines in V formation like migrating geese. Colette took her place at the apex of the V, as the rest of the group waited at the top of the steps.

---

* Not only is she China's most renowned contemporary folk singer, she's also the First Lady, being married to President Xi Jinping.

Colette turned around and made a final inspection. "Who has the towels? The hot towels?"

One of the younger maids stepped out of the line holding a small silver chest.

"What are you doing? Get back in formation!" Roxanne screamed, as the convoy of black Audi SUVs came speeding up the driveway.

The doors on the lead SUV flung open, and several men in black suits and dark sunglasses emerged, one of them approaching the middle car and opening the door. Judging by how thick the door was, Nick surmised it was a reinforced bombproof model. A short, stocky man in a bespoke three-piece suit was the first to emerge.

Roxanne, who was standing next to Nick, let out a barely audible gasp.

Seeing that the man appeared to be no older than his mid-twenties, Nick asked, "I take it that's not Colette's father?"

"It's not," Roxanne said curtly, before stealing a quick glance at Carlton.

# MICHAEL AND ASTRID

SINGAPORE

"Is that all you're wearing?" Michael asked, lurking by the doorway of Astrid's dressing room.

"What do you mean? Am I too scantily clad for you?" Astrid joked as she struggled to fasten the delicate clasp on her sandals.

"You look so casual."

"I'm not *that* casual," Astrid said, standing up. She was wearing a short black tunic dress with crochet panels and black fringe.

"We're going to one of the best restaurants in Singapore, and it's with the IBM people."

"Just because André is a top restaurant doesn't mean it's formal. I thought this was just a casual business dinner with a few of your clients."

"It is, but the bigwig is flying in and he's bringing his wife, who's supposedly very chic."

Astrid shot Michael a look. Had aliens secretly abducted her husband and replaced him with some finicky fashion editor? In the six years they had been married, Michael had never made a single comment about what she wore. He had, on certain occasions, grunted that something looked "sexy" or "pretty" on her, but he had never used a word like "chic." Until today, it wasn't part of his vocabulary.

Astrid dabbed a little rose essential oil onto her neck and said, "If the wife is as chic as you say, she will probably appreciate this Altuzarra dress—it's a runway look that never went into production, which I'm wearing with Tabitha Simmons silk stripe sandals, Line Vautrin gold earrings, and my Peranakan gold bracelet."

"Maybe it's all the gold. It looks a bit *kan chia*\* to me. Couldn't you swap it out for diamonds or something?"

"There's nothing *kan chia* about this bracelet—it's actually part of an heirloom suite that my great-aunt Matilda Leong bequeathed to me, which is now on loan to the Asian Civilisations Museum. They are dying for me to let them display this piece too, but I held on to it for sentimental reasons."

"Sorry, I didn't mean to offend your auntie. And I'm not a fashion guerrilla or whatever like you. This is one of the most important business deals I've ever been involved in, but please wear what you want. I'll be downstairs waiting," Michael said in a patronizing tone.

Astrid sighed. She knew all this fuss had something to do with that silly Hong Kong gossip columnist's barb about Michael needing to upgrade his wife's jewelry. Even though he denied it, the comment must have gotten under his skin. She made her way to the vault, punched in the nine-digit code to open the door, and peered inside. Damn, the earrings she was thinking of were at the big vault at OCBC Bank. The

---

\*   The literal translation is "pull vehicle," but this Hokkien term refers to rickshaw pullers or anything that is deemed low-class. (Of course, Michael has never been to Manhattan, where pedicab drivers tend to be out-of-work male models who charge more than Uber Black Cars.)

only thing she had of any significant size at home was a pair of gargantuan Wartski diamond-and-emerald pendant earrings that her grandmother had inexplicably handed her after mah-jongg at Tyersall Park the other day. The emeralds on each side were almost the size of walnuts. Apparently the last time her grandmother had worn them was at King Bhumibol of Thailand's coronation in 1950. *Well, if Michael really wants a Busby Berkeley showstopper, that's what he's going to get. But what outfit could possibly go with these earrings?*

Astrid scanned her closet and pulled out a black Yves Saint Laurent jumpsuit with a drawstring waist and jet beaded sleeves. This was just dressy and yet simple enough to complement a pair of outrageously bling earrings. She would wear them with a pair of Alaïa ankle boots to give the whole look an extra edge. Astrid felt a little lump in her throat as she put the jumpsuit on—she had never worn it before because it was too precious to her. It was from Yves's final couture collection in 2002, and though she was only twenty-three when she had her fitting for this, it still draped against her body more perfectly than almost anything else she owned. *God, I miss Yves.*

Astrid headed downstairs to the nursery, where she found Michael keeping Cassian company at the children's dining table while he ate his spaghetti with meatballs.

"*Wow, vous êtes top, madame!*" Cassian's nanny exclaimed as Astrid entered.

"*Merci, Ludivine.*"

"Saint Laurent?"

"*Qui d'autre?*"

Ludivine placed her hand on her chest and shook her head in awe. (She could not wait to try it on as soon as madame left the house tomorrow.)

Astrid turned to Michael. "Is this good enough to impress your IBM bigwig?"

"Where on earth did you get those earrings? *Tzeen* or *keh*?"* Michael exclaimed.

"*Tzeen!* My grandmother just gave them to me," Astrid replied, slightly annoyed that Michael only noticed the earrings and failed to appreciate the subtle genius of her jumpsuit.

"*Wah lan!*† Van Cleef and Ah Ma strikes again."

Astrid winced. Michael had punished Cassian for using cuss words, and yet here he was swearing like a sailor right in front of him.

"Look—doesn't Mummy look pretty tonight?" Michael said to Cassian, pinching a meatball from his bowl and popping it into his mouth.

"Yes. Mummy always looks pretty," Cassian said. "And stop stealing my meatballs!"

Astrid melted instantly. How could she be annoyed at Michael when he looked so cute sitting in the little chair next to Cassian? Things had gotten much better between father and son since she returned from Venice. After kissing Cassian goodbye, the two of them headed outside to the front driveway, where their chauffeur, Youssef, was doing a final polish on the chrome work of Michael's 1961 red Ferrari California Spyder.

*Jesus, he's really out to impress tonight*, Astrid thought.

"Thanks for changing, hon. It really means a lot to me," Michael said as he held open the car door.

Astrid nodded as she climbed in. "If you think it makes any difference, I'm happy to help."

They drove in silence at first, enjoying the balmy breeze through the open top, but as he turned onto Holland Road,

---

* "Real or fake?" in Hokkien.
† Literally "My cock!," this Hokkien swear is comparable to the American "Fucking hell!"

Michael picked up the conversation again. "How much do you think your earrings are worth?"

"Probably more than this car."

"I paid $8.9 mil for this 'Rari. You really think your earrings are worth more? We should get them valued."

Astrid found his line of questioning slightly tacky. She never thought of jewelry in terms of prices and wondered why Michael even brought it up. "I'm never going to sell them, so what's the point?"

"Well, we do want to insure them, don't we?"

"It all goes under my family's umbrella policy. I just add it to a list that Miss Seong keeps at the family office."

"I didn't know about this. Can my vintage sports cars get on the policy too?"

"I don't think so. It's just for Leongs," Astrid blurted out, instantly regretting her choice of words.

Michael didn't seem to notice and continued chattering away. "You're really getting all of your Ah Ma's biggest jewels, aren't you? Your cousins must be envious as hell."

"Oh, there's plenty to go around. Fiona got the Grand Duchess Olga sapphires, and my cousin Cecilia got some superb imperial jade. My grandmother is very discerning—she gives the right pieces to whoever she knows will appreciate them the most."

"Do you think she feels she's going to conk off soon?"

"What a thing to say!" Astrid exclaimed, giving Michael a look of horror.

"Come on, *lah*, it must be going through her mind, which is why she's begun divesting all her stuff. Old people can sense when they are going to die, you know."

"Michael, my grandmother has been around all my life, and I can't even begin to imagine the day when she won't be here."

"Sorry—I was just making conversation."

They lapsed into silence again, Michael focusing on the client dinner and Astrid contemplating their disagreeable conversation. Michael had always shied away from anything to do with money when they first got married, especially if it involved her family, and went to great pains to show that he had absolutely no interest in her financial affairs. Indeed, their marriage had been rocked to its core by his insecurities over her fortune and his ill-conceived attempt to set her free, but thankfully that awful period was well behind them.

But ever since his business had exploded into a huge success, he had become the proverbial mouse that roared. It dawned on Astrid that at family gatherings these days, her husband always seemed to be at the center of the financial debates with the men. Michael relished being the go-to guy for advice about the tech industry and the newfound respect he was forging with her father and brothers, who had for years treated him with barely veiled condescension. He had also discovered his acquisitive side, and Astrid had watched in wide-eyed wonder as his tastes had upgraded faster than you could say "Do you take Amex?"

She glanced over at him now, cutting such a dashing figure in his dark gray Cesare Attolini suit and his perfectly knotted Borrelli tie, the face of his Patek Philippe Nautilus Chronograph glinting under the flash of streetlamps as he shifted gears forcefully on his iconic automobile, the one that every hot-blooded male from James Dean to Ferris Bueller had coveted. She was proud of all he had achieved, but part of her missed the old Michael, the man who was happiest lounging at home in his soccer kit enjoying his plate of *tau you bahk*[*] with white rice and his Tiger beer.

---

[*]  Pork belly cooked in soy sauce, a simple Hokkien dish.

As they drove along palm-tree-lined Neil Road, Astrid gazed at all the colorful heritage shophouses. Then she realized they had just sped past the restaurant. "Hey, you missed the turn. That was Bukit Pasoh we just passed."

"Don't worry, I did that on purpose. We're going to circle the block for a while."

"Why? Aren't we already late?"

"I've decided to give them a little more time to cool their heels. I instructed the maître d' to make sure they get drinks at the bar first, and that they are seated right by the window so that they will have the best view of us pulling up. I want all the guys to see me get out of this car, and then I want them to see *you* getting out of this car."

Astrid almost wanted to laugh. Who was this man next to her talking this way?

Michael continued, "We're playing this game of chicken right now, and I know they want to see who blinks first. They have raging hard-ons to acquire this new proprietary technology that we've developed, and it's really important that I am able to convey the right image to them."

They finally pulled up outside the elegant white colonial-era shophouse that had been converted into one of the island's most acclaimed restaurants. As Astrid got out of the car, Michael looked her over and said, "You know, I think you made a mistake changing out of that first cocktail dress. It showed off your sexy legs. But at least you have those earrings. That's really going to make their jaws drop, especially the wife. It'll be great—I want them to know that I'm not going to be a cheap date."

Staring at him in disbelief, Astrid stumbled for a moment on the pristine wooden deck leading to the front door.

Michael grimaced. "Shit, I hope they didn't see you do that. Why the hell are you wearing those ridiculous boots anyway?"

Astrid breathed in deeply. "What's the wife's name again?"

"Wendy. And they have a dog named Gizmo. You can talk about the dog with her."

A wave of nausea churned like acid at the base of her throat. For the first time in her life, she had a true appreciation of how it felt to be treated like a cheap date.

# 10

## THE BINGS

SHANGHAI

Nick, Rachel, Carlton, and Roxanne stood on the wide stone steps of the Bing estate, watching Colette give a warm hug to the man that had just stepped out of the convoy of SUVs.

"Who's that?" Nick asked Roxanne.

"Richie Yang," Roxanne replied, before adding in a whisper, "one of Colette's suitors, who's based in Beijing."

"He's rather dressed up for tonight."

"Oh, he is always very fashionable. *Noblest Magazine* ranked him the best-dressed man in China, and his father is ranked the fourth richest man in China by *The Heron Wealth Report*, with a net worth of US$15.3 billion."

A short, slight man in his early fifties emerged from the armored SUV. His face had a slightly punched-in look, something that his neatly trimmed Errol Flynn mustache only served to accentuate. "Is that Colette's father?" Nick asked.

"Yes, that is Mr. Bing."

"What's he ranked?" Nick asked in jest. He found these rankings to be rather ridiculous and more often than not wildly inaccurate.

"Mr. Bing is ranked fifth richest, but *The Heron* is wrong.

At current share prices, Mr. Bing should be ranked higher than Richie's father. *Fortune Asia* has it correct—it ranks Mr. Bing at number three," Roxanne said earnestly.

"What an outrage. I should write a letter to *The Heron Wealth Report* to protest the error," Nick joked.

"Oh no need, sir, we already have," Roxanne replied.

Mr. Bing helped a woman with shoulder-length bouffant hair, dark-tinted sunglasses, and a blue surgical mask over her face out of the car.

"That's Mrs. Bing," Roxanne whispered.

"I figured. Is she ill?"

"No, she is just an extreme germaphobe. This is why she spends most of her time on the Big Island of Hawaii, where she thinks the air is freshest, and why this estate has a state of-the-art air-purifying system."

Everyone watched as Colette gave her parents polite half hugs, after which the maid bearing the chest of hot towels prostrated herself in front of them as if she were offering gold, frankincense, and myrrh. Colette's parents, who wore matching navy blue cashmere Hermès tracksuits, took the steaming towels and began wiping their hands and faces methodically. Mrs. Bing then stretched out her hands, and another maid rushed up and squirted hand sanitizer onto her eager palms. After they had finished, Wolseley offered his greetings, and then Colette gestured for the group to approach.

"Papa, Mama, meet my friends. You know Carlton, of course. This is his sister, Rachel, and her husband, Nicholas Young. They live in New York, but Nicholas is from Singapore."

"Carlton Bao! How is your father doing these days?" Colette's father said as he clapped him on the back, before turning to Nick and Rachel. "Jack Bing," he said, shaking their hands vigorously. He eyed Rachel with much interest, saying in Mandarin, "You look unmistakably like your brother."

Colette's mother, by contrast, did not extend her hands but nodded quickly as she peered at them from behind her surgical mask and Fendi sunglasses.

"Richie's plane was parked next to ours when we landed," Jack Bing said to his daughter.

"I just flew in from Chile," Richie explained.

"I insisted he join us for dinner," Colette's father said.

"Of course, of course," Colette said.

"And look who's here—Carlton Bao, the man with nine lives!" Richie cracked.

Rachel noticed Carlton's jaw tense up the same way hers did whenever she was annoyed, but he laughed politely at Richie's comment.

Everyone made their way into the grand salon. Upon entering, they were met by a man who Rachel thought looked rather familiar. He stood by the door bearing a tray that held a sparkling decanter and a freshly poured glass of scotch. It suddenly dawned on her that she had seen him at Din Tai Fung, where he had been introduced as the sommelier. She realized now that the Frenchman didn't work for the restaurant—he was the Bings' personal master sommelier.

"Would you care for the twelve-year-old sherry to welcome you home, sir?" he said to Mr. Bing.

Nick had to bite his tongue to keep from cracking up— the man sounded like he was offering Colette's father the services of a child prostitute.

"Ah Baptiste, thank you," Jack Bing said in heavily accented English as he grabbed the heavy cut-glass tumbler from the tray.

Mrs. Bing removed her surgical mask, headed for the nearest sofa, and plopped down with a satisfied sigh.

"No, Mother, let's not sit here. Let's sit on the sofa by the windows," Colette said.

"*Aiyah*, I've been flying all day and my feet are so swollen. Why can't you just let me sit here?"

"Mother, I had the maids specially fluff the lotus silk pillows on that sofa for you, and the magnolia trees are in full bloom this week. We must sit by the windows so you can enjoy them," Colette said sharply.

Rachel jumped at Colette's tone. Mrs. Bing got up reluctantly and the whole group made their way to the wall of glass at the end of the grand salon.

"Now, Mother, sit here so you can face the topiaries. Dad, you sit here. Mei Ching will bring little stools for your feet. Mei Ching, where are the pillow-top stools?" Colette demanded. Colette made herself comfortable on the chaise lounge facing in from the windows, but for everyone else sitting in that spot, the setting sun cast a blinding glare. It began to dawn on Rachel and Nick that the elaborate welcoming ritual they had witnessed outside wasn't something that Colette did out of fear or filial respect for her parents. Rather, Colette was just an absolute control freak and liked everything done precisely her way.

As everyone leaned at awkward angles to avoid the glare, Jack Bing gave Nick a discerning look. *Who is this man married to Bao Gaoliang's love child? He has a jaw so chiseled it could slice sushi, and he carries himself like a duke.* He nodded at Nick and said, "So, you are from Singapore. Very interesting country. What line of work are you in?"

"I'm a history professor," Nick replied.

"Nick studied law at Oxford, but he teaches at New York University," Colette added.

"You went to all the trouble of getting a law degree at Oxford, but you don't practice?" Jack asked. *Must be a failed lawyer.*

"I've never practiced. History was always my first passion." *Next he's going to ask me how much money I make or what my parents do.*

"Hmmm," Jack said. *Only these crazy Singaporeans can waste money sending their children to Oxford for nothing. Maybe he comes from one of those rich Indonesian Chinese families.* "What does your father do?"

*And there it is.* Nick had met innumerable Jack Bings over the years. Successful, ambitious men who were always looking to make connections with people they deemed worthy. Nick knew that by simply dropping a few of the right names, he could easily impress someone like Jack Bing. Since he had no interest in doing that, he answered politely, "My father was an engineer, but he's retired now."

"I see," Jack said. *What a waste of a man. With his height and looks, he could have been a top banker or a politician.*

*Now he's either going to dig further about my family, or move on to Rachel's inquisition.* Nick asked out of courtesy, "And what do you do, Mr. Bing?"

Jack ignored Nick's question and turned his attention to Richie Yang. "So Richie, tell me what you were doing in Chile, of all places. Scouting for more mining companies that your father can acquire?"

*Oh very nice—I've been deemed inconsequential, and he obviously couldn't give a damn what Rachel does.* Nick chuckled to himself.

Richie, who was staring intently at his titanium Vertu phone, scoffed at Jack's words. "Good God no! I'm training for the Dakar Rally. You know, that off-road vehicle endurance race? It's held in South America now—the course starts in Argentina and ends in Peru."

"You're *still* racing?" Carlton piped in.

"Of course!"

"Unbelievable!" Carlton shook his head, his voice laced with anger.

"What? You think I go running home to Mommy after just one little wreck?"

Carlton went red in the face, and he looked like he was

about to leap out of his chair and lunge at Richie. Colette placed her hand on his arm and said in a cheery voice, "I've always wanted to visit Machu Picchu, but you know I get terrible altitude sickness. I went to St. Moritz last year and got so ill, I could hardly do any shopping."

"You never told me that! See how you constantly put your life in danger by going to dangerous places like Switzerland?" Mrs. Bing admonished her daughter.

Colette turned to her mother and said in an irritated tone, "It was fine, Mother. Now, who died and made you Jackie Onassis? Why are you wearing those sunglasses in the house?"

Mrs. Bing sighed dramatically. "Hiyah, you don't know my latest suffering." She took off her sunglasses and revealed puffy, swollen eyes. "I can't open my eyes properly anymore. See, see? I think I have this very rare disease called mayo . . . mayonnaise gravies."

"Oh, you mean myasthenia gravis," Rachel offered.

"Yes, yes! You know it!" Mrs. Bing said excitedly. "It affects the muscles around your eyes."

Rachel nodded sympathetically. "I've heard it can be very debilitating, Mrs. Bing."

"Please, call me Lai Di," Colette's mother said, warming up to Rachel.

"You do not have mayonnaise gravy, or whatever you call it, Mother. Your eyes are all swollen because you sleep too much. Anyone would look like that if they slept fourteen hours a day," Colette said disdainfully.

"I have to sleep fourteen hours a day because of my chronic fatigue syndrome."

"Another disease you do not have, Mother. Chronic fatigue syndrome does not make you sleepy," Colette said.

"Well, I'm going to see a specialist for mayonnaise-athena gravies next week in Singapore."

Colette rolled her eyes and explained to Rachel and Nick, "My mother keeps ninety percent of all the doctors in Asia employed."

"Well, she's probably seen quite a few of my relatives, then," Nick quipped.

Mrs. Bing perked up. "Who are your doctor relatives?"

"Let's see . . . the one you might know is my uncle Dickie—Richard T'sien, he's a GP who has many society clients. No? Then there's his brother Mark T'sien, an ophthalmologist; my cousin Charles Shang, a hematologist; my other cousin Peter Leong, a neurologist."

Mrs. Bing gasped. "Dr. Leong? Who shares a clinic in K.L. with his wife, Gladys?"

"Yes, that's him."

"*Aiyah!* Small world—I went to see him when I thought I had a brain tumor. And then I went to see Gladys for a second opinion."

Mrs. Bing began rattling away excitedly to her husband in a Chinese dialect that Nick couldn't recognize. Jack, who had been listening to Richie describe the special off-road vehicle he was designing with Ferrari, immediately circled back to Nick. "Peter Leong is your cousin. So Harry Leong must be your uncle?"

"Yes, he is." *Now he thinks I'm a Leong. My market value is rebounding again.*

Jack eyed Nick with renewed interest. *My God, this boy is one of the Leong Palm Oil people! Ranked number three on* The Heron Wealth Report*'s list of richest families in Asia! No wonder he can afford to be a teacher!* "Is your mother a Leong?" Jack asked excitedly.

"No, she's not. Harry Leong married my father's sister."

"I see," Jack said. *Hmm. Family name Young. Never heard of them. This kid must come from the poor side of the family.*

Mrs. Bing leaned toward Nick. "What other doctors are in your family?"

"Er . . . do you know Dr. Malcolm Cheng, the Hong Kong cardiologist?"

"Oh my God! Another one of my doctors!" Mrs. Bing said excitedly. "I went to see him for my irregular heartbeat. I thought maybe I had micro-valve relapse, but it turned out I just needed to drink less Starbucks."

Richie, who was getting increasingly bored of all the doctor talk, turned to Colette. "When's dinner?"

"It's almost ready. My Cantonese chef is making her famous parchment chicken with white truffles."*

"Yum!"

"And as a special treat, I've also asked my French chef to make your favorite Grand Marnier soufflé for dessert," Colette added.

"You sure know the way to a man's heart, don't you?"

"Only certain men," Colette said, lifting one eyebrow.

Rachel glanced at Carlton to see how he was reacting to this exchange, but he seemed to be staring intently at his iPhone. He then looked up and nodded quickly at Colette, who caught his gesture but said nothing. Rachel couldn't decipher what was going on between them.

Wolseley soon announced that dinner was ready, and the party adjourned to the dining room, which was a glassed-in terrace up a short flight of steps overlooking the big reflecting pool. "It's just a casual family dinner tonight, so I thought we could dine informally on our little air-conditioned terrace," Colette explained.

Of course, the terrace was neither little nor informal.

---

* A delicacy where chicken pieces are mixed with a hoisin sauce and five-spice garnish, wrapped envelope-style into square packets of parchment paper, and left to marinate overnight (white truffles, an ingredient not normally found in classical Cantonese cuisine, are an extra touch of decadence added by the Bings' wildly ambitious chef). The packets are then deep-fried, allowing the delicious marinade to caramelize onto the chicken. Finger-lickin' good!

Lining the perimeter of the tennis-court-size space were tall silver hurricane votive lamps filled with flickering candles, and the round zitan-wood dining table that seated eight was elaborately set with "casual" Nymphenburg china. Maids stood at attention behind every chair, waiting as if their life depended on it to help ensure that each guest could properly manage the feat of sitting down.

"Now, before we start dinner, I have a special treat for everyone," Colette announced. She glanced at Wolseley and nodded. The lights were dimmed, and the first strains of the classic Chinese folk song "Jasmine Flower" began to boom from the outdoor loudspeakers. The trees around the great reflecting pool outside suddenly lit up in brilliant shades of emerald, and the waters of the pool, lit in deep purple, started to churn. Then, as the operatic singing began, thousands of water jets shot up into the night sky, choreographed to the music and morphing into elaborate formations and a rainbow riot of colors.

"My goodness, it's just like the Bellagio dancing fountain in Las Vegas!" Mrs. Bing squealed in delight.

"When did you have this put in?" Jack asked his daughter.

"They've been working on it in secret for months. I wanted it to be ready in time for my summer garden party with Pan TingTing," Colette proudly explained.

"All this just to impress Pan TingTing!"

"Nonsense—I did this for Mother!"

"And how much is this costing me?"

"Oh—it was much less than you might think. Only around twenty bucks."

Colette's father sighed, shaking his head in resignation.

Nick and Rachel exchanged looks. They knew that among the wealthy Chinese, "bucks" meant "millions."

Colette turned to Rachel. "Do you like it?"

"It's spectacular. And whoever is singing sounds a lot like Celine Dion," Rachel said.

"It *is* Celine. It's her famous duet in Mandarin with Song Zuying," Colette said.

As the water spectacle ended, a line of maids entered the dining terrace, each bearing an antique Meissen platter. The lights came on again, and in perfect unison the maids placed a platter of parchment chicken in front of each dinner guest. Everyone began undoing their parchments, which had been adorably knotted in butcher's twine, and tantalizing aromas came seeping out of the golden-brown paper. As Nick was about to take his first bite into the succulent-looking chicken thigh, he spied the trusty Roxanne creep up to Colette and whisper something into her ear. Colette grinned broadly and nodded. She looked across the table at Rachel and said, "I have one final surprise for you."

Rachel saw Bao Gaoliang coming up the stairs to the dining room. Everyone at the table rose in deference to the high-ranking minister. Gasping in delight, Rachel got up from her seat to greet her father. Bao Gaoliang looked just as surprised to see Rachel. He hugged her warmly, much to Carlton's astonishment. He had never seen his father display physical affection for anyone like that before, not even his mother.

"I am so sorry to interrupt your dinner. I was in Beijing a few hours ago, and I suddenly got strong-armed by these two conspirators and put onto a plane," Gaoliang said, gesturing toward Carlton and Colette.

"No interruption at all. It is an honor to have you here with us, Bao *Buzhang*,"* Jack Bing said, getting up and patting Gaoliang on the back. "This calls for a celebration. Where's Baptiste? We need some very special Tiger Bone wine."

"Yes, tiger power for everyone!" Richie cheered, getting up to shake Bao Gaoliang's hand. "That was a very insight-

---

* Mandarin for "minister," the correct form of address for a high-ranking official.

ful speech you gave last week about the dangers of monetary inflation, *Lingdao*."*

"Oh, were you there?" Bao Gaoliang asked.

"No, I watched it on CCTV. I'm a politics junkie."

"Well, I'm glad some of you younger generation pay attention to this country's affairs," Gaoliang said, casting a sideways glance at Carlton.

"I only pay attention when I feel like our leaders are being on the level with me. I don't watch any of the speeches that are all hype or rhetoric."

Carlton had to resist rolling his eyes.

A place setting next to Rachel was swiftly arranged for Gaoliang, and Colette graciously gestured, "Bao *Buzhang*, please do sit down."

"I'm sorry to see that Mrs. Bao couldn't join us. Is she still held up in Hong Kong?" Rachel asked.

"Yes, unfortunately. But she sends her regards," Gaoliang said quickly.

Carlton let out a snort. Everyone at the table looked at him momentarily. Carlton looked like he was about to say something, but then he changed his mind and chugged a full glass of Montrachet in several quick gulps.

As the meal resumed, Rachel filled her father in on everything they had done since arriving in Shanghai, while Nick chatted amiably with the Bings and Richie Yang. Nick was relieved that Bao Gaoliang had finally shown up, and he could see how excited Rachel was to spend time with him. But he couldn't help noticing that a few seats away, Carlton sat stone-faced while Colette seemed to be getting more and more agitated as each course was served. *What's the deal? Both of them look like they could spontaneously combust at any moment.*

---

* Mandarin for "boss," the correct form of address for really sucking up to a high-ranking official.

Suddenly, while everyone was in the midst of savoring the Lanzhou-style hand-pulled noodles with lobster and abalone, Colette put down her chopsticks and whispered into her father's ear. The two of them abruptly got up. "Please excuse us for a moment," Colette said with a forced smile.

Colette marched her father downstairs and as soon as they were out of earshot, she began to scream: "What is the point of hiring the best butler in England to teach you proper manners, when you just won't learn? You were slurping your noodles so loudly, it made my teeth ache! And the way you spit out your bones onto the table, my God, Christian Liaigre would have a heart attack if he knew what was happening on his beautiful table! And how many times have I told you not to kick your shoes off when we are dining with company? Don't lie to me—I could smell something from a mile away, and I know it wasn't the snow-pea shoots simmered in stinky tofu!"

Jack laughed at his daughter's tantrum. "I am the son of a fisherman. I keep telling you, you cannot change me. But don't worry, it doesn't matter how good my manners are. As long as *this* remains fat," he patted the wallet in his back pocket, "even in China's best dining rooms, no one will care if I spit on the table."

"Rubbish! Everyone can change! Look how well Mother is doing—she hardly chews with her mouth open anymore, and she wields her chopsticks like an elegant Shanghainese *lady*."

Colette's father shook his head in amusement. "Hiyah, I really pity that idiot Richie Yang. He doesn't know what he's getting himself into."

"What on earth do you mean?"

"Don't try to deceive your own father. Your plan of dangling Carlton Bao in front of Richie has paid off like a charm. I have a feeling he's planning to propose to you any day now."

"That's ridiculous," Colette said, still fuming at her father's negligent etiquette.

"Really? Then why did he beg his way onto my plane to ask my permission for your hand in marriage?"

"How silly of him. I hope you told him exactly where he could stuff that proposal."

"Actually, I gave Richie my blessing. I think it will be a brilliant match, not to mention that I will finally be able to stop fighting over companies with his father." Jack grinned, flashing the crooked incisor that Colette was constantly begging him to get fixed.

"Don't start getting any fantasies of mergers, Dad, because I have no interest in marrying Richie Yang."

Jack laughed, and then he said in a low whisper, "Silly girl, I never asked if you were interested in marrying him. Your *interest* is not my concern."

Then he turned and headed back upstairs.

## 11

CORINNA AND KITTY

*She's late again.* Corinna stood fuming by the revolving doors outside Glory Tower. She had specifically told Kitty to arrive no later than ten thirty, but it was now almost eleven. *I'm going to have to give her my punctuality lecture—the one I haven't had to use since working with that Burmese family in 2002,* Corinna thought as she nodded politely at all the nicely dressed people rushing past her into the building.

A few minutes later, Kitty's modest new pearl white Mercedes S-Class sedan pulled up at the curb, and Kitty emerged from the car. Corinna jabbed at her watch anxiously, and Kitty quickened her pace across the plaza. At least Kitty had diligently followed her advice in the appearance department and gone were the complicated up-do, the overly whitened face, and the burlesque-red lipstick.

In their place, the immaculately transformed Kitty only had a dusting of blush on her cheeks, a light apricot gloss on her lips, and a relaxed mane of chestnut-highlighted hair cut four inches shorter. She wore a baby-chicken-yellow Carolina Herrera dress with silk faille puff sleeves, low-heeled beige pumps of indeterminate brand, and a simple Givenchy green crocodile clutch, with her only jewelry being a pair of pearl stud earrings and a dainty diamond sideways cross necklace by Ileana Makri. The overall effect rendered her virtually unrecognizable.

"You're very late! Now we will be *noticed* when we enter, as opposed to blending in with the crowd," Corinna scolded.

"I'm sorry—this whole church thing has got me so nervous, I changed six times. Does this look okay?" Kitty asked, readjusting the pleats on her skirt.

Corinna scrutinized her for a moment. "The cross might be overdoing it a bit for your first visit, but I will let it pass. Otherwise, it looks quite appropriate—you no longer remind me of Daphne Guinness."

"The church is inside this office building?" Kitty asked, a little confused as they entered the peach-marble-clad lobby of Glory Tower.

"I told you, this is a very special church," Corinna replied as they went up an escalator to the main reception hall. There, a greeting table draped with ruffled blue bunting was manned by a trio of teenage greeters and several security guards. An American girl with a headset and an iPad came bounding toward them with a big toothy grin. "Good morning! Are you joining us for the main service or the Seekers' Class?"

"The main service," Corinna answered.

"Your names, please?"

"Corinna Ko-Tung and Kitty—I mean—Katherine Tai," Corinna replied, using the name Kitty had used before she became a soap-opera star.

The girl scrolled through her iPad and said, "I'm sorry, I don't see you on the list for Sunday services."

"Oh, I forgot to mention—we're guests of Helen Mok-Asprey."

"Okay, yes, I see you here. Helen Mok-Asprey plus two."

A female security guard approached and presented each of

them with lanyards with freshly printed name badges attached in plastic sleeves. Printed in a vibrant purple font were the words "Stratosphere Church Sunday Worship—Guest of Helen Mok-Asprey," followed by the church's motto in italics: *Communing with Christ at a Higher Level.*

"Put these on and take the first elevator up to the forty-fifth floor," the guard instructed.

When Kitty and Corinna reached the forty-fifth floor, another greeter with a headset stood waiting to escort them to an elevator bank across the hall, this one taking them up to the seventy-ninth floor.

"We're almost there—just one more set of elevators," Corinna said as she straightened the collar on Kitty's dress.

"Are we going all the way to the top?"

"The very top. See—I told you to be early precisely because it takes fifteen minutes just to get up there."

"All this trouble for a church!" Kitty grumbled.

"Kitty, you are about to enter the most exclusive church in Hong Kong—Stratosphere was started by the billionaire Pentecostal Siew sisters, and it is strictly by invitation. Not only is it the highest church in the world, at ninety-nine stories above the earth, but it boasts more members on the *South China Morning Post*'s rich list than any other private club on the island."

With that introduction, the elevator doors opened onto the ninety-ninth floor, and Kitty was momentarily blinded by the light. She found herself standing in the apex of the tower under a soaring atrium, its cathedral-like ceilings constructed almost entirely of glass flooding the space with intense sunlight. Kitty wanted to put on her sunglasses, but she suspected this would elicit another scolding from Corinna.

The next thing to assault her senses was the blaring rock music. As they took a seat in one of the back rows, Kitty saw hundreds of worshippers with their hands raised and wav-

ing in unison as they sang along to the Christian rock band.
The band was made up of a strapping blond lead singer who
could have passed for a Hemsworth brother, a Chinese female
drummer with a buzz cut, another white guy on bass guitar,
three college-age Chinese girls singing backup, and a scrawny
teenage Chinese boy in a green Izod shirt three sizes too big
pounding away frantically on a Yamaha keyboard.

Everyone sang: "*Jesus Christ, come into me! Jesus Christ, come
fill me up!*"

Kitty took in the whole spectacle with childlike awe—none
of this was anything like what she ever imagined a Christian
church service to be: the celestial light, the thumping music,
the hunky rock god onstage, and best of all, the view. From
her seat, she had a jaw-dropping bird's-eye view of Hong
Kong Island, from Pacific Place mall in Admiralty all the way
to North Point. If this wasn't heaven on earth, what was? She
took out her phone and began snapping a few covert pictures.
She had never seen the top of 2IFC up close before.

"What on earth do you think you're doing? Put that away!
You're in the house of God!" Corinna hissed into her ear.

Kitty put away her phone red-faced, but whispered to
Corinna, "You lied to me—look how everyone is dressed to
the nines except me!" Kitty said, pointing to the young woman
in the front row in a white Chanel suit, the three enormous
Bulgari gemstone rings on her fingers sparkling brightly as
she waved her arms back and forth.

"She's the pastor's wife. She is entitled to dress like that,
but as a new visitor, you can't."

Kitty was aggravated at first, but as she gazed at the gigantic cumulus clouds in the crisp azure sky, with the roar of the
catchy chorus in her ears and everyone around her singing
their guts out, she began to feel strange new emotions stirring within. The dapper guy in the houndstooth jacket and
tight Saint Laurent jeans next to her was screeching off-key,

"*Everything I need is right here, Jesus! Everything I neeeeed*," tears of joy streaming down his face. She found it strangely sexy to see this young hipster crying so openly. After half an hour of singing, the blond lead singer—who turned out to be the pastor—said to the congregation in an American accent, "It fills me with so much joy to see all your bright happy faces today. Let's share the love! Let's share the joy by passing it along to the person next to you! How about that?"

Before Kitty knew what was happening, the crying hipster turned to her and gave her a big bear hug. Then the middle-aged *tai tai* in front of her turned around and embraced her warmly. Kitty was stunned. Hong Kongers—*hugging each other*! How was this possible? And not just one or two friends who knew each other. *Perfect strangers* were hugging each other and introducing themselves. This was a miracle. My God, if this was what it was like to be a Christian, she wanted in right now!

. . .

When the service finally concluded, Corinna turned to Kitty. "At last, time for coffee and cake. Follow me."

"I don't want to spoil my appetite. Aren't we going to Cuisine Cuisine for lunch?"

"Kitty, the whole reason I brought you here is so you can socialize with these people over coffee and cake. This is the main event. Many of the members are the younger generation of Hong Kong old-guard families, and this is the best chance you have of getting to know them. They will be much more accepting of you because they are born-again Christians."

"Born again? How can you be born twice?"

"Hiyah, I'll explain later. But the important thing you need to know about being a born-again Christian is that once you repent and accept Jesus into your heart, you are forgiven for all your sins no matter what they are. Whether you mur-

dered your parents, slept with your stepson, or embezzled
millions to fund your singing career—these people *have* to
forgive you. Now what I hope to accomplish today is to get
you into one of the Bible Study Fellowships. The group that
everyone wants to join is Helen Mok-Asprey's, but it's a very
closed circle of only the top ladies. To begin with, I would
aim for the group led by my niece Justina Wei. It's a younger
crowd, and there are quite a few girls from good families in
that one. Justina's paternal grandfather, Wei Ra Men, started
Yummy Cup Noodles, so everyone calls her the Instant Noodle Heiress."

Kitty was steered toward a moon-faced woman in her
early thirties. She couldn't believe that this person dressed in
a secretary-like navy pantsuit was the noodle heiress she had
heard so much about. "Justina—hiyah, *gum noi moh gin*!* Meet
my friend Katherine Tai."

"Hello. Are you related to Stephen Tai?" Justina asked,
immediately trying to place Kitty on her social map.

"Um, no."

Justina, who was usually only comfortable talking to people she knew from birth, was forced to resort to her default
question. "So, which school did you go to?"

"I didn't go to school in Hong Kong," Kitty responded,
a little flustered. Justina's long, frizzy, limp hair reminded her
of instant noodles. She wondered what would happen if you
poured boiling water over them and let them sit for three
minutes.

"Katherine went to school abroad," Corinna quickly
interjected.

"Oh—is this your first time worshipping with us?" Justina
cocked her head.

"Yes."

---

* Cantonese for "long time no see."

"Well then, welcome to Stratosphere. Which church do you normally attend?"

Kitty tried to think of all the churches she passed every single day on the way down from her apartment on The Peak, but her mind temporarily went blank. "Er, the Church of Volturi," she blurted out, picturing the church-like space from the *Twilight* movies where those scary old vampires sat on thrones.

"Oh, I don't know that one. Is it over on Kowloon side?"

"Yes it is," Corinna said, coming to the rescue again. "I really must introduce Kit—I mean Katherine to Helen Mok-Asprey. I see Helen already grabbing the flowers from the church altar, so I know she's about to leave."

Pulling Kitty off to the side, Corinna said, "My God, that was an utter disaster! What is wrong with you today? Where is the girl who charmed the socks off Evangeline de Ayala?"

"Sorry, sorry, I don't know what's happening. I guess I'm just not used to all this—my new name, pretending to be a Christian, dressing this way. Without my normal makeup or proper jewelry, I feel like I don't have my armor on. People always used to ask me about what I was wearing, and now I can't even talk about that."

Corinna shook her head in dismay. "You're an actress! It's time you put your improv skills to the test. Just think of it as playing a new role. Remember, you are no longer the evil twin sister. You are the good wife now. You spend all your time taking care of your invalid husband and your young daughter, and this is the only time all week you get to socialize with people. So you must be animated and grateful. Now let's try again with Helen Mok-Asprey. Helen was born a Mok, divorced a Quek, and is now married to Sir Harold Asprey. You should address her as Lady Asprey."

Corinna steered Kitty toward the hospitality table, where a woman with an enormous coiffed helmet of hair was furtively wrapping up six enormous slices of Black Forest cake in paper napkins and stuffing them into her big black Oroton handbag. "Helen, thank you so much for putting us on your list today!" Corinna chirped.

Helen jumped a little. "Oh, hi, Corinna. I'm just taking home a little bit of cake for Harold. You know what a sweet tooth he has."

"Yes, Harold's just like you when it comes to sweets, isn't he? Before you leave, I wanted to introduce my guest Katherine Tai. Katherine used to belong to the Volturi Church in Kowloon, but she's thinking of changing."

"I love your church! Thank you so much for inviting us today, Lady Asprey," Kitty said sweetly.

Helen looked Kitty up and down. "What a lovely little cross that is," she complimented, before turning to Corinna and saying, sotto voce, "I had one very similar to that, but I think one of the new maids stole it. Those new girls from *youknowwhere* are just so untrustworthy. My God, I miss my Norma and Natty. You know, I paid them so well that now they've abandoned me to start a beach bar in Cebu."

A lady chicly attired in a celadon-colored A-line dress came up to the table with two carafes freshly refilled with coffee. "My goodness, what happened to all the cake? I guess I have to go down to the kitchen again." She sighed.

"Oh Fi—before you run off, meet my friend Katherine Tai. Katherine, this is my cousin Fiona Tung-Cheng," Corinna said.

"Pleased to meet you, Katherine," Fiona said, before giving Kitty a more discerning look. "You look so familiar. Are you by any chance related to Stephen Tai?"

"They're distant cousins," Corinna cut in, trying to stop her from asking more questions.

Kitty smiled calmly at Fiona and said, "You know I just adore your dress. Narciso Rodriguez, isn't it?"

"Why yes, thank you," Fiona beamed. It wasn't often that anyone complimented her clothes.

"I met him a few years ago," Kitty continued, ignoring Corinna's glare. She was going to talk about fashion at church even if it gave Corinna a stroke.

"Really? You met Narciso?" Fiona said.

"Yes, I went to his fashion show in New York. Don't you think it's wonderful that a boy from a family of Cuban immigrants can become such a successful fashion designer? It's like the message of today's sermon—anyone with a willing heart can be born again."

Helen Mok-Asprey beamed in approval. "How true. My goodness, why don't you join my Bible study group? We could use another fresh young perspective like yours."

Kitty's face lit up, as Corinna looked on like a proud mother. My God, Kitty had hit pay dirt on her very first try! Maybe Corinna had misjudged her capabilities. At this rate, Kitty was bound to win the ladies over at Bible study and would be getting invited to all sorts of other old-guard events by the time the festive season began.

Just then, Eddie Cheng came strolling over to his wife, Fiona. "Are you done with your coffee duties yet?" Turning to Helen and Corinna, he bragged, "We are expected to lunch at the Ladoories, and it would be very bad form to be late."

"I'm almost finished. I just need to make one more kitchen run for cake—it's disappeared so fast today. Eddie, meet Corinna's friend Katherine."

Eddie made an obligatory nod in Kitty's direction.

"Help me with the cake and then we can get out of here faster," Fiona said. Walking toward the kitchen with Eddie, she said, "That nice lady is going to join our Bible study. I love her dress. If only you would let me wear a bright color like that."

Eddie stared at Kitty again, suddenly narrowing his eyes. "What did you say her name was again?"

"Katherine Tai—she's a distant cousin of Stephen's."

Eddie snorted. "Maybe on Mars they might be related, but here on earth they certainly aren't. Take a good look at her, Fi."

Fiona stared searchingly at Kitty's face. Suddenly she let out a gasp of recognition and dropped the empty metal cake tray onto the floor with a loud clang. All eyes in the room were on them. Relishing the attention, Eddie made a beeline to where Corinna, Kitty, and Helen were standing and announced smugly, "Corinna, I know you have always tried to take on these charity cases, but this time you've really been had. This woman who's trying to pass herself off as Stephen Tai's cousin is an imposter. She's actually Kitty Pong—the gold digger who broke my brother Alistair's heart and eloped with Bernard Tai two years ago. Hello, Kitty."

Kitty lowered her eyes. Stung with hurt, she wasn't quite sure how to react. Why was she being called an imposter? None of this was her doing—Corinna was the one who had told Fiona she was related to this Stephen person. She turned to Corinna, hoping she would come to her defense, but the woman just stood there.

Helen Mok-Asprey glared at Kitty and said in a sharp voice, "*You're* that Kitty Pong? Carol Tai is a good friend of mine. What have you done with her son? And why won't you let Carol see her own granddaughter? *Gum hak sum!*"*

---

* Cantonese for "so black-hearted."

## ASTRID

"Are you going for a run now?" Astrid asked Michael as he came downstairs in nothing but a pair of black Puma running shorts.

"Yeah, I need to blow off some steam."

"Don't forget we have Friday-night dinner in an hour."

"I'll join you later."

"We can't be late tonight. My Thai cousins Adam and Piya are visiting, and the Thai ambassador has arranged a special perform—"

"I don't give a fuck about your Thai cousins!" Michael snapped as he ran out the door.

*He's still upset.* Astrid got up from the sofa and headed upstairs to her study. She logged on to Gmail and saw Charlie's name lit up. *Thank God.* She immediately pinged him:

**ASTRID LEONG TEO:** Still at work?

**CHARLIE WU:** Yup. Never leave my office these days, except for juice breaks.

**ALT:** Question for you . . . when you are in the midst of negotiating major deals with potential clients, do you also entertain them?

CW: What do you mean by "entertain"?

ALT: Do you take them out to business dinners?

CW: LOL! I thought you meant get them laid! Yes, there are always business dinners . . . more lunches actually. We sometimes do a celebratory dinner when a deal closes. Why?

ALT: I'm just trying to educate myself. It's funny—I've had to deal with all kinds of social events with intricate protocols my whole life, but when it comes to the corporate dinner, I'm totally ignorant.

CW: Well, you've never had to be a corporate wife.

ALT: Does Isabel usually come to your work dinners?

CW: Isabel at a client dinner? Ha! Hell would freeze over. Client entertaining rarely involves spouses.

ALT: Even for international clients who are visiting Asia?

CW: When international clients come to Asia, they generally don't bring their wives. Back in my dad's time in the 1980s and '90s, yes, maybe some wives wanted to come to Hong Kong or Singapore to shop. But not so much anymore. On the rare occasions that they do, we really try to roll out the red carpet, so that clients can concentrate on work and not worry that their wives are getting ripped off at Stanley Market.

ALT: So you don't feel that a crucial component of deal-making involves a "dinner with the wives."

CW: Not at all! These days, most of my clients are single twenty-two-year-old monosyllabic Zuckerbergs. And many of them are women! What's up? I'm assuming Michael is trying to enlist your help with some clients?

ALT: It already happened.

CW: So why are you asking?

ALT: Well, it was a total disaster, the deal fell through, and guess who got the blame?

CW: Huh? Why would you get the blame for a botched deal? Last time I checked, you weren't his employee. Did you spill scalding hot *bak kut teh*[*] onto the client's lap or something?

ALT: It's a long story. Pretty funny, actually. I'll tell you about it when I see you in Hong Kong next month.

CW: C'mon, you can't leave me hanging like this!

Astrid took her hands off the keyboard. For a moment, she debated whether to make some excuse and beg off or to continue with her story. She didn't want to trash her husband to Charlie, knowing he already had a colored impression of Michael, but her need to vent got the better of her.

ALT: Michael has apparently been cultivating these clients for a while, and the bigwig and his whole team flew in to finalize the deal. He brought his wife, so Michael asked me to organize a nice dinner someplace that would impress all of them. The couple are really into food, so I chose André.

CW: Not bad. For out-of-towners I also like Waku Ghin.

ALT: I love Tetsuya's cooking, but I felt it wouldn't be right for this crowd. Anyway, for the first time ever, Michael was obsessing over what I wore to dinner. I had on what I felt to be the perfect outfit,

---

[*] Literally translated as "meat bone tea," this is not the name of a summer event on Fire Island but rather a popular Singaporean soup that consists of melt-in-your-mouth pork ribs simmered for many hours in an intoxicatingly complex broth of herbs and spices.

but he wanted me to change into something more
ostentatious.

cw: But that's not your style!

alt: I wanted to be a team player. So I wore this irre-
sponsibly large pair of earrings—emeralds and diamonds that really should not be seen in public unless
you're going to a state dinner at Windsor Castle or a
wedding in Jakarta.

cw: Sounds amazing.

alt: Well, it ended up being the wrong choice. We get
to the restaurant late, and Michael insisted on driving
his new vintage Ferrari and parking it right outside.
So everyone is already staring at us as we walked
in. Then it turns out the bigwig is from Northern
California. Lovely, low-key couple—the wife was
chic but in an understated way. She was wearing a
beautiful tunic dress, strappy sandals, and these artsy
earrings that some kid had made for her. I looked
outrageously overdressed by comparison and it made
everyone uncomfortable. Everything went south
from there, and today Michael came home pretty
upset. They nixed the whole deal.

cw: And Michael blames YOU?

alt: He blames himself more, but I do see it was partly
my fault. I should have followed my gut and stuck to
the first outfit. Truth be told, I was a little cheesed
off that Michael was second-guessing my choice, so I
really put my foot on the accelerator to up the bling
quotient with the second outfit. But it was way too
much, and it put off the client.


Astrid's phone started to ring, and she picked it up when
she saw it was Charlie on the line.

"Astrid Leong, that's the most ridiculous thing I've ever

heard! Clients don't give a shit how the wives of their business partners are dressed, especially in the tech world. I'm sure there are many reasons why this deal did not work out, but trust me, your accessories had nothing to do with it. You see that, don't you?"

"I get what you're saying, and I agree . . . partly. But it was an unusual night, and a strange confluence of events. You just had to be there."

"Astrid, that's total BS. I'm mad at Michael that he would try to make you feel like you were in any way responsible!"

Astrid sighed. "I know I am not ultimately responsible, but I do see that if I had done things a little differently, the outcome might have been more positive. I'm sorry it's upset you. I didn't mean to do that—I guess I was just selfishly venting after Michael and I got into a fight. I feel bad for him, I really do. I know he worked so hard to try to get this deal off the ground."

"Cry me a river! Michael's company is still doing fantastic—his stock hasn't lost a single point over this. But he's somehow managed to make *you* feel bad about it, and that's what worries me. You just don't see how preposterous this whole line of reasoning is. You did nothing wrong, Astrid. NOTHING."

"Thank you for saying that. Hey, I gotta run. Cassian is screaming about something." Hanging up the phone, Astrid closed her eyes and let the tears seep out. She didn't dare tell Charlie what Michael had really said when he came home that afternoon. He had come into Cassian's bedroom, where Astrid was crouched under the desk with three chairs barricading her in, and she was wearing the emerald earrings, pretending to be a captured Guinevere to Cassian's King Arthur.

"Those goddamn earrings again! You lost me the biggest deal because of those earrings!" Michael scoffed.

"What on earth are you talking about?" Astrid asked, peering out from her hiding place.

"The deal fell through today. They weren't anywhere near my asking price."

"I'm so sorry, hon." Astrid emerged from underneath the desk and tried to give him a hug, but he pulled away after a second. She followed him down the hallway to their bedroom.

As Michael began changing out of his work clothes, he continued: "We really screwed up that client dinner. I don't blame you, I blame me. I was the fool who asked you to change. Apparently, your look didn't go over so well with everyone."

Astrid couldn't believe her ears. "I don't understand why any of that would matter anyway. Who really cares what I was wearing?"

"In this business, perception is everything. And a crucial component of deal-making is the all-important client dinner with the wives."

"I thought we had a lovely time. Wendy was raving about every dish, and we even swapped numbers."

Michael sat down on the bed and put his head in his hands for a moment. "Don't you see? It doesn't really matter what the wife thinks. I was trying to show the guys that I run *the* leading tech company in Singapore. That we are the blue-chip choice, and we have the blue-chip lifestyle to match it. And they needed to pay us what we're worth. But it all backfired."

"Maybe you shouldn't have driven the Ferrari. Maybe that was too obvious," Astrid said.

"No, that's not it. Everyone loved the Ferrari. What they didn't get was your style."

"My style?" Astrid said incredulously.

"All this strange vintage stuff, no one gets it. Why can't you just wear Chanel once in a while like everyone else? I've been doing a lot of thinking, and I think we need to make some big changes. I really need to revamp my image completely. People don't take me seriously because of how we live. They think, 'If he has one of the most successful tech companies in Asia, why doesn't he live in a bigger house? Why isn't he in the press more? Why does his wife still drive an Acura, and why doesn't she have better jewels?'"

Astrid shook her head in disbelief. "Every serious jewelry collector knows about my family's collection."

"That's part of the problem, hon—no one outside of a tiny inbred circle has even *heard* of your family because they are so goddamn private! At dinner my client couldn't imagine that those rambutan-size rocks you had on were real. So instead of making you look more expensive, it looked like you were wearing cheap costume jewelry. Do you know what their general counsel told Silas Teoh over drinks last night? He said that when we first walked into dinner, all the guys thought my date was some girl from Orchard Towers."

"Orchard Towers?" Astrid was confused.

"That's where all the escorts work. With those boots and earrings you were wearing the other night—the guys thought you were a high-class whore!"

Astrid stared at her husband, too stung to speak.

"We need to go big or go home. I need to hire a new PR consultant, and you need a new look. And I think tomorrow you should call that MGS friend of yours who is a realtor, what's her name again? Miranda?"

"You mean Carmen?"

"Yes, Carmen. Tell her we need to start looking at new houses. I want a place that will make everyone who comes over *lao nua*\* the moment they drive up."

---

\* Literally translates as "dribble saliva" in Hokkien. In other words, to drool over something with envy.

# SAVE THE SEAMSTRESS FASHION SHOW

JUNE 2013, PORTO FINO ESTATES, SHANGHAI

---

**NOBLESTMAGAZINE.COM.CN—**
*Society columnist Honey Chai live-blogs from her front-row seat as two of China's most influential fashion forces come together tonight for the worthiest of causes.*

5:50 p.m.
I've just arrived at heiress and fashion blogger **Colette Bing's** heavenly country estate, where she's hosting a very special fall fashion preview with her best friend, superstar **Pan TingTing**. This is the coveted invitation that only three hundred of China's chicest have received. **Prêt-à-Couture** has flown in the most decadent looks from the top fashion houses in Europe. As Asia's top supermodels, including **Du Juan** and **Liu Wen**, strut the runway, the outfits will be auctioned off to benefit **Save the Seamstress**, a foundation started by Colette and TingTing that fights to improve working conditions for garment workers throughout Asia.

5:53 p.m.

As guests walk up the long pebble driveway to the house, a line of French waiters in black Napoleon-collared jackets welcome us with French Blonde cocktails* served in vintage Lalique stemware. Now that's class.

6:09 p.m.

This place resembles the Puli Hotel, only much bigger. We are now inside the Bing Family Museum, and everywhere I look, I see Warhols, Picassos, and Bacons, and standing in front of them are some of China's most fabulous living works of art: **Lester Liu** and his wife, **Valerie**, in a va-va-voom vintage Christian Lacroix pouf dress; **Perrineum Wang** sporting a Stephen Jones fascinator of glittery gold sunrays with a Sacai shredded dress; **Stephanie Shi** rockin' it in royal blue Rochas; and **Tiffany Yap** as au courant as ever in Carven. *Le tout* Shanghai is here tonight!

6:25 p.m.

I just met **Virginie de Bassinet**, the chic founder of Prêt-à-Couture, who promises that we will be swooning in our seats when the fashion show starts. **Carlton Bao** just walked in with a pretty girl who looks a lot like him. Who could she be, and who is the hottie with them? OMG—is he that actor from the hit Korean TV series *My Love from the Star*?

6:30 p.m.

It's not the guy from *My Love from the Star*. Turns out he's some history professor friend of Carlton's visiting from New York. How disappointing.

---

* St. Germain elderflower liqueur, gin, and white Lillet mixed with grapefruit juice create this classic effervescent aperitif. Chin-chin!

6:35 p.m.

**Lester** and **Valerie Liu** are standing in the gallery where some beautiful antique scrolls hang, and Valerie is sobbing on Lester's shoulder. Whatever could be wrong?

6:45 p.m.

In the garden now, where seats have been arranged along the sides of an immense reflecting pool. Could this garden actually be air-conditioned? We're in the middle of a June heat wave, and yet I feel a cold draft blowing and detect the scent of honeysuckle.

6:48 p.m.

There are iPads on every seat, with a special app installed so we can view close-ups of each outfit as it comes down the runway and place our bids. Now *this* is useful technology!

6:55 p.m.

Everyone awaits the arrival of Colette and Pan Ting-Ting. What will they be wearing?

7:03 p.m.

Colette just made her entrance, with **Richie Yang** rushing up to take her arm and escort her to her seat. (Are the rumors that they are back together true?) This is what Colette has on: a Dior Couture daffodil strapless gown with a striking see-through panel at the thigh, worn with ridiculously sexy red Sheme heels that feature a heavily beaded snake winding around her ankles. You're reading about it here FIRST, before she has time to blog about it herself!

7:05 p.m.
**Roxanne Wang**, Colette's fabulous assistant, who is just killing it in a Rick Owens DRKSHDW black denim suit, just informed me that the beading on the snake is actually rubies. I DIE!!!!

7:22 p.m.
Still waiting for Pan TingTing, who is more than an hour late. We're being told that her plane has just landed from London, where she has been filming some top-secret new movie with director Alfonso Cuarón.

7:45 p.m.
Pan TingTing is in da house! I repeat, Pan TingTing is in da house! She's sporting a high ponytail and dressed in a white silk charmeuse jumpsuit and knee-high riding boots in distressed gray leather. Designer names to come the moment I find out. Jewelry: colorful beaded African Maasai Mara tribal earrings. Not much bling factor, but who cares—she looks beyond amazing, like she just came from a motorbike rally across the Gobi desert. The crowd is going crazy!!!

. . .

Observing the commotion on the other side of the reflecting pool, Rachel said to Carlton, "So that's the Jennifer Lawrence of China?"

"Oh, she's a much bigger star than Jennifer. She's like Jennifer Lawrence, Gisele Bündchen, and Beyoncé put together," Carlton declared.

Rachel laughed at the analogy. "Until tonight, I'd never heard of her."

"Trust me, you will soon. Every director in Hollywood is trying to get her in their films, because they know it will mean hundreds of millions in box-office gold over here."

Pan TingTing stood at the entrance to the garden as all eyes locked onto her. Every guest wanted to study the translucent marble complexion that *Shanghai Vogue* had likened to Michelangelo's *Pietà*, those celebrated Bambi eyes, and her Sophia Loren–esque curves. TingTing put on the beatific smile she was so famous for and scanned the crowd quickly as the first camera flashes went off. *No surprises tonight—it's all the usual suspects. Why did I ever agree to leave London for this event? Good exposure, my agent says. Considering that I am already on six magazine covers this month, why do I need more exposure? I could be enjoying that amazing butternut squash salad at Ottolenghi right now and bicycling through Notting Hill totally unrecognized (except for the Chinese tourists shopping on Ledbury Road), but here I am, being dissected like an insect under a microscope. Speaking of insects, what in Guanyin's name is Perrineum Wang wearing on her head? Don't make eye contact. Oh look, here comes photographer Russell Wing. How does he manage to be at every party in Asia at the same time? Stephanie Shi just leaped out of her seat like an electrocuted poodle. Just watch, she's going to try to stand on my right again so that when the photograph appears anywhere, the caption will read "Stephanie Shi and Pan TingTing." She always wants her name to come* first. *Thank God her grandfather isn't in power anymore. I hear that these days the old man has to use a colostomy bag. And of course, right behind Stephanie come two other Beijing princesses, Adele Deng and Wen Pi Fang. God help them, they're both wearing those Balmain basket-weave dresses that make them look like a pair of walking rattan chairs.*

The ladies greeted TingTing with cloying hugs and interlocked their arms around her as if they were the closest of friends while Russell snapped his pictures. *My God, in the photo I'm going to look like the meat in a Balmain sandwich. Would these* *guanerdai** girls have even spit in my direction five years ago? God, the things I do in the name of charity!*

As they returned to their seats, Adele whispered to Pi Fang, "I tried to look for the scars on her eyelids this time—I really don't believe those huge raccoon eyes of hers can be real. The problem is she has fake eyelashes on, and she uses very good concealer. In pictures, she appears to have very little makeup on, but in reality she has gobs on in all the right places."

Pi Fang nodded. "I looked at the nose. No one's nostrils are that perfect! Ivan Koon swears that she used to be a KTV hostess in Suzhou until some tycoon there paid for her to go to Seoul to get everything redone. The plastic surgeon had to issue her one of those certificates with 'before' and 'after' pics because she looked nothing like her passport photo after all the bandages came off."

"*Pi hua!*"† Tiffany Yap shot back. "Can't you just accept the fact that she was born with natural beauty? Not everyone has gone to Seoul to get their noses broken on purpose like the both of you. And TingTing isn't from Suzhou—she comes from Jinan. She's very open about the fact that before Zhang Yimou discovered her, she sold makeup at an SK-II counter."

"Well, I'm partly right then. This is how she has access to all the best concealers," Adele declared.

TingTing arrived at her seat of honor, between Colette and Colette's mother. She shook Mrs. Bing's hands respectfully before taking her seat, and Colette leaned in to give her a double-cheek kiss. *Colette looks fab, as always. People say she only looks good because she can afford anything on the planet, but I disagree. She's got a style that money can't buy. It's funny how the press labels us "best friends," when this is maybe the fifth time I've met her. Still, she's*

---

\*   A Mandarin term for the children of top government officials.
†   Mandarin for "Bullshit!"

*one of the few out of this bunch that I can actually stand. She's not pre-*
*dictable like the rest of them, and the way she keeps all these guys running*
*laps around her like desperate gigolos—it's pretty damn funny. Now I'm*
*going to ignore the fact that Mrs. Bing just slathered on an entire bottle*
*of hand sanitizer right after shaking my hand.*

The lights in the garden suddenly went black. After a brief
pause, the bamboo grove behind the reflecting pool lit up in a
vibrant Yves Klein blue, while yellow-hued lights submerged
deep in the water began pulsating dramatically like an airport
runway. Serge Gainsbourg and Brigitte Bardot's "Bonnie and
Clyde" began blaring on the sound system, as the first model
in a golden gown with a long chiffon train glided across the
vast pool, appearing to magically walk on water.

The crowd broke into rapturous applause, but Colette sat
with her arms crossed and her head tilted appraisingly. As more
models dressed in fancily embellished outfits continued to
prance down the catwalk, several of the ladies in the front row
started exchanging agitated looks. Valerie Liu shook her head
disapprovingly, while Tiffany Yap raised her eyebrows at Stephanie Shi as a model in a biker jacket festooned with silk peonies
stomped past. When a trio of girls in mermaid fishtail gowns
with bejeweled bodices appeared, Perrineum Wang leaned over
and whispered loudly to Colette, "Is this really a fashion show,
or are we at the Miss Universe evening-wear competition?"

"I'm as mystified as you are," Colette said agitatedly. A few
moments later, when a model took to the catwalk in a pearles-
cent satin coat embroidered with a scarlet dragon, Colette
had seen enough. She stood up imperiously and stormed to
the edge of the runway, where the fashion show's producer,
Oscar Huang, was frantically directing the models.

"Stop the show!" Colette demanded.

"What?" Oscar said, confused.

"I said stop the damn show!" Colette said. She glanced at
Roxanne, who had already sprinted over to the audio booth

where the sound engineer stood. The music was abruptly cut, the house lights came up, and the models stood awkwardly in their places in inch-deep water, unsure of what to do.

Colette grabbed Oscar's headset angrily, tore off her ruby-encrusted stilettos, and jumped onto the Plexiglas catwalk that hid just beneath the surface of the water. She strolled to the middle of the pool and announced, "I'm so sorry, everyone. This fashion show is over. This was not the show I was expecting, and this was not what I had promised you. Please accept my sincere apologies."

Virginie de Bassinet, the founder of Prêt-à-Couture, came rushing onto the runway. "What is the meaning of this?" she screeched.

Colette turned to Virginie. "I should be asking *you* that question. You assured me that you would be sending over the hottest looks from London, Paris, and Milan."

"These clothes are straight off the runway!" Virginie insisted.

"Which runway would that be? Ürümqi airport? Tell me, what's with all this dragon and phoenix rubbish and the excessive beading? I feel like I'm looking at Russian ice-skater outfits! Would Hubert de Givenchy ever have embroidered pavé crystals on a cashmere cape? This is the sort of fashion that panders to ignorant *fu er dai*[*] from the western provinces, and it is an insult to my guests! I invited the most stylish brand influencers and key opinion leaders in the country to come here tonight, and I think I can speak for all of them: There isn't a single dress I've seen so far that we would even let our *maids* be caught dead in!"

Virginie stared at Colette, utterly dumbstruck.

---

[*] A Mandarin term that means "second generation of the rich." Generally a derogatory term for the sons and daughters of the Chinese nouveaux riches who profited from the early years of China's reform-era boom.

. . .

After most of the guests had dispersed, Colette invited Carlton, Rachel, Nick, TingTing, and a few of her closest friends
back to the house for a light supper.

"Where's Richie?" Perrineum Wang asked Colette as they
entered the grand salon.

"I sent him packing after the stunt he pulled earlier. Imagine presuming I would need him to escort me to my seat, as if
he owned me or something!" Colette said in a huff.

"Bravo, Colette!" Adele Deng said. "I couldn't agree with
you more. And you also did the right thing by shutting down
that fashion show. It would have ruined your reputation as a
style icon to let it go on any longer."

Rachel gave Nick a look of bafflement, before venturing to
ask, "Forgive my ignorance, but I still don't really understand
what happened. What was wrong with the show? From my
iPad guide, it seemed like we were looking at clothes from all
the top designers."

"They *were* the top designers. But we were seeing only the
clothes that they specifically designed to appeal to the Chinese market. It was extremely patronizing. This is part of
a rather alarming trend where brands are sending all these
China-centric pieces to Asia, but not giving us access to the
truly fashion-forward pieces that women in London, Paris, or
New York get to buy," Colette explained.

"Every week, all the top designers send me racks and racks
of these outfits, hoping I will wear them, but most of them
remind me of what we just saw coming down that runway,"
TingTing said.

"I had no idea this was happening," Rachel said.

"Where was the Gareth Pugh, I ask you? Where was the
Hussein Chalayan? If one more one-shouldered sequin gown
came down that catwalk, I was going to projectile vomit!"

Perrineum huffed, the gold antennae on her head wobbling in fury.

Sprawled out on one of the sofas, Tiffany Yap sighed. "I was hoping to do all my shopping for next season tonight, but this has been an utter failure."

"You know, I've completely given up trying to shop in China these days. I just go straight to Paris," Stephanie Shi sniffed.

"We should all go to Paris one of these days. That'd be a fun trip," Adele said.

A spark came into Colette's eyes. "Why don't we go now? Let's take my plane and go straight to the source!"

"Colette, are you serious?" Stephanie said excitedly.

"Why wouldn't I be?" Turning to Roxanne, Colette asked, "What's the jet schedule like? Is Trenta in use next week?"

Roxanne began scrolling through her iPad. "Your father has Trenta on Thursday, but I have you scheduled on Venti on Monday. You're supposed to fly to Guilin with Rachel and Nick."

"Oh I forgot about that," Colette said, glancing at Rachel a little sheepishly.

"Colette, you should absolutely go to Paris. Nick and I can see Guilin on our own," Rachel insisted.

"Nonsense. I promised to show you my favorite mountains in Guilin, and we'll definitely go. But first, you and Nick must come to Paris with us."

Rachel shot Nick a glance he could tell translated as, *Jesus, not another private jet trip!* He responded, carefully, "We really wouldn't want to impose."

Colette turned to Carlton. "*Aiyah*, tell Nick and Rachel to stop being so polite with me!"

"Of course they're coming with us to Paris," Carlton said matter-of-factly, as if it was a foregone conclusion.

"How about you, TingTing? Can you come?" Colette asked.

For a split second, TingTing looked like a deer caught in headlights. *I'd rather get a scorching case of herpes than be trapped on a plane with these girls for twelve hours.* "Wow—I wish I could come to Paris, but I'm due back on the set in London first thing next week," said the actress, giving everyone a mournful look.

"That's too bad," Colette said.

Roxanne cleared her throat loudly. "Ahem, there's one little snag . . . your mother is using Trenta tomorrow."

"What for? Where's she going?" Colette demanded.

"Toronto."

"Mother!" Colette shouted at the top of her lungs.

Mrs. Bing came waddling into the grand salon holding a bowl of fish congee.

"Why do you need to go to Toronto, of all places?" Colette asked.

"There's a foot doctor there that Mary Xie recommended."

"What's wrong with your foot?"

"*Aiyah*, it's not just my feet. It's my calves and my thighs. They burn like fire every time I walk for more than ten minutes. I think I have spinal phimosis."

"Well, if you really have foot problems, you shouldn't be going to Toronto—you should go to Paris."

"Paris, France?" Mrs. Bing said dubiously as she continued to eat her congee.

"Yes, don't you know the best foot doctors in the world are in Paris? They have to deal with all those women killing their feet trying to walk on cobblestone streets in their Roger Viviers. We want to go to Paris tonight. You should come with us and I'll get you to the top specialist there."

Mrs. Bing stared at her daughter with a mixture of shock and delight. This was the first time Colette had taken an interest in any of her ailments. "Can *Nainai*\* and Auntie Pan Di

---

\*   Mandarin for "Grandmother."

come too? She's always wanted to visit Paris, and *Nainai* needs to do something about her bunions."

"Of course. We have plenty of room! Invite anyone you want."

Mrs. Bing gave Stephanie a thoughtful look. "Why don't you invite your mother too? I know she's been so sad ever since your brother got kicked out of Yale."

"What a fantastic idea, Mrs. Bing! I'm sure she'd love to come along, especially if you're going," Stephanie replied.

Colette turned to Roxanne as soon as her mother had left the room. "You need to google 'foot doctor Paris.'"

"Already done," Roxanne replied. "And Trenta can be fully staffed and ready in three hours."

Colette turned to her friends. "Why don't we all meet at Hongqiao Airport at midnight?"

"Everybody get out your Goyards! We're going to Paris!" Perrineum cheered.

## TRENTA

SHANGHAI TO PARIS ON THE BINGS' PRIVATE JET[*]

The security guard at the Hongqiao International Airport Private Aviation entrance handed Carlton, Rachel, and Nick their passports and waved them through. As Carlton's SUV approached a Gulfstream VI surrounded by arriving cars, Rachel commented, "I have a bit of a phobia of private jets, but I gotta admit, Colette's got a beautiful plane."

"That's a nice plane, but it's not Colette's. *That* one is," Carlton said, steering the car to the right. Parked in the distance on the tarmac was an alpine white Boeing 747 jumbo jet with one undulating scarlet stripe painted along its fuselage like a giant calligraphy brushstroke. "This Boeing 747-81 VIP was a fortieth-birthday present for Colette's mother."

"You've got to be kidding me!" Rachel said, staring at the humongous plane glistening under floodlights.

Nick chuckled. "Rachel, I don't know how you can still be surprised. Bigger is always better for the Bings, isn't it?"

---

[*] The passenger list included Rachel, Nick, Carlton, Colette Bing, Mrs. Bing, Grandma Bing, Auntie Pan Di, Stephanie Shi, Mrs. Shi, Adele Deng, Wen Pi Fang, Mrs. Wen, Perrineum Wang, Tiffany Yap, Roxanne Ma, and six maids (every one of Colette's girlfriends brought along a personal maid).

"They spend so much time crisscrossing the globe, it makes sense for them. And especially for businessmen like Jack Bing, time is money. With the long delays at the airports in Shanghai and Beijing these days, it's an advantage to have your own plane—you can just pay to jump the runway queue," Carlton explained.

"Isn't that precisely what's causing the flight delays at Chinese airports? All the private jets getting to skip ahead of commercial airliners?" Nick asked.

"No comment," Carlton said with a wink as he pulled up to the red carpet that extended from the airplane's staircase onto the tarmac. The ground crew immediately bustled around the car, opening doors and removing the luggage while Carlton handed off his car to the valet. Along the length of the carpet, fifteen flight crew members stood at attention like troops ready for inspection, attired in the same crisp black James Perse uniforms seen at Colette's house.

"I feel like Michelle Obama about to board Air Force One," Rachel whispered to Nick as they walked along the plush red carpet.

Overhearing them, Carlton quipped, "Wait till you get on board. This plane makes Air Force One look like a sardine tin."

At the top of the steps, they entered the cabin door and were immediately greeted by the chief purser. "Welcome aboard, Mr. Bao. Good to see you again."

"Hi, Fernando."

Next to Fernando stood a flight attendant who bowed deeply before asking Rachel and Nick, "Your shoe sizes, please?"

"Er . . . I'm a size six, and he's a ten and a half," Rachel said, wondering why she asked.

Moments later, the flight attendant returned with velvet drawstring bags for everyone. "A gift from Mrs. Bing," she announced. Rachel looked inside and saw a pair of Bottega Veneta leather slippers.

"Colette's mum prefers for everyone to wear these on board," Carlton explained, slipping off his loafers. "Come, let me give you a quick tour before everyone else gets here." He led them down a hallway paneled in a lacquered gray maple wood and tried to open a set of double doors. "Bugger, I guess it's locked. This is a staircase that leads downstairs to the clinic. There's an operating theater with a full life-support system, and there's always a doctor on board."

"Let me guess . . . Mrs. Bing's idea?" Nick asked.

"Yes, she's always worrying that she'll fall ill on the plane on the way to visit her doctors. Let's try going this way."

They followed Carlton along another passage and down a wider set of steps. "Here's the main cabin, or the Grand Lounge, as they call it."

Rachel's jaw dropped. She knew, on an intellectual level, that she was still on an airplane. But what she was seeing was something that couldn't possibly exist on a plane. They were standing in a vast, semicircular room filled with sleek Balinese teak sofas, consoles that looked like antique silver chests, and silk-covered lamps in the shape of lotus blossoms. But the focal point of the space was a three-story rock wall carved with ancient-looking Buddhas. Growing out of the wall were live ferns and other exotic botanicals, while off to the side, a spiral glass-and-stone staircase wound its way to an upper floor.

"Mrs. Bing wanted the Grand Lounge to feel like an ancient Javanese temple," Carlton explained.

"It's just like Borobudur," Nick said in a hushed whisper as he touched the moss-covered stone.

"You got it. I think she fell in love with some resort there many years ago and wanted it replicated on her plane. The wall is an actual temple façade from an archaeological dig. They had to smuggle it out of Indonesia, from what I'm told."

"I guess you can do whatever you want with a 747 if you don't need to fit four hundred seats," Nick surmised.

"Yeah, and having five thousand square feet of space to play with also helps. These sofas, by the way, are upholstered in Russian reindeer leather. And up those stairs, there's a karaoke lounge, a screening room, a gym, and ten bedroom suites."

"Sweet Jesus! Nick, come over here right now!" Rachel said in a panicked voice from across the room.

Nick rushed over to her. "Are you okay?"

Rachel stood dead in her tracks at the edge of what appeared to be a lap pool, shaking her head in disbelief. "Look—it's a koi pond."

"God, you scared me. For a moment I thought something was wrong," Nick said.

"You don't think anything's wrong? THERE'S A FRIG-GING KOI POND IN THE MIDDLE OF THIS PLANE, NICK!"

Carlton came over, highly amused by his sister's reaction. "These are some of Mrs. Bing's prized koi. You see that fat white one over there with the big red spot right in the middle of its back? Some Japanese tosser who was a guest on the plane once offered the Bings $250,000 for that fish. It reminded him of the Japanese flag. I do wonder if these poor koi ever get jet-lagged."

Just then, Colette entered the main cabin swathed in a hooded angora poncho, trailed by a large entourage that included her mother, grandmother, Roxanne, a few of the girls from earlier, and a retinue of maids. "I can't believe those idiots let you on board! I wanted to give Nick and Rachel the tour myself," Colette said with a little pout.

"We haven't seen anything except this room," Rachel said meekly.

"Okay, great! Knowing your love of bathrooms, I wanted

to show you the hydromassage room myself." Lowering her voice, she said to Rachel, "I wanted to warn you ahead of time. My parents bought and designed this plane while I was away at Regent's. So I can't be held responsible for the decor."

"I don't know what you're talking about, Colette. This plane is unfathomably gorgeous," Rachel assured her.

Colette looked genuinely relieved. "Here, come meet my grandmother. *Nainai,* these are my friends from America, Rachel and Nick," Colette announced to a plump septuagenarian with a standard-issue Chinese-grandma perm.

The old lady smiled tiredly at them, baring a couple of gold teeth. She looked as if she had been hastily yanked out of bed, shoved into a St. John knit jacket two sizes too small, and hustled aboard the plane.

Colette surveyed the cabin, looking rather displeased. She glanced at Roxanne and said, "Send for Fernando right now."

The man arrived momentarily, and Colette gave him a lethal glare. "Where's the tea? There should always be cups of steaming-hot Bird's Tongue Longjing tea[*] waiting for my mother and grandmother the minute they get on board! And little plates of *hua mei*[†] to suck on during takeoff! Hasn't *anyone* read the Aircraft Standards Manual?"

"I apologize, Miss Bing. We only landed a little over an hour ago and haven't had time to turn around the plane properly."

"What do you mean you just landed? Wasn't Trenta here all weekend?"

---

[*] The mountains of Hangzhou are famed for Longjing tea, also known as Dragon Well tea. It is said that 600,000 fresh tea leaves are required to produce one kilogram of this precious tea that is prized above all else by Chinese tea connoisseurs.

[†] Salted dried plums, fervently sucked on by generations of Chinese like martini olives. Supposedly great for combating nausea but has the reverse effect on me.

"No, Miss Bing. Your father just returned from Los Angeles."

"Really? I had no idea. Well, get us the tea and tell the captain we're ready for takeoff."

"Right away, Miss Bing," the chief purser said, turning to leave.

"One more thing . . ."

"Yes, Miss Bing?"

"There is something in the air tonight, Fernando."

"We'll readjust the cabin climate right away."

"No, that's not it. Can you smell the air, Fernando? It's nothing like Frédéric Malle's Jurassic Flower. Who changed the cabin scent without my permission?"

"I'm not sure, Miss Bing."

After Fernando left the room, Colette turned to Roxanne again. "When we get to Paris, I want new copies of the Aircraft Standards Manual printed and bound for every member of the flight crew. I want them to memorize every page, and then we're going to give them a pop quiz during the return flight."

## 28 CLUNY PARK ROAD

Carmen Loh had just stretched into *sarvangasana* pose in the middle of her living room when she heard her answering machine kick in.

"Carmen, ah. Mummy here. Geik Choo just called to tell me that Uncle C.K. has been checked in to Dover Park Hospice. They say if he makes it through the night, he can probably last through the week. I'm going to pay a visit today. I think you should come with me. Can you come and pick me up at Lillian May Tan's around six? We should be finished with mah-jongg by then, unless Mrs. Lee Yong Chien shows up. In that case the game will take longer. Visiting hours at Dover Park end at eight, so I want to make sure we have ample time. Also, I ran into Keng Lien today at NTUC, and she said she heard from Paula that you are selling your Churchill Club membership to fund some new scuba-diving venture. I said 'What rubbish, there is no way my daughter would ever do a thing like . . .'"

Grunting in frustration, Carmen eased her body down from its shoulder stand. Why the hell didn't she remember to turn off the machine? Thirty minutes of pure bliss ruined by one call from her mother. She walked slowly to the phone and picked it up. "Ma, why on earth is Uncle C.K. in a hospice and not at home? Won't they get him twenty-four-hour home-hospice care even in his final days? I can't believe the family is as *giam siap*\* as that."

"*Aiyah*, it's not that. Uncle C.K. wants to die at home, but the children won't let him. They think it will affect the value of the house, *lor*."

Carmen rolled her eyes in exasperation. Even before the tin-mining tycoon C. K. Wong's MRI results came in showing that his cancer had spread all over, everyone had already begun plotting. In the old days, real estate agents would scour the obituaries every morning, hoping to see the name of some prominent tycoon appear, knowing that it was only a matter of time before the family put the big house up for sale. Now, with Good Class Bungalows† becoming rarer than unicorns, the top agents were resorting to "well-placed contacts" at all the hospitals. Five months ago, Carmen's boss, Owen Kwee, at MangoTee Properties had called her into his office and said, "My *lobang*‡ at Mount E. saw C. K. Wong come in for chemo. Aren't you related to him?"

"Our fathers are cousins."

"That house of his on Cluny Park Road is on a three-acre plot. It's one of the last Frank Brewer houses still standing."

"I know. I've been going there my whole life."

Owen leaned back in his tufted-leather office chair. "I only

---

\* Hokkien for "cheap, stingy."
† Believe it or not, this is the Singapore real estate industry term for luxury properties that have a minimum lot size of 15,070 square feet and a height of only two stories. On an island of 5.3 million, there remain only about 1,000 Good Class Bungalows. They are located exclusively in the prime residential districts 10, 11, 21, and 23, and a nice starter-level GCB can be yours for around US$45 million.
‡ Malay slang for "contact, connection."

know the oldest son, Quentin. But there are other siblings, right?"

"Two younger brothers and one daughter." She knew exactly where he was going with this.

"Those two brothers live abroad, don't they?"

"Yes," Carmen said impatiently, wishing he would get to the point.

"The family will probably want to sell after the old man conks off, won't they?"

"Jesus, Owen, my uncle is still very much alive. He was golfing at Pulau Club last Sunday."

"I know, *lah*, but can I safely assume that MangoTee will get the exclusive listing if the family ever decides to sell?"

"Stop being so *kiasu*.* Of course I will get the listing," Carmen said in annoyance.

"I'm not being *kiasu*, I just wanted to make sure you are prepared. I hear Willy Sim over at Eon Properties is already circling like a hawk. He went to Raffles with Quentin Wong, you know."

"Willy Sim can circle all he wants. I'm already in the nest."

· · ·

Six months later, this was precisely where Carmen found herself—standing in the crow's nest, a small room tucked away in the attic of her late uncle's old bungalow—as she showed her friend Astrid around the property.

"What a cute space! What did they use this room for?" Astrid asked as she peered around the little nook.

"The original family that built this house called it the crow's nest. The story is that the wife was a poetess, and

---

*    Hokkien for "afraid to lose out" to something or someone.

she wanted a quiet place away from her children to do her writing. From the window, she had a bird's-eye view of the front garden and the driveway, so she could always keep an eye on who was coming and going. By the time my uncle bought the house, this was just a storeroom. My cousins and I used it as a clubhouse when we were kids. We called it Captain Haddock's Hideout."

"Cassian would love this. He would have so much fun up here." Astrid peered out the window and saw Michael's 1956 black Porsche 356 Speedster pulling up the driveway.

"James Dean just arrived," Carmen deadpanned.

"Haha. He does look like quite the rebel in it, doesn't he?"

"I always knew you'd end up with a bad boy. Come, let's give him the grand tour."

As Michael got out of his classic sports car, Carmen couldn't help but notice the transformation. The last time she had seen him was two years ago at a party at Astrid's parents' house, where he was in cargo pants and a polo shirt and still had his commando buzz cut. Now, striding up to the front steps in his steel-gray Berluti suit, Robert Marc sunglasses, and trendy disheveled haircut, he seemed like a totally different man.

"Hey, Carmen. Love your new hairstyle," Michael said, giving her a kiss on the cheek.

"Thanks," Carmen said. She'd had her long straight hair layered into a chin-length bob a few weeks ago, and he was the first man to pay her a compliment.

"My condolences about your uncle—he was a great man."

"Thank you. The silver lining to this unfortunate event is that you are getting to preview the place before it officially goes on the market tomorrow."

"Yes, Astrid hassled me to leave the office and come see this place right now."

"Well, we anticipate a feeding frenzy as soon as the listing goes live. A property like this hasn't come on the market in years, and it will most likely go straight to auction."

"I can only imagine. What is this—two, three acres? In this neighborhood? I'm sure every developer would love to get their hands on this," Michael said, surveying the expansive front lawn framed by tall, lush traveler's palms.

"That's precisely why the family has allowed me to show it to you exclusively. We don't want this house to be torn down and turned into some huge condo development."

Michael glanced quizzically at Astrid. "This isn't a tear-down? I thought you wanted to hire some hot-shit French architect to design something on this land."

"No, no, you're confusing this with the place I wanted you to see on Trevose Crescent. This should never be torn down—it's a treasure," Astrid said emphatically.

"I like the grounds, but tell me what's so special about this house—it's not like it's one of those historic Black and Whites."

"Oh, it's much rarer than a Black and White house," Carmen said. "This is one of the few houses built by Frank Brewer, one of Singapore's most prominent early architects. He designed the Cathay Building. Come, let's take a walk around the outside first."

As they circled the house, Astrid began pointing out the distinctive half-timbered gables that gave the house its stately, Tudor-esque feel, the elegant exposed-brick arches in the porte cochere, and other ingenious details like the Mackintosh-inspired ventilation grilles that kept the rooms feeling cool even in the sweltering tropical heat. "See how it combines the Arts and Crafts esthetic with Charles Rennie Mackintosh and Spanish Mission style? You're not going to find such a fusion of architectural styles in one house anywhere else on the planet."

"It's nice, hon, but you're probably the only person in Singapore who would even care about those details! Who lived here before your relatives?" he asked Carmen.

"It was built originally in 1922 for the chairman of Fraser and Neave, and later it became the Belgian ambassador's residence," Carmen replied, adding rather unnecessarily: "This is a rare chance to own one of Singapore's truly historic gems."

The three of them entered the house, and as they wandered through the elegantly proportioned rooms, Michael began to appreciate the place more and more. "I like how high the ceilings are on the ground floor."

"It's a bit creaky in places, but I know just the architect to help give this place a gentle restoration—he worked on my uncle Alfred's place in Surrey and just redid Dumfries House in Scotland for the Prince of Wales," Astrid said.

Standing in the living room, with sunlight flooding through the oriel windows and casting origami shadows onto the parquet wood floors, Michael was suddenly reminded of the drawing room at Tyersall Park and the feeling of unutterable awe that came over him the first time he entered that room to meet Astrid's grandmother. He had originally envisioned his new house as something resembling the contemporary wing of a museum, but now he had another vision of himself in thirty years as a silver-haired eminence, presiding over this grand and historic showplace as business colleagues from all over the world came to pay their respects. He pounded his hand against one of the buttressed walls and said to Astrid, "I like all this old stonework. This house feels rock solid, not like your father's rickety Black and White."

"I'm glad you like it. It has a very different feel from my father's place," Astrid said measuredly.

*It's also bigger than your father's house*, Michael thought. He could already imagine what his brothers would say when they

drove up: *Wah lan eh, ji keng choo seeee baaay tua!** He turned to
Carmen and asked, "So, what will it take to get the keys to the
front door?"

Carmen considered his question for a moment. "On the
open market, this house would go for sixty-five, seventy million, easily. You'd have to make a compelling enough offer for
the family to stop the listing tomorrow morning."

Michael stood at the top of the staircase and fingered
the carved woodwork on the banister. Its art deco sunrays
reminded him of the Chrysler building. "C. K. Wong had four
children, right? I'll offer seventy-four. This way every sibling
gets an extra million for their trouble."

"Let me just call my cousin Geik Choo," Carmen said,
reaching into her Saint Laurent handbag for her phone and
walking discreetly out of the living room.

A few minutes later, she returned. "My cousin thanks you
for the offer. But factoring in stamp duties and my commis-
sion, the family is going to need more. At eighty million, you
have a deal."

"I knew you were going to say that," Michael said with a
laugh. He looked over at Astrid and said, "Honey, how badly
do you want this?"

*Wait a minute—it's you who wants to move*, Astrid thought.
Instead, she said, "I will be very happy in this house if
you are."

"Okay then, eighty it is."

Carmen smiled. This was so much easier than she had
imagined. She disappeared into a bedroom down the hallway
again to call her cousin back.

"How much do you think it's going to take to decorate this
place?" Michael asked Astrid.

"Really depends on what we want to do. It reminds me

---

*    Hokkien slang for "Fucking hell, this house is friggin' HUGE!"

of the sort of country houses you see in the Cotswolds, so I could picture some simple English pieces mixed with Geoffrey Bennison fabrics perhaps. I think it would go well with your historic artifacts and some of my Chinese antiques. And downstairs, maybe we can—"

"The entire downstairs is going to be converted into a state-of-the-art car museum for my collection," Michael interrupted.

"All of it?"

"Of course. That's the first thing I pictured when I walked in the front door. I was like, let's tear all these reception rooms down and make it one vast hall. Then I could put car turntables into the floor. It will be so cool to see my cars revolving around between all those columns."

Astrid looked at him, waiting for him to say, *Just kidding*, but then she realized he was dead serious. "If that's what you want," she finally managed to squeak out.

"Now, what is taking that friend of yours so long? Don't tell me those Wongs are getting greedy and want to take me for another ride."

Just then, Carmen reentered the room, looking rather flushed in the face. "I'm sorry—I hope I wasn't shouting too loudly?"

"No. What happened?" Astrid asked.

"Er, I don't quite know how to say this, but I'm afraid the house has been sold to someone else."

"WHAAAT? I thought we had an exclusive first bid," Michael said.

"I'm very sorry. I thought you did too. But my asshole cousin Quentin played me out. He used your offer to bid up another one that was already in the works."

"I'll top whatever offer your cousin got," Michael said defiantly.

"I already suggested that, but it's apparently a done deal.

The buyer doubled your price to take the house off the market completely. It sold for $160 million."

"$160 million? That's ridiculous! Who the hell bought it?"

"I don't know. My cousin doesn't even know. Some limited liability company in China, obviously as a cover."

"Mainlanders. Of course," Astrid said softly.

"*Kan ni na bu chao chee bye!*"* Michael shouted, kicking the wooden banister in frustration.

"Michael!" Astrid exclaimed in shock.

"What?" Michael looked at her defiantly. "This is all your damn fault! I can't believe you would waste my time like this!"

Carmen huffed. "Why are you blaming your wife? If there's anyone you should be blaming, it's me."

"You're *both* to blame. Astrid, do you have any idea how busy I was today? You shouldn't have demanded I drop everything to come see this godforsaken house if it wasn't really available. Carmen, how the hell did you ever get your real estate license when you can't even do a simple deal like this? Fucking unbelievable!" Michael swore, before storming out of the house.

Astrid sank down onto the top step of the staircase and buried her head in her hands for a moment. "I am so, so sorry."

"Astrid, please, you have nothing to apologize for. I'm sorry."

"Is the banister okay?" Astrid asked, gently patting the scuff mark that Michael's foot had left.

"The banister will be fine. I'm a little more worried about you, to tell the truth."

"I'm perfectly fine. I think this is a beautiful house, but to be honest, I couldn't have cared less if we lived here or not."

---

* A popular and charmingly eye-watering Hokkien phrase that translates literally as "Fuck your mother's smelly rotten pussy."

"I'm not talking about that. I'm just . . ." Carmen paused for a moment, pondering whether to open a Pandora's box. "I'm just wondering what happened to *you*?"

"What do you mean?"

"Okay, I'm going to be very frank with you because we're such old friends: I can't believe the way Michael talks to you, and how you let him get away with it."

"Tsk, that was nothing. Michael just got angry for a moment because he got outbid. He's used to getting what he wants."

"You don't say. But I'm not referring to the fit he threw before he stormed out. I didn't like the way he was talking to you from the moment he arrived."

"How do you mean?"

"You really don't see it, do you? You don't see how much he's changed?" Carmen sighed in frustration. "When I first met Michael six years ago, he seemed like such a gentle soul. Okay, he didn't say very much, but I saw the way he looked at you, and I thought, 'Wow, this guy truly worships her. This is the kind of guy I want.' I was so used to all these spoiled mama's boys who expected to be waited on hand and foot, like my ex, but here was this *man*. This strong, reserved man who was always doing thoughtful little things for you. Do you remember the day we were shopping at Patric's atelier, and Michael ran all around Chinatown for an hour trying to hunt down *kueh tutu*[*] just because you mentioned that your nanny used to take you there to buy it from the *kueh tutu* man who sold it out of those old metal carts?"

"He still does nice little things for me—" Astrid began.

---

[*]   This traditional Singaporean delicacy consists of a small, flower-shaped steamed cake of pounded rice flour filled with brown sugar and either ground peanuts or grated coconut. It is served on a pandan leaf for extra fragrance. The "*kueh tutu* man" used to be a familiar sight in Singapore's Chinatown district but these days is an increasing rarity.

"That's not the point. The man who came to look at this house today was a completely different person than the one I first met."

"Well, he's gained much more confidence. I mean, he's made such a huge success of his business. It's bound to change anyone."

"Clearly. But has he changed for better or worse? When Michael first got here, he gave me a kiss on the cheek. That was the first thing that surprised me—it was so Continental, so unlike the *chin chye*[*] guy I know. And then to top it off he pays me a compliment. But then you're standing there right next to me in the prettiest Dries Van Noten floral dress I've ever seen and he doesn't even say a thing to you."

"Come on, I don't expect him to gush over me every time we see each other. We've been married for so many years now."

"My father gives a million compliments to my mother all day long, and they've been married over forty years. But aside from that, it was his whole manner to you the entire time he was here that got to me. His body language. His little asides. There was this undercurrent of . . . of . . . contempt to everything."

Astrid tried to laugh off her comment.

"This is no joke. The fact that you don't even see it is what's alarming. It's like you've got Stockholm syndrome or something. What happened to "The Goddess"? The Astrid I know would never have put up with this."

Astrid remained silent for a few moments, and then she looked up at her friend. "I do see it, Carmen. I see it all."

"Then why are you letting it happen? Because take it from me, this is a slippery slope you're on. First it's just a few digs here and there, but then one morning you wake up and realize

---

[*]  Hokkien for "easygoing, down-to-earth."

that every conversation you have with your husband is a shouting match."

"It's more complicated than that, Carmen." Astrid took a deep breath and then continued. "The truth is Michael and I hit a big speed bump a few years ago. We were separated for a while and on the brink of divorce."

Carmen's eyes widened. "When?"

"Three years ago. Right around the time of Araminta Lee's wedding. You're the only person on this entire island I've told this to."

"What happened?"

"It's a long story, but it basically boiled down to the fact that Michael was having a hard time coping with the power dynamic in our marriage. Even though I tried my best to be supportive, he felt emasculated by . . . you know, the whole money thing. He felt like a trophy husband, and the way my family treated him wasn't helping much either."

"I can see how being married to Harry Leong's only daughter can't be easy, but come on, most men can only dream of being so lucky," Carmen said.

"That's exactly it. Michael's not like most men. And that's what attracted me to him. He is so smart, and so driven, and he really wanted to make it on his own terms. He's never wanted to use a single family connection to help him get a leg up in his business, and he's always insisted on not taking a cent from me."

"Is that why you guys were living in that little place on Clemenceau Avenue?"

"Of course. He bought that flat with his own money."

"No one could figure that out! I remember everyone was talking about it—*Can you believe Astrid Leong married this ex-army guy and moved into some TINY OLD FLAT? The Goddess has really come down to earth.*"

"Michael didn't marry me because he wanted some goddess. And now that he's finally made it, I'm trying to be more like a traditional wife. I'm trying to let him have his way more, and to win some battles, some of the time."

"Just as long as you don't lose yourself in the process."

"Come on, Carmen, would I ever let that happen? You know, I'm happy that Michael's finally taken an interest in some of the things that matter to me. Like how he dresses. And how we live. I'm glad that he's developed strong opinions, and that he challenges me sometimes. It's quite a turn-on, actually. It reminds me of what originally drew me to him."

"Well, as long as you're happy," Carmen conceded.

"Look at me, Carmen. I'm happy. I've never been happier."

## PARIS

*Excerpts from Rachel's Diary*

*Sunday, June 16*

Traveling to Paris Colette Bing–style was like entering an alternate universe. I never thought I'd eat the best Peking duck of my life at an altitude of 40,000 feet in a dining room more lavish than Empress Cixi's Summer Palace, or get to see *Man of Steel* in the plane's IMAX-designed screening room (it just opened in the U.S., but Adele Deng's family owns one of the biggest cinema chains in the world, so she gets advance screeners of everything). I never imagined I'd witness the sight of six extremely sloshed Chinese girls doing a rendition of "Call Me Maybe" off-key in Mandarin in the plane's karaoke lounge, which had marble walls embedded with pulsating LED lights. Before we knew it, we had landed at Le Bourget Airport, and it was all so civilized—no lines, no customs, no fuss, just three officials who came aboard to stamp our passports and a fleet of black Range Rovers waiting on the tarmac. And, oh yeah, six bodyguards who all looked like Alain Delon in his prime. Colette hired this security detail of ex–French Foreign Legionnaires to follow us around 24/7. "It'll be a fun sight gag," she said.

The gleaming black cars whisked us to the city in no time at all and deposited us at the Shangri-La Hotel, where Colette bought out all the rooms on the two top floors. The whole place had the feel of a private residence, precisely because it used to be the palace of Prince Louis Bonaparte, Napoleon's grandson,* and four years were spent painstakingly restoring it. Everything in our ginormous suite is done in splendid shades of cream and celadon, and there's the prettiest dressing table with a three-way folding mirror that I took a million pictures of from every angle. Somewhere in Brooklyn, I know there's a hipster carpenter/literary agent who can replicate it. I tried to get some shut-eye like Nick but I'm too excited, jet-lagged, and hungover at the same time. 11 hours on a plane + 1 genius Filipino bartender = bad combo

*Monday, June 17*

Woke up this morning to the sight of Nick's cute naked butt silhouetted against a view of the Eiffel Tower and thought I was still dreaming. Then it finally hit me—we're really in the City of Lights! While Nick spent the day poking around bookshops in the Latin Quarter, I joined the girls on their first big shopping expedition. In the motorcade of SUVs, I ended up in a car with Tiffany Yap, who gave me the lowdown on all the other girls: impeccably mannered Stephanie Shi hails from a top political family, and her mother's family has huge mining and property holdings throughout the country. Adele Deng, who has had the same pageboy haircut since kindergarten,

---

* Actually, it was Prince Roland Bonaparte, and he was Napoleon Bonaparte's grandnephew (Rachel is still too hungover to get her facts straight).

is the shopping mall and cinema heiress, and she's married to the son of another party patriarch. Wen Pi Fang's father is the Natural Gas King, and Perrineum Wang, whose chin, nose, and cheekbones are apparently rather new, also possesses the newest fortune. "Ten years ago her father started an e-commerce company in their living room, and now he's China's Bill Gates." And Tiffany herself? "My family's in beverages" was all the girl with the beguiling overbite would say. But guess what? All these girls work at P. J. Whitney Bank, and all have very impressive-sounding titles—Tiffany is an "Associate Managing Director—Private Client Group." So it wasn't a problem for all of you to take off at a moment's notice and come to Paris? "Of course not," Tiffany said.

We arrived at rue Saint-Honoré and everyone scattered to different boutiques. Adele and Pi Fang made a beeline for Balenciaga, Tiffany and Perrineum went mad for Mulberry, Mrs. Bing and the aunties glided toward Goyard, and Colette did Colette. I accompanied Stephanie into Moynat, a leather goods boutique that I'd never even heard of until today. The most exquisite Rejane clutch bag was calling my name, but there was no way I was shelling out €6,000 for a piece of leather—even if it's from a cow that's never known the existence of mosquitoes. Stephanie circled around the curved wall filled from floor to ceiling with bags, studying everything intently. Then she pointed out three handbags. "Would you like to see those three bags, mademoiselle?" the saleswoman asked. "No, I will take everything on that wall *except* those three," Stephanie said, handing over her black palladium credit card. #OMFG #thisjustgotreal

*Tuesday, June 18*

I guess word got out that six of China's biggest weapons of mass consumption were in town, because emissaries from the top boutiques began hand-delivering invitations to the Shangri-La this morning, all offering exclusive perks and dedicated suck-up time. We started out the day on avenue Montaigne, where Chanel opened early for us and hosted a sumptuous breakfast in Colette's honor. As I stuffed my face with the fluffiest omelet I've ever tasted, the girls ignored the food and instead began stuffing themselves into these fluffy fringe dresses. Then it was time for lunch at the Chloé boutique, followed by tea at Dior.

I thought I knew some major shoppers in Goh Peik Lin and Araminta Lee, but I have never seen this level of spending in my entire life! The girls were like a plague of locusts, descending on every boutique and decimating everything in sight, while Colette breathlessly posted every purchase on social media. Swept up in all the excitement, I made my first high-fashion purchase—a pair of beautifully tailored navy slacks I found on the sale rack at Chloé that will go with everything. Needless to say, the sale rack is invisible to the other girls. For them, it's next season's looks or nothing.

Nick decided that he'd had enough after Chanel and took off to visit some taxidermy museum, but Carlton, who had the patience of Job, stayed and watched adoringly as Colette hoovered up every chic object. He won't admit it, but you know it's true love when a dude will go shopping for fifteen hours straight with a bunch of women and their mothers. Of course, Carlton was shopping up a storm too, but he was much quicker about it: While Mrs. Bing was having an existential crisis over whether to buy a €6.8 million ruby necklace at Bulgari or an €8.4 million canary diamond necklace across the street at Boucheron, Carlton ducked out quietly. Twenty minutes later he returned carrying ten shopping bags from Charvet, covertly handing me one. Back at the hotel, I opened it to find a tailored blouse that was pale pink with white stripes, in the softest cotton you can imagine. Carlton must have thought it would go perfectly with my new Chloé pants. What a sweetie!

*Wednesday, June 19*

Today was Couture Day. In the morning, we visited the ateliers of Bouchra Jarrar and Alexis Mabille for private fashion shows. At Bouchra, I witnessed something I've never seen in my life: women going into multi-orgasmic frenzies over *trousers*. Apparently Bouchra's ingeniously cut trousers are like the second coming of, well, your second coming. At the next atelier, Alexis actually appeared at the end of the fashion show and the girls suddenly transformed into frothing tweens at a One Direction concert, trying to impress him and one-up each other in ordering outfits. Nick even encouraged me to get something but I told him I'd rather save the €€€ for our bathroom refurbishment fund. "The bathroom is fully funded, okay. Now please pick out a dress!" Nick insisted. I looked at all the fantastical ball gowns and selected this beautifully structured black jacket that's hand-painted with an ombré effect at the sleeves and tied together at the waist with the most elegant blue silk bow. It's original yet classic, and it's something I can wear until I'm a hundred.

When it was time for them to take my measurements, the vendeuse insisted on measuring every inch of my body. Apparently Nick told them that I needed the matching hand-painted trousers too! It was so fun to watch the artistry of these seamstresses in action—never in my life could I imagine that I'd ever own a couture outfit! I think of Mom, and the backbreaking long hours she had to work in the early years, but how she still found the time to alter the hand-me-downs that came from our cousins so that I'd always look decent at school. I need to get her something really special in Paris.

After an overly froufrou lunch at a restaurant on place des

Vosges that cost more than my bonus last year (thank God Perrineum paid), Carlton and Nick headed off to Molsheim to visit the Bugatti car factory, while Mrs. Bing insisted on visiting the Hermès boutique on rue de Sèvres. (BTW, her feet didn't seem to hurt anymore, even after seventy-two hours of nonstop pavement pounding.) I've never understood the fascination with Hermès, but I had to admit the store was pretty cool—it's set in the Hôtel Lutetia's former indoor pool, with all the merchandise scattered around different levels of the vast atrium. Perrineum was indignant that the store wouldn't close to the public for her and decided to boycott the place. She then proceeded to walk around making disparaging remarks about the other Asian shoppers. "Don't you feel self-conscious trying to shop around *these people*?" she said to me. "Do you have something against rich Asians?" I joked. "These people aren't rich—they're just Henrys!" Perrineum scoffed. "What are Henrys?" She gave me a withering look. "You're an economist—don't you know what HENRY stands for?" I racked my brains, but I still didn't have a clue. Perrineum finally spat it out: "High Earners, Not Rich Yet."

*Thursday, June 20*

Nick and I decided to take a break from shopping today and do something cultural instead. As we were sneaking out early in the morning to visit the Musée Gustave Moreau, we ran into Colette in the elevator. She insisted that we join her for the special breakfast she had planned for everyone at the Jardin du Luxembourg. Since the garden is one of my favorite discoveries from our last trip, I happily agreed.

It was so lovely in the morning—nothing but chic mothers pushing their babies around in prams, dapper old men reading the morning paper, and the plumpest, most contented-looking pigeons I've ever seen. We climbed the steps next to the Medici fountain and sat at a lovely outdoor café. Everyone got café crème or Dammann tea, and Colette ordered a dozen *pains au chocolat*. The waiters soon brought out twelve plates of pastries, but as I was about to bite into mine, Colette hissed, "Stop! Don't eat that!" My coffee hadn't quite kicked in yet, and before I could figure out what was going on, Colette jumped out of her chair and whispered to Roxanne, "Quick, quick! Do it now, while the waiters aren't looking!" Roxanne opened up this big S&M-looking black leather satchel and took out a paper bag filled with *pains au chocolat*. The two women began frantically swapping out the pastries on everyone's plates with the stuff from the bag, while Nick and Carlton laughed hysterically and this very proper-looking couple at the next table stared at us like we were crazy.

Colette declared, "Okay, now you can eat." I took the first bite of my *pain au chocolat*, and it was *amazing*. Airy, flaky, buttery, oozing rich bittersweet chocolate. Colette explained: "These *pains au chocolat* are from Gérard Mulot. They are my favorite, but the problem is they don't have a sit-down café there. And I can only eat my *pain au chocolat* while sipping a good cup of tea. But the decent tea places don't have *pain au chocolat* as good as this, and of course they won't allow you to bring anything in from another bakery. So the only way to solve this quandary was to resort to a switcheroo. But isn't this perfect? Now we get to enjoy the best morning tea, with the best *pains au chocolat*, in the best park in the world." Carlton shook his head and said, "You're raving bonkers, Colette!" And then he consumed his chocolate croissant in two bites.

In the afternoon, some of the girls went to a private shopping party at L'Eclaireur while Nick and I accompanied Stephanie and her mother to the Kraemer Gallery. Nick knew of this antiques dealer and wanted to see it. He jokingly called it "the billionaire's IKEA," but when we got there I realized he wasn't kidding—it was a palatial mansion by the Parc Monceau filled with the most astounding furniture and objets. Every piece was museum quality and seemed to have once been owned by a king or queen. Mrs. Shi, this mousy woman who until now hadn't joined in the fashion frenzy, suddenly transformed into one of those QVC shopping addicts and started buying up the place like a whirling dervish. Nick stood on the sidelines, chatting with Monsieur Kraemer, and after a few minutes the man ducked away. He soon returned bearing one of their historical ledgers and, much to Nick's delight, showed us some old receipts for purchases made by Nick's great-grandfather in the early 1900s!

*Friday, June 21*

Guess who showed up in Paris today? Richie Yang. Obviously he just couldn't bear to miss out on the action. He even tried to stay at the Shangri-La, but with all the suites booked by our party, he ended up "making do" with the penthouse at the Mandarin Oriental. He came by the Shangri-La bearing baskets of expensive-looking fruit from Hédiard—all for Colette's mother. Meanwhile, Carlton conveniently announced that he was offered an incredible vintage sports car and had to go meet with the owner somewhere outside of Paris. I offered to accompany him, but he mumbled some quick excuses and rushed off alone. I'm not sure if I buy his excuses—it's so strange that he would run off like this. Why would he flee the match just as his chief competitor entered the ring?

In the evening, Richie insisted on inviting everyone to "the most exclusive restaurant in Paris. You've practically got to kill someone to get a reservation," he said. The restaurant was inexplicably decorated like a corporate boardroom, and Richie arranged for all of us to have the chef's tasting menu—the "Amusements and Tantalizations in Sixteen Movements."

Despite how unappetizing this sounded, the food turned out to be quite spectacular and inventive, especially the artichoke-and-white-truffle soup and the razor clams in a sweet garlic sabayon, but I could see that Mrs. Bing and the aunties weren't half as thrilled. Colette's grandmother looked especially puzzled by the seafood "raw-cooked in cold steam," the startlingly colored foams, and the artfully composed dwarf vegetables, and kept asking her daughter, "Why are they giving us all the vegetable scraps? Is it because we're Chinese?" Mrs. Bing replied, "No, everyone gets the same dishes. Look how many French people are eating here—this place must be very authentic."

After the meal, the elders headed back to the hotel while Pied Piper Richie announced that he was taking us to some ultra-exclusive club started by the director David Lynch. "I've been a member since day one," he boasted. Nick and I begged off and took a lovely evening stroll along the Seine. Arriving back at the hotel, we passed Mrs. Bing, who was standing at the door of her suite talking furtively to a Chinese maid from housekeeping. Catching my eye, she beckoned us over excitedly. "Rachel, Rachel, look what this nice maid gave me!" In her hand was a white plastic trash bag filled with dozens of bottles of the hotel's Bulgari bath gel, shampoo, and conditioner. "Do you want some? She can get more!" I told her that Nick and I used our own shampoos and didn't touch the hotel toiletries. "Can I have yours, then? And the shower caps too?" Mrs. Bing asked eagerly. We gathered up all our toiletries and headed back to her suite. She came to the door and acted like a junkie who had just been handed free premium-grade heroin. "*Aiyah!* I should have been asking you to collect these bottles for me all week long! Wait a minute, don't go away!" She returned with a bag containing five plastic bottles of water. "Here, take some water! We boil it fresh every day in the electric kettle so we don't have to pay for the hotel's bot-

tled water!" Nick was desperately trying to maintain a straight
face when Grandma Bing came to the door and said, "Lai Di,
why don't you invite them in?"

We entered her massive suite and discovered Auntie Pan
Di, Mrs. Shi, and Mrs. Wen huddled over a large portable hot
pot in the dining room. On the floor was a huge Louis Vuit-
ton trunk filled with packets of ramen in all kinds of flavors.
"Shrimp and pork ramen?" Auntie Pan Di asked, stirring a
big batch of noodles with a pair of chopsticks. Mrs. Bing
whispered conspiratorially, "Don't tell Colette, but we do this
every night! We're so much happier eating ramen than all this
fancy French food!" Mrs. Wen said, "*Aiyah*, I've had constipa-
tion every single day from all this cheese we've been forced to
eat." I asked them why they didn't just go downstairs to Shang
Palace, the hotel's Michelin-starred Chinese restaurant, for
dinner. Mrs. Shi, who earlier today bought an antique clock*
for €4.2 million at the Kraemer Gallery after looking at it for
less than three minutes, exclaimed, "We tried going there after
that awful French dinner, but all the dishes were so expensive
we walked out! Twenty-five euros for fried rice? *Tai leiren le!*"†

*Saturday, June 22*

Colette knocked on our door at the crack of dawn and woke
us up. Had we seen Carlton? Had he called? Apparently he
didn't return to the hotel last night, and he wasn't answering his phone. Colette seemed worried, but Nick didn't think
there was anything to worry about. "He'll turn up. Sometimes
it takes a while to negotiate with these car collectors—he's
probably still in the middle of doing his deal." In the mean-

---

*  An exceptional Louis XV long-case clock by Jean-Pierre Latz, almost iden-
tical to the one made for Frederick the Great of Prussia at Neues Palais in
Potsdam.
†  Mandarin for "That's insane."

time, Richie invited everyone over to his penthouse suite for sunset cocktails on the roof terrace. "A little party in Colette's honor," he called it. While the girls spent the afternoon getting spa treatments, Nick and I took a blissful nap on the grass at the Parc Monceau.

In the early evening, we arrived to Richie's party at the Mandarin Oriental only to find that the security men posted by the VIP elevator wouldn't let us through—our names were apparently "not on the list." After a phone call to Colette, we managed to clear things up and were whisked to the roof terrace, where we discovered that this wasn't just a "little cocktail party" for our group. The penthouse was packed with an extremely glam crowd and decorated like a high-tech product launch. Giant obelisk topiaries festooned with lights lined the parapet, an elaborate stage was set up on one end, and along one side of the terrace stood half a dozen celebrity chefs manning different food stations.

I immediately felt underdressed in my cornflower blue silk shirtdress and strappy sandals, especially when guest of honor Colette made an entrance wearing the enormous canary diamond necklace her mother had just bought and a stunning black strapless Stéphane Rolland gown with a long ruffled skirt that seemed to go on for miles and miles. Mrs. Bing, meanwhile, was virtually unrecognizable with her expertly painted face, her hair swept up into a beehive do, and the biggest set of sapphires set against a red Elie Saab cocktail dress with a plunging neckline.

But the biggest surprise of all—Carlton was there! He made no mention about being MIA for twenty-four hours and seemed his usual charming self. Turns out he knew plenty of people at the party—many friends from the London-Dubai-Shanghai party axis had flown in, and soon I was swept up in a frenzy of introductions. I met Sean and Anthony (two charming brothers who were DJing the party), an Arab prince Carlton knew from Stowe, some French countess who wouldn't stop telling me how disgusted she was with U.S. foreign policy, and then things really got crazy when some famous Chinese pop star showed up. Little did I realize the night was about to get a whole lot crazier.

# THE MANDARIN ORIENTAL

PARIS, FRANCE

Nick climbed the steps to the uppermost deck of the roof
terrace, trying to find a quiet spot away from the crowd below.
He didn't particularly enjoy these raucous parties, and this
affair seemed even more over the top than usual—every squil-
lionaire within private-jet flying radius was here, and there
were far too many outsize egos filling up the space.

A carefully planted row of Italian cypresses started shaking
fitfully behind him, and Nick could hear some guy moaning,
"Baby . . . baby . . . baby ohhh!" He turned around discreetly
to leave, but Richie suddenly ducked out from behind the
trees, tucking his shirt back into his trousers as a girl skulked
off sheepishly in the other direction.

"Oh, it's you," Richie said unabashedly. "You having a
good time?"

"The view's terrific," Nick said diplomatically.

"Isn't it? If only these stupid Parisians would allow skyscrapers to be built in their city. The views would be unbelievable, and they'd make a killing selling them. Hey, you never
saw me up here, okay?"

"Of course."

"You didn't see that girl, okay?"

"What girl?"

Richie grinned. "You're A-plus on my list now. Hey, I'm sorry for that mix-up downstairs, but I can see why my security wouldn't let you up. No offense, but you don't exactly look like you're dressed for this crowd."

"My apologies—we were in a park all day and fell asleep. Rachel wanted to go back to the hotel to change, but I thought this party was just going to be drinks on a rooftop. If I knew you were going to be wearing a burgundy velvet smoking jacket, we would have dressed up."

"Rachel looks slammin'. Girls can get away with anything, but we guys have to make more of an effort, don't we? You can only get away with dressing this casually if you're flashing a Billionaire Wristband."

"What's that?"

Richie gestured to Nick's wrist. "Your watch. I see you're wearing a new Patek."

"New? Actually, this watch was my grandfather's."*

"Nice, but you know Pateks are basically considered middle-class watches these days. It wouldn't qualify as a Billionaire Wristband like mine. Here, check this out, my latest Richard Plumper Tourbillon," Richie said, thrusting his wrist within several millimeters of Nick's nose. "I'm a VIC—very important client—of Richard Plumper, and they let me buy it straight off the display at the Baselworld Watch Show. It's not even going to be available till October."

"Looks very impressive."

"This Plumper's got seventy-seven complications, and it's made from a titanium-and-silicon compound that is spun in

---

* An exceedingly rare Patek Philippe 18K gold single-button chronograph with a vertically positioned register and sector dial. Ref. 130, manufactured in 1928, given to Nick by his grandmother when he turned twenty-one.

a centrifuge at such high speeds that it bonds on a molecular level."

"Wow."

"I could be wearing a T-shirt and torn jeans with my balls hanging out but still get into any of the hottest clubs or restaurants in the world just by sporting this. Every doorman and maître d' is trained to spot a Richard Plumper from a mile away, and they all know it costs more than a yacht. That's what I mean by Billionaire Wristband, heh heh!"

"Tell me, how exactly do you read the time on that?"

"See those two little spokes with the green stars at the tips?"

Nick squinted his eyes. "I think so . . ."

"When those green stars align with those gears on the cable-and-pulley system, that's how you tell the hour and the minute. The gears are actually made of unclassified experimental metals that are intended for the next generation of spy drones."

"You don't say."

"Yes, the entire watch is constructed to withstand forces up to ten thousand Gs. That's equivalent to being strapped to the outside of a rocket while it's breaking through the earth's outer atmosphere."

"But if you were actually exposed to such forces, wouldn't you be dead?"

"Heh heh! Indeed. But just knowing your watch would survive makes it worth having a Plumper, doesn't it? Here, I'll let you try it on."

"I couldn't possibly."

Richie was momentarily distracted by a text message on his phone. "Wow, guess who just arrived? Mehmet Sabançi! That guy's family basically owns all of Greece."

"Turkey, actually," Nick said almost reflexively.

"Oh, you've heard of him?"

"He's one of my best friends."

Richie looked momentarily shocked. "*He is?* How in the world do you know him?"

"We were at Stowe together."

"You guys met at a ski resort?"

"Not Stowe, Vermont. *Stowe*—it's a school in England."

"Oh. I went to Harvard Business School."

"Yes, you've mentioned that a number of times."

Just then, Mehmet stepped out of the elevator and onto the terrace. Looking down at the late arrival, Richie said excitedly, "Whew—who is that spectacular babe he brought with him?"

Nick glanced down. "My God . . . I don't believe it!"

. . .

On the main terrace, Carlton leaned against a railing alongside his Cambridge chum Harry Wentworth-Davies, surveying the scene. "You need to try these foie gras cronuts," Harry yelled into his ear. "Better than crack cocaine. And I couldn't believe that bloke on the telly who goes around the world terrorizing other people's restaurants served it to me."

"This is how Richie draws his crowd. Heaps of pretentious food and pricey booze," Carlton said with barely veiled contempt.

"Quite right—this Romanée-Conti isn't shabby at all," Harry said, swirling his goblet.

"It's a bit too obvious for me, but I will help to deplete as much of these reserves as I possibly can," Carlton said.

"Not sure you want to get too sloshed tonight, mate," Harry cautioned. "Shouldn't you be in tip-top condition for the main event later?"

"Quite right. The smart thing to do would be to stop drinking now, wouldn't it?" Carlton deliberated, before downing another glassful in several quick gulps. He scanned the

crowd, recognizing most of Richie's cronies who had gathered here. It was a wonder Colette didn't suspect anything. He
shouldn't have come tonight. Being here—seeing everyone
trying way too hard to have fun—only made him angrier, and
he could feel the blood pounding in his temples. Four hours
ago he was in Antwerp, and he wished he'd stayed there, or
continued on to Brussels and caught the next flight back to
Shanghai. Actually, what he really wanted to do was go to England, but Mr. Tin had advised him not to enter the UK for a
few years. How did he ever fuck things up to this extent? To
be banned from the one place where he felt like he could truly
breathe?

"Colette's looking rather spectacular," Harry said to Carlton, eyeing her as she posed for a picture with Rachel by the
pyramid of champagne glasses.

"She always does."

"That girl she's posing with looks rather like you."

"That's my sister," Carlton replied. Rachel was the reason he had come back today. Part of him resented her for
it, but he found himself strangely protective of her at the
same time. He just couldn't ditch her in Paris like that. It had
been like this from the moment they met. He was all ready
to hate her, this girl who had come out of nowhere and set
off an atomic bomb in the midst of his family, but she had
turned out to be nothing like what he had expected. She was
different from all the other women in his life, and Nick was
one of the few guys he could actually stand being around.
What was it? he wondered. Was it that Nick had also gone
to Stowe? Or was it the way Nick didn't feel the need to vie
for position with Richie like all the other party parasites here
tonight?

"You never told me you had a sister," Harry interrupted
his thoughts again.

"I do. She's quite a bit older, though."

"You look like you could be twins. That's the trouble with you chinks—you never bloody age."

"We don't for a while, but then there's a tipping point where we go from looking twenty one night to two hundred the next morning."

"Well, if they all look like your sister or Colette at first, sign me up. Now tell me, what's the deal with you and Colette these days? One minute you're on, one minute you're off, I just can't keep track anymore."

"I can't either," Carlton said. He was so sick of the games Colette was playing. All week long, she had been dropping hints every time they passed by a jeweler. He knew that when he refused to go into Mauboussin with her on Tuesday, she had put Plan Richie into action and sent for him to come to Paris. She could be so fucking childish sometimes. As if having Richie here throwing her a party with his daddy's dirty money was going to make him jealous.

Carlton felt Harry jabbing his ribs. "Hey, do you know that girl over there? White dress, nine o'clock."

"Harry, someday you're going to realize that not all Asians know each other."

"You can't blame me for getting excited—that's quite possibly the fittest bird I've ever seen! I'm going in."

"Race you there," Carlton said. If Colette wanted to play games, he could play too. He gave his jacket lapel a tug, grabbed two glasses of wine from a passing server, and strode confidently across the terrace toward the girl in white. Just as he got to her, Nick suddenly cut in front of him and, to his astonishment, wrapped her in a warm embrace.

"Astrid! What the hell are you doing here?" Nick said excitedly.

"Nicky!" Astrid squealed. "But I thought you and Rachel were in China."

"We were, but we flew to Paris on the spur of the moment

with Rachel's brother and some new friends. Oh, speak of the devil, here's Carlton. Carlton, this is my cousin Astrid from Singapore."

"Pleasure to meet you." Astrid extended her hand to Carlton, who was completely stunned by the sudden turn of events. *This extraordinary creature he was about to hit on was Nick's cousin?*

"And this is my great friend, Mehmet," Nick said, introducing Carlton. "You rascal—what are you doing hanging out with my cousin in Paris?"

Mehmet patted Nick on the back heartily. "It's a complete coincidence! I'm here on business, and we ran into each other at Le Voltaire. I was sitting down at a lunch meeting and who should come through the door but Charlotte Gainsbourg . . . with Astrid! Of course I had to say hello—I couldn't resist making all my associates sick with envy. Then Astrid invited me to dinner, and I talked her into making this pit stop."

By this point, Rachel and Colette had joined the group. "Astrid! Mehmet? This can't be happening!" Rachel shrieked, hugging both of them in utter delight.

Colette was introduced all around, and she couldn't help but scrutinize every inch of Astrid. So this was the couture-wearing cousin that Rachel had told her about. Astrid's sexy gold sandals she recognized as being handmade in Capri by Da Costanzo. Her white patent-leather clutch was vintage Courrèges. Her gold Etruscan-style cuff bracelets with the facing lion heads were Lalaounis. But that little white pleated dress she just couldn't place. My God, it was perfection, the way the linen skimmed her body, just tight enough to drive all the men wild but not so tight it looked vulgar. And those sundial pleats at the neckline to accentuate the sensuality of the collarbone—pure genius. She just HAD to know who designed it.

"I am a fashion blogger—would you mind if I took a picture of you?" she asked.

"Colette's being modest. She is THE most popular fashion blogger in China," Nick bragged.

"Um, of course," Astrid replied in surprise.

"Roxanne!" Colette yelled. Her trusty assistant came running over and snapped a few pictures of Colette and Astrid posing together. Then Roxanne began to take notes as Colette quizzed Astrid on everything she was wearing.

"Now, I just need some caption info. I recognize your shoes and your handbag, of course, and the bracelets are Lalaounis—"

"Actually, they're not," Astrid interrupted.

"Oh. Who did them?"

"They're Etruscan."

"I know, but who designed them?"

"I have no idea. They were made in 650 BC."

Colette stared in wonder at the museum artifacts dangling so casually on Astrid's wrists. Now she wanted some herself. "Okay then, most important, tell me which genius designed your fabulous dress. It's Josep Font, isn't it?"

"Oh, this? I bought it today at Zara."

For the rest of her life, Roxanne would never forget the look on Colette's face.

· · ·

A few hours later, Rachel and Nick found themselves having a late supper with Astrid and Mehmet at Monsieur Bleu, the brasserie tucked away at the back of the Palais de Tokyo. As Rachel took the first bite of her sole meunière, she looked around the room, taking in the intriguing light fixtures, the marble-backed banquettes, and the shimmering bronze bas-reliefs. "Astrid, we've been eating at super-fancy places all week, but this is by far my favorite meal. Thanks for bringing us here."

Mehmet chimed in. "I quite agree! There's something

about this place that manages to be simple and yet envelop-
ingly luxurious at the same time. It doesn't compete with the
food, but one does feel more special just being here."

Astrid smiled. "I'm so happy you all like it. I wanted to
come here because I'm thinking of commissioning the architect of this space—Joseph Dirand—to build our next house.
It's actually why I came to Paris."

"I can't wait to see what he does for you," Mehmet said.

"Didn't you just move into a new house last year?" Nick
asked.

"We did, but we're quickly outgrowing it. We almost
bought a historic Frank Brewer house on Cluny Park Road,
but it fell through at the last minute. So we've decided to build
on a piece of land I have in Bukit Timah."

Nick looked around the table and chuckled. "I still can't
believe the four of us are here together. It's such a small
world!"

"And to think, I almost wanted to skip the party. But with
my family doing business with the Yangs, I felt like I needed
to show my face," Mehmet said.

"I'm so glad we went," Astrid said. "It was total seren-
dipity! I'm just sorry your brother and his girlfriend couldn't
join us."

"I think Carlton wanted to, but he felt obligated to stay at
the party with Colette. And she couldn't leave, being the guest
of honor."

"Colette's quite a character. I've never had someone want
to know about every single thing I'm wearing. I was half afraid
she was going to end up asking what brand of underwear I
had on."

"She very well might have, if she hadn't been so shocked
that you bought your dress at Zara!" Rachel laughed.

"I don't know why anyone would be shocked by that. I
buy clothes everywhere—vintage shops, street vendors . . ."

"Colette and her friends live and breathe for high fashion. Frankly, I've hit my limit with them," Nick admitted.

"It has been nonstop shopping since the minute we arrived. It was fascinating for the first couple of days, but then it just got tedious," Rachel explained. "I don't want to complain, since Colette's been so generous with us, but I only came because I thought I'd get to spend more time with my brother."

Astrid leaned closer in. "What's it been like getting to know your new family?"

"Quite frustrating, actually. I've only managed to see my father once since arriving in China."

"Only once?"

"We can't quite figure out what's happening, but we think it has something to do with my father's wife. We haven't met her at all since setting foot in China. Rather odd, don't you think?"

"Maybe you should take a break from China and come down to Singapore for a week," Astrid suggested.

Nick's brow furrowed. It was already challenging enough getting Rachel through this trip with her family. He didn't want to complicate things any further by going to Singapore and facing all those minefields. Where would he and Rachel even stay?

As if reading his mind, Astrid said, "You're welcome to stay with me. Cassian would be thrilled to see you. As I'm sure many others will," she couldn't help adding.

Nick went quiet for a few moments, and Rachel didn't know quite what to say.

"Or you two could always come back to Istanbul with me," Mehmet said, breaking the awkward silence.

"Ohh! I would love to visit Istanbul!" Rachel said.

"It's only three hours from Paris on my plane, and we're having the most glorious weather this summer," Mehmet

said tantalizingly. "You should come too, Astrid. Come for a
few days."

. . .

After dinner, the four of them strolled leisurely along the
terrace steps of the Palais de Tokyo leading up to avenue du
Président Wilson. Rachel checked her phone and saw that
Colette had left a number of text messages.

> 10:26 p.m.—Sat.
> Is Carlton with you at restaurant?

> 10:57 p.m.—Sat.
> If Carlton calls you, please let me know!

> 11:19 p.m.—Sat.
> Never mind . . . found him.

> 11:47 p.m.— Sat.
> Please call me ASAP.

> 12:28 a.m.—Sun.
> URGENT!!! CALL ME PLEASE!!!

Rachel gasped upon reading the last message and immediately dialed Colette's cell number.

"Hello?" a muffled-sounding voice answered.

"Colette? It's Rachel. Is this Colette?"

"Rachel! Oh my God! Where have you been? Where
are you?"

"What's wrong, Colette? What happened?" Rachel said,
alarmed by Colette's near-hysterical tone.

"It's Carlton . . . You *must* help me. Please."

# THE SHANGRI-LA

"Oh thank God you're here! Thank God!" Colette cried as she opened the door, letting Rachel, Nick, Astrid, and Mehmet into her sprawling duplex suite. Rachel gave her a concerned hug, and Colette immediately broke down in sobs against her shoulder.

"Are you okay? Is Carlton okay?" Rachel asked, leading the suddenly fragile girl to the nearest sofa.

"Where's everyone?" Nick asked, noticing that Colette was unusually sans entourage.

"I told everyone I was exhausted and sent them to their rooms. I couldn't let them find out what was happening!"

"What *is* happening?" Rachel asked.

Trying to compose herself, Colette said, "Oh, it's been terrible! Just terrible! After you guys left the party, this baby grand piano was wheeled out on the stage. Then John Major appeared and asked me to stand next to him while he serenaded me—"

"The former prime minister of Britain serenaded you?" Nick cut in, utterly bewildered.

"I'm sorry, I mean John Legend."

"I'm so relieved," Mehmet remarked drily to Astrid.

"So John began to sing 'All of Me,'" Colette continued tearfully, "and at the end of the song, Richie got onstage, dropped to his knees dramatically, and asked me to marry him."

Rachel and Nick both gasped.

"He ambushed me right in front of everyone! Apparently my mother and the girls were in on this—that's why so many friends from China showed up at the party. I didn't know what to say. I just stood there and noticed Gordon Ramsay over by the carrot truffle fries and all I could think was, *What is Gordon going to think if I say no?*"

"What did you do?" Rachel asked.

"I tried to laugh it off. I said, 'Oh come on, Richie, this is a prank, right?' And Richie said, 'Does this look like a prank?' He takes a velvet box out of his pocket and thrusts this ring in my face. I'm looking at it, this thirty-two-carat blue diamond from Repossi, and I'm thinking, 'AS IF I would ever wear a ring from Repossi! This man doesn't know me, and I'm not in love with him.' So I said, 'I'm so honored, but you're going to have to give me time.' Richie said, 'What do you mean *give you time*? We've been dating exclusively for three years now.' And I said, 'Come on, we haven't exactly been exclusive,' and all of a sudden Richie's face got all twisted up and he began ranting, 'What the hell do you mean by that? You've strung me along for three years now! I'm sick of waiting, and I'm sick of your games. Do you have any idea how much I've spent on tonight? Do you think John Legend flies to Paris for just anyone?' Then suddenly Carlton, who had been standing right in front of the stage, hollered, '*Hundan!*[*] Can't you get the message? SHE'S JUST NOT THAT INTO YOU!' And before I knew what

---

[*]    Mandarin for "prick."

was happening, Richie screamed '*Nong sa bi suo luan!*,'* leaped off the stage onto Carlton, and started punching him in the face!"

"Jesus! Is Carlton okay?" Rachel asked.

"He's a bit battered, but he's okay. Mario Batali, though—"

"What happened to Mario?" Astrid cut in, alarmed.

"As Carlton and Richie were rolling on the ground trying to kill each other, my bodyguards tried to get in there and break it up, but it just made things worse, because the four of them bashed into Mario's food station, and this vat of olive oil where he was deep-frying the fritto misto got toppled over and burst into flames. The next thing you know Mario's ponytail was on fire!"

"Oh no! Poor Mario!" Astrid clasped her hands to her face in horror.

"Thank God Mrs. Shi was standing nearby. She knew exactly what to do—she grabbed the can of baking soda and immediately emptied it onto Mario's head. She saved his life!"

"I'm so glad Mario's all right." Astrid sighed in relief.

"So what happened after that?" Nick asked.

"The fight pretty much ended the party, and I managed to drag Carlton back to the hotel, but as I was trying to help him clean up his wounds, we got into the biggest row we've ever had. Oh Rachel, I know he was drunk, but he started spewing such hurtful things . . . he accused me of playing him against Richie . . . he said I had no one to blame for this whole fiasco but myself, and then he stormed out of the room."

Rachel thought her brother's accusations weren't actually that far off the mark, but she tried to be sympathetic. "You probably need to just let him cool down a bit. Things will be better by the morning."

"But we can't wait until morning! After Carlton left, I got

---

*   Shanghainese for "bastard with shrunken testicles."

a call from Honey Chai, the gossip columnist. She's in Shanghai, but she had already heard all about Richie and Carlton's fight. Then she told me something even more alarming—apparently several months ago, Richie challenged Carlton to a drag race, and it's happening tonight!"

"Drag race? You must be joking," Rachel said.

"Do I look like I'm joking?" Colette frowned.

"Aren't they a little old for this?" Rachel asked. Drag racing sounded so juvenile to her, like something out of *Rebel Without a Cause*.

"Hiyah, you don't understand! This isn't some kiddie race—they'll be driving these super-fast cars through the streets at night, evading police all the way. It's going to be so dangerous! Honey Chai heard that Richie and Carlton are staking ten million dollars against each other, and people all over Asia are betting on this race—that's why so many of Richie's friends are here in Paris! Almost every guy I know is obsessed with racing these days."

Nick chimed in, "Actually, I read an article about this in the paper. All these Chinese kids from rich families are taking part in illegal drag races around the world—Toronto, Hong Kong, Sydney—getting into huge wrecks and damaging millions of dollars in property along the way. Now I know why Carlton was doing so many test laps around the track at Bugatti the other day!"

Colette nodded grimly. "Yes, I thought he was just buying cars for his side business, but now we know the real reason. And he's been so emotionally erratic these past few days—the disappearing act, the drinking, the fighting—it's all because of this goddamn race! I feel so stupid, I should have seen this coming from a mile away."

"Come on, none of us suspected either," Rachel said.

Colette looked around the room uneasily, trying to decide how much of the story she wanted to tell. "You know, this isn't the first time Richie and Carlton have tried this. This happened before in London."

"That's how Carlton got into that car wreck, wasn't it?" Nick asked.

Colette nodded sadly. "He was racing Richie down Sloane Street, and his car"—her voice was suddenly cracking—"his car spun out of control and crashed into a building."

"Wait a minute, I think I read about this . . . wasn't it a Ferrari that smashed into the Jimmy Choo boutique?" Astrid piped in.

"That was it! But that's not the whole story. There were other passengers with Carlton. Two girls were inside the car—a British girl who will never walk again and a Chinese girl who . . . who *died*. It was a horrible tragedy, all covered up by the Baos."

Rachel's face went pale. "Carlton told you all this?"

"*I was there*, Rachel. I was in the other car—the Lambor-rhi~ghini that Richie was driving. The girl who died was a friend of mine who went to LSE," Colette tearfully revealed.

Everyone stared in shock at Colette.

"It's all beginning to make sense now," Nick said in a hushed tone, thinking back to what his mother had told him about the accident.

Colette continued. "Carlton hasn't been the same since the crash. He's never been able to get over it—he blames himself and he blames Richie. I think he feels like he can somehow redeem himself by winning this race. But we can't let him get into any car tonight. He's in no condition—not physically and especially not mentally. Rachel, can you please talk some sense into him? I've been calling him nonstop, and of course he isn't picking up my calls. But I think he'll listen to you."

With the full gravity of the situation finally sinking in, Rachel picked up her phone and dialed Carlton's number. "It's gone straight to voice mail."

"I was hoping he'd pick up if he saw your number." Colette sighed.

"We'll just have to go to him. Where's this race taking place?" Nick asked.

"That's the thing—I have no idea. Everyone's just disappeared. Roxanne's off with my security team trying to track them down, but she hasn't had any luck so far."

Astrid suddenly spoke up. "What's Carlton's phone number?"

"It's 86 135 8580 9999."

Taking out her phone, Astrid began dialing Charlie Wu's private line. "Hey you! No, no, everything's fine, thank you. Um, hope you don't mind, but I have a big favor to ask. Does that security whiz still work for you?" She paused, lowering her voice. "The one who tracked *youknowwho* down with just a mobile-phone number a couple of years ago? Great. Could you help me track down the location of this phone? No, really, I'm absolutely fine. I'm just trying to help some friends out—I'll tell you the whole story later."

A few minutes later, Astrid's phone buzzed back with a text message. "Found him," she said with a grin. "Right now, it looks like Carlton's at a commercial garage on avenue de Malakoff, right next to Porte Maillot."

PARIS—2:45 A.M.

Rachel, Nick, and Colette huddled in the backseat of the Range Rover as it sped toward Carlton's location. Sitting in silence, Rachel gazed out at the mostly empty boulevards of the Sixteenth Arrondissement, the streetlamps illuminating the elegant façades with that particular golden hue only to be found in Paris. She thought about how best to handle Carlton in his current state and wondered whether they would even get to him in time.

Suddenly they had arrived at avenue de Malakoff, and the chauffeur gestured toward the lone garage that seemed to be a hive of activity. Rachel stared in astonishment as the full extent of the race operation that had been months in the planning finally became clear to her. Through the partially raised garage door, a team of mechanics bustled around a carbon blue Bugatti Veyron Super Sport* as if it were being prepared for the Formula One final, and several guys she recognized from the party stood outside the garage smoking. Rachel whispered to Nick, "Can you believe this? I had no idea it would be this much of a production!"

"You've seen how the women in this crowd spend their money; this is how the guys spend it," Nick commented discreetly.

"Look, look! There's Carlton standing over there with Harry Wentworth-Davies. Ugh, I should have known that wanker was part of all this!" Colette said.

Rachel took a deep breath. "I think it's best that I try to talk to Carlton on my own. He might be more receptive if the three of us aren't ganging up on him."

"Yes, yes, we'll just stay in the car," Colette anxiously agreed.

Rachel got out of the car and approached the garage, and Carlton suddenly looked up and noticed them. Grimacing, he staggered out to the middle of the street and blocked Rachel from coming any farther. "You guys shouldn't be here. How did you even find me in the first place?"

"Does it really matter?" Rachel said, studying her brother with concern. His left eye was blackened, he had a bruise on

---

\*  The Veyron, also proclaimed "the fastest street-legal production car in the world," set a top speed of 267.856 mph. Park one in your garage today for $2.7 million.

his jaw, a nasty cut on his bottom lip, and God knows what other injuries under his racing overalls. "Carlton, please don't go through with this—you know you're not in any condition to race tonight."

"I've sobered up—I know what I'm doing."

*Like hell you have*, Rachel thought. Knowing it was useless arguing with someone who had clearly had too much to drink, she tried a different tactic. "Carlton, I know what happened tonight. I can totally understand your anger, I really can."

"I don't know how you could possibly understand at all."

Rachel grasped his arm encouragingly. "Look, you have nothing to prove to Richie anymore! Can't you see that he's already lost? He's been totally humiliated by Colette. Can't you see how much she loves you? Be the bigger man and walk away from this race now."

Jerking his arm away, Carlton said gruffly, "This isn't the time to big sister me. Just get out of here, please."

"Carlton, I know about London," Rachel said, looking him in the eyes. "Colette told me the whole story . . . I know what you're feeling."

Carlton looked taken aback for a moment, but then his eyes narrowed in anger. "You think you know everything, don't you? You come to China for two weeks and you think you're the expert on all of us. Well, you don't know a thing! You have no idea how I really feel. You have no clue how much trouble you've caused me, caused my family!"

"What do you mean?" Rachel looked at him in surprise.

"You don't even know the damage you've done to my father just by coming to China! Can't you get the hint that he's been avoiding you like the plague? Haven't you figured out why you're staying at the Peninsula? It's because my mother would rather die than let you set foot in her house! Do you know I've been spending time with you just to piss her off? Why can't you mind your own business and leave us alone?"

His words hit her like a ton of bricks, and she took a few steps back, feeling momentarily winded. Colette sprang out of the car, stomped over to Carlton in her black-and-gold Walter Steiger Unicorn heels, and began yelling right in his face. "How dare you talk like that to your sister! Do you know how lucky you are to have someone like her looking out for you? No, you don't. You take everyone for granted and only love feeling sorry for yourself. What happened in London was a tragedy, but it wasn't just your fault. It was my fault, it was Richie's fault—we were all to blame. Winning this race isn't going to bring anyone back from the dead, and it's not going to make you feel any better. But go ahead, get into your car. Go and race Richie. The both of you can go measure your dicks and crash your million-dollar sports cars into the Arc de Triomphe for all I care!"

Carlton stood stock-still for a moment, not looking at either of them. Then he yelled, "Fuck you! Fuck all of you!" before heading back toward the garage.

Colette threw up her hands in resignation and started to walk back to the SUV. Unexpectedly, Carlton sank down onto the curb, clasping his head as if it were about to explode. Rachel turned and looked at him for a moment. All of a sudden, he seemed like a lost little boy. She sat down on the curb next to him and put her hand on his back. "Carlton, I'm sorry for causing your family so much pain. I had no idea about any of this. All I ever wanted was to get to know you, and to get to know your father and mother better. I won't go back to China if it's been that hurtful to you. I promise you I'll go straight home to New York. But please, *please* don't get in that car. I don't want to see you get hurt again. *You're my brother, goddamit, you're the only brother I've got.*"

Carlton's eyes brimmed with tears, and bowing his head, he said in a muffled voice, "I'm sorry. I don't know what's come over me. I didn't mean to say those things."

"I know, I know," Rachel said softly as she patted his back.

Seeing that things had calmed down, Colette approached the two of them gingerly. "Carlton, I called off Richie's proposal. Will you *please* call off this stupid race?"

Carlton nodded wearily, and the women glanced at each other in relief.

# PART THREE

*Behind every fortune lies a great crime.*

—HONORÉ DE BALZAC

# SHEK O

## HONG KONG

"Oh good, you're early," Corinna said, as Kitty was shown outside to the table by the butler.

"My God! The view! I don't even feel like I'm in Hong Kong anymore," Kitty exclaimed as she stared at the sparkling azure waters of the South China Sea from the dramatic cliff-side terrace of the Ko-Tung villa at Shek O, a peninsula on the southern coast of Hong Kong Island.

"Yes, that's what everyone always says." Corinna nodded, glad to see that Kitty was duly impressed. She had arranged the lunch here today specifically because she knew she needed to do something special to make up for the whole Strato-sphere Church debacle.

"This is the most beautiful house I've ever been to in all of Hong Kong! Does your mother live here?" Kitty asked, tak-ing her appointed seat beneath the arch at the outdoor dining table.

"No. No one lives here full-time. This was originally my grandfather's weekend retreat, and when he died he very clev-erly left it to the Ko-Tung Corporation so that his children couldn't fight over it. It's shared among the whole family—we use it like our own private club, and the company also uses it for very special functions."

"So this is where your mother hosted the ball for the Duchess of Oxbridge a few months ago?"

"Not just the duchess. My mother threw a dinner party here for Princess Margaret when she came with Lord Snowdon in 1966, and Princess Alexandra has visited too."

"Where are those princesses from?"

Corinna had to refrain from rolling her eyes. "Princess Margaret is the younger sister of Queen Elizabeth II, and Princess Alexandra of Kent is a cousin of the queen."

"Oh, I didn't realize there were so many princesses in England. I just thought there was Princess Diana and Princess Kate."

"Actually, her name is Catherine, the Duchess of Cambridge, and she is not officially a princess of the blood royal. As consort to Prince Will . . . oh never mind," Corinna said dismissively. "Now, Ada and Fiona will be here in a few minutes. Remember to be extra gracious to Fiona, because she was the one who convinced Ada to come today."

"Why is Fiona Tung-Cheng being so nice to me?" Kitty asked.

"Well, for one thing, unlike some of the members of Stratosphere, Fiona is a true Christian who believes in the power of redemption, and she's also my cousin, so I could twist her arm into helping me. Of course, it doesn't hurt that Ada's been dying to see this house for years."

"I don't blame her. I thought only Repulse Bay and Deep Water Bay had a few big mansions—I didn't know big houses on the water still existed in Hong Kong."

"That's how we prefer it. Shek O is where all the old families have their houses tucked away on the secluded headlands."

"I should get a place here, shouldn't I? You've been telling me to move out of Optus Towers. This would be like having a place in Hawaii!"

Corinna gave her a patronizing smile. "You can't just buy a house here, Kitty. First of all, there are only a handful of houses, and most have been in families for generations and will always remain that way. In the rare instance that a property does come on the market, new residents need to be approved by Shek O Development, which controls most of the land around here. Living here is like being accepted into a very exclusive club—in fact, I would say that Shek O home-owners are part of *the* most exclusive club in Hong Kong."

"Well, can't you help me get in? Isn't that the whole point of our working together?" *And my paying you so goddamn much money every month*, Kitty thought.

"We'll see how things go. This is why it is so important to rehabilitate your image—in time, perhaps your grandchildren might be allowed to buy here."

Kitty absorbed all this in a sulky silence. *My grandchildren? I want to live here now, when I can still sunbathe in the nude on a private terrace like this one.*

"Now, do you have the apology to Ada memorized by heart?" Corinna asked.

"I do. I was practicing it all morning with my maids. They thought it was very convincing."

"Good. I really want this to come from the heart, Kitty. You need to deliver it like this is your one and only chance to win an Oscar. I don't expect Ada and you to become instant best friends, but I do hope that this gesture will soften her and mark a turning point. Her forgiveness will go a long way toward your being accepted into society again."

"I will try my best. I even wore exactly what you told me to." Kitty sighed. She felt like a lamb being led to the slaughter in the muted floral Jenny Packham dress and peach Pringle cardigan that Corinna had chosen for her.

"I'm glad you listened. Just do me a favor and button one more button on that cardigan. Now it's perfect!"

A few minutes later, the butler announced, "Madame—Lady Poon and Mrs. Tung-Cheng." The ladies stepped onto the terrace, Fiona giving polite air-kisses to both Corinna and Kitty, while Ada barely looked in Kitty's direction and hugged Corinna extravagantly. "My goodness, Corinna, what a place! It's just like the Hotel du Cap out here!"

After the Niçoise salads had been served and a few pleasantries had been exchanged, Kitty took a deep breath and gazed earnestly at Ada. "Lady Poon, there's no easy way to say this, but I so regret what happened at the Pinnacle Ball. I haven't been able to forgive myself for my actions ever since. It was so terribly foolish of me to dash up on stage like that when Sir Francis was receiving his award, but you see—I was just so overcome with emotion. I have to tell you something that I've never told anyone before . . ." Kitty paused, looking the ladies in the eye one by one before she continued. "You see, when Sir Francis started talking about all those children in Africa that have been getting tuberculosis, I couldn't help but remember my own childhood. I know everyone thinks I am from Taiwan, but the truth is, I grew up in a tiny village in Qinghai, China. We were the poorest peasants . . . we didn't even have enough money to stay in the village—I lived in a little hut made out of metal and cardboard scraps beside the river with my grandmother. My grandmother raised me all by herself, you see, because my parents were working at a clothing factory in Guangzhou. We grew vegetables in the marshes by the river's edge. That's how we fed ourselves and earned a meager existence. But then when I was twelve, my grandmother . . ." Kitty paused again, as tears welled up in her eyes. "My grandmother contracted TB . . . and . . ."

"You don't have to continue," Fiona said softly, putting her hand on Kitty's shoulder.

"No, no I must," Kitty said, shaking her head and swallowing back her tears.

"Lady Poon, I want you to understand why I was so overcome that night when your husband started talking. My *nainai* contracted tuberculosis, and I had to stop going to school to nurse her. For three months I did this . . . until she died. This is why I was so touched by your husband's efforts to combat TB in Africa. This is why I jumped onstage and wanted to write my twenty-million-dollar check right there and then! I just felt so lucky that a girl like me, who grew up in a hut by the river, could now be in the position to help others with TB. I really had no idea what I was doing . . . I wasn't thinking . . . I never imagined how disrespectful it was. That was the last thing I wanted to do to your husband . . . your husband is such a hero to me. And you, if you only knew how much I admire you. Everything you do for the people of Hong Kong, your work on behalf of breast cancer awareness . . . it's made me become aware of my breasts in a whole new way, and when I realized what I had done to offend you and offend all the Poons, my God, I just . . . I just wanted to bury myself in shame," Kitty said sadly, as she cast her eyes downward and shook violently with sobs.

*My God, she's better than Cate Blanchett!* Corinna thought, transfixed at the sight of Kitty with tears streaming down her face and snot running from her nose.

Ada, who had been sitting stone-faced through Kitty's entire performance, suddenly broke out a tight smile. "I understand now. Please say no more. It is all in the past."

Fiona's eyes were moist as she reached across the table and grasped Kitty's hands tightly. "You have been through so much in your life. I never knew! And now with Bernard as ill as he is—you poor girl . . ."

Kitty gave her a look. *What the hell is she talking about?*

"I want you to know that I have been praying for Bernard.

I don't know him very well, but he and my husband go way back. I know Eddie looks at him like another brother."

"Really? I never knew they were that close."

"The two of them did stints at P. J. Whitney in New York early in their careers, and they used to frequent some sporting club called Scores. Whenever I called Eddie, he was always having a match there with Bernard—he would sound so out of breath. Anyway, I will pray even harder now for Bernard, that he makes a full recovery. Jesus can work miracles."

"Yes, I hope so," Kitty said softly. *It'll take a miracle to help Bernard.*

"If I might ask," Ada said as she leaned in closer, "what is the prognosis like? And is it really as contagious as they say?"

Kitty stared at them blankly. "Um, we really don't know . . ."

. . .

After Ada and Fiona had departed, Corinna summoned for a bottle of champagne. "Here's to you, Kitty! That was a brilliant success," she said as she clinked glasses with her protégée.

"No, no. You did all the work! Where in the world did you come up with that whole story about the grandma and the shack by the river?" Kitty asked.

"Oh, I got all of that from some documentary film I saw last year. But my goodness, you really brought my writing to life—even I was feeling a lump in my throat."

"So you knew all along this would work with Ada? Just making that heartfelt apology and flattering her was enough?"

"I've known Ada for many years now. I don't think she really gave a damn about the apology, quite honestly. All she needed to hear was you admitting that you come from some shitty village in China. She needed to feel superior to you, and it didn't hurt that you groveled so nicely at her feet for a bit. Now she will feel much more comfortable around you. Just you watch—more doors are going to start opening to you now."

"I can't believe your cousin Fiona invited me to that charity party next week. Am I allowed to go?"

"The King Yin Lei Mansion fund-raiser? Of course. Fiona will be expecting you to write a big, fat check."

"She was really so nice to me today. I think she felt sorry for me because of Bernard."

"Yes, but you know the sympathy for you will only last so long. I think you were almost seen through today. Ada isn't as gullible as Fiona, you know. Really, Kitty, you need to address all the whisperings going on about Bernard and your daughter."

Kitty turned toward the ocean and stared at a small island in the distance. "Let them whisper all they want."

"Why can't you just tell me what's going on? Is Bernard *really* ill? Did he really infect your daughter with some strange genetic disorder?"

Kitty suddenly burst into tears, and Corinna could tell that this time, her tears were all too real. "I can't explain . . . I don't know if I even have the words to explain," she said softly.

"Then can you show me? If you want me to help you, I need to understand. Because until we can put a full stop to all the rampant rumors about Bernard, things are not going to get much better for you here in Hong Kong," Corinna said gently.

Dabbing away her tears with an embroidered handkerchief, Kitty nodded. "Okay, I'll show you. I'll take you to Bernard."

"I can go to Macau with you anytime after Thursday."

"Oh no, we won't be going to Macau—we haven't lived there in years. You'll need to come with me to LA."

"Los Angeles?" Corinna said in surprise.

"Yes," Kitty said through clenched teeth.

## CHANGI AIRPORT

SINGAPORE

Astrid had just gotten off her flight from Paris, and as she strolled past the Times Travel shop in Terminal 3 toward the exit, a clerk was placing a stack of the latest *Pinnacle* onto the magazine rack. There was a man hugging a young boy on the cover, and as Astrid walked by, she glanced at the cover from afar and thought, *What a cute kid.* Then she stopped, turned around, and headed back to the newsstand. It wasn't often that *Pinnacle* would publish a cover that didn't involve some overly photoshopped woman in a ball gown, and she was intrigued to see who these people were. She went up to the magazine rack and gasped in horror.

Staring back at her on the cover of *Pinnacle*'s "Special Fathers and Sons Edition" were her husband and son. MICHAEL & CASSIAN TEO SAIL TO CONQUER, it said on the cover. Michael was pictured at the prow of some mega-yacht, wearing a striped sailor tee with an electric blue cardigan draped fussily over his shoulders, his arm awkwardly positioned on the railing to show off his vintage Rolex "Paul Newman" Daytona to full advantage. Crouched between his knees was Cassian, dressed in a blue checked shirt and a gold-buttoned navy blazer, with what looked like a gallon of gel in his hair and a hint of rouge on his cheeks.

*Oh my God, what have they done to my son?* Astrid grabbed the magazine and began flipping furiously through the five hundred pages of jewelry and watch ads, desperate to find the article. And there it was. The opening spread featured a completely different photo shoot of Michael and Cassian, this time in matching suede Brunello Cucinelli driving jackets and Persol sunglasses, shot from above as they sat in Michael's Ferrari 275 GTB convertible. *When the hell did they take these pictures?* Astrid wondered. In bold white type, the title of the article ran along the bottom of the picture:

**FATHER OF THE YEAR: MICHAEL TEO**

*It's hard to imagine someone with more of a charmed life than Michael Teo. The founder of one of Singapore's most visionary companies has a picture-perfect family, a gorgeous house, and a growing collection of classic sports cars. Did we mention that he has the physique of a Calvin Klein underwear model and cheekbones you could cut diamonds on? Olivia Irawidjaya digs a little deeper, and discovers that there's far more to the man than meets the eye . . .*

"Do you know what this is?" Michael Teo asks as he points to an old yellowing document in a simple titanium frame hanging on the wall of his ultramodern dressing room, in between rows of bespoke suits from the likes of Brioni, Caraceni, and Cifonelli. I scrutinize the writing and discover to my astonishment that it's signed "Abraham Lincoln." "This is an original copy of the Emancipation Proclamation. There are only seven copies in existence and I own one of them," Teo says proudly. "I've hung it right across from the mirrored wall in my closet so that I can see it every day while I'm putting on my clothes, and be reminded of who I am."

It's only fitting, since Teo is an emancipated man himself—a few years ago, he was a virtual unknown toiling away at his tech start-up in Jurong. This son of schoolteachers grew up "very middle class in Toa Payoh," he shamelessly admits, but through hard work and perseverance gained a place at St. Andrew's School, and from there became a standout commando in the Singapore Armed Forces.

"From the very beginning, Teo proved himself to be one of the bravest cadets of his generation," his former commanding officer Major Dick Teo (no relation) recalls. "His endurance level was almost superhuman, but it was his intelligence that propelled him to the top of military intelligence." Teo won a government scholarship to study computer engineering at the prestigious California Institute of Technology, and after graduating summa cum laude, he returned to work at the Ministry of Defence.

Another high-ranking official I spoke to, Lt. Col. Naveen Sinha, says, "I can't tell you exactly what he did, because that's classified information. But let's just say that Michael Teo has been instrumental in helping to bolster our intelligence capabilities. We were sorry to see him go."

What led Teo to leave a promising career with MINDEF to go into the private sector? "Love. I fell for a beautiful woman, got married, and decided that I needed to start acting like a married man—all the constant travel visiting army bases around the world and working through the night was no longer for me. Plus, I needed to build my own empire for the sake of my son and my wife," Teo says, his piercing hawk-like eyes flickering with emotion.

When I quiz him about his wife, he remains somewhat evasive. "She prefers to stay out of the limelight." Spying a black-and-white portrait of a stunning woman in his bedroom, I ask, "Is that her?" "Yes, but that was taken quite a few years ago," he says. I take a closer look and discover that the photograph is signed "To Astrid—who still eludes me, Dick." "Who's 'Dick,'" I ask? "It's actually some photographer named Richard Burton who died a while back," Michael says. Wait a minute, was this picture taken by the legendary fashion photographer Richard Avedon? "Oh yeah, that's his name."

Intrigued by this astonishing tidbit, I went sleuthing into Astrid Teo's past. Was she a high-fashion model in New York? As it turns out, Astrid is not just another pretty Methodist Girls School girl who married well and became a pampered housewife. *Pinnacle* can now reveal that she is the only daughter of Henry and Felicity Leong—names that are quite meaningless to most readers of this magazine, but who are apparently influential in their own right.

An expert on Southeast Asian lineage (who wished to remain unnamed) says, "You won't ever find the Leongs on any list because they are far too smart and far too discreet to be visible. They are an exceedingly private Straits Chinese family that goes back generations and has diversified holdings all over Asia—raw materials, commodities, real estate, that sort of thing. Their wealth is vast—Astrid's great-grandfather S. W. Leong used to be called 'the Palm Oil King of Borneo.' If Singapore had an aristocracy, Astrid would be considered a princess."

Another grande dame of Singapore's old-money crowd who will only talk off the record tells me, "It's not just her Leong blood that makes her important. Astrid is loaded on both sides. Her mother is Felicity Young, and let me just tell you, the Youngs make everybody else look like paupers, because they intermarried with the T'siens and the Shangs. *Alamak*, I've already told you too much."

Can this mysteriously powerful family be responsible for Teo's meteoric success? "Absolutely not!" Teo says angrily. Then, catching himself, he breaks into a laugh. "Originally, I was the one who married up, I'll admit that. But nowadays I fit in very well with her family *specifically* because I never asked for their help—I was determined to succeed entirely on my own."

And succeed he has—by now everyone knows how Teo's fledgling tech firm was suddenly acquired by a Silicon Valley company in 2010, increasing his net worth by several hundred million dollars. While most men might have been content to spend the rest of their lives staring out at the ocean view from one of Annabel Lee's luxury resorts, Teo doubled down and started his own tech-focused venture capital firm.

"I had no interest in retiring at thirty-three. I felt like I had been handed this golden opportunity, and I didn't want to take it for granted. There is so much talent and ingenuity right here in Singapore, and I wanted to find Asia's next generation of Sergey Brins and provide them with the wings to fly," Teo says. So far, his bets haven't just soared like eagles, they've rocketed to the moon. His apps Gong Simi? and Ziak Simi? have revolutionised the way Singaporeans communicate and argue about food, and several of the start-ups he has funded have been acquired by behemoths like Google, Alibaba Group, and Tencent. *The Heron Wealth Report* estimates that Teo is now worth close to a billion dollars—not bad for a thirty-six-year-old who shared a bedroom with two of his brothers until he went to college.

So how does a man like Teo enjoy the spoils of his fortune? For starters, there is the contemporary villa in Bukit Timah that anyone driving past could easily mistake for an Aman Resort. Built around several reflecting pools and Mediterranean-style gardens, the sprawling house is already getting a bit cramped for Teo's growing collection of war artifacts and sports cars. "We are in the process of building a new home, and have been interviewing prospective architects like Renzo Piano and Jean Nouvel. We really want something revolutionary, a home like nothing Singapore's ever seen."

Until then, Teo takes me on a tour of his exclusive booty. On the ground-floor gallery, samurai swords from the Edo period and a massive cannon from the Napoleonic War are displayed alongside his sparklingly restored Porsches, Ferraris, and Aston Martins. "I'm taking my time, but I hope to amass the finest collection of vintage sports cars outside the Western Hemisphere. See this 1963 Ferrari Modena Spyder over here?" Teo says, as he rubs the chrome work lovingly with his index finger. "This is the actual Ferrari that Ferris Bueller drove on his day off."

And just home from kindergarten is Teo's adorable son, Cassian, who enters the room doing a series of cartwheels. Teo grabs him by the collar of his shirt and lifts the boy into his arms. "All these things I possess, though, are nothing to me without this little rascal here." Cassian, a high-spirited boy who has inherited his parents' extraordinary looks, will turn six later this year, and Teo is determined to pass on the secrets of his success to his son. "I'm a true believer in the adage 'spare the rod and spoil the child.' I think kids need a great deal of discipline, and they need to be trained to function at their highest level. For example, my son is exceedingly smart, and I don't feel that he's being challenged at his kindergarten, and this will be very bold of me to say, but I don't think he'll be challenged at any primary school in Singapore either."

So does that mean that the Teos plan to send their child abroad to a boarding school at such an early age? "We haven't made up our minds yet, but we think we'll either send him to Gordonstoun in Scotland [the alma mater of both Prince Philip and Prince Charles] or Le Rosey in Switzerland. For my son, nothing is more important than the best education that money can buy—I want him to go to school with future kings and world leaders, people who really shake up the world," he fervently declares. Michael Teo is undoubtedly one of these people, and with such a dedicated vision and love for his son, it's no wonder he is *Pinnacle*'s Father of the Year!

. . .

Rushing home from the airport, Astrid entered the front door and saw Michael standing on a ladder, adjusting the spotlight that was shining on his marble bust of the Emperor Nero.

"Jesus, Michael! What have you done?" she said angrily.

"Well hello to you too, honey."

Astrid held up the magazine. "When did you do this interview?"

"Oh—it's out already!" Michael said excitedly.

"Damn right it's out! I can't believe you let this happen."

"I didn't let it happen, I *made* it happen. We did the photo shoot while you were at Nick's wedding in California. You know, it was supposed to be Ang Peng Siong and his son on the cover, but they yanked it at the last minute in favor of me. My new publicist, Angelina Chio-Lee at SPG Strategies, engineered that. What do you think of the pictures?"

"They are absolutely ridiculous."

"You don't have to be such a bitch about it, just because you weren't in them," Michael suddenly snapped.

"Jesus, do you think that's what I'm upset about? Have you even read the article?"

"No—how could I? It just came out. But don't worry, I took extra care not to say anything about you or your crazy paranoid family."

"You didn't have to—you let the writer into our house! Into our *bedroom*! She found things out for herself!"

"Stop being so hysterical. Can't you see that this is good for me? That this will be good for our family?"

"I'm not sure you'll think that after you've read it. Well, you'll have to reckon with my father when he gets wind of this, not me."

"Your father! Everything's always about your father," Michael grumbled as he fiddled with the screw on the light.

"He is going to be *furious* when he sees this. More than you can possibly ever imagine," Astrid said ominously.

Michael shook his head in disappointment as he came off the ladder. "And to think, this was supposed to be a present to you."

"A present to me?" Astrid struggled to grasp the logic behind this.

"Cassian was so excited about the photo shoot, he was so looking forward to surprising you."

"Oh believe me, I'm surprised."

"You know what's surprising me? You've been away for

almost a week, but you seem to care much more about this magazine article than seeing your own son."

Astrid stared at him incredulously. "Are you actually trying to make me the bad person here?"

"Actions speak louder than words. You're still standing here ranting at me, while upstairs there's a child who's been waiting all night for his mother to come home."

Astrid left the room without another word and headed upstairs.

# JINXIAN LU

SHANGHAI

A couple of hours after returning to Shanghai from their Paris trip, Carlton called Rachel at the Peninsula Hotel. "All settled in?"

"Yes, but now I'm jet-lagged all over again. Nick, of course, put his head on the pillow and immediately started snoring. It's so unfair," Rachel sighed.

"Er . . . think Nick would mind if I took you out to dinner? Just the two of us?" Carlton asked timidly.

"Of course not! Even if he wasn't dead to the world for the next ten hours, he wouldn't mind."

That evening, Carlton drove Rachel (this time in a very sensible Mercedes G-Wagen) to Jinxian Lu, a narrow street lined with old shophouses in the French Concession. "Here's the restaurant, but where to park—that is the question," Carlton muttered. Rachel glanced at the modest storefront with pleated white curtains and noticed a row of luxury vehicles parked outside. They found a space halfway down the block and walked leisurely toward the restaurant, passing a few enticingly quaint bars, antique shops, and trendy boutiques along the way.

Arriving at their dining spot, Rachel discovered a tiny space with only five tables. It was a fluorescent-lit room completely devoid of decor save for a plastic rotating desk fan bolted to the dingy white wall, but it was packed with a decidedly posh crowd. "Looks like quite the foodie destination," Rachel commented, eyeing an expensively dressed couple dining with two small kids still in their gray-and-white private-school uniforms, while at a table by the door sat two hipster Germans in their regulation plaids, wielding chopsticks as expertly as any locals.

A waiter in a white singlet and black trousers approached them. "Mr. Fung?" he asked Carlton in Mandarin.

"No, Bao—two people at seven thirty," Carlton answered. The man nodded and gestured for them to enter. They navigated their way to the back of the room, where a woman with dripping-wet hands pointed toward a doorway. "Up the stairs! Don't be shy!" she said. Rachel soon found herself climbing an extremely narrow, steep staircase whose wooden steps were so worn that they dipped in the center. Halfway up, she passed a small landing that had been converted into a cooking space. Two women crouched in front of sizzling woks, filling the whole staircase with a tantalizing smoky aroma.

At the top of the stairs was a room with a bed against one wall and a dresser piled high with neatly folded clothes on the opposite side. A small table had been placed in front of the bed along with a couple of chairs, and a small television set buzzed in the corner. "Are we actually eating in someone's bedroom?" Rachel asked in astonishment.

Carlton grinned. "I was hoping we'd get to eat up here—it's considered the best table in the house. Is it okay with you?"

"Are you kidding? This is the coolest restaurant I think I've ever been in!" Rachel said excitedly, looking out the window at the line of hanging laundry that stretched across to the other side of the street.

"This place is the definition of 'hole-in-the-wall,' but they are famous for preparing some of the most authentic home-style Shanghainese food in the city. There's no menu—they just bring you whatever they're cooking today, and everything's always in season and very fresh," Carlton explained.

"After our week in Paris, this is such a welcome change."

"You take the place of honor on the bed," Carlton offered. Rachel gleefully made herself comfortable on the mattress— it felt so strange and a little naughty to be eating on some-one's bed.

Soon two women entered the bedroom-cum-dining room and started placing a multitude of steaming-hot dishes onto the Formica table. Arrayed before them was *hongshao rou*— thick slices of fatty pork in a sweet marinade with green pep-pers; *jiang ya*—braised duck leg covered in thick, sweetened soy sauce; *jiuyang caotou*—seasonal vegetables stir-fried in fra-grant wine; *ganshao changyu*—deep-fried whole pomfret; and *yandu xian*—a typical Shanghainese soup of bamboo shoots, pressed tofu, salted ham, and fresh pork.

"Sweet Jesus! How are we going to finish all this by our-selves?" Rachel laughed.

"Trust me, the food here is so good you'll be eating more than you normally would."

"Uh, that's what I'm afraid of."

"We can wrap up whatever we don't finish and Nick can enjoy a late-night snack," Carlton suggested.

"He's gonna love that."

After clinking their bottles of ice-cold Tsingtao beer, they dove into the dishes without any ceremony, savoring the food in silence for the first few minutes.

After his first round of sweet fatty pork, Carlton looked earnestly at Rachel and said, "I wanted to take you to dinner tonight because I owe you an apology."

"I understand. But you already apologized."

"No, I didn't. Not properly, anyway. I've been thinking about it nonstop, and I still feel horrible about what happened in Paris. Thank you for stepping in and doing what you did. It was rather stupid of me to think I could ever race Richie in the condition I was in."

"I'm glad you see that."

"I'm also sorry for everything I said to you. I was just so shocked—ashamed, really—that you found out about London, but it was bloody unfair of me to lash out at you like that. I wish I could take it all back."

Rachel was silent for a moment. "I'm actually very grateful for what you told me. It's given me some insight into a situation that's been puzzling me since we arrived."

"I can only imagine."

"Look, I think I understand the position I've put your father in. I truly am sorry if I've caused your family any trouble. Especially your mother. I see now that it must be very hard on her—this whole situation is just something none of us could ever have prepared for. I really hope she doesn't hate me for coming to China."

"She doesn't hate you—she doesn't know you. Mum's just had a tough year with my accident and all. Finding out about you—discovering this side of my father's past—has just compounded that stress. She's someone who's used to a very orderly way of life, and she's spent so many years planning things out perfectly. Like the company. And Dad's career. She really has been the force behind his political rise, and now she's trying to propel my future as well. My accident was a huge setback in her eyes, and she's so afraid that any more scratches to that façade will destroy everything she's planned for me."

"But what has she planned for you? Does she want you to get into politics too?"

"Ultimately, yes."

"But is that even something you want?"

Carlton sighed. "I don't know what I want."

"That's okay. You have time to figure it out."

"Do I? Because sometimes I feel like everyone my age is ahead of the game and I'm just totally fucked. I thought I knew what I wanted, but then the accident changed everything. What were *you* doing when you were twenty-three?"

Rachel thought about it as she drank some of the pork-and-bamboo soup. She closed her eyes, momentarily transported by the subtle flavors.

"Good, isn't it? They're famous for this soup," Carlton said.

"It's amazing. I think I could drink the whole pot!" Rachel exclaimed.

"Go right ahead."

Collecting herself, Rachel continued, "When I was twenty-three, I was in Chicago going to grad school at Northwestern. And I spent half the year in Ghana."

"You were in Africa?"

"Yep. Doing field research for my dissertation about microlending."

"Brilliant! I've always dreamed of going to this place in Namibia called the Skeleton Coast."

"You should talk to Nick—he's been there."

"Really?"

"Yeah—he went with his best friend Colin when he was living in England. They used to travel to all these extremely hard-to-get-to places. Nick used to have quite the life before he met me and settled down."

"You guys seem to have quite the life now," Carlton said wistfully.

"You can have any type of life you want, Carlton."

"I don't know about that. You haven't met my mother. But you know what? You will soon. I'm going to have a talk with Dad—he needs to stand up to her and end this idiotic blockade that she's imposed. Once she meets you, once you are no longer this mysterious entity to her, she'll see you for who you are. And she'll come to appreciate you, I just know it."

"It's very kind of you to say that, but Nick and I were discussing it earlier today and we're thinking of changing our travel plans. Peik Lin, my friend from Singapore, is flying up to visit me on Thursday. She wants to take me to Hangzhou for a spa weekend while Nick is off in Beijing doing his research at the National Library. But when we get back next week, I think we'll head home to New York."

"Next week? You were supposed to be here until August—you can't leave so soon!" Carlton began to protest.

"It's better that way. I realize that it was a huge mistake for me to make this trip so soon. I never gave your mother enough time to adjust to the idea of me. The last thing I want to do is cause a lasting wound between your parents. Really."

"Let me talk to them. You can't leave China without seeing Dad again, and I want my mum to meet you. She *has* to."

Rachel pondered things for a moment. "It's up to you. I don't want to impose on them any more than I already have. Look, we've had a fantastic time in China. And Paris, of course. Getting to spend all this time with you is already far more than I could have ever hoped for."

Carlton locked eyes for a moment with his sister, and nothing more needed to be said.

# RIVERSIDE VICTORY TOWERS

SHANGHAI

For many Shanghainese who had been born in Puxi—the historic city center—the glittering new metropolis on the other side of the river called Pudong would never be part of the real Shanghai. "Puxi is like Pu-*York*, but Pudong will always be Pu-*Jersey*," the cognoscenti snidely remarked. Jack Bing, who hailed from Ningbo in Zhejiang Province, had no time for such snobberies. He was proud to be part of the new China that built Pudong, and whenever guests came to his triplex penthouse at Riverside Victory Towers—a hulking trio of ultra-luxurious apartment complexes that he had developed on the riverfront of Pudong's financial district—he would proudly walk them around the sprawling rooftop garden of his 8,888-square-foot penthouse and point out the new city that stretched as far as the eye could see. "A decade ago, all this was farmland. Now it is the center of the world," he would say.

Today, as Jack sat on the titanium and Mongolian gazelle lounge chair Marc Newson had custom designed for him, sipping his glass of 2005 Château Pétrus on the rocks, his thoughts lingered on the memory of an afternoon spent alone at the Palace of Versailles at the end of a business trip, where he delighted in stumbling upon a small exhibition devoted to Chinese antiquities in the court of Louis XIV. He was admiring a portrait of the Emperor Qianlong in a small gallery tucked behind the Hall of Mirrors when a large tour group of Chinese tourists crowded into the space. A man in head-to-toe Stefano Ricci pointed at the portrait of the emperor dressed in a Manchu-style fur cap and murmured excitedly, "Genghis Khan! Genghis Khan!"

Jack left the gallery hastily, afraid he might be associated with this group of ignorant Chinese. Imagine these heathens not knowing one of their greatest emperors, who ruled for more than sixty years! But as he strolled along the grand canal that bisected the majestic gardens of Versailles, he began to wonder whether the French themselves might today recognize a portrait of their own king who had built such an impressive monument to his power. Now, as Jack stared out at the curving crescent of golden lights along the Pudong waterfront, counting the buildings that belonged to him, he pondered his own legacy, and how the people of this new China might remember him in centuries to come.

The familiar click-click of his daughter's high heels soon broke the silence, and Jack quickly removed the ice cubes from his wine and tossed them into the potted *tan hua* plant nearby. He knew Colette would scold him if she saw them. A couple of ice cubes missed the Ming ceramic planter and skidded across the floor, leaving faint red streaks along the Emperador marble.

Colette barged into his study all a-huff. "What's wrong? Is Mother okay? Is Nainai okay?"

"Your grandmother is still alive as far as I know, and your mother is at her reflexology appointment," Jack said calmly.

"Then why did you need me so urgently? I was in the middle of a very important dinner with the world's most acclaimed chefs!"

"And *that's* more important than seeing your own father? You come back from Paris and you would rather dine with the help?"

"This top truffle dealer was about to offer me his prized white Alba truffle when you called, but now I think that sneaky Eric Ripert has snagged it. I was going to surprise you with the truffle."

Jack let out a snort. "What really surprises me is the way you keep disappointing me over and over again."

Colette stared at her father quizzically. "What have I ever done to disappoint you?"

"The fact that you don't even know is so telling. I went to such lengths to help Richie Yang orchestrate the perfect proposal to you, and look what you did in return."

"*You* were part of that whole scheme? Of course you were—if I had planned the affair, it would have been so much more tasteful!"

"That's not the point. The point is that you were supposed to say yes, like any normal girl who is being serenaded by one of the most expensive singers in the world."

Colette rolled her eyes. "I like John Legend, but even if you had paid John Lennon to rise from the grave and sing 'All You Need Is Love' to me, the answer would still be no."

Colette saw something move out of the corner of her eye and turned to find her mother standing by the doorway. "What are you doing skulking in the shadows? Have you been home all this time? You knew Dad was involved all along, didn't you?"

"*Aiyah*, I couldn't believe it when you turned Richie down! We have both wanted this for you ever since you started dating him three years ago," her mother said with a deep sigh, planting herself down on the gilded settee.

"It's not like I've been seeing him exclusively. I've been dating many other men."

"Well, you've had your fun, and now it's high time you got married. I had you by the time I was your age," Mrs. Bing chastised.

"I can't even believe we're having this conversation! Why did you send me to the most progressive schools in England if all you expected out of me was to get married at such a young age? Why did I bother studying so hard at Regent's? I have so many goals, so many things I want to accomplish before I become anyone's wife."

"Why can't you accomplish your goals while you're married?" Jack argued.

"It's not the same, Father. Besides, my situation is so different than when the both of you were young. Sometimes I wonder if I even need to get married at all—it's not like I need a man to look after me!"

"How long do you intend to make us wait until you are ready for marriage?" her mother demanded.

"I think I won't be ready for at least another decade."

"*Wo de tian ah!*\* You'll be thirty-three. What will happen to your eggs? Your eggs will get old and your babies might be born retarded or deformed!" Mrs. Bing screeched.

"Mother, stop being so ridiculous! With all the damn doctors you see every day, you should know that such things don't happen anymore. They have special genetic tests now, and women are having babies well into their forties!"

"Listen to her!" Mrs. Bing said incredulously to her husband.

Jack leaned forward in his chair and remarked wryly, "I don't think this has anything to do with age, actually. I think our daughter is in love with Carlton Bao."

"Even if I was, I wouldn't want to get married to him right now," Colette shot back.

---

\*   Mandarin for "Oh my God!"

"And what makes you think I would ever approve of your marrying him?"

Colette looked at her father in exasperation. "Why is Richie so much more special than Carlton? They both have degrees from top universities, and both come from respectable families. Why, I'd even say that Carlton comes from a higher-status family than Richie."

Mrs. Bing harrumphed. "I don't like that Bao Shaoyen. Always acting so uppity, like she's so much better and smarter than me!"

"That's because she IS smarter than you, Mother. She has a PhD in biochemistry and runs a multibillion-dollar company."

"How dare you say that to me! Don't you think I'm partly responsible for your father's success? I was the one who spent all those years—"

Raising his voice to be heard over his arguing wife and daughter, Jack interjected, "CARLTON BAO'S family has two billion dollars at most. The Yangs are on a whole other level. Our level. Don't you see that this is the perfect dynastic match? The two of you together would make our families the most powerful and influential in China. Do you not see the unique position that you are in to be part of history?"

"I'm sorry, I didn't realize that I was a chess piece in your plan for world domination," Colette shot back sarcastically.

Jack banged his fist on the desk and stood up from his chair, pointing at her angrily. "You are not my chess piece! You are my prized possession. And I want to see that you are treated like a queen and married off to the best possible man in the whole world!"

"But the fact that I don't agree with your idea of the best man means nothing to you!"

"Well if Carlton Bao is the best man for you, then why hasn't he proposed to you?" Jack challenged her.

"Oh, he'll propose whenever I want him to. Don't you

understand? I keep telling you, *I'm just not ready!* WHEN I want to get married and IF I choose Carlton, you can be sure he will exceed your expectations. The Baos might have more money than the Yangs by then. You have no idea how smart Carlton is! Once he really devotes his attention to his family's business, there's no telling how well he can do."

"Is that going to happen in my lifetime? Your mother and I are not getting any younger—I want to see my grandsons grow up while we are still healthy enough to enjoy them!"

Colette's eyes narrowed as she stared at her father, seeing things in a whole new light. "So this is what it's really all about . . . you are just dying for grandsons, aren't you?"

"Of course! What grandparents wouldn't want lots and lots of grandsons?" Mrs. Bing said.

"This is just too funny . . . it's like I'm trapped in some time warp." Colette laughed to herself. "And what if I only produce girls? What if I don't want any children at all?"

"Don't talk nonsense," her mother snapped.

Colette was about to argue back when it hit her—her mother's very name, *Lai Di*, meant "hoping for a son." Her mother couldn't escape her mind-set—it had literally been branded on her since the day she was born. Colette looked at her parents squarely and said, "The two of you might have grown up like peasants, but I am not a peasant, and you did not raise me to be one. It is 2013, and I am not going to get married and pump out babies just because you want a barrel full of grandsons."

"Ungrateful child! After all we've given you in life!" Mrs. Bing blurted out.

"Yes, thank you, you've given me a great life, and I intend to live it!" Colette declared, storming out of the room.

Jack gave a sharp little laugh. "Let's see how she intends to live her life once I put a freeze on her accounts."

# PULAU CLUB

SINGAPORE

Michael was huddled in his office preparing for a big presentation with his head venture partner and his chief technology adviser when his phone buzzed with a text message from Astrid:

> WIFEY: Mum called—she's having a meltdown about the magazine article.
>
> MT: Big shocker.
>
> WIFEY: My dad's requested that you meet him at Pulau club at 10:30 a.m.
>
> MT: Sorry, I'll be in a meeting then.
>
> WIFEY: You're going to have to face him sooner or later.
>
> MT: I know, but I'm busy right now. Some of us HAVE TO WORK FOR A LIVING.
>
> WIFEY: I'm just passing along the message.
>
> MT: Tell him I have a very important meeting with the Monetary Authority of Singapore this AM. My assistant will call his assistant to set up another time to meet.
>
> WIFEY: Okay. Good luck at your meeting.

Several minutes later, Michael's executive assistant, Krystal, buzzed on the intercom. "Michael, ah? I just receive call from your father-in-law's seck-ree-teh-ry Miss Chua. He wants you to meet him at Pulau Club in half an hour."

Michael rolled his eyes in frustration. "I already know about this, Krystal. It's been dealt with. Now, no more interruptions, please. We only have an hour left before our big pitch."

He turned back to his partners. "Sorry, guys. Now, where were we? Yes, we can reinforce that our new finance-data app is a quarter of a second faster than Bloomberg's terminals—"

The intercom buzzed again. "Michael—I know you said not to *kachiao** you, but—"

"So why the hell did you?" Michael raised his voice angrily.

"I just got an-nah-der call . . . the meeting with *gahmen*[†] people postpone, *lah.*"

"The Monetary Authority meeting?" Michael tried to clarify.

"Yah *lah.*"

"Until what time?"

"Postpone, postpone, *lor!* They never say."

"What the fuck?"

"And your father-in-law's office call again with an-nah-der message. Miss Chua said to read it aloud to you. Wait, ah! I get message. Okay, here it is: *Please meet Mr. Leong at Pulau Club at 10:30 a.m. No more excuses.*"

"*Kan ni nah!*" Michael swore, kicking his desk.

. . .

Anyone standing at the third hole of the Island Course at Pulau Club—quaintly referred to as the "old course"—would

---

*   Singlish for "disturb" (Malay origin).
†   Correct Singlish pronunciation for "government."

feel as if they were transported back to an earlier time. Carved out of natural virgin jungle in 1930, the undulating green hills gave way to tropical groves of casuarinas and tembusus on one side and the oasis-like Peirce Reservoir on the other. Not a hint of the densely packed skyscrapers that were modern Singapore could be seen from this vantage point. Harry Leong, dressed in his usual golfing outfit of short-sleeved white cotton shirt, khaki pants, and a faded blue Royal Air Force cap* to protect his thinning silvery hair, was watching his golf buddy adjust a swing when his son-in-law came storming up the fairway.

"Oh—here he comes, looking blacker than the devil. Let's have some fun with him, shall we?" Harry said to his friend. "Lovely day, isn't it?" he called out.

"It might have been, had you not . . ." Michael began in a surly tone, before catching sight of the man standing next to his father-in-law. It was Hu Lee Shan, the minister of commerce, nattily dressed in a brightly striped Sligo golf shirt.

"Good morning, Mr. Teo," the minister said jovially.

Forcing a smile, Michael said, "Good morning, sir." *Bloody hell! No wonder he was able to sabotage my meeting so quickly. He's golfing with the friggin' boss of the boss of the Monetary Authority!*

"Thank you for meeting me on such short notice," Harry continued politely. "Now, I'll get right to the point: this matter over the silly magazine story."

"I'm sorry, Dad. It was never my intention for your name to get mentioned," Michael began.

"Oh I don't care about my name. I mean, who am I in the grand scheme of things, right? I'm a public servant—people can print any sort of nonsense they want about me. It's all much ado about nothing in my opinion, but, you see, other names were mentioned in that article. Other people who are

---

* A gift from his friend His Royal Highness the Duke of Kent.

touchy about such things. Like my wife and my mother-in-law. That side of the family. You know how we mustn't ever upset Astrid's grandmother, or Uncle Alfred."

"Heh heh heh—no one should *ever* upset Alfred Shang," chuckled the minister.

Michael wanted to roll his eyes. What was the big deal about Alfred Shang that made every man so *bo lam pa*[*] in his presence? "I really had no idea that reporter was going to go digging. It was only supposed to be a flattering stor—"

Harry cut him off mid-word. "The *Tattle* people know never to write about us. So you went to the other magazine, *Pompous* or whatever it's called. Tell me, what did you hope to achieve?"

"I thought the article would allow me to increase my company's profile while respecting Astrid's—and your family's—need for privacy."

"And do you think it does? I'm assuming you've read the article by now."

Michael swallowed hard. "It doesn't quite do what I had hoped."

"Makes you out to be a pretentious buffoon, doesn't it?" Harry said, as he reached for another putter. "Try this Honma, Lee Shan."

Michael's jaw tightened. If the minister wasn't right there, he would give this old man a piece of his mind!

The minister executed a precise chipping swing and the golf ball rolled smoothly into the hole.

"Nice shot, sir," Michael said.

"Do you play, Mr. Teo?"

"I do when I can."

The minister glanced at Harry as he stepped up to the tee box and said, "You're a lucky man—you have a son-in-law

---

[*]   A Hokkien term for cowards that literally means "no balls."

who golfs. My kids are far too preoccupied with their important lives to ever play with me."

"We should all play at my club at Sentosa sometime. The
ocean views are spectacular," Michael offered.

Harry paused in the middle of his golf swing. "You know,
I've never set foot in that club and I plan to *die* never having
set foot there. If I'm not at St. Andrews or Pebble Beach, the
only place I play is the old course right here."

"I feel the same way, Harry," the minister said. "Didn't
you use to catch Concorde to London on Fridays after
work and then hop over to Edinburgh just to play a round at
St. Andrews?"

"Those were the old days when I only had the weekends
to spare. Now that I'm semiretired, I can go a whole week at
Pebble Beach."

Michael fumed in silence, wondering when this audience
was ever going to end. As if reading his mind, his father-in-
law looked him in the eye and said, "I need you to do something for me. I need you to go in person and apologize to your
mother-in-law."

"Of course. I'll even write a letter to the magazine dis-
avowing the article, if that's what you want."

"There's no need—I've bought up the entire print run and
had every issue of the magazine pulled from the bookstores
and pulped," Harry said lightly.

Michael's eyes widened.

"Heh heh heh. All those subscribers are going to wonder
why *Pinnacle* is missing from their mailboxes this month," the
minister cracked.

"Now, don't let me keep you, Michael. I know you're a
very busy man. You have to get over to see my wife before she
heads to Salon Dor La Mode for her wash and set at eleven
thirty."

"Of course," Michael said, grateful to be getting away relatively unscathed. "Once again, I apologize. At the end of the day, I was only trying to do my best for the family. A feature article about my success can only benefit—"

Harry suddenly snapped in fury. "Your success is absolutely irrelevant to me! What have you succeeded at, really? You've sold a few meaningless companies and made some insignificant money. It's all been handed to you! Your *only* mission in life as far as I'm concerned is to protect my daughter, and that means protecting her privacy. Your second mission is to protect my grandson. And on both scores you have failed."

Michael, his face boiling in embarrassment and fury, stared at his father-in-law. He was about to say something when six black-suited security guards suddenly appeared out of nowhere and began carrying off the golf bags.

Harry Leong turned to his friend. "Now, on to the fourth hole?"

. . .

Michael sped down Adam Road in his Aston Martin DB5, seething with rage. *How dare that shitbag humiliate me in front of the minister of commerce! Calling me a pretentious buffoon, when he's the one bragging about his weekend trips to golf at Pebble Beach! What fucking bullshit to say it's all been handed to me, when he inherited every cent of his obscene fortune and I've worked so goddamn hard my whole life!*

Suddenly it was as if a flare went off inside his head. He had been going to his mother-in-law's house on Nassim Road, but now he slammed on the brakes, made a U-turn, and raced back to his office.

Krystal was on her computer surfing websites for cheap travel deals to the Maldives when he came bursting into the office and started going through the filing cabinets.

"Where are all the files related to the sale of Cloud Nine Solutions, my first company?"

"*Acherley*,* wouldn't those old files be in the archive room on forty-third floor?" Krystal suggested.

"Come with me, we need to find those files now!"

They raced down to the archive room, which Michael had never even entered before, and began digging through the file drawers. "I need to find the original contracts from 2010," he said urgently.

"Wah, so many files here! Search and search until vomit blood!" Krystal complained.

After searching for twenty minutes, they came across a set of large orange binders that contained all the relevant documents. "Here it is!" Michael said excitedly.

"Wah, you damn *heng*!† I thought we never find!"

"Okay, Krystal, you can go back upstairs now." Michael began rifling through the pages until he came to the one he was looking for. It was the Share Purchase Agreement authorizing the sale of his company to Promenade Technologies of Mountain View, California. There, buried within the dozens of various entities that were involved in the buyout of his tech firm, one name stood out—the ultimate parent company of the acquisition vehicle, some shell corporation based in Mauritius. He held the piece of paper in his hands, staring intently at the name in disbelief and denial, his heart pounding more furiously than it ever had before: Pebble Beach HoldCo IV-A, LTD.

*It's all been handed to you!* His father-in-law's words suddenly took on a whole new meaning.

---

* Correct Singlish pronunciation for "actually."
† Hokkien for "lucky," "fortunate."

## IMPERIAL TREASURE RESTAURANT

SHANGHAI

"I hope you don't mind—I invited Colette to join us," Carlton said breezily to his parents as the two of them entered the private dining room of Imperial Treasure. The Baos, who had summoned their son to dinner as soon as the gossip about Paris had reached their ears, couldn't mask their looks of surprise when Colette walked in, followed by the ubiquitous Roxanne with a large beribboned hamper full of gifts from Paris.

"It's always a pleasure to have you with us, Colette," Gaoliang said, forcing a smile as he stared grimly at Carlton's purplish eye. *So the story about his fight with Richie Yang was true.*

Shaoyen was less restrained. She got up from the table and rushed toward her son, putting her hands on his face. "Look at you! You look like a raccoon that went for lip fillers! My God, after all you went through with your reconstructive surgeries, how could you let this happen?"

"I'm fine, Mother. It's nothing," Carlton said gruffly, trying to shrug her off.

"Mrs. Bao, I brought you some presents from Paris. I know how much you love the *pâtés de fruits* at Hédiard." Colette gestured to the hamper, hoping to distract them.

"Hiyah, had I known you were coming, I would have arranged dinner at someplace special. This was just a last-minute family dinner," Shaoyen said, hoping her emphasis on the word *family* would make the girl feel especially unwelcome.

"Oh, this is one of my family's favorite restaurants too! I know the menu very well," Colette chirped, seemingly oblivious to the tension in the room.

"Why don't you do the ordering then? Be sure to get all your favorite dishes," Shaoyen replied solicitously.

"No, no, I'll just keep it simple." Colette turned to the waiter and smiled. "Let's start with the deep-fried crab claws stuffed with minced shrimp, followed by the live Venus clams steamed in XO sauce, the barbecued roast pork with honey sauce, the sautéed scallops with Italian white truffle oil, and the stewed chicken with diced abalone and salted fish in clay pot. Oh, and of course we must have the roasted suckling pig—make sure it's a fat one—and the steamed sliced garoupa with mushroom in lotus leaf, the stir-fried diced vegetables with walnut served in crispy nest, and of course the braised e-fu noodles with crab roe and crabmeat in soup. And for dessert, the double-boiled bird's nest with rock sugar."

Standing behind Colette's chair, Roxanne leaned toward the waiter's ear. "Please tell the chef it's for Miss Bing—he knows she likes the bird's nest dessert spiked with nine drops of amaretto di Saronno and sprinkled with shavings of twenty-four-carat gold."

Gaoliang exchanged looks with his wife. This Colette Bing was just too much. Glaring at Carlton, Shaoyen quipped, "Now I know why our banker called me up last week. They noticed some highly elevated spending patterns on your accounts. Looks like you two had quite a time in Paris, didn't you?"

"Ooh, it was pure heaven," Colette said with a sigh.

"We had a lovely time," Carlton said a little uncomfortably.

"And that racing competition with Richie Yang, was that lovely too?" Shaoyen asked, her voice dripping with sarcasm.

"What do you mean? I didn't race him," Carlton replied carefully.

"But you were going to, weren't you?"

"It never happened, Mother," Carlton protested.

Gaoliang sighed heavily. "Son, what really disappoints me is your complete lack of judgment. I can't believe you would even consider doing something like that after your accident! And to make things worse, this callous bet you made over the race—I never imagined you would have the audacity to make a bet with Richie Yang for *ten million dollars*."

Colette spoke up in Carlton's defense. "Mr. and Mrs. Bao, I don't mean to intrude, but you should know that Richie was the one who came up with the challenge and the bet. Richie was the one provoking Carlton every chance he could for the past few months. He did all this to try to impress me. If anyone should be blamed for everything that happened in Paris, it should be me. You should be proud of your son— Carlton did the right thing. He was the bigger man and walked away from that race. Can you imagine if Richie had won the race? I mean, I know ten million dollars is not that much money, but still, what a loss of face it would have been for you Baos!"

Gaoliang and Shaoyen looked at Colette, too stupefied to say anything. Just then, Colette's phone began to buzz. "Haha—speak of the devil, it's Richie. He still won't give up and has been calling me a dozen times a day! Should I turn on the speakerphone and bring him into the conversation? I'm sure he would confirm everything."

The Baos shook their heads, mortified by the suggestion.

"Then I will just hit Ignore," Colette said lightly, placing her phone on the empty chair next to her.

The dinner dishes began to arrive, and the four of them

started to eat in an uncomfortable silence. When the roasted suckling pig was finally brought in on a silver platter with much fanfare, Carlton decided it was time to speak up. "Father, Mother, I take full responsibility for what happened in Paris. It was foolish of me to get dragged into the mud with Richie. Yes, I was prepared to race him, but thankfully Rachel talked some sense into me."

Shaoyen flinched at the mention of Rachel, but Carlton continued talking. "Rachel knows all about London. She understood what an emotional state I was in, and she still managed to convince me to walk away from the race. And I'm awfully grateful she did, because otherwise I might not even be here telling you this right now."

"She knows everything about your accident?" Shaoyen asked Carlton, trying to make it sound casual. *She even knows about the girl who died?*

"Yes, *everything*," Carlton said, looking his mother straight in the eye.

Shaoyen said nothing, but her glare spoke volumes. *Stupid boy stupid boy stupid boy!*

As if reading her mind, Carlton responded, "We can trust her, Mother. Whether you like it or not, Rachel is going to be part of our lives. She's visiting Hangzhou now with a friend from Singapore, but once she returns to Shanghai, I really think you need to invite her over. This freeze-out has gone on for far too long. Once you meet her, I know you'll come to like her as well."

Shaoyen stared down at the uneaten crisp of golden pork skin on her plate, saying nothing, so Carlton tried another tactic. "If you don't believe me, ask Colette. All your friends were charmed by Rachel in Paris, weren't they? Stephanie Shi, Adele Deng, Tiffany Yap."

Colette nodded diplomatically. "Yes, she was a big hit with all my friends. Mrs. Bao, Rachel's nothing like what you're expecting—she's American, but in the best possible way. I think that in time, Shanghai and Beijing society would come to accept her, especially if she carries a different handbag. You should give her one of your Hermès bags, Mrs. Bao. She will be like the daughter you never had."

Shaoyen sat stone-faced, while Gaoliang addressed his son. "I'm glad Rachel was able to help you, but it still doesn't excuse your behavior. The profligate spending in Paris, the public fights, the drag racing, it's all an indication to me that you are not ready to—"

Carlton got up abruptly from his chair. "Look, I apologized. I'm very sorry for disappointing you. For always disappointing you. I'm not going to sit here any longer and continue this inquisition. Especially when the two of you can't even sort out your own problems! Colette, let's get out of here."

"But the bird's nest? The bird's nest dessert isn't even here yet," Colette protested.

Rolling his eyes, Carlton left the dining room without another word.

Colette pursed her lips awkwardly. "Um, I think I better follow him. But first, allow me to treat tonight."

"That's a very nice gesture, Colette, but we'll take care of dinner," Gaoliang responded.

"I did all the ordering—I really should pay," Colette said matter-of-factly, gesturing to Roxanne, who ceremoniously handed the head waiter a credit card.

"No, no, we insist," Shaoyen said, getting up from her chair and attempting to thrust her credit card in the waiter's hand.

"Absolutely not, Mrs. Bao!" Colette shrieked, leaping up and snatching Shaoyen's card away from the hapless waiter.

"*Aiyah*, it's no use fighting you," Gaoliang said.

"You're right, it's no use," Colette said with a triumphant smile.

A few moments later, the waiter returned. Glancing sheepishly at Colette, he whispered something in Roxanne's ear.

"That's not possible. Try again," Roxanne said dismissively.

"We tried several times, ma'am," he said in a low voice. "Perhaps it has exceeded its limit?"

Roxanne stepped outside of the private dining room with the waiter and barked, "Do you know what this is? It's a P. J. Whitney Titanium card, and it's only available to ultra-high-net-worth individuals. There is no limit. I could buy an airplane with this card if I wanted to. Run it one more time."

"What is the problem?" Colette asked, coming out of the room.

Roxanne shook her head in disgust. "He is saying the card's been rejected."

"I don't understand. How can a credit card ever be rejected? It's not like it's a kidney!" Colette laughed.

"No, no, it's a billing term. Sometimes, other people's cards can be 'rejected' if they exceed a certain spending limit, but that's not possible with you," Roxanne explained.

A moment later, the head waiter returned with the manager, who was ornately dressed in a Gianni Versace patterned shirt and black Jeggings. He smiled apologetically and said, "I'm very sorry, Miss Bing, but we tried everything. It just would not work. Perhaps you'd like to use another card?"

Colette looked at Roxanne in utter bafflement. Nothing like this had ever happened to her in her entire life. "Do I even have another card?"

"I'll just pay for it first," Roxanne huffed, handing the manager her own black card.

. . .

After Roxanne and Colette had left the room, the Baos sat in silence for a few moments.

"I suppose you're feeling very satisfied about all this," Shaoyen finally said.

Gaoliang frowned. "What do you mean?"

"We get to hear about how your virtuous daughter saved the day, and you think everything is fine now."

"Is that what you think?"

Shaoyen glared at him icily and said in a soft, deliberate voice, "No, that's not what I think. I'm thinking that all of China's top families now know that you sired a bastard child. I'm thinking that our family is going to become the laughing-stock of society. I'm thinking that your political life as you know it will be over, and that Carlton won't stand a chance now either."

Gaoliang gave a weary sigh. "Right now, I'm more concerned about Carlton as a human being, not his political career. I'm wondering where we went wrong with him. How did we manage to raise a child who would find it acceptable to wager ten million dollars on a race? I don't recognize this son of mine anymore!"

"So now what? You're going to throw him out of the house?" Shaoyen said facetiously.

"I could do more than that. I could threaten to disinherit him. Knowing he may no longer have a fortune to gamble away might help knock some sense into him," Gaoliang mused.

Shaoyen's eyes widened in alarm. "You can't be serious."

"I won't disinherit him completely, but after all that's happened, I think that giving him absolute control of everything would be a big mistake. Tell me, what is going to happen to everything we've worked so hard for? You especially— you took my father's medical supplies company and single-handedly transformed it into a billion-dollar empire. Do you really think Carlton's capable of taking the reins anytime soon? I'm thinking of getting Rachel more involved in the business.

She's a highly respected economist—at least *she* won't run the company into the ground!"

Just then the door opened and Roxanne walked in. "Oh— you're still here? I'm sorry to intrude, but I think Colette left her cell phone in here."

Gaoliang saw it lying on a nearby chair and handed it to Roxanne. The minute the door closed behind her, Shaoyen began to speak again. "How dare you even think of bringing that girl into the company? How would Carlton feel?"

"I think Carlton couldn't care less. He has shown no interest at all in doing anything serious with his life, and—"

"He's still recovering from his accident!"

Gaoliang shook his head in frustration. "Carlton has done nothing but screw up over the past few years, but you keep making excuses for him every time. He races his car in London and almost gets himself killed, and you forbid me to criticize him because you think it will upset his recovery. He comes back to China and does nothing but party every night of the week with Colette Bing, and we say nothing. Now he goes to Paris and has the audacity to try to compete in *another* reckless race, and you're still defending him."

"I'm not defending him! But I can appreciate his inner struggle," Shaoyen protested. *If Gaoliang only knew what really happened in London, he would understand. But he couldn't know.*

"What inner struggle? The only struggle I've witnessed is how you've smothered him with all your pampering."

Stung by his remark, Shaoyen let out an angry laugh. "So it's all my fault then? You are too blind to see it, but your own actions are to be blamed! You let that girl come to China. *She* is the one who has destroyed the harmony in our family. *She* is the reason Carlton is acting so recklessly!"

"That is such nonsense! You heard it yourself from him tonight—Rachel was the one who talked sense into him, when he didn't even value his own life!"

"How could he, when his own father has never valued him? Even when he was a baby, I could sense that you never loved Carlton the same way I did. And now I know why . . . it's because you've never stopped loving that *shabi*[*] Kerry Chu, isn't it? You've never stopped pining after her and your long-lost daughter!"

"You're being ridiculous. You know very well I had no idea Kerry was even alive until a few months ago. I had no idea I had a daughter!"

"Then you're even more pathetic than I thought! You are willing to give away your family's legacy to a girl you barely know! I've bled for this goddamn company for over twenty years, and you'll have to kill me before I see you hand it over to that . . . that bastard girl!" Shaoyen screamed, grabbing the half-empty teapot from the table and flinging it against the mirrored glass wall.

Gaoliang stared grimly at the smashed pieces of cracked porcelain and the amber lines of tea streaking down the mirrored wall. "I can't talk to you when you're like this. You're clearly out of your mind," he said, getting up from the table and leaving the room.

Shaoyen shouted after him, "I'm out of my mind because of you!"

---

[*]   Mandarin for "stupid cunt."

# THE WEST LAKE

As the last vapors of early-morning mist hovered over the still waters, the only sound to be heard was the discreet splish of the boatman's single wooden oar as he rowed Rachel and Peik Lin through a secluded inlet of Hangzhou's West Lake.

"I am so glad you dragged me out of bed to do this. This is beyond exquisite!" Rachel sighed contentedly as she stretched her legs out on the cushioned lounge seat of their traditional Chinese rowboat.

"I told you the lake is at its most beautiful right at dawn," Peik Lin said, gazing at the poetry of lines created by the converging mountains. Far off, she could make out an ancient hilltop temple silhouetted against the pearl gray sky. There was just something about this landscape that touched her beyond words, and she suddenly understood how over the centuries all the great Chinese poets and artists were inspired by the West Lake.

As the boat drifted slowly under one of the romantic stone bridges, Rachel asked the boatman, "When were these bridges built?"

"There's no telling, miss. Hangzhou was the favored

retreat of the emperors for five thousand years—Marco Polo called it the City of Heaven," he replied.

"I would have to agree with him," Rachel said, taking another long, slow sip of the freshly roasted Longjing tea that the boatman had prepared for her. As the boat drifted through a watery grove of wild lotuses, the girls caught sight of a small kingfisher perched on the tip of a lotus stalk, waiting for the right moment to strike.

"I wish Nick could see this," Rachel said wistfully.

"Me too! But you'll be back with him before too long. I think you've been bitten by the Hangzhou bug, haven't you?"

"Jesus, I wish I'd come sooner! When you first told me this place was China's answer to Lake Como, I had my doubts, but after visiting that glorious tea plantation yesterday, followed by the amazing dinner at the mountaintop temple, I'm completely sold."

"And here I thought I needed to arrange for George Clooney to pop up from under those willows over there," Peik Lin quipped.

Arriving back at the elegant wooden dock of the Four Seasons Hangzhou, they climbed out of the boat slowly, still lulled by the sybaritic boat ride. "Just in time for our spa appointments. Get ready, this place is going to rock your world," Peik Lin said excitedly as they walked along the pathway to the palatial gray-walled villa that housed the resort's spa. "Which treatment did you end up scheduling first?"

"I thought I'd start the day with the Jade and Lotus massage," Rachel answered.

Peik Lin raised an eyebrow. "Hmm . . . what parts of your body are they massaging, exactly?"

"Oh, stop! Apparently they buff your body with lotus seeds and crushed jade and then give you an intensive deep-tissue rubdown. What are you getting?"

"My favorite—the Imperial Consorts and Concubines

Perfumed Water Ritual. It's inspired by the bathing ritual that was reserved for whichever woman the emperor chose to spend the night with. You're immersed in a perfumed bath of orange blossoms and gardenia, followed by a gentle pressure-point massage. Then they do this awesome body scrub with crushed pearls and almonds, before cocooning you in a white-china-clay body wrap. It all ends with a long nap in a private steam room. I tell you, I always come out of it feeling a decade younger."

"Oooh. Maybe I'll do that one tonight. Oh wait, I think I scheduled the luxury caviar facial tonight. Shoot, we don't have enough days for all the treatments I want to try!"

"Wait a minute, when did Rachel Chu, who wouldn't even go for a pedicure back in her college days, become a spa whore?"

Rachel grinned. "It's all the time I've been spending with those Shanghai girls—I think it's catching."

. . .

After several hours of pampering treatments, Rachel and Peik Lin met for lunch at the resort's restaurant. Naturally, they were shown to one of the private dining rooms, which were in pagoda-style structures overlooking a serene lagoon. Admiring the massive Murano glass chandelier that hovered over their lacquered walnut table, Rachel mused, "After this trip, New York is going to seem like a dump. Every place I go to in China seems to be more luxurious than the last. Who would have ever guessed? Remember when I was teaching in Chengdu in 2002? The place where I roomed had one communal indoor toilet, and *that* was considered a luxury."

"Ha! You wouldn't recognize Chengdu now. It's become the Silicon Valley of China—one fifth of the world's computers are made there," Peik Lin said.

Rachel shook her head in wonder. "I just can't get over it—all these megacities springing up overnight, this nonstop economic boom. The economist in me wants to say 'This can't last,' but then I'll see something that totally blows my mind. The other day in Shanghai, Nick and I were trying to get back to our hotel from Xintiandi. All the taxis had their signs lit up, but we couldn't figure out why they wouldn't stop for us. Finally, this Australian girl standing on the corner said to us, 'Don't you have the taxi app?' We were like, *The what?* Turns out there's an app you use to bid on taxis. Everyone uses it, and the highest bidder ends up getting the taxi."

Peik Lin laughed. "Free-market enterprise at its best!"

A server entered the room and lifted the lid off the first course with a flourish. It was a heaping plate of tiny shrimp that glistened like pearls. "These are the famous Hangzhou freshwater shrimp flash fried in garlic. You don't find them anywhere else on the planet. I've been craving this dish since we first talked about meeting up here," Peik Lin said, scooping a generous portion onto Rachel's plate.

Rachel tried a mouthful and smiled at her friend in surprise. "Wow . . . they're *sweet*!

"Pretty amazing, right?"

"I haven't had seafood this good since Paris," Rachel said.

"I always say that only the French can compete with the Chinese when it comes to preparing seafood. I'm sure you guys ate your way through Paris."

"Nick and I did, but food wasn't really the focus for Colette and her friends. Remember how I used to accuse you of 'irrational exuberance' whenever Neiman Marcus invited you to a trunk show? Well, these girls went completely batshit insane in Paris! They hit the shops from morning till night, and we had three extra Range Rovers tailing us everywhere we went just to carry the shopping bags alone!"

Peik Lin smiled. "Sounds familiar. These PRCs* come to Singapore on crazy shopping sprees too. You know, for many of them, shopping on a massive scale is how they validate their success. It's a way to make up for all the suffering their families had to endure in the past."

"Look, I get it. I come from an immigrant family that's done well, and I married a guy who's well-off. But I feel that there's a certain limit I would never go over when it comes to shopping," Rachel said. "I mean, when you're spending more money on a couture dress than it takes to vaccinate a thousand children against measles or provide clean water to an entire town, that's just unconscionable."

Peik Lin gave Rachel a thoughtful look. "Isn't it all relative though? To someone living in a mud hut somewhere, isn't the $200 you paid for those Rag & Bone jeans you're wearing considered obscene? The woman buying that couture dress could argue it took a team of twelve seamstresses three months to create the garment, and they are all supporting their families by doing this. My mother wanted an exact re-creation on her bedroom ceiling of a Baroque fresco she saw at some palace in Germany. It cost her half a million dollars, but two artists from the Czech Republic worked on it every day for three months. One guy was able to buy and furnish a new house in Prague, while the other one sent his kid to Penn State. We all choose to spend our money in different ways, but at least we get to make that choice. Just think—twenty years ago, these girls you went to Paris with would only have two choices: Do you want your Mao jacket in shit brown or shit gray?"

Rachel laughed. "Okay, point taken, but I still wouldn't

---

* The younger generation of Singaporeans have taken to referring to Mainland Chinese as "PRCs" (for People's Republic of China), while many of the older generation still use the term "Mainlanders."

spend that kind of money. Now I don't think I can eat any of these braised meatballs. They're reminding me too much of a steaming pile of Mao."

After lunch, Rachel and Peik Lin decided to do some exploring around the resort, which was set on seventeen acres of landscaped grounds designed to resemble the gardens of an imperial summer palace from the Qing dynasty. As they meandered along the covered walkways, inhaling the fragrant cherry blossoms and admiring interconnected lily ponds, Rachel started to feel a little queasy. When they reached a garden filled with carved scholar's rocks, she took a seat on one of the benches.

"Are you okay?" Peik Lin asked, noticing how pale Rachel suddenly looked.

"I'm going to head back to my room. I think it's getting a little too humid for me."

"You're not used to this. This is paradise compared to Singapore this time of the year. Wanna cool down in that infinity pool by the lake?" Peik Lin suggested.

"I think I just need to lie down for a while."

"Okay, let's go back."

"No, no, you should stay and enjoy the gardens," Rachel insisted.

"Shall we meet for afternoon tea on the terrace around four?"

"That sounds perfect."

Peik Lin lingered in the gardens a while longer, discovering a tranquil little grotto that sheltered a large stone carving of a very fat laughing Buddha. She decided to burn a few of the joss sticks that were sitting in an urn in front of the sculpture and then headed back to her room to change into her bikini. Upon entering her room, she noticed that the green message light on the telephone was blinking. She hit the button to listen to the message. It was Rachel, sounding extremely out of breath: "Um, Peik Lin, could you please come to my room? I think I need help."

Alarmed, Peik Lin instinctively grabbed her cell phone and saw that Rachel had called three times. She rushed out of her room and ran down the long corridor toward Rachel's room. Arriving outside the room, she began knocking on the door, but there was no answer. A hotel employee walked by, and Peik Lin grabbed him urgently. "Can you open this door? My friend is sick and needs help!"

Within a few minutes, a desk manager arrived with a security guard.

"Can we help you, miss?"

"Yes, my friend left me an urgent message asking for help. She wasn't feeling well, and now she's not answering," Peik Lin said frantically.

"Er, maybe she's asleep?" the manager said.

"Or maybe she's dying! Open the fucking door now!" Peik Lin screamed.

The manager swiped his pass key over the door, and Peik Lin rushed in. There was no sign of anyone in the bed or on the private terrace, but in the marble bathroom beside the deep soaking tub, she found Rachel lying unconscious in a pool of dark green bile.

# NATIONAL LIBRARY OF CHINA

BEIJING, CHINA

*3:54 p.m.*

Nick was poring over an old biography about the Sassoon family in the Western Languages Reading Room of the National Library when his cell phone started buzzing. He put a manila folder over the open book to hold his page and went out to the corridor to take the call.

It was Peik Lin, sounding close to tears. "Oh my God, Nick! I don't know how to tell you this, but I'm at the emergency room with Rachel. She passed out in her hotel room."

"What? Is she okay? What happened?" Nick asked in shock.

"We don't really know. She's still unconscious, but her white cell count is extremely low and her blood pressure is through the roof. They have her on an IV of magnesium to stabilize her, but they think she maybe has an extreme case of food poisoning."

"I'll get on the next flight to Hangzhou," Nick said decisively.

*4:25 p.m.*

Racing through Beijing Capital International Airport, Nick had just reached the China Airlines counter when Peik Lin called again.

"Hey, Peik Lin, I'm trying to get on the 4:55 flight."

"I don't want to alarm you, but the situation has gotten progressively worse. Rachel's still unconscious, and her kidneys have shut down. The doctors are running tests, but so far they have no clue what's happening. Frankly, I'm losing confidence and I think Rachel should be medically evacuated to Hong Kong, where she can get the best care in the region."

"I trust you. Do what you think is best. Should I charter a plane?" Nick asked.

"Don't worry—I've already arranged that."

"I don't know what we'd do without you, Peik Lin!"

"Just get to Hong Kong."

"I will. Listen, I'm going to call my uncle Malcolm, who is a heart surgeon in Hong Kong. He might be of help."

*6:48 p.m.*

When Peik Lin's Gulfstream V landed in Hong Kong's Chek Lap Kok International Airport, there was already a medical helicopter waiting on the tarmac to airlift Rachel to the hospital. Peik Lin emerged from the aircraft to find a man in mustard yellow jeans and a cobalt blue Rubinacci blazer awaiting her.

"I'm Nick's cousin Edison Cheng! There's no room in the chopper for you, so come in my Bentley," he said over the roar of the helicopter's propellers. Peik Lin followed Eddie to his car numbly, and as they began making their way to the hospital, Eddie said, "My father is in Houston getting an award at the DeBakey Medical Foundation, but he's already put in a call to Queen Mary Hospital—that's our top emergency care center. I'm told the whole kidney team is waiting for her arrival."

"I'm so glad," Peik Lin said.

"Now, Leo Ming happens to be my best friend, so his father, Ming Kah-Ching, who I'm sure you've heard of, has already put in a call to the hospital's chief executive to add even more pressure. The emergency medical ward, by the way, is in the Ming Kah-Ching wing. So Rachel will be treated like a VVIP from the moment she arrives," Eddie boasted.

*Like Rachel cares about that right now!* Peik Lin thought. "As long as they treat her EFFECTIVELY, that's all I care about."

They drove in silence for a few minutes, and then Eddie asked, "So was that your GV, or did you charter the plane?"

"It's my family's," Peik Lin answered. *I bet he's going to ask who my family is.*

"Very nice. And if I might ask, what line of business is your family in?" *She looks Hokkien, so I'd guess either banking or real estate.*

"Construction and property development." *Now he'll want to know which company. I'm going to make him work for it!*

Eddie smiled at her cordially. *Damn Singaporeans! If she was from Hong Kong or China, I would have known everything about her family the moment she stepped off the plane.* "Commercial or residential?"

*Okay, let's put him out of his misery.* "My family started the Near West Organization."

Eddie's face lit up. *Ding ding ding! The Gohs are ranked number 178 on* The Heron Wealth Report. "Oh, you guys built that new condo in Singapore with the sky garages, didn't you?" he said nonchalantly.

"That was us." *Now he's going to tell me what he does. Based on the outfit, I'm guessing either weatherman or hairdresser.*

"I'm the managing director of Leichtenburg Group Asia."

"Ah, yes." *Another banker. Yawn.*

Eddie flashed Peik Lin his Cheshire cat grin. "Tell me, are you satisfied with your private wealth management team?"

"Very much so." *I don't believe this fucker! Rachel's being rushed to the hospital in critical condition and he's trying to land a new client!*


*7:45 p.m.*

Peik Lin and Eddie ran up to the reception counter at the emergency medical ward. "Yes, can you tell us where Rachel Young has been taken? She would have been admitted in the past hour. She came in by air ambulance."

"Are you relatives of the patient?" the woman at the counter asked.

"Yes, we are."

"Let me see . . ." The woman began typing into her computer terminal. "What is the name again?"

"Rachel Young. Or maybe she was admitted as Rachel Chu," Peik Lin said.

The woman scanned her computer screen. "I'm not finding anything here. You should go to the main reception hall at—"

Eddie banged on the counter in frustration. "Stop wasting our time! Do you know who I am? I'm Edison Cheng! My father is Dr. Malcolm Cheng—he used to be head of cardiology! The cafeteria is named after him! I demand to know where they've taken Rachel Young right now or you will be out of a job by tomorrow!"

Just then, they heard someone call out behind them, "Hey, Eddie! Over here!" They turned to see Nick poke his head out from behind a pair of swinging double doors.

"Nick! How the hell did you get here before we did?" Peik Lin said in shock as she rushed to him.

"I called in a favor," Nick said as he hugged her tightly.

"You know Captain Kirk or something? Beijing's an hour farther from Hong Kong!"

"I managed to catch a military transport jet. We didn't have to deal with any airspace delays, and I swear we were flying at Mach 3."

"Let me guess . . . Uncle Alfred made a call?" Eddie asked.

Nick nodded. He ushered the two of them into the waiting room of the adult intensive care unit, which was lined with comfortable leather chairs. "I was able to see Rachel for a few minutes, and then they made me leave. They're trying to restore her renal function right now. The doctor needs to ask you some questions, Peik Lin."

Several minutes later, the doctor entered the waiting room.

"Everyone, this is Dr. Jacobson," Nick said.

Eddie got up from his chair and extended his hand with a flourish. "Edison Cheng—I'm Malcolm Cheng's son."

"I'm sorry, am I supposed to know that name?" the raven-haired doctor asked.

Eddie looked at her in astonishment. The doctor grinned. "Just kidding. Of course I know your father."

Eddie was never more relieved in his life.

"How is she?" Nick asked, trying to remain calm.

"Her vitals have been stabilized for the time being, and we're running a range of tests. This is a very perplexing case. We're still not able to pinpoint what led to such rapid multi-organ failure, but obviously there is something extremely toxic in her system." Looking at Peik Lin, she asked, "Can you tell me everything your friend ate or drank in the last twenty-four hours?"

"I can try. Let's see, when we first arrived last night at the Four Seasons, Rachel had a Cobb salad, and then a straw-berry and lychee mousse dessert. This morning we skipped breakfast, but we had a very simple lunch of Hangzhou river shrimp, sautéed young bamboo shoots, and roast duck noodle soup. There was also some chocolate-dipped ginger in our rooms that Rachel might have eaten. I didn't eat those. Oh wait a minute—she had a massage this morning that supposedly used pieces of crushed jade and lotus seeds."

"Hmm . . . let me look into that. We'll put in a call to the resort and get a full list of anything she might have possibly ingested or been exposed to."

"What do you think it could have been, doctor? We've basically eaten the same foods, and as you can see I'm totally fine," Peik Lin said.

"Everyone's body reacts differently. But I don't want to jump to any conclusions until we finish running all the toxicology tests," the doctor explained.

"What's your prognosis?" Nick asked worriedly.

The doctor paused, hunching her shoulders. "I'm not going to kid you— things are quite critical at the moment. We may have to put in a TIPS* to staunch the worsening liver failure. And if she develops encephalopathy, we will have to put her in a medically induced coma in order to give her body more of a fighting chance."

"Medically induced coma?" Peik Lin said in a hushed tone, promptly bursting into tears. Nick held her in his arms, desperately trying not to lose it himself.

Eddie went up to the doctor. "You do everything you possibly can. Remember, Dr. Malcolm Cheng and Ming Kah-Ching will hold you personally responsible if anything happens to her."

Dr. Jacobson gave Eddie a slightly annoyed look. "We do

---

* TIPS is an acronym for transhepatic intrahepatic portosystemic shunt. Try saying that five times fast.

the best we can for *all* our patients, Mr. Cheng, regardless of who they are."

"Can we please see her?" Peik Lin asked.

"I can only let you in one at a time," the doctor replied.

"You go, Nick," Peik Lin said, sinking back down onto the couch.

*8:40 p.m.*

Nick stood at the foot of Rachel's bed, watching helplessly as a team of doctors and nurses hovered over her. Two days ago they had been in their suite at the Peninsula, where she had been excitedly packing for her spa weekend with one of her best friends. *Don't you have too much fun in Beijing now! No flirting with any sexy librarians, unless it's Parker Posey,* Rachel had teased, before giving him the sweetest goodbye kiss. Now her complexion had turned yellow and there were cables, cords, and tubes in her neck and abdomen. It was just so unreal. What happened to his beautiful wife? Why wasn't she getting any better? He couldn't even begin to imagine losing her. No, no, no, he had to wipe that thought out of his mind. She was so strong, so healthy. She was going to be okay. She had her whole life ahead of her. Their whole life together. Nick left the room and walked toward the waiting room. Passing a handicapped toilet, he let himself in and locked the door. He took a few deep breaths, splashed some water on his face, and looked at himself in the mirror. Then he noticed the mirror itself—a round, backlit mirror that looked like it came from some pricey design showroom. He glanced around and saw that the whole space had recently been redecorated. Tears started streaming down his face uncontrollably. If Rachel pulled through—no—*when* Rachel pulled through this, he was going to build her the most insanely beautiful bathroom the world had ever seen.

*9:22 p.m.*

Nick reentered the waiting room and found Peik Lin and
Eddie huddled over Styrofoam bowls of wonton noodles.
His aunt Alix and cousin Alistair were sitting in the chairs
across from them. Alistair got up and gave his cousin a
warm hug.

"Oh Nicky! This is so vexing! How is Rachel?" Alix asked
anxiously.

"There's not been much change," Nick said wearily.

"Well, I know Dr. Jacobson very well. She's the best, really,
so Rachel is in very capable hands."

"I'm glad to hear that."

"And your uncle Malcolm called— the hospital has been
updating him, and he's asked his colleague who is Hong
Kong's top hepatobiliary specialist to come in and give a second opinion."

"I can't thank him enough."

"He only wishes he could be here. *Gum ngaam,*\* ah, the
one time you have a medical emergency in Hong Kong and
Malcolm is away! We brought some *siew yook* and *wonton meen.*†
Are you hungry?"

"Sure. I think I should eat something." Nick sat in a daze
while his aunt proceeded to arrange assorted takeout containers of food and plastic utensils around him.

"Now, we haven't called anyone yet, Nicky. I wasn't sure
what you wanted people to know, so I held off on calling your
mother. Once she knows, the whole world will know."

"Thanks, Auntie Alix. I can't deal with my mum at the
moment."

"Have you spoken to Rachel's mom?" Peik Lin asked.

---

\*  Cantonese for "too fitting."
†  Barbecued roast pork and wonton noodles.

Nick sighed. "I'll call her in a little while. I just don't see the need to alarm her until we know what's going on."

The door opened and in walked Eddie and Alistair's sister, Cecilia, carrying an elaborate arrangement of white lilies.

"Looks like the gang's all here," Nick said, trying to force a smile.

"You know me—I couldn't miss out on a party," Cecilia said, giving Nick a peck on the cheek as she set the floral arrangement on the seat next to him.

"My God, look at that! Thanks so much, but you really didn't need to bring anything."

"Oh, I didn't bring this. The receptionist outside told me to bring it in for you."

"That's strange. Who could it be from? No one knows we're here aside from you all," Nick wondered aloud as he slurped down some noodles.

Peik Lin started undoing the ribbons around the vase, and as the plastic wrappings came undone, a note card fell out. She opened the card and started reading it. "HOLY SHIT!" Peik Lin gasped, shoving the vase away from her reflexively. The vase of flowers landed on the floor with a crash, as water spilled everywhere.

Nick leaped out of his chair. "What happened?"

Peik Lin handed him the card, which read:

Rachel,

You have been poisoned with a potentially lethal dose of Tarquinomid. Your doctors will be able to reverse the side effects once they know this.

If you value your life, you will not mention this incident to anyone.

Never set foot in China again.

This is your last warning.

9

# RIDOUT ROAD

SINGAPORE

Astrid turned on her laptop and composed an e-mail:

Dear Charlie,

Sorry to keep bothering you like this, but I need to ask another favor. Wondering if you can help me get to the bottom of something . . .

What do you know about Promenade Technologies? Based in Mountain View, CA? Have you ever worked with them before? They acquired Michael's first company—Cloud Nine Solutions. I need to find out more about this company; specifically, who the people are that own it.

Thanks!

xo, Astrid

She sent the e-mail, and one minute later, Charlie popped up on Google Chat.

CHARLIE WU: Hey! Happy to look into this for you.

ASTRID LEONG TEO: Really appreciate your help.

CW: Any special reason why?

ALT: Trying to get some answers for myself. Have you
   heard of them?

CW: Yes. But doesn't Michael know everything you'd
   need to know?

ALT: Apparently not. Do you know if they are
   fully owned or partially owned by some Asian
   conglomerate?

CW: What's going on, Astrid?

Astrid paused for a few minutes, not sure whether she was
prepared to get into it with Charlie about everything that had
happened with Michael.

ALT: I'm trying to help Michael get to the truth. It's a
   bit complicated . . . don't want to drag you into it.

CW: I'm already in it. But okay, I won't press further.
   But if you really want my help, it would be better if I
   had the big picture.

She sat on the edge of her bed, thinking, *What do I have to
hide from Charlie? He's the only person who will understand.*

ALT: Okay, here goes. Michael's gotten it into his head
   that my father—or someone at one of the companies controlled by my family—actually bought Cloud
   Nine Solutions, using Promenade as a cover.

CW: Why would he suddenly think that?

ALT: Long story, but basically he came across some
   old papers listing the buyer as Pebble Beach Holding Company, and knowing how much my dad loves
   golfing there, he's made this huge assumption.

CW: Sorry to state the obvious, but did you ask your
dad if he bought the company?

ALT: I did. And of course he denied it. "Why the
bloody hell would I want Michael's company? I
thought it was absurdly overvalued to begin with."

CW: Classic Harry Leong!

ALT: Indeed.

CW: I don't think your father has anything to do with
this, but would it really matter if he does?

ALT: Are you kidding? Michael's story has always been
that he made it on his own. This suspicion that
my family had something to do with his success is
driving him up the wall. He thinks my father is trying
yet again to control him, control us, etc. We had the
biggest fight ever last night.

CW: Sorry to hear that.

ALT: I ended up leaving the house. It was either that or
call the police. I'm now at the Marina Bay Sands hotel.

Fifteen seconds later, Astrid's cell phone rang. It was Charlie calling, so she picked it up and mischievously answered,
"Housekeeping?"

"Er, yes, I need someone to come deal with a big problem
in my room right now," Charlie responded, not missing a beat.

"What kind of problem?"

"These cake fetishists had a party in my room, and there
are about thirty crushed cakes from Lana Cake Shop all over
the carpet, smeared on the walls, on the bed. It looks like people have been rolling around in the cake and frosting, trying
out different Kama Sutra positions."

Astrid giggled. "Sicko! Where do you come up with this
kind of stuff?"

"I was surfing the web last night and came across this article on people who get turned on by sitting on cakes."

"I'm not going to ask what sort of websites you've been surfing in Hong Kong—no doubt ones that would be blocked in Singapore."

"And I'm not going to ask why you're sitting in a room at Marina Bay Sands, of all places!"

Astrid sighed. "There are very few hotels where I can be sure no one will recognize me. MBS is one of those—it's mainly tourists."

"No locals? Really?"

"No one I would know, anyway. When they first opened, my mother tried to go up to the SkyPark with Mrs. Lee Yong Chien and the Queen Mother of Borneo to see the view, but when they found out there was a twenty-dollar entry fee for seniors, Mrs. LYC said, '*Ah nee kwee! Wah mai chut!*'* So they ended up going to Toast Box in the mall instead."

Charlie laughed. "You can't change those women! It's funny—my mother used to be so extravagant, but the older she gets, the more she seems to be turning into an obsessive tightwad. You know she won't let her cooks turn on the lights in the kitchen until seven thirty now? I go over there and they are bumbling around in complete darkness, trying to make dinner for her."

"That's crazy! When we go to restaurants nowadays, my mum gets them to *tah pow*† leftover gravy from the dishes. I kid you not. I tell her she's insane and she says, 'We paid for it! Why waste all this great gravy? Rosie can put it into tomorrow's lunch and it will taste so much better!'"

Charlie chuckled. "So really, how long are you planning to hide out at the hotel?"

"I'm not hiding. I'm just taking a little break. Cassian

---

*    In Hokkien: "So expensive! I'm not coming out with the money!"
†    Hokkien for "put in a doggie bag."

and his nanny are with me, and he's loving the SkyPark pool."

"You know, the husband is the one that's supposed to leave. Whenever I got into really bad fights with Isabel, I would either go over to my brother's or get a hotel room. I couldn't ever imagine making my wife and children leave the house."

"Well, you're a different species than Michael. Besides, he didn't make me leave. I *chose* to leave. He got so angry that he began getting physical."

"What? With you?" Charlie said in shock. *I'm going to fucking kill him if he touched her.*

"No, come on, Michael would never hurt me, but he completely trashed one of his Porsches. Took a samurai sword and began bashing the hood. I couldn't bear to stick around and watch."

"Damn! All because of his issue over who bought the company?" Charlie asked, getting more alarmed by the minute.

"It's not just that. Things have been bad for him lately. He blew that deal with IBM, he lost the house he really wanted, there was this whole magazine article thing that I won't even get into, and it seems like all we ever do these days is . . ." Astrid's voice trailed off for a minute. *I've said too much. It's not fair of me to keep burdening Charlie like this.*

Charlie could hear Astrid's discreet sniffling away from her phone's mouthpiece. *She's crying. She's sitting in a hotel room crying.*

"I'm sorry, it's so inappropriate of me to be bothering you with all this when you're at work." Astrid sniffled again.

"I'm not really doing much today, but don't worry, no one can fire me. You know you can call me anytime at all, don't you?"

"I know. You are the one person who truly understands

me. You know what I have to go through with my family. They don't get what it's like to have marriage problems."

"Do you honestly think your brothers are perfectly content in their marriages?"

"Are you kidding me? I think they are all miserable in one way or another, but none of them would ever admit it. No one is allowed to be unhappy in my family. I think only Alex in LA is truly happy—he got away and got to be with the love of his life. It's just pathetic that Salimah's not accepted. So ironic, isn't it, when you think that all the family money originally comes from Malaysia."

"At least they make each other happy. That's the only thing that matters," Charlie said.

"You know, when I visited them a few months ago, I thought to myself, 'I wish I could do this too.' Sometimes I wish I could just pack a bag and move to California, where no one knows me and no one cares. Cassian can grow up far away from all the pressures he's going to have to start facing very soon. And I would be perfectly happy, I swear to God, living in a beach shack."

*I could be too*, Charlie thought to himself.

They were both silent for a moment, and then Charlie spoke up. "So what are you going to do?"

"There's nothing to do, really. Michael will calm down in a couple of days and we'll go home. If you can help me prove that my father had nothing to do with the acquisition of his company, I'm sure that will go a long way toward making him happier."

Charlie was silent for a moment. "I'll see what I can do."

"You're the best, Charlie, you really are."

The minute he was off the phone with Astrid, Charlie placed a call to his chief financial officer: "Hey, Aaron. Remember the Michael Teo Cloud Nine acquisition back in 2010?"

"How could I ever forget? We're still writing down the losses on that one," Aaron replied.

"Why in God's name did you name the holding company Pebble Beach LTD?"

"Dude, I was standing on the eighteenth hole when you called to tell me to buy the company. It's the greatest finishing hole in the world. Why are you asking?"

"Never mind."

## QUEEN MARY HOSPITAL

POK FU LAM, HONG KONG

Nick was doing the *New York Times* crossword puzzle on his iPad when the police officer on guard outside the room poked his head in.

"Sir, there's a couple at reception demanding to see Ms. Chu. They have two cartfuls of food products with them, and the man says he's her brother."

"Oh yes." Nick smiled, leaning over and whispering softly into Rachel's ear. "Baby . . . you awake? Carlton and Colette are here. Are you up for seeing people?"

Rachel, who had been napping intermittently all morning, opened her eyes groggily. "Um, sure."

"Send them up," Nick instructed the officer.

It had been two days since Rachel had been moved from the intensive care unit to the private ward, and her condition had been steadily improving ever since the doctors discovered the precise drug that had been used to poison her and swiftly administered an antidote.

Soon there was a knock on the door, and Carlton and Colette entered the room. "Hey, Sis! This isn't exactly what I thought the Four Seasons Hangzhou was going to be like,"

Carlton teased, coming up to her bedside and squeezing her hand gently.

Rachel smiled weakly. "You guys really shouldn't have taken the trouble—"

"Oh, come on! We caught the first flight out the minute Nick called," Carlton said. "Besides, there's a sale at Joyce that Colette wanted to get to."

Colette smacked Carlton's arm. "When we hadn't heard from you guys by Monday, we thought you were just having too good a time in Hangzhou without us."

"A marvelous time, as you can see," Rachel said drolly, extending her arms to show off her IV tubes.

"I still can't believe you can get an attack of gallstones when you're this young! I thought it only happened to old people," Colette said.

"Actually, it can happen to anyone," Nick said.

Colette perched on the edge of Rachel's hospital bed and said, "Well, I'm so glad you're back on the mend."

"Did you guys fly down on your smaller plane . . Grande?" Rachel asked Colette.

"Oh, you mean Venti? No, no we didn't," Colette said, rolling her eyes. "My father has cut off my fleet privileges. Ever since I turned down Richie Yang's proposal, my parents have been furious and they have this idea that they're going to teach me some kind of lesson. Can you believe they put a freeze on my bank account, and my Titanium card got revolted? Well, guess what? The joke's on them, because I can survive just fine without their help—you are now looking at the new international brand ambassador for Prêt-à-Couture!"

"Colette just signed a multimillion-dollar contract with them," Carlton boasted.

"Congratulations! How fantastic!" Rachel said.

"Yes, I patched things up with Virginie de Bassinet, and now she's throwing me a party next week at the Johnnie

Walker House to make the big announcement. I'll be in all
the ads for Prêt-à-Couture next season, and Tim Walker will
shoot the campaign. I hope you'll be well enough to make it
to the party."

Nick and Rachel remained silent.

"Hey, this crazy girl here insisted on bringing you more
food from Daylesford Organic, but the warden wouldn't let
us bring the carts up to this floor," Carlton said.

"Well, I'm sure the hospital food must be insipid," Colette
remarked.

"Actually, you'd be surprised. I had a beef pie in the cafeteria yesterday that was rather good," Nick said.

"Thank you so much, Colette. I just started back on
solid foods this morning, and I'm craving something sweet,"
Rachel said.

"OMG—let's smuggle up some of the white-chocolate-
dipped lemon biscuits for you!" Colette squealed.

"Maybe if I go downstairs with you, they'll let us bring
some stuff up," Nick suggested to Carlton.

The two of them headed to the lobby. In the elevator,
Carlton said, "I'm so relieved to see that Rachel is out of the
woods. But why are there police all over the place?"

Nick looked Carlton in the eye. "I'm going to tell you
something, but you have to promise it's strictly between
us, okay?"

"Of course."

Nick took a deep breath. "Rachel didn't have an attack of
gallstones—she was poisoned."

"Like food poisoning?" Carlton asked, confused.

"No, someone intentionally poisoned her with a toxin."

Carlton stared at Nick in horror. "You must be joking."

"I wish I was. She doesn't want to make a big deal out of
it, but you know she could have died. Her organs were shut-

ting down one by one, and the doctors were hopelessly trying to figure out what was wrong until we found out she was
poisoned."

"Un-fucking-believable! How did you find out?"

"We got an anonymous letter."

Carlton gasped. "What? Who would want to poison
*Rachel*?"

"That's what we're trying to find out. Thanks to my aunt
Alix, who knows the chief executive of Hong Kong very well,
it's become an official investigation involving both the Hong
Kong and Chinese police." The elevator reached the lobby,
and Nick pulled Carlton to a quiet corner. "Let me ask you . . .
honestly, do you think Richie Yang is capable of something
like this?"

Carlton paused for a moment. "Richie? Why would he
have anything to do with this?"

"You humiliated him in front of all his friends in Paris.
Colette made it clear to everyone that she prefers you—"
Nick began.

"You think he poisoned Rachel to get back at me? Bloody
hell, that would make him even sicker than I thought! I'd
never forgive myself if that were true."

"It's just one theory. We've been trying to come up with
anyone who might have the slightest motive. I think the police
are going to want to talk to both you and Colette at some
point."

"Of course, of course," Carlton said, his brow furrowed
in shock. "Do they know what kind of toxin was used?"

"It's called Tarquinomid. It's a very hard-to-get pharmaceutical that's normally used to treat people with multiple sclerosis,
manufactured only in Israel. They say it's sometimes used by
Mossad agents for assassinations."

Carlton's face suddenly went pale.

# Bao Residence, Shanghai

Bao Gaoliang and his wife were standing under the portico of their elegant garden mansion in the French Concession, waving goodbye to departing guests, when Carlton's car came racing up the circular driveway.

"My goodness, the emperor has decided to grace us with his presence! To what do we owe this honor?" Shaoyen said sarcastically as Carlton walked up the stone steps toward them.

"I need to see you both in the library. Now!" he said through gritted teeth.

"Don't speak to your mother in that tone!" Gaoliang chastised.

"What, you guys kissed and made up?" Carlton said, as he stormed into the house.

"We had a dinner for the Mongolian ambassador. Unlike you, your father and I still know how to be civil around each other when the occasion warrants it," Shaoyen said, sinking into the tufted leather sofa and taking off her Zanotti heels with a sigh of relief.

Carlton shook his head in disgust. "I don't know how you can sit there in that ball gown of yours, pretending that nothing's wrong when you know very well what you've done!"

"What are you talking about?" Gaoliang asked wearily.

Carlton gave his mother a withering look. "Do you want to tell him, or should I?"

"I have no idea what you're referring to," Shaoyen said icily.

Carlton turned to his father, his eyes black with anger. "While you've been sitting in this house hosting a dinner party with your wife, your daughter—*your flesh and blood*—has been lying in a hospital in Hong Kong—"

"Rachel's in the hospital?" Gaoliang interrupted.

"You haven't heard? They had to airlift her from Hang-zhou to Hong Kong."

"What happened?" Gaoliang stared at Carlton in alarm.

"She was poisoned by someone. She was in the ICU for three days and almost died."

Gaoliang's jaw dropped. "Who would poison her?"

"I dunno . . . why don't you ask *Mother*?"

Shaoyen bolted upright on the sofa. "*Ni zai jiang shen me pi hua?*\* Did you stop taking your medication, Carlton? Is this some hallucination of yours?"

"I know you were just trying to send her a warning, but you almost killed her! I don't understand you, Mother. *How could you do something like that?*" Carlton said, his eyes brimming with tears.

Shaoyen turned to her husband in astonishment. "Can you believe this? Our son is accusing me of being a murderer. How on earth do you think I had any part in this, Carlton?"

"I know precisely how you did it. Not you, of course, but one of your lackeys. Rachel was poisoned with Tarquinomid—which we so conveniently just started manufacturing for Opal Pharmaceuticals of Tel Aviv!"

"Oh my God," Shaoyen said in a whisper, while Gaoliang looked stunned.

"You don't think I keep up with what's happening at the company? Well surprise, surprise, I do. I know all about that secret deal you made with Opal."

"We have so many secret deals with companies all over the world. Yes, Opal outsourced Tarquinomid to us, but do you actually think I would poison Rachel? Why would I do that?"

Carlton looked at his mother accusingly. "Oh come on! You have been so hell-bent against Rachel since day one! Do I need to spell it out for you?"

---

\*    Mandarin for "What the fuck are you saying?"

Gaoliang spoke up, finally fed up with his son's accusations. "Don't be ridiculous, Carlton. SHE DID NOT POISON RACHEL! How dare you say such a thing about your own mother?"

"Dad, you don't know half the things Mother has been telling me. If you could only hear what she's said about Rachel!"

"Your mother may have issues with Rachel, but she would never do anything to harm her."

Carlton started to laugh bitterly. "Oh, that's what you think? You don't have a clue what Mother is capable of, do you? Of course you don't—you have no idea what she did in—"

"CARLTON," Shaoyen said as a warning.

"What Mother did *in London*!"

"What are you talking about?" Gaoliang asked.

"The big cover-up in London . . . all to protect you."

Shaoyen rushed up to her son and grabbed his shoulders in a panic. "SHUT UP, CARLTON!"

"NO! I WON'T SHUT UP! I'm sick of shutting up and not talking about it!" Carlton exploded.

"Then talk! What happened in London?" Gaoliang demanded.

"Please, Carlton, if you know what's best for you, please don't say any more," Shaoyen pleaded frantically.

"A girl died in my car wreck!" Carlton spat out.

"DON'T LISTEN TO HIM! He's drunk! He's sick in the head!" Shaoyen screamed as she struggled to put her hands over Carlton's mouth.

"What on earth are you talking about? I thought the girl was paralyzed," Gaoliang said.

Carlton shook his mother off and ran to the other side of the room. "There were two girls in the Ferrari with me, Dad! One girl survived, but the other girl died. And Mother had it all covered up. She got Mr. Tin and your banker in Hong Kong to pay everyone off. She wanted you to remain blissfully ignorant about what happened—all to protect your precious position! She's never allowed me to talk about it. She's never wanted you to know what a fuckup I am. But I'm admitting it now, Dad—I killed a girl!"

Gaoliang stared at both of them in horror, as Shaoyen sank to the floor sobbing.

Carlton continued, "I will never forgive myself, and it will haunt me for the rest of my life. But I'm trying to take responsibility for what I've done, Dad. I can't change the past, but I'm trying to change myself. Rachel helped me realize all this when we were in Paris. But Mother found out that Rachel knows this secret about my accident, and that's the *real* reason she wanted her killed!"

"No, no! That's not true!" Shaoyen cried.

"How do you feel now, Mother? The big secret is out, and your worst nightmare is coming true. Our family name will be ruined just like you thought it would—not by Rachel or by me, but when the police come and haul you off to jail!"

Carlton stormed out of the house, leaving his mother on the floor of the library and his father seated next to her with his head buried in his hands.

# BUKIT BROWN CEMETERY

Every year, on the anniversary of their father's death, Shang Su Yi and her brother, Alfred, would visit the grave where their parents were buried. Su Yi's immediate family and a few close relatives would traditionally gather at Tyersall Park for breakfast before heading to the cemetery, but this year everyone met at Bukit Brown first. Astrid arrived early, coming straight from dropping Cassian off at Far Eastern Kindergarten, and hardly anyone was around as she strolled through Singapore's oldest cemetery.

Since the cemetery had stopped accepting burials in 1970, the forest had grown unchecked around it, making this final resting place of Singapore's founding fathers a lush, Edenic nature preserve for some of the rarest plants and wildlife on the island. Astrid loved meandering and admiring the ornate graves that were unlike anywhere else in the world. The larger, more ostentatious Chinese-style tombs were built into the sides of gentle sloping mounds, and some were as big as palace gatehouses, boasting their own tiled courtyards where mourners could gather, while others were decorated with colorful Peranakan tiles and life-size statues depicting Sikh

guards, Quanyin, or other Chinese deities. Astrid began reading the gravestones, and every now and then, she recognized
the name of a pioneer Singaporean: Tan Kheam Hock, Ong
Sam Leong, Lee Choo Neo, Tan Ean Kiam, Chew Boon Lay.
They were all here.

At precisely ten o'clock, a small convoy of cars invaded the
quiet of the cemetery. At the front was the 1990s-era Jaguar
Vanden Plas ferrying Astrid's mother, Felicity Leong—Su Yi's
eldest child—and her husband, Harry, followed by the small
Kia Picanto driven by Astrid's brother Henry Leong Jr.* Then
came the vintage black-and-burgundy Daimler with Su Yi's
younger daughter, Victoria, who rode with Rosemary T'sien,
Lillian May Tan, and the Bishop of Singapore. A few minutes later, a black Mercedes 600 Pullman with tinted windows
pulled up, and before the humongous limousine had come
to a full stop, the middle doors flung open and two Gurkha
guards jumped out.

Alfred Shang, a short, portly man in his late seventies
with a careful comb-over of gray hair, emerged from the car,
squinting in the bright morning light even with his rimless
sunglasses on. He helped his older sister, Su Yi, out of the
car, followed by her two lady's maids in elegant iridescent
peacock-blue silk dresses. Su Yi was dressed in a cream-colored
blouse, a thin saffron-colored cardigan, and light brown trousers. With her round tortoiseshell sunglasses, straw cloche
hat, and brown suede gloves, she looked like she was ready for
a day of gardening. Su Yi caught sight of Bishop See Bei Sien

---

*    Henry Leong Jr.'s personal net worth is conservatively estimated at $420
million, since his father is still very much alive and he has yet to inherit any of
his real fortune. For that reason, and because he commutes daily to the Wood-
lands for his job, Harry drives a very fuel-economical car. His wife, the attorney
Cathleen Kah (herself an heiress to the Kah Chin Kee fortune), walks from
their consulate-like house on Nassim Road to the bus stop and takes Bus 75 to
her office at Raffles Place every day.

and muttered angrily to Alfred, "Victoria invited that busy-body bishop again when I specifically told her not to! Father is going to spin in his grave!"

After a flurry of quick greetings, the family made their way along one of the more manicured paths, forming a rather stately procession as Su Yi led the way, walking under an embroidered yellow silk umbrella held by one of the Gurkha guards. The tomb of Shang Loong Ma was on the highest hill, a secluded spot completely encircled by a thicket of trees. The tombstone itself was not particularly monumental compared to some of the others, but the large circular plaza of glazed tiles and the exquisite bas-reliefs depicting a scene from *The Romance of the Three Kingdoms* on the tomb made it uniquely beautiful. Awaiting them at the grave were several Buddhist monks in dark brown robes, and in front of the plaza, a marquee had been set up with a long banquet table that gleamed with silver and the pale yellow nineteenth-century Wedgwood service that Su Yi always used for al fresco entertaining.

"Oh my goodness! Are we lunching here?" Lillian May Tan exclaimed, eyeing the fat suckling pig with a cherry in its mouth and the line of uniformed staff from Tyersall Park standing at attention beside the marquee.

"Yes, Mother thought it would be nice to eat here for a change," Victoria said.

The family assembled in front of the gravestone, and the Buddhist monks began chanting. After they were finished, the bishop stepped up and said a short prayer for the souls of Shang Loong Ma and his wife, Wang Lan Yin, for even though they were never baptized, he hoped that their good deeds and contributions to Singapore would mean that they would not suffer from too much eternal damnation. Victoria nodded approvingly while he prayed, ignoring her mother's daggerlike glare.

When the bishop had moved offstage, the Thai lady's

maids handed Su Yi and Alfred small silver buckets of soapy water and toothbrushes, and the two elderly Shang siblings approached the grave and began scrubbing the headstones. Astrid was always deeply moved by this simple gesture of filial piety, as her ninetysomething-year-old grandmother got on her hands and knees and painstakingly cleaned the tiny crevices in an intricately carved tomb panel.

After the cleaning ritual was over, Su Yi placed a bouquet of her prized dendrobium orchids in front of her father's headstone, while Alfred placed a vase of camellias next to his beloved mother's. Then each of the family members took turns coming forward and placing offerings of fresh fruit and sweets by the grave. When the cornucopia of food had been laid out like a Caravaggio still life, the Buddhist monks lit joss sticks and said some final prayers.

The family then adjourned to lunch underneath the tent. As Alfred Shang passed Harry Leong on the way to the table, he took a folded piece of paper out of his trouser pocket and said, "Oh, here's that info you wanted. What's this all about? I had to twist a few more arms than I expected."

"I'll explain later. You'll be at Tyersall for Friday night dinner, right?"

"Do I have a choice?" Alfred sniggered.

Harry sat down at the table and scanned the paper quickly. He then put it away and began digging into the first course of chilled mung bean soup.

"Now Astrid, I heard you were just in Paris. Was it as lovely as always?" Lillian May Tan asked.

"It was wonderful. The biggest surprise was running into Nicky."

"Nicky! Really? I haven't seen him in ages!"

Astrid glanced a few paces down to make sure her grandmother was safely out of earshot. "Yes, he was there with Rachel, and we had a rather exciting evening together."

"Tell me, what's his new wife like?" Lillian May asked in a lowered voice.

"You know, I really like Rachel. Even if she wasn't married to Nicky, she's the sort of person I would definitely be friends with. She's quite—"

Just then, Astrid felt a gentle nudge on her shoulder. It was one of Su Yi's lady's maids, who whispered, "Your grandmother wants you to stop talking about Nicholas *right now* or leave her table."

. . .

After the luncheon, as everyone made their way back to the cars, Harry walked alongside Astrid and asked, "Do you keep up with that Charlie Wu?"

"I do from time to time—why?"

"Uncle Alfred just supplied me with the most intriguing tidbit. You know how you asked the other day if I acquired Michael's first company? I decided to dig deeper, since it did always strike me as odd how he was able to sell that company for so much money."

"Oh, did Charlie lend you a hand?"

"No, Astrid—Charlie was the one who bought the company."

Astrid stopped dead in her tracks. "You're joking, right?"

"Not at all. The real joke is Charlie Wu secretly paying three hundred million dollars for a tiny tech start-up."

"Dad, are you absolutely sure about this?"

Harry took out the piece of paper and showed it to Astrid. "Listen, this was really tough info to come by. Even our top finance guys turned up nothing but dead ends, so I had to ask Uncle Alfred to help, and you know he is never wrong. Charlie obviously went to great lengths to hide his ownership in a complex web of shell corporations, but you can see the proof in this document as clear as day. Now, what is he plotting at? That's what I want to know."

Astrid stared at the paper in disbelief. "Dad, do me a favor—please don't mention a word of this to Michael or anyone else until I find out more."

After everyone had departed, Astrid remained at the cemetery. She sat in her car with the air-conditioning on full blast for a few minutes, preparing to leave, but then she turned off the engine and got out. She needed to walk a bit. Her head was spinning, and she desperately needed to make sense of the startling news she had just learned. Why in the world had Charlie bought her husband's company? And why had he never told her? Did Charlie and Michael have some secret agreement all along? Or was there a darker scheme that she couldn't even begin to fathom? She didn't know what to think, but she couldn't help feeling strangely betrayed by Charlie. She had poured out her heart and soul to him, and he had deceived her. Could she ever trust him again?

Astrid wandered down an overgrown path into a deeper part of the woods, passing long creepers dangling from the limbs of towering rain trees and old graves covered in moss. Birds cackled loudly in the trees overhead, and small butterflies darted in and out of gigantic ferns. Finally she could breathe again. She felt totally at ease in these woods—they were almost the same as the woods she had spent her childhood playing in at Tyersall Park. At a clearing where rays of sunlight filtered through the verdant foliage, Astrid came upon a small gravestone nestled by the sprawling roots of a large banyan tree. There was a distinctive sculpture of a cherubic angel crouched on top of the tomb, its huge wings unfurled and arching all the way over its head. A tiny oval sepia-toned portrait of an earnest-looking little boy dressed in a white suit was centered behind glass on the headstone. He would have been around Cassian's age when he died. There

was something so tragic and yet beautiful about that gravestone, and Astrid was reminded of the graves at Père Lachaise
Cemetery in Paris.

On one of their frequent trips back when they were living
in London during their university days, Charlie had shown her
the tomb of Abelard and Héloïse. When they finally arrived
at the grand tomb, they found it strewn with love letters, and
Charlie explained: "Abelard was a great philosopher in the
twelfth century who was hired to teach Héloïse, a young noble-
woman who was the niece of Notre Dame's Canon Fulbert.
They fell in love and had an affair, which led to Héloïse becoming pregnant and the two of them getting married in secret.
When Héloïse's uncle discovered the affair, he had Abelard
castrated and Héloïse sent to a nunnery. They could never see
each other again, but they sent each other passionate letters
for the rest of their lives, letters that have become among the
most famous in history. The bones of the lovers were finally
reunited here in 1817, and ever since, lovers from all over the
world have been leaving letters on this tomb."

"Ohh—how romantic!" Astrid sighed. "Will you promise
you'll never stop sending me love letters?"

Charlie kissed her hands and declared, "I promise I will
never stop sending you letters of love, Astrid. Until my
dying day."

As Astrid stood alone in the middle of the forest recall-
ing his words, it was as if she could suddenly hear the trees
speaking to her. In the deepest hollows of bark, in the rus-
tling of leaves, she could hear them whisper, *He did it out of
love, he did it out of love.* And suddenly it all became so clear.
Charlie had bought Michael's company to help save her marriage. He had overpaid by hundreds of millions because he
wanted Michael to have a fortune of his own, to give him a
chance to overcome his feelings of inadequacy. It was an act
of pure, unselfish love. Everything Charlie had done three

years ago began to make sense now—advising her to wait at least a year before agreeing to a divorce, telling her, *I have a feeling Michael could have a change of heart.* Michael did have a change of heart, but not in the way that anyone could have anticipated. He had transformed into a completely unrecognizable man. The modest, unassuming soldier had become a brash, maniacal billionaire. And he wanted her to become a different type of wife to match him. Astrid realized how much she had struggled to change for Michael, and how much she no longer wanted to. What she truly wanted, what she had always wanted but failed to realize until this moment, was someone who loved her just the way she was. Someone like Charlie. Oh, Charlie. In another lifetime they could have been happy together. If only she hadn't broken his heart the first time. If only she had been stronger and stood up to her parents the first time. If only he wasn't married with two beautiful kids of his own. If only.

## MAR VISTA

"When was the last time you saw them?" Corinna asked Kitty when they were comfortably seated in the Tesla that had come to fetch them from the airport.

"Three weeks ago. I try to spend a week every month here, but honestly, it's become a huge challenge lately because of my daughter's regimen."

"So it *is* true. Bernard and your daughter are here in LA for medical treatment?"

Kitty let out a weary laugh. "I have no idea how that rumor got started. Bernard was here for treatments, but not the kind you're thinking of."

"What kind of rare disorder is it?" Corinna asked, her eyes widening.

Taking a deep breath, Kitty began her story: "It all started right after we got married in Las Vegas. We stayed there for a few days, and one night we went to see the latest Batman film. I didn't realize then how obsessed Bernard was with Batman, how he saw himself as an Asian version of Bruce Wayne. With his obsession for exotic cars and creepy interior design, I should have guessed. So when we got back to Hong Kong, Bernard was fixated on wanting to look like that actor from Batman. He found this top plastic surgeon who supposedly specialized in making people look like celebrities, this doctor in Seoul. We had long talks about it, and hey, I didn't mind if my husband wanted to look like some handsome actor. I thought it was quite exciting, actually. But then . . ."

"My God, they botched the surgery, didn't they?" Corinna said, on the edge of her bucket seat.

"No, the surgery actually turned out perfect. But a colossal mistake was made by the prep team before the surgery took place. It was a computer mistake—the most advanced plastic surgery in Korea is all computer-aided these days, and the AutoCAD 3D imaging program that was 'designing' Bernard's new face received the wrong information. It was a language issue—the nurse heard the name wrongly from the doctor before the surgery and she typed the wrong actor's name into the computer. So all the anatomical impressions they made were a mistake, and all the implants were fabricated for the wrong face. Bernard came out of the surgery looking nothing like what he intended to."

"I have to ask, who was the actor the nurse confused him with?"

Kitty sighed. "It was supposed to be Christian Bale, but instead the nurse heard *Kristen Bell*."

Corinna's jaw dropped. "That perky blond actress?"

"Yes. Turns out they had another patient from Hong Kong that was transitioning from male to female. It was an honest mistake."

"Is this why Bernard has been hiding from everyone in Asia?"

"No. I mean, at first, yes, but that's not really the reason anymore. Bernard and I came to Los Angeles so he could get corrective plastic surgery. He found a great doctor who has been slowly transforming his face back to normal. But now the problem goes far beyond his surgery."

"What do you mean?"

"This experience has completely changed Bernard. Not just physically but psychologically. You'll understand when you see him."

At this point, they arrived at a small two-story English cottage–style house in Mar Vista where a little girl and a man were doing yoga in the front yard with a tall blond instructor.

"Oh my goodness—is that cute little girl your daughter?" Corinna asked, staring at the girl with the long braided hair executing a perfect downward-facing dog.

"Yes, that's Gisele. Here, put on some of this organic hand sanitizer before you meet her."

As soon as the car came to a stop, Gisele broke from her yoga pose and came running toward them.

"Did you put on the Dr. Bronner's?" Bernard yelled urgently at Kitty.

"Of course," Kitty yelled back, as she hugged her daughter tightly. "My darling! I've missed you so much!"

"You're not supposed to say that! We don't want to implant attachment issues," Bernard chastised. "And you're supposed to speak to her in Mandarin only. I get English and Cantonese, remember?"

"*Hoy es el día de español, no?*"* the little Chinese girl said, furrowing her brow.

"My goodness, she can speak Spanish so well already! How many languages is she learning?" Corinna inquired.

"Just five right now—she has a part-time Colombian nanny who only speaks to her in Spanish, and our live-in chef

---

*    "Today is Spanish day, right?" (Said in perfect Spanish.)

is French," Kitty replied. "Gisele, this is Auntie Corinna. Can you say hello to Auntie Corinna?"

"*Buenos días, Tía Corinna,*" Gisele said sweetly.

"We're going to start her on Russian when she turns three," Bernard said, coming up to greet the ladies.

"Bernard, my goodness, it's been much too long!" Corinna said, trying not to appear too shocked as she studied his new face. The man she had seen at so many galas was transformed in a way she could never have possibly imagined. His round-ish Cantonese features had been replaced with an angu-lar jawline, but it was incongruously paired with the tiniest birdlike nose. His cheekbones were newly chiseled, but his eyes were strangely elfin and upturned at the corners. *He looks like the love child of Jay Leno and that Hermione girl from the Harry Potter movies,* Corinna thought, unable to stop staring at his face.

"Come now, it's time for Gisele's cranial-sacral session, and then we can have lunch," Bernard said as he shepherded the girl indoors.

Corinna was already quite shocked that Bernard Tai, who grew up in huge mansions and on the biggest superyachts, would be living in such modest surroundings, but nothing prepared her for what she saw upon entering the house. The living room had been turned into a kind of clinic, with all sorts of unusual therapeutic contraptions everywhere, and Gisele lay quietly on a professional massage table as her cranial-sacral specialist gently stroked her scalp. Next to this was an alcove room that resembled a Scandinavian classroom, with simple blond-wood stools and little tables, hemp fabric cushions on the floor, and a corkboard wall where dozens of children's drawings and finger paintings were pinned up.

"This used to be the dining room, but since we always have mealtime in the kitchen, we've turned it into a learn-ing space. Gisele's coding class meets here three times a week now. Come, let me show you to your guest room, where you can freshen up before lunch," Bernard said to Corinna.

Corinna tried to do a bit of unpacking in her cramped bedroom. She took out the tin of Almond Roca candies that she had splurged on and went downstairs, where she found the family was already seated around a wooden farm table on the small patio deck.

"I brought you a little present, Gisele," Corinna said. She handed her the shiny pink tin with the plastic lid, and the two-and-a-half-year-old stared at it in absolute puzzlement.

"*Wah lao!* Plastic! Put that down now, Gisele!" Bernard gasped in horror.

"Oh I'm sorry, I forgot to tell you—there's no plastic in this house," Kitty whispered to Corinna.

"Not a problem. I'll just take the candies out for her and you'll never see the container again," Corinna said calmly.

Bernard gave Corinna a withering look. "Gisele is on a sugar-free, gluten-free organic farm-to-table Paleo diet."

"I am terribly sorry—I had no idea."

Seeing the look on Corinna's face, Bernard softened a little. "I'm sorry. I don't think guests, especially those visiting from Asia, are prepared for our lifestyle. But I hope you will appreciate the conscious, nourishing food we consume in this house. We have our own farm up in Topanga where we grow all our produce. Here, try some of this fennel-stuffed acorn squash. We just harvested it yesterday. Gisele plucked the fennel with her own hands, didn't you, Gisele?"

"*Sólo comemos lo que cultivamos*,"[*] Gisele chirped, as she began chewing carefully on her tiny slices of medium-rare grass-fed-and-finished filet mignon.

"I guess you probably won't be drinking the Johnnie Walker Black Label I brought for you," Corinna remarked.

---

[*]   Spanish for "We only eat what we grow."

"I honor your gesture, but I only drink reverse-osmosis water these days," Bernard said.

*"I honor your gesture?" My God, look what happens to Hong Kong men when they move to California,* Corinna thought in horror.

After Corinna had politely swallowed down the blandest meal of her entire life, she stood in the foyer watching as Bernard helped Gisele put on her TOMS sneakers and her little hemp sun hat.

Kitty pleaded with Bernard. "We just arrived. Can't Gisele skip one session today and be with us? I want to take her to buy some cute clothes at Fred Segal."

"You're not buying her any more clothes from that temple of materialism. The last time you got her those frilly pink princess dresses, we ended up donating all of it to Union Rescue Mission. I really don't want her to be wearing clothes that reinforce gender stereotypes and fairytale narratives."

"Okay, then, can we just take her to the beach or something? The beach is still allowed, right? Isn't sand gluten-free or whatever?"

Bernard took Kitty around the corner and said in a hushed tone, "I don't think you really understand how much Gisele needs these biweekly mindfulness sessions in the sensory deprivation float tank. Her Reiki practitioner tells me that she still struggles with retained trauma and anxiety related to her passage through the birth canal."

"Are you kidding me? In case you don't remember, I was there when she was born, Bernard. The real trauma was how she murdered *my* birth canal because you wouldn't let me have an epidural!"

"Shhh! Do you want to add to her repressed guilt?" Bernard said in hushed whisper. "Anyway, we'll be back by six. Her float session in Venice Beach only lasts forty-five minutes, and then she has an hour of undirected play with her real-world-immersion friends in Compton."

"So why would that take five hours?"

Bernard gave Kitty an exasperated look. "Traffic, of course. Do you know how many times I have to get on the 405?"

After saying *adiós* to Gisele as she was being carefully strapped into the custom-designed car seat in Bernard's Tesla, Kitty and Corinna sat down to talk.

"I understand now why you said I had to see this with my own eyes. When did things get this bad?" Corinna asked.

Kitty looked at Corinna sadly. "The problem began when Bernard started getting his corrective surgeries in LA. He would spend a great deal of time at Dr. Goldberg's clinic, and he became friends with some of the patients in the waiting room—mainly these super-competitive young Westside mothers. One of them invited him to a weekend retreat in Sedona, and that was all it took. He came back to Singapore a changed person, declaring that he wanted to stop all the surgeries and embrace his new face. He talked about his terrible childhood and how he had a father who ignored him and just threw money in his direction and a mother who was too obsessed with her church to care. He wanted to undo all the generations of damage by becoming an enlightened, conscious parent. The first year after Gisele was born was the worst. Bernard moved us to Los Angeles when Gisele was just two months old—claiming that Singapore was toxic for her, that his parents were toxic for her. Here, I was totally isolated, with Bernard hovering over us every second of the day, policing every single thing I did. Nothing I ever did was right—I was always exposing the baby to something. I mean, the only thing I was exposing her to were my tits! We went to about fifty different specialists a week for every little problem. The last straw was when he redesigned the master bedroom to suit Gisele's sleep patterns. I couldn't sleep in there with all those strange glowing LED lights, the over-purified air, and the Mozart playing in her crib throughout the night. That's when I started coming back to Hong Kong every month. I couldn't take it anymore. I mean, just look at how we live!"

"I was very surprised when we pulled up to this house," Corinna said.

"We moved out of our mansion in Bel Air because Bernard wants Gisele to experience 'real-world preparedness.' And he thinks that by living in this lower-income zip code, she'll have a better chance of getting into Harvard."

"Does Bernard ever ask you what you want for your daughter?"

"I have no say in any of this, because apparently I'm too stupid to understand anything. You know, I actually think Bernard prefers it when I'm in Asia. I think he's afraid I will somehow make this child more stupid. He doesn't even care if I exist anymore. It's all about his precious daughter, twenty-four hours a day."

Corinna looked at Kitty sympathetically. "Take it from me, speaking not as your social consultant but from one mother to another, if you really want your daughter to grow up normal, if you ever want her to take her rightful place in Asian society, you have to put a stop to all this."

"I know. I have been working on a plan," Kitty said softly.

"I'm glad to hear that. Because if *Dato'* Tai Toh Lui could see how his only granddaughter was being raised, he would be spinning in his grave! This little girl should have a bedroom in Queen Astrid Park or Deep Water Bay that's bigger than this whole house, not sleeping with her parents every night!" Corinna declared, her voice quivering with conviction.

"Amen."

"This little girl needs to be raised properly—by a team of sensible Cantonese nannies, not interfering parents!" Corinna pounded on the table.

"You got that right!"

"This little girl should be dressed in the prettiest clothes from Marie-Chantal and taken to the Mandarin for afternoon tea and bright pink macarons every week!"

"Fuck yeah!" Kitty roared.

# TRIUMPH TOWERS

THE PEAK, HONG KONG

Nick and Rachel sat beside each other on deck chairs on the balcony, holding hands as they gazed at the magnificent view. Eddie's penthouse apartment was like a falcon's lair high up on The Peak, and below them sprawled the city's dramatic skyscrapers, followed almost too startlingly soon by the sparkling blue waters of Victoria Harbour.

"This ain't half bad," Nick commented, enjoying the cool breeze blowing against his sun-warmed skin.

"Definitely ain't bad," Rachel said. It had been two days since she was discharged from the hospital, and she was relishing every moment outdoors. "You know, when Eddie first insisted that we stay with him since Fiona and the kids were away, I got a bit scared. But this has turned out to be such a treat. He wasn't kidding when he said that staying with him would be like staying at Villa d'Este."

As if on cue, Laarni, one of the domestic helpers, came onto the balcony with two tall tumblers of Arnold Palmers, complete with oversize ice cubes and paper umbrellas.

"Oh my God, Laarni, you shouldn't have!" Rachel said.

"Sir said you need to drink more liquids and get well," Laarni said with a gracious smile.

"You know, I never thought I'd ever say this, but I could get used to this. Laarni is just amazing. Do you know what she tried to do yesterday when I went to meet Carlton for lunch? She insisted on coming downstairs to the driveway with me, where Eddie's chauffeur was waiting. Then she opens the car door and after I got in, she suddenly leaned into the car, reached over me, and PUT MY SEAT BELT ON FOR ME!"

"Oh yeah, the seat belt thing. I guess you've never had that done for you before," Nick said nonchalantly.

"Jesus, for a split second I thought she was trying to make a pass at me—I was so shocked! I said, 'Laarni, do you do this for Eddie and Fiona too?' She said, 'Yes ma'am, we do it for the whole family.' Your cousins are so pampered they can't even put their own seat belts on!" Rachel said in mock outrage.

"Welcome to Hong Kong," Nick quipped.

Rachel's cell phone rang, and she picked it up. "Oh! Hello, Father . . . Yes, yes, thank you—I feel a million times better . . . You'll be in Hong Kong today? . . . Oh, definitely. Around five? Yes, we're free . . . Okay then. Safe travels."

Rachel put down the phone and looked at Nick. "My dad's coming to Hong Kong today, and he's wondering if we can meet him."

"How do you feel about that?" Nick asked. Over the past few days, Carlton had shared with them everything that had happened when he had rushed back to Shanghai to confront his parents, and there had been nothing but silence from the Baos since then.

"I *would* like to see him, but it's going to be rather awkward, isn't it?" Rachel said, her face clouding over a bit.

"Well, I'm sure he feels even more awkward than you do. I mean, his wife is one of the prime suspects in your poisoning. But at least he's making an overture to come and see you."

Rachel shook her head sadly. "God, this is all so fucked up. Why do things always get fucked up when we come to Asia? Don't answer that."

"Would it make you feel more comfortable if he just came over here? I'm sure Eddie would relish the opportunity to show off his Biedermeier furniture or his humidity-controlled shoe closet."

"Sweet Jesus, that shoe closet! Did you notice that all his shoes were arranged alphabetically according to brand?"

"I sure did. And you think *I'm* obsessive with my shoes."

"I will never say anything about your weird OCD habits again, not after meeting Edison Cheng."

. . .

At four forty-five, Eddie was rushing around his apartment like a madman, yelling at his maids. "Laarni, that's the wrong one! I said *Bebel* Gilberto, not Astrud Gilberto!" Eddie screamed at the top of his lungs. "I don't want the Girl from fucking Ipanema to be playing when Bao Gaoliang arrives— he's one of my most important clients! I want track two of *Tanto Tempo!*"

"Sorry, sir," Laarni called from the other room as she nervously tried to find the song on the Linn music system. She scarcely knew how the damn thing worked, and it was even harder to use the remote with the cotton gloves that Mr. Cheng made her wear whenever she came near his precious stereo, which he kept harping was worth more than her entire village in Maguindanao.

Eddie stormed into the kitchen, where the two Chinese

maids were sitting by the small television watching *Fei Cheng Wu Rao*.* They jumped up from their barstools when he entered. "Li Jing, is the caviar ready?" he asked in Mandarin.

"Yes, Mr. Cheng."

"Let me see it."

Li Jing opened the Subzero fridge and proudly took out the sterling silver caviar server that filled up an entire shelf.

"No, no, no! You're not supposed to refrigerate the whole thing! Only the caviar gets refrigerated! I don't want the whole damn caviar tray to be sweating like a Cambodian whore when it comes out of the fridge! Now wipe it dry and leave it out. Right when our very important politician guest arrives, you put the ice in here, see? And then you lay the glass caviar bowl over it. Like this, see? And make sure you use crushed ice from the fridge, not the cubed ice from the ice machine, okay?"

*These maids are useless, absolutely useless*, Eddie lamented to himself as he walked back to his dressing room. It didn't help that his maids never seemed to renew their contracts after the first year. He had tried to steal away some of his Ah Ma's impeccably trained staff while he was in Singapore, but those servants were more loyal than the Nazis.

Eddie checked for lint on his herringbone jacket for the tenth time in his gilt Viennese Secession mirror. He had paired it with his tight DSquared jeans, thinking it made him look more casual. The doorbell suddenly chimed. Fucky fuck, Bao Gaoliang was early!

"Laaaarni, cue the music! Charity, turn on the accent lights! And Charity, you're having a better hair day—you answer the door!" Eddie yelled, as he rushed into the formal living room.

---

* An immensely popular Chinese dating game show, known in English as *If You Are the One*. A national uproar occurred after a poor suitor asked a female contestant whether she would ride a bicycle with him on a date and she famously replied: "I would rather cry in a BMW than smile on a bicycle!"

Nick looked on in amazement as his cousin began doing karate chops on all the tasseled throw pillows, frantically trying to create the perfect fluffed-up look.

Rachel, meanwhile, went to the front door. "I'll get it, Charity."

"Nicky, you really need to train your wife to let the maids do what they're supposed to do," Eddie said to his cousin sotto voce.

"I wouldn't dream of trying to change her," Nick responded.

"Hiyah, this is what happens when you go and live in America," Eddie said disparagingly.

Rachel opened the door, and standing in front of her was her father looking like he'd aged ten years. His hair wasn't as meticulously combed as it normally was, and there were heavy bags under his eyes. He reached out and hugged her tightly, and Rachel knew at that moment that there was nothing to feel uncomfortable about around him. They entered the formal living room arm in arm.

"Bao *Buzhang*, such an honor to have you in my home," Eddie said cordially.

"Thank you so much for inviting me over on such short notice," Gaoliang said to Eddie, before turning back to Rachel with a tender look. "I am so relieved to see you looking so well. I'm very sorry that this trip has turned out so badly for you. It was truly not what I had intended when I invited you to come to China. I'm not just talking about your, er, incident. I'm talking about myself, and all the complications that have prevented me from spending more time with you."

"That's okay, Father. I have no regrets about this trip— I've enjoyed getting to know Carlton."

"I know he feels the same as well. By the way, I really must thank you for what you did for Carlton in Paris."

"It was nothing," Rachel said modestly.

"Which brings me to what I'm really here to talk about. Listen, I realize what a strange situation this must be for both of you. I've had many meetings over the past few days with the commissioner of police in Hangzhou, and I just came from meeting his counterpart Commander Kwok in Hong Kong. Now, I believe with all my heart that my wife has nothing to do with your poisoning. I don't think it's any surprise to you at this point that Shaoyen has been harboring some issues around your visit, and I can only blame myself for that. I handled things badly with her. However, she's just not the sort of person who would ever harm a soul."

Rachel nodded diplomatically.

Gaoliang let out a sigh. "I'm going to do everything in my power to help bring whoever was responsible for this terrible crime to justice. I know that the Beijing police have Richie Yang under twenty-four-hour surveillance now, and the entire city of Hangzhou has been turned inside out with this investigation. I have every confidence that the police are getting closer to the truth with every hour that passes."

Everyone else remained silent, unsure of what to say after Gaoliang's monologue, and Li Jing chose this moment to enter the living room pushing a gleaming silver cart with the caviar. Eddie noticed in annoyance that the bottom was filled with ice cubes, and not crushed ice as he had specifically requested. Now the glass bowl sat on the cubes at a slight angle, and he tried not to be distracted by it. Charity followed along with a just-opened bottle of Krug Clos d'Ambonnay and four champagne flutes. Fucky fuck, he'd told the maids to get out the vintage Venini glasses, not the everyday Baccarat!

"Some caviar and champagne?" Eddie said, trying to lighten the mood, all the while shooting daggers at Charity, who wondered what he was so upset about. Did she bring the champagne in too early? He did say to bring it in eight minutes after the important guest arrived, and she had timed it exactly on the grandfather clock. Sir kept glaring at the champagne flutes. Oh shit, she'd used the wrong glasses.

Rachel and Nick helped themselves to some caviar and champagne, but when Gaoliang was offered a glass, he shook his head politely.

"No champagne, Bao *Buzhang*?" Eddie said, rather disappointed. He would only have served Dom had it been just Nick and Rachel.

"No, but I wouldn't mind a glass of hot water."

*These Mainlanders and their hot water!* "Charity, could you see to it that Mr. Bao gets a glass of hot water at once."

Gaoliang gazed intently at Nick and Rachel. "I want you both to know that Shaoyen has cooperated one hundred percent with the investigators. She has submitted herself to countless hours of questioning, and she's even handed over all the surveillance videos in our plant in Shenzhen, where the drug is manufactured, so that the police can analyze everything."

"Thank you for making this trip to tell me all this, Father. I know how difficult this must be for you," Rachel said.

"My goodness, it's nothing compared to what you had to go through!"

Charity entered the living room bearing a tray with a carafe of boiling hot water and one of the antique Venini flutes. She set the tray down next to Bao Gaoliang, and before Eddie could fully process what was happening, she began to pour the boiling hot water into the eighty-year-old venetian glassware. A high-pitched cracking sound could be heard as the glass began to crack down its side.

"Nooooooooooooooooooooo!" Eddie suddenly screamed, leaping off the sofa and knocking over the caviar server. A million tiny black fish eggs went flying across the faded antique Savonnerie carpet, and as the other maids ran in to see what

the commotion was, Eddie looked down in panic and began
to pant. "Don't move! This rug cost me nine hundred and
fifty thousand euros at auction! Nobody move!"

Rachel turned to Laarni and said calmly, "Do you have a
Dustbuster?"

. . .

After the caviar incident had been resolved safely with nary
a casualty to a single knot of carpet, the group took their
aperitifs onto the terrace to enjoy the sunset view. Now that
Gaoliang had unburdened himself of all he needed to say,
the mood had lightened considerably. Eddie stood at one
end with Gaoliang, pointing out the houses of every famous
tycoon who lived on Victoria Peak and estimating the value
of their properties, while Rachel and Nick perched at the corner looking down toward the water.

"How are you feeling, hon?" Nick asked, still concerned
about how Rachel was handling everything.

"I feel good. I'm so glad I've cleared the air with my father.
I'm just ready to go home now."

"Well, Commander Kwok said we could leave at the end of
the week if nothing new develops. I promise, we'll go home as
soon as we possibly can," Nick said, wrapping his arms around
her as they looked at the lights coming on all over the city.

Later that evening, while Nick, Rachel, and Gaoliang were
in the middle of dinner with Eddie and his mother, Alix, at
the Locke Club, Gaoliang's cell phone began to ring. Seeing
that it was the Shanghai chief of police calling, he excused
himself from the table and went out to the foyer to take the
call. A few moments later, he came back to the table with an
urgent look on his face. "There's been a huge break in the
case, and an arrest has been made. They want us to come back
to Shanghai immediately."

Rachel felt her gut tense up. "Do I really need to be there?"

"Apparently they need you to identify someone." Gaoliang said gravely.

A little over three hours later, Rachel, Nick, and Gaoliang were back in Shanghai, speeding along in a chauffeured Audi to the Central Police Station on Fuzhou Lu.

"Still no word from Carlton?" Rachel asked.

"Er, no," Gaoliang said tersely. He had been trying to contact Carlton and Shaoyen even before the chartered jet had departed from Hong Kong, but their phones were both going straight to voice mail. Now he was nervously hitting the redial button to no avail.

They arrived at the station and were escorted upstairs to a reception room ablaze in fluorescent lights. An officer with magnificently droopy jowls came into the room and bowed to Rachel's father. "Bao *Buzhang*, thank you for returning so speedily. Is this Ms. Chu?"

"Yes," Rachel said.

"I'm Inspector Zhang. We are going to take you into an interrogation room, and we would like you to tell us if the person we are holding appears familiar to you. You will see them behind a two-way mirror, and they will not be able to see or hear you, so please do not be afraid to speak up. Am I making myself clear?"

"Yes. Can my husband come in with me?"

"No, that won't be possible. But don't worry, you will be with me and several other officers. Nothing is going to happen."

"We'll be right out here, Rachel." Nick squeezed her hand encouragingly.

Rachel nodded and went along with the officer. There were two other detectives already in the first room when she entered. One of them pulled at a cord, and the blinds over a viewing window were lifted. "Do you recognize this person?" Inspector Zhang asked.

Rachel could feel her heart beating furiously in her throat. "Yes. Yes, I do. He was the man who was rowing our boat on the West Lake in Hangzhou."

"He's not a real boatman. He paid off the regular boatman so that he could poison the tea you drank while you were on the boat ride."

"Oh my God! I forgot all about that Longjing tea!" Rachel said in astonishment. "But who is he? Why in the world would he want to poison me?"

"We're not done yet, miss. Come into the next room."

Rachel walked into the adjoining room, and the officer opened up another set of blinds. Rachel's eyes widened in disbelief. "I don't understand. What's she doing here?"

"Do you know her?"

"That's . . ." Rachel stammered. "That's Roxanne Ma— Colette Bing's personal assistant."

# CENTRAL POLICE STATION

FUZHOU LU, SHANGHAI

Nick and Gaoliang were allowed to join Rachel in the viewing booth as Roxanne was subjected to the official interrogation.

"For the millionth time, I keep telling you it was a horrible mistake. I was just trying to send Rachel a little message, that's all," Roxanne said wearily.

"You thought poisoning a woman with a highly potent drug that shut down her kidneys and liver and could have led to her death was a way to *send someone a little message*?" Inspector Zhang asked incredulously.

"It wasn't supposed to be like that. The drug was just supposed to make her vomit for a while and have really bad stomach cramps. It makes you feel like you're dying, when you're not actually. The plan was to send Rachel the flowers along with the note right when she arrived at the hospital in Hangzhou. But before we could get the lilies to her, she had been checked out of the hospital and evacuated to Hong Kong. How the hell was I supposed to know that was going to happen?"

"So why did you wait so long after she was admitted to Queen Mary Hospital in Hong Kong before you sent the note?"

"I had no idea where they took her. She just disappeared! We were frantically searching for her everywhere—I had people in Shanghai, Beijing, all the top regional hospitals looking for her. But we had to wait till her admission record popped up somewhere. It was never the intention to let things get as bad as they did. I just wanted to scare her and make her leave the country. The plan went terribly wrong."

"But why would you want to try to scare Rachel Chu in the first place?"

"I told you this already. Colette was extremely distraught that Carlton Bao might lose part of his inheritance to Rachel."

Gaoliang's jaw dropped when he heard this, while Rachel and Nick looked at each other in confusion.

"Why would this happen?" Inspector Zhang continued.

"Bao Gaoliang and his wife were furious after finding out all the reckless things their son did in Paris."

"Reckless things that were discussed during the dinner at Imperial Treasure?"

"Yes, the Baos got into a fight about Carlton, and Bao Gaoliang threatened to disinherit him."

"This fight occurred in the presence of Colette Bing and yourself?"

"No, the fight happened after we left the room. I had intentionally left Colette's iPhone in the room with the record mode on, and I went back to collect it later."

Gaoliang put his hands to his forehead, shaking his head in disgust.

"And that's when you discovered the Baos talking about disinheriting Carlton?"

"Yes. It was a tremendous shock for Colette. She thought she was helping to smooth things out between Carlton and his parents, but instead it made things far worse. See, I told her, no good deed goes unpunished!"

"Why would Colette Bing care if Carlton Bao gets disinherited?"

"Isn't it obvious? She's pathetically in love with the loser."

"So Colette Bing ordered all this to happen?"

"No, she didn't! I keep telling you she didn't. Colette was just very upset after realizing that she had put Carlton in jeopardy. She couldn't stop crying, and she couldn't stop cursing Rachel Chu, so I told her I would fix things."

"Then she *did* know of your plan to poison Rachel."

"No! Colette never knew what I was going to do. I just told her I would handle it."

"This was such an important mission, and Colette had nothing to do with it?"

"NOTHING AT ALL! And it wasn't an 'important mission.'"

"Stop trying to protect Colette Bing! She *ordered* you to do this, didn't she? This was her plan all along and you were just the minion who did all the dirty work."

"I am not her minion. I am her personal assistant! Do you know what that entails? I manage a direct staff of forty-two employees and a support staff of countless more. I make $650,000 a year."

"Colette Bing pays you so much money, and yet she does not know everything that you do for her? I find that very hard to believe."

Roxanne glared at the inspector contemptuously. "What do you know about billionaires? Do you even know one? Do you have any idea how they live? Colette Bing is one of the richest women in the world, and she is an extremely busy and influential person. Her fashion blog is followed every minute of the day by more than thirty-five million people, and she's about to become the international brand ambassador for one of the biggest fashion companies. Her schedule is packed—she has at least three or four social functions that she is required to show her face at every single night. She has six residences, three planes, ten cars, and she is traveling somewhere every week. Do you think she keeps track of everything that's going on all the time? She's too busy having important meetings with world-famous people like Ai Weiwei and Pan TingTing! My job is to make sure that everything in her professional and personal life goes smoothly. I post all her pictures to her blog! I negotiate all her contracts! I make sure her dogs' feces are the correct shade of maple sugar brown! I see to it that every floral arrangement in six houses and three planes is exquisitely perfect at all times! Do you even know how many floral designers we have on the payroll, and the dramas *they* have? Those bitches could have their own reality show with all the conniving and backstabbing that goes on just to get one compliment out of Colette about some fucking delphiniums! Every single day, I have to make a million and one annoying little problems she is never even aware of go away!"

"So Rachel Chu was just an annoying little problem that needed to go away?"

Roxanne gave Inspector Zhang an indignant look. "I was just doing my job."

Nick turned to Rachel in utter disgust. "Let's get out of here. I've heard more than enough."

The three of them left the police headquarters, and as their SUV drove along the darkened roads of Huangpu, they sat in silence, each contemplating everything that had just transpired. Sitting in the front passenger seat, Bao Gaoliang was a jumble of emotions. He was sickened by Roxanne and Colette, but even more angry at and ashamed of himself. It was all his fault. He had allowed things to spiral out of control with Shaoyen, and as the secrets and lies spun around Carlton became a dangerously tangled web, Rachel was the innocent victim who got caught in it. Rachel, who wanted nothing from him except to get to know him and his family. She deserved so much better. She didn't deserve to be exposed to a family as diseased as his.

Nick appeared to be sitting placidly in the backseat with his arm around Rachel, but inside he was seething with fury. That fucking Colette. *She* was the one who was ultimately culpable for causing Rachel so much pain, and he wanted her to feel the heat along with Roxanne. It was an outrage that Roxanne would be going to jail while Colette got away scot-free. The rich and well-connected were always untouchable, he knew that only too well. But if Rachel hadn't been sitting beside him right now, he would've hightailed it to Colette's house and shoved her face into that ridiculous reflecting pool, with Celine Dion blaring full blast.

Leaning her head against Nick's broad shoulder, Rachel remained the calmest of the trio. From the moment Roxanne began talking in that interrogation cell, Rachel started to feel a tremendous sense of relief. The ordeal was over. There wasn't some crazy irrational stranger after her. It was just the crazy personal assistant of her brother's girlfriend, someone she now felt only intense pity for. All she wanted at this moment was to get to their hotel. She wanted to slip into that luscious bed with the down pillows and silken Frette sheets and just go to sleep.

As their Audi turned onto Henan South Road, Nick noticed that they were going in the opposite direction of their hotel. "Aren't we heading away from the Bund?" he asked Gaoliang.

"Yes, we are. I'm not taking you to the Peninsula. You're going to be staying at my house tonight—where you should have been all along."

They entered a quieter residential area lined with plane trees whose branches created leafy archways over the streets, and the car pulled up outside a gatehouse by a high stone wall. A black wrought-iron gate was opened by a police guard, and the car proceeded along a short curving driveway to a beautiful French manor–style house ablaze in lights. As the SUV rolled up the circular front driveway, the tall oak doors opened and three women came scurrying down the steps.

"Hello, Ah Ting. Is my wife home?" Gaoliang said to his head housekeeper.

"Yes, she's retired upstairs for the evening."

"This is my daughter and her husband. Could you please call the Peninsula and make sure their luggage is brought here immediately? And see that a late supper is prepared for them. Maybe some fish-ball noodle soup?"

Ah Ting gawked at Rachel in utter shock. *His daughter?*

"Please see that the blue bedroom is made comfortable for them," Gaoliang instructed.

"The *blue* bedroom?" Ah Ting asked. The blue bedroom was used only for honored guests.

"That's what I said," Gaoliang said forcefully, glancing up at the second floor and noticing his wife's silhouette in the window.

Ah Ting hesitated for a moment, as if she was going to say something, but then she turned and started barking orders at the two younger maids.

Gaoliang smiled at Rachel and Nick. "It's been a very long day. I hope you don't mind if I bid you good night now. See you in the morning."

"Good night," Rachel and Nick said in unison, as they watched Gaoliang disappear into the house.

. . .

Rachel found herself woken up by a shrill chirping outside the window. Sunlight filtered through the curtains, casting gauzy shadows onto the soft lilac blue walls. Rolling out of the four-poster bed, she walked toward the window and discovered a bird's nest tucked in the eave of the gabled roof. Three hungry little chicks arched their tiny beaks skyward, eager to be fed breakfast by their mother, who fluttered around the nest protectively. She ran to get her iPhone, and leaning daringly out the dormer window, she tried to capture a good shot of the mama bird, which had a distinctive black head, gray body, and a smart dash of blue along her wings. Rachel took a few snaps, and as she put her camera phone down, she was startled by the sight of a lady in a pale yellow mandarin-collared dress standing in the middle of the garden staring up intently at her. It had to be Carlton's mother.

Caught off guard, Rachel blurted out, "Good morning."

"Good morning," the lady replied a little tersely. Then she said in a more relaxed tone, "You found the magpies."

"Yes. I took some pictures," Rachel said, immediately feeling a little foolish for stating the obvious.

"Coffee?" the woman said.

"Thank you. I'll be right down," Rachel replied. She tiptoed around the room for a few minutes, trying not to disturb Nick as she brushed her teeth, pulled her hair into a ponytail, and fretted about what she should wear. Oh, this was ridiculous—the lady had already seen her in her oversize Knicks jersey and Nick's old boxers. A thought occurred to her: Was that lady even Carlton's mother? She threw on a simple embroidered white cotton summer dress and walked gingerly down the graceful curving staircase. Why was she suddenly so nervous? She knew that the Baos had talked till the early hours—there were muffled voices echoing every now and then down the hallway from their guest room.

Where was she supposed to meet the lady? As she peeked around the stately reception rooms on the ground floor, which were filled with an elegant mix of French and Chinese antiques, she wondered what Carlton's mother was going to say to her now, after all that had happened. Carlton's words in Paris suddenly echoed in her mind: *My mother would rather die than let you set foot in her house!*

A maid passing along a corridor with a silver coffee carafe stopped when she saw Rachel poking around. "This way, ma'am," she said, leading her through a set of French doors onto a wide flagstone terrace, where the lady from the garden sat at a dark rosewood bistro table. Rachel walked toward her slowly, her throat suddenly going dry.

The lady watched the girl come out onto the terrace. *So this is my husband's daughter. The girl who almost died because of Carlton.* And as the girl came into focus, a revelation: *My God, she looks just like him. She's his sister.* And just like that, all the fears she had bottled up so deeply, all the thoughts that had been tearing her up inside instantly became meaningless.

Rachel approached the table, and the lady stood up and extended her hand. "I'm Bao Shaoyen. Welcome to my home."

"I'm Rachel Chu. It's a pleasure to be here."

# RIDOUT ROAD

SINGAPORE

When Astrid returned from Friday night dinner at Tyersall Park, Led Zeppelin was blasting at an eardrum-shattering level on the sound system in Michael's study. She carried a sleepy Cassian upstairs to his bedroom and handed him over to his au pair. "How long has it been like this?" she asked.

"I only got home an hour ago, madame. It was Metallica then," Ludivine dutifully reported. Astrid shut the door to Cassian's bedroom firmly and went back downstairs. She peeked into the study and found Michael sitting in the dark in his Arne Jacobsen armchair. "Do you mind turning it down a little? Cassian's sleeping and it's past midnight."

Michael turned off the stereo with one click and remained motionless in his chair. She could tell he had been drinking, and not wanting to pick a fight, she ventured cheerily, "You missed a good time tonight. Uncle Alfred suddenly had a mad craving for durians, so we all dashed off to 717 Trading on Upper Serangoon Road to get some. I wish you could have been there—everybody knows you pick the best durians!"

Michael snorted derisively. "If you think I'm going to sit there and make idle conversation with Uncle Alfred and your father about durians . . ."

Astrid came into the room, turned on a lamp, and sat down on the ottoman facing him. "Listen, you can't keep avoiding my father like this. Sooner or later you're going to have to make peace with him."

"Why should I make peace when he was the one who started the war?"

"What war? We've been over this so many times, and I've told you I know for a fact that my father did not buy your company. But let's say for argument's sake that he did. What difference would that make at this point? You took that money and quadrupled it. You've already proven to everyone—to my father, to my family, to the world—what a genius you are. Can't you be happy with that?"

"You weren't there that morning on the golf course. You didn't hear the things your father said to me, the contempt in his voice. He has looked down on me from the very beginning, and he will never stop."

Astrid sighed. "My father looks down on *everyone*. Even his own children. That's just the way he is, and if you haven't figured that out by now, I don't know what to tell you."

"I want you to stop going to Friday night dinner. I want you to stop seeing your parents every damn week," Michael announced.

Astrid paused for a moment. "You know, I would do that if I thought it made any difference. I know you've been unhappy, Michael, but I also know that your unhappiness actually has very little to do with my family."

"You're right about that. I think I'd be happier if you would also stop cheating on me."

Astrid laughed. "You really are drunk."

"I'm not drunk at all. I've only had four whiskeys. Either way, I'm not drunk enough to ignore the truth when I see it."

Astrid looked him in the eye, unsure if he was being serious or not. "You know, Michael, I am trying so hard to be patient with you, for the sake of our marriage, but you really aren't making it easy."

"So you've been fucking Charlie Wu for the sake of our marriage?"

"*Charlie Wu?* What in the world would make you think I'm cheating on you with Charlie?" Astrid asked, wondering if he had somehow discovered the real truth about his company.

"I've known about you and Charlie from the very start."

"If you're talking about that weekend road trip we took in California with Alistair, you're being ridiculous, Michael. You know we're just old friends."

"Just old friends? *'Oh Charlie, you are the one person who truly understands me,'*" Michael said in a mocking, girlish voice.

Astrid felt a chill go up her spine. "How long have you been eavesdropping on my phone calls?"

"Since the beginning, Astrid. And your e-mails too. I've read every e-mail you've ever exchanged with him."

"How? *Why?*"

"My wife spent two weeks in Hong Kong with one of my top competitors back in 2010. You don't think I'm going to look into that? I was a surveillance specialist for the government—I have all the resources right at my fingertips," Michael bragged coldly.

For a long moment, Astrid was too shocked and outraged to move. She stared at Michael, wondering who this man was in front of her. She used to think he was the most handsome man on the planet, but now he looked almost demonic. At that moment, Astrid realized she could no longer live under the same roof with him. She bolted out of her seat and walked down the breezeway past the reflecting pool to the staircase that led to Cassian's bedroom. She ran up the stairs and knocked on Ludivine's door.

"Yes? Come in." Astrid opened the door and saw Ludivine lying on her bed FaceTiming with some surfer dude on her laptop.

"Ludivine, please pack an overnight bag for yourself and for Cassian. We are leaving for my mother's house."

"When?"

"Right now."

From there, Astrid ran to her bedroom and grabbed her wallet and car keys. As she came downstairs with Ludivine and Cassian, Michael was standing in the middle of the great hall leering at them. She handed the car keys to Ludivine and whispered, "Get in the car with Cassian. If I'm not out in five minutes, drive straight to Nassim Road."

"Ludivine, don't you dare fucking move or I'll mother-fucking break your neck!" Michael shouted. The au pair froze, and Cassian stared at his father wide-eyed.

Astrid glared at him. "Nice language in front of your son, Michael. You know, for the longest time I tried, I really tried. I thought we could save this marriage, for the sake of our son. But the fact that you would invade my privacy in such a fundamental way has shown me how broken our marriage is. You don't respect me, and more importantly, you don't trust me. You've never trusted me! So why do you want to stop us now? Deep down, you know I'm no longer the wife you want. You just won't admit it to yourself."

Michael ran to the front door and blocked it. He grabbed a fifteenth-century Bavarian poleax from the wall and waved it threateningly at Astrid. "You can go to hell for all I care, but you are not taking my son! If you leave this house now, I am going to call the police and tell them you have kidnapped him. Cassian, get over here!"

Cassian started to cry, and Ludivine held on to him tightly, muttering under her breath, "*C'est des putains de conneries!*"*

"Stop it! You're scaring him!" Astrid said angrily.

"I'm going to drag you and your entire family through the mud! You're going to see yourself on the front page of *The Straits Times*! I'll sue you for adultery and desertion—I have all the e-mails and phone recordings to prove it!" Michael snarled.

"If you've read all my e-mails, you should know that I haven't written a single inappropriate thing to Charlie. Not one word! He has been nothing but a good friend to me. He's been a better friend than you could possibly ever imagine," Astrid said, her voice cracking with emotion.

"Yes, I know you've been very careful in covering your tracks. But that home-wrecker Charlie hasn't."

"What do you mean?"

"It's so obvious, Astrid. The guy is so crazy in love with you it's fucking sad. All his e-mails read like pathetic love letters."

In a flash, it occurred to Astrid that what Michael said was true. Every casual e-mail, every text message Charlie had ever written to her was a testament to his love. He had never broken his promise. Not since the day they were at Abelard and Héloïse's tomb in Paris. Suddenly, Astrid was flooded with a power that made her more courageous than ever. "Michael, if you don't move away from the front door right now, I swear to God I will call the police myself!"

"Go ahead! We can both be in the fucking papers tomorrow morning!" Michael screamed.

Astrid got out her phone and dialed 999, all the while smiling calmly. "Michael, don't you know by now that my grandmother and Uncle Alfred are the largest private shareholders of Singapore Press Holdings? We're not going to be in the papers. We're *never* going to be in the papers."

---

* "This is fucking bullshit!" (Sounds so civilized in French, doesn't it?)

# 188 TAIYUAN ROAD

SHANGHAI

"Why do I have to find out from Eleanor Young that my own daughter almost died?" Kerry Chu scolded into the phone.

"I didn't almost die, Mom," Rachel said, stretched out on a chaise lounge in her bedroom at the Bao residence.

"Hiyah, Eleanor said you were on your deathbed! I'm going to catch the first flight to Shanghai tomorrow!"

"You don't need to come, Mom. I can assure you I was never in any danger, and I'm perfectly fine now." Rachel laughed, trying to downplay it.

"Why didn't Nick call me sooner? Why am I the last to know everything?"

"I was only in the hospital for a few days, and since I got back to normal so quickly I really didn't see any reason to worry you. And since when have you started believing everything Eleanor tells you? Are you best buddies now?"

"We are nothing of the sort. But she calls me several times a week now, and I have no choice but to take her calls."

"Wait a minute, why is she calling you several times a week?"

"Hiyah! Ever since she found out at the wedding that I sell houses to all the tech people in Cupertino and Palo Alto, she's been calling me for hot tips on tech stocks. And then she keeps hassling me for news about you. Every few days she wants to know if there's any news."

"News about our trip?"

"No, she couldn't care less about your trip. She wants to know if you're pregnant, of course!"

"Oh God! Now it begins," Rachel muttered under her breath.

"Seriously, wouldn't it be nice to say you conceived a baby in Shanghai? I hope you and Nick have been trying very hard."

Rachel made a sound like she was choking. "Ack! Stop, stop! I don't want to be having this conversation with you, Mom. Please. Boundaries!"

"What do you mean, 'boundaries'? You came out of my vagina. What kind of boundaries do we have? You are already thirty-two, and if you don't start having your babies now, when are you going to start?"

"Duly noted, Mom. Duly noted."

Kerry sighed. "So what happened to the girl who tried to poison you? Are they going to hang her?"

"Oh God, I have no idea. I hope not."

"What do you mean you hope not? She tried to kill you!"

Rachel sighed. "It's more complicated than that. I can't really explain it all over the phone, Mom. It's a long story, one that could only happen in China."

"You keep forgetting I'm from China, daughter! I know much more about the country than you do," Kerry said in annoyance.

"Of course, Mom, I didn't mean it that way. But you just don't know the people and the circumstances that I've been exposed to since getting here," Rachel said, feeling a sadness come over her, as she thought about her encounter with Colette earlier that week.

The morning after they had returned to Shanghai, Rachel had been bombarded with voice mails from Colette: "Oh my God, Rachel, I am so, so sorry. I don't know what to say. I just found out about Roxanne and everything. Please call me back."

Followed very shortly by: "Rachel, where are you? Can I please see you? I called the Peninsula and they said you never checked in. Are you with the Baos? Call me back, please."

Half an hour later: "Hi, it's me again, Colette. Is Carlton with you? I'm really worried for him. He's completely disappeared and not returning my calls or texts. Please call me."

And then in the afternoon, a tearful voice message: "Rachel, I really hope and pray that you know I had NOTHING to do with this. Nothing at all. Please believe me. This is just horrible. Please let me explain."

Nick felt strongly that Rachel should not return any of Colette's calls. "You know, I really don't believe that she's as innocent as Roxanne claims. She's ultimately responsible for what happened to you, and I'd just as soon never see or hear from her again."

Rachel was more sympathetic. "Say what you want about her being an obscenely spoiled princess, but you can't say she hasn't been nice to us."

"I just don't want to ever see you get hurt again, that's all," Nick said, his brow furrowed with worry.

"I know. But I don't believe Colette really wanted to see me hurt, and I certainly don't think she's going to hurt me now. I feel like I owe it to her to at least hear her out."

At five o'clock the next afternoon, Rachel walked into the Waldorf Astoria Hotel on the Bund, tailed discreetly by two of Bao Gaoliang's security men that Nick insisted accompany her. She made her way to the Grand Brasserie, a magnificent space framed by an elliptical mezzanine, tall marble columns that rose up to the second floor, and a stunningly landscaped interior courtyard. Colette got out of her seat and rushed toward Rachel the minute she saw her.

"I'm so glad you came! I didn't know if you would," Colette said, hugging her tightly.

"Of course I would," Rachel said.

"They have a fabulous high tea here. You must try the scones—they're just like the ones at Claridges. Now, what tea do you feel like today? I think I'll have the Darjeeling, that's always the best." Colette fluttered nervously.

"I'll have whatever you're having," Rachel said, trying to put her at ease. She noticed that Colette was dressed in a completely different manner than she had ever seen her—in an austerely elegant gray-and-white dress accessorized with nothing but a Maltese cross made out of old cabochon emeralds. She wore less makeup than usual, and her eyes appeared to be swollen from crying.

"Rachel, you must believe me when I say that I had no idea Roxanne was going to do what she did. It was as much a shock to me as it must have been to you. I never, ever ordered Roxanne to do anything that would harm you. Nothing at all. You believe me, don't you? Please say you believe me."

"I believe you," Rachel said.

"Oh thank God. Thank God." Colette sighed. "For a while there I thought you were going to hate me forever."

"I could never hate you, Colette," Rachel said gently, placing her hand over Colette's.

Two steaming pots of tea arrived, along with a tall silver stand overflowing with daintily cut triangles of sandwiches, scones, and a decadent array of sweet confections. As Colette began piling glistening pastries and fluffy warm scones onto Rachel's plate, she continued to explain herself.

"Roxanne was the one who came up with the idea of eavesdropping on the Baos after we left—it was all her idea. But then, when we heard their conversation, I was in shock, that's all. All I could think of was that I had hurt Carlton, that I had made things far worse for him. And in that moment, just that one moment, I got really upset—not at you, but at the whole situation—and Roxanne misinterpreted my feelings."

"Boy, she *really* misinterpreted," Rachel remarked.

"Yes she did. Roxanne and I . . . we have a complicated relationship. She's worked for me for five years now—she was an eighteenth-birthday present from my father—and she knows me inside out. Before she came to work for me, she had a miserable job at P. J. Whitney, and she's so thankful to me, she doesn't have anything else—I'm her whole life. She's like that Helen Mirren character in *Gosford Park*, the ultimate housekeeper—she can anticipate my needs even before I know what they are, and she does things all the time that she thinks are good for me, even when I don't ask her. But she crossed the line, she really crossed the line. I hope you know I fired her. I sent her a text message firing her the minute I found out everything."

*Yeah, I'm sure she gets great Wi-Fi in her prison cell,* Rachel thought. "What I'm not clear on, Colette, is why you got so upset over Carlton potentially losing some of his inheritance. Why does it matter to you so much?"

Colette looked down at her plate and began to pick at the raisins on a scone. "I don't think you know the pressures I've had to face in my life. I know how fortunate I am, believe me I do, but with this fortune has come tremendous burdens. I'm the only child, and ever since I was born, my parents have had these great expectations of me. They gave me the best of everything, the best schools, the best doctors—you know, my mother sent me to get my eyelids done when I was six? Through my teens, there was always some surgery done on me every year to make me look prettier. But in return they have always expected me to be the best. To be the top performer in school. To be the best of everything. I thought that they were priming me to succeed in business, but it turns out all they want is for me to get married and start giving them grandsons. To them, I am a crown princess, and they only want me to marry a crown prince. Richie Yang was their handpicked choice, and they were so angry when I turned him down. But I don't love him, Rachel. I love Carlton—I'm sure you've always known that—and even though I'm not ready to get married, I want Carlton to be the one when I am ready. I can picture myself with him—he's got that wonderful accent, and the height, and that beautiful face—we would have the most beautiful children together. My father doesn't see any of that. He doesn't understand someone like Carlton, he only gets traditional types like Richie. So Carlton is already in a tough spot, and if he were to lose his fortune—even a small part of it—it would only further diminish my father's view of him. And it would make it even more impossible for me to marry him one day."

"But your family already has so much. More than enough for a hundred lifetimes."

"I know it can't make much sense to you—coming from where you do—but believe me, my father does not think he has enough. Nowhere near."

Rachel shook her head in disgust. "I hope you realize that you're going to have to stand up to your father at some point."

"I realize that. I've already been doing that—I said no to Richie, remember? And now I'm trying to prove to my father that I can do just fine, thank you very much, without his money. I know he's testing me—he's always doing such things—and I know he's not going to cut me off for long. I mean, it's not like he's really going to stop paying the landscape architect at my country estate. But now I need your help."

"What can I do?"

Colette's eyes brimmed with tears. "Carlton finally picked up the phone. He told me to stop calling him. He said so many horrid, horrid things, I don't even want to tell you. And he told me that he never wants to see me again! Can you believe it? I know he's just upset about what happened to you. I know he's feeling guilty, blaming himself in some way. Please, you've got to convince him that you're fine, and that we're friends, and that he doesn't have to be angry at me anymore. I have something very important to discuss with him, and I need to see him as soon as possible. Will you please help me?"

Rachel sat quietly, watching the tears spill down Colette's cheeks. "You know, I haven't seen Carlton since getting back to Shanghai. He hasn't spoken to me or his parents. I don't think he's ready to talk to anyone yet."

"He'll talk to you, Rachel, and I know where he is. He's in the Presidential suite at the Portman Ritz-Carlton—that's where he always hides out. Will you go and see him for me? Please?"

"I can't do that, Colette. I don't want to force Carlton into seeing me until he's ready. And I really don't think I should be getting in the middle of your relationship. Nothing I can say will make him stop feeling the way he wants to feel. You need to give him time to heal, and he needs to figure out for himself what he wants."

"But he never knows what he wants. You have to tell him!" Colette pleaded. "I think the longer he broods about this, the more it will fester—like his accident. He was already such a mess all the time when he was recovering from his accident, I don't want him to get into another mess in his head about this."

"I don't know what to tell you, Colette. People are messy. Life gets messy. Things are not always going to work out perfectly just because you want them to."

"That's not true. Things always end up working out for me," Colette said impetuously.

"Well then I suppose you'll just have to trust that they will this time."

"So you're really not going to go over to the Portman?"

"I just don't see the point."

Colette's eyes narrowed for a moment. "Oh, I get it. You don't want me to get back with Carlton, do you?"

"That's not true."

"Yes, I see now. You want to punish me, don't you?"

"I don't understand—"

"You're still angry about what happened to you."

Rachel gave Colette a look of frustration. "I'm not angry at you. I felt sad for you, maybe, but I was never truly angry."

"You felt *sad* for me?"

"Yes, I felt sad about the whole situation, that things would ever get to a point where Roxanne would feel the need—"

Colette suddenly slammed her fist onto the table. "How dare you feel sad for me! Who do you think you are?"

Rachel jerked back in alarm. "Um, I didn't mean it as an insult, Colette, I just meant—"

"I took pity on you, Rachel Chu! I thought, here is this poor, pathetic orphan girl from America. I paid for your meals, I invited you to my house, you flew on my plane, I paid for the whole damn Paris trip. I gave you special access to the most exclusive places in the world and introduced you to all my important friends, and you can't even do one small favor for me?"

*My God, she's losing it.* Rachel tried to remain calm. "Colette, I think you are being unreasonable here. I am grateful for all the generosity you have shown Nick and me, but I just don't think it's my place to tell Carlton to do anything, especially if it concerns his relationship with you."

"You've never really been my friend, have you? I see you clearly now, in your cheap American clothes and your cheap little jewelry!" Colette spat contemptuously.

Rachel stared at her in shock. *Was this really happening?* She could see that all the other well-manicured women in the dining room were gawking at them now. The two security guards rushed up behind Rachel's chair. "Is everything okay, miss?"

"You brought *security*? Who do you think you are? Oh this is funny, are you trying to imitate me now? Well, I have *double* the security detail that you do! Roxanne was right about you all along—you've been envious of me from day one, and you've been plotting to get Carlton away from me and away from his family. This works out perfectly for you, doesn't it? You want their money all to yourself. Well you can have their pathetic one-point-five billion dollars for all I care—that's nothing compared to what my family has. You're never in your life going to come close to touching me! All the money in the world is never going to buy you my style or my taste because you'll always be common. You're nothing but a common little bastard!"

Rachel sat completely still for a moment, feeling her face get white hot. Deciding that she wasn't going to endure one more second of Colette's deranged abuse, she pushed her chair back and got up from the table. "You know, this is beyond absurd. For a while there I actually felt bad for you, even though I was violently ill for a week because of your actions. But now I have nothing but pity for you. You're right, I will never be like you—thanks so much for the compliment! You're nothing more than a spoiled, entitled little shit. And unlike you, I'm *proud* of my roots—I'm not talking about my birth father, I'm talking about the honest, hardworking mother who raised me, and the amazing family that supported her. We didn't make some crazy fortune overnight, and we won't ever need to hire some fancy butler to teach us manners. You don't live in the real world, you never have, so I'm not even going to try arguing with you—it's way below my pay grade to bother. You sit in your perfect little eco-luxury bubble, while your father's companies are the biggest polluters in China. You may have all the money in the world, but you are the most morally impoverished *child* I've ever met! Grow up, Colette, and get a life!"

With that, Rachel walked out of the hotel and onto the Bund, followed closely by the two bodyguards. "Shall we call the car, miss?" one of them asked.

"You know, if you don't mind, I'd like to get some fresh air. I think I'll be fine from here—I'll see you guys back at the house."

Rachel began walking down the famous curved boulevard, looking up at the gleaming art deco buildings and the red Chinese flags fluttering above them. As she passed a happy bride and groom getting their picture taken outside the Peace Hotel, her phone began to ring. It was Carlton.

"Rachel! Are you okay?" he said, sounding anxious and euphoric at the same time.

"Of course. Why?"

"That fight you just had with Colette   "

"How did you know about that?" Rachel gasped.

"Someone videoed the whole thing on their phone from the mezzanine right above your table. It's gone viral on WeChat! 'Spoiled Bitch Epic Takedown,' that's what they've named it. Blimey—nine million views already!"

# NEWSPAPERS AROUND THE WORLD

*LOS ANGELES DAILY NEWS*

**MAR VISTA CHILD KIDNAPPED IN PRIVATE JET**

*Breaking News*—Van Nuys Airport was the scene of a high-speed chase last night at around 9:50 when LAPD officers pursued a private jet containing a two-and-a-half-year-old kidnapping victim as it sped down runway 16R. At least four squad cars were involved in pursuing the jet but failed to prevent it from taking off and leaving U.S. airspace.

Minutes before, the child's father, Bernard Tai, had made a frantic 911 call reporting that his daughter, Gisele, had been kidnapped from their home at 11950 Victoria Avenue in Mar Vista. Gisele's babysitter allowed an unidentified woman into the home while Tai was out, and the woman departed with the child. By the time the police had tracked down Gisele at Van Nuys Airport, she was already aboard the private aircraft.

Tai, who is a Singapore citizen but resides in Los Angeles, gave his occupation as unemployed and told LAPD that he was Gisele's full-time caregiver. Tai was unreachable for further comment. LAPD would not release any more information about the jet pending further investigation.

*LOS ANGELES TIMES*

## CHILD HEIRESS KIDNAPPED BY HER MOTHER

*Los Angeles*—In a startling new development in the mysterious "private jet kidnapping" of a Mar Vista child two days ago, the *Los Angeles Times* has learned that the kidnapping victim, Gisele Tai, was taken by her mother, former Hong Kong soap opera actress Kitty Pong. Gisele is the sole heiress and only daughter of Bernard Tai, the president and non-executive vice chairman of TTL Holdings, which is headquartered in Hong Kong.

Tai, who told LAPD that he was "unemployed," is said to be worth over $4 billion and maintains lavish residences around the world. He is also the owner of the 388-foot megayacht *Kitty's Galore*. However, for the past two years Tai and his family have quietly resided in a 2,807-square-foot house in the upper-middle-class neighborhood of Mar Vista. "I always suspected Bernard had money, but I never knew he had *that* kind of money. I knew he moved to Mar Vista because he wanted to raise his daughter in the most conscious way possible. He's a terrific father. I never once met the wife," said Linda C. Scout, who took a Nia class with Tai.

Two nights ago, Tai's personal chef, Milla Lignel, who resides at the house and was babysitting that evening, allowed the child's mother, Kitty Pong, into the home. Pong, who is currently estranged from her husband and lives in Hong Kong, removed her daughter from the house. "Madame asked me to make her an omelet, and it only took me *cinq* minutes, but by the time the omelet was ready, madame and Gisele had disappeared," said a tearful Lignel.

Tai knew something was wrong when he was served with divorce papers in the middle of a sound-bath healing workshop in Santa Monica. After speaking with Ms. Lignel, he immediately suspected that his wife intended to leave the country with their daughter. LAPD has confirmed that Tai activated a secret GPS tracking device in Gisele's TOMS shoes that also alerted the police. The police pursued the child to Van Nuys Airport, but it was too late to stop the private Boeing 747-81.

Officer Scot Ishihara, who was on the scene, calmly noted, "We gave chase, but it's hard to stop a 450-ton jumbo jet from taking off if it wants to."

Tai, who has filed kidnapping charges against his wife in Los Angeles, has apparently left the country. Calls to TTL's corporate headquarters in Hong Kong were unreturned.

*SOUTH CHINA MORNING POST*

## KITTY TAI ESCAPED WITH DAUGHTER ON MAINLAND BILLIONAIRE'S PLANE

*Hong Kong*—The Los Angeles Police Department, together with officials at Van Nuys Airport in Los Angeles, can now confirm that the Boeing 747-81 used in the alleged "kidnapping" of heiress Gisele Tai by her mother, Kitty Tai, was owned by Chinese industrialist Jack Bing.

Mr. Bing, who is said to be worth upward of $21 billion, apparently lent Mrs. Tai his $350 million jet at the behest of a mutual friend. Mr. Bing's spokesperson today issued this statement: "Mr. Bing lends his planes from time to time to various individuals and organizations on humanitarian grounds. Mr. Bing is not acquainted with Mrs. Tai in any way, but was urged to provide the plane for what he understood to be a humanitarian rescue mission. Neither Mr. Bing nor his family has played any role whatsoever in what is a private family matter between the Tais."

After a brief refueling stop in Shanghai, Bing's jet landed in Singapore, where representatives for Mrs. Tai say she intends to divorce Bernard Tai and sue for shared custody of her daughter. Tai, who arrived in Singapore earlier today, has already countersued and filed kidnapping charges in both Los Angeles and Singapore.

Giving a brief statement after landing at Changi Airport, Tai, whose face appears to be drastically altered by cosmetic surgery, said, "My wife has never played an active role in the raising of our daughter, and this is a well-documented fact that can be confirmed just by looking at any society magazine to see all the events my wife attends in Asia while her daughter has been in Los Angeles. Gisele has spent most of her conscious life in Los Angeles, and she is missing out on valuable learning and developmental opportunities. This is a tragedy of epic proportions and Gisele needs to be immediately returned to those who truly love her and care for her."

Mrs. Tai was unavailable for comment.

**NOBLESTMAGAZINE.COM.CN**
*The latest scoop from China's most trusted*
*society columnist, Honey Chai*

Is everyone sitting down? Because I have so many scoops for you that we might as well make a giant banana split! First scoop, and you heard it here FIRST: **Mrs. Bernard Tai**, aka **Kitty Pong**, is the mistress of **Jack Bing!** Extremely reliable sources tell me that Pong and Bing have been carrying on for quite a while now; they met two years ago at—get this—*the funeral of Kitty's father-in-law*, **Dato' Tai Toh Lui!** Tai was a great mentor of Bing's, and apparently sparks *really* flew at the crematorium when Jack met Kitty. Meanwhile, a devastated Mrs. Bing has reportedly checked into the health spa at Brenners Park-Hotel in Baden-Baden, Germany. **Colette Bing**, who by all accounts is furious with her father, has also left Shanghai and was last seen canoodling with a certain notorious playboy at a club in Ibiza.

Which brings me to my next hot scoop: Everyone on the planet has by now seen the leaked video of Colette's epic takedown by an unidentified woman. It's the video that made Prêt-à-Couture cancel the multimillion-dollar endorsement deal with Colette. I can now reveal that this woman, whose monologue has become a rallying cry for every non-billionaire in China (and unfortunately, there are still quite a few of us who didn't make it onto the *Heron Wealth List*!), is none other than **Rachel Chu**, the *sister* of Colette's ex-paramour **Carlton Bao**. (Everyone still with me here?) Anyway, the video also led to Carlton and Colette's breakup, and when I asked Carlton how he felt the other night at DR Bar, he gave me a frown and said,

"What breakup? I've always said that Colette wasn't my girlfriend. But she was a good friend at a time I really needed one, and I wish her the best." That's a classy response in my book.

Speaking of classy, Carlton's parents, **Bao Gaoliang** and his wife, **Bao Shaoyen**, hosted a farewell dinner party at Yong Foo Elite last night for his daughter, Rachel Chu, and her husband, **Professor Nicholas Young**, who would be heading back to New York shortly. There wasn't a dry eye in the splendid art deco room when Bao made an emotional toast to his "long lost" daughter, recounting the harrowing story of his youth and how he rescued his infant daughter and her mother from the clutches of an abusive family. The glittering crowd of China's top political and financial powerhouse families clapped wildly after his speech, including Hong Kong's tech titan **Charles Wu**. Wu, who stunned le tout Hong Kong by announcing his separation from his wife, Isabel, just weeks ago, spent the whole night glued to the side of a beautiful lady wearing the most drop-dead-gorgeous pleated white dress. Many at the party seemed to know her, but I was never able to catch her name.

When I can mention Yong Foo Elite, abusive families, and girls in white dresses in the same breath, I know it's time to end my column. In the meantime, stay tuned for more updates on the Bing-Pong affair. I just know there will be more bombshells hurtling our way once all the legal teams get involved!

. . .

"What in God's name are you doing?" Corinna screeched when she was finally able to reach Kitty.

"I take it you've read this morning's paper? Or did you read Honey Chai's latest post?" Kitty said with a giggle.

"You sound almost as if you're proud of yourself!"

"I *am* proud of myself! I finally got Gisele away from Bernard."

"But you've completely sabotaged all the work we've done! This scandal is going to do untold damage to your reputation in Hong Kong!" Corinna moaned.

"You know, I no longer care about all that. Ada Poon can have Hong Kong all to herself—I'm in Singapore now, and there are all these lovely international people here who have lots of fun and don't give a damn about local society. And I've just moved into a fabulous new house on Cluny Park Road. Actually, it's a very old house, but you know what I mean."

"Oh my goodness—you're the mysterious buyer of the Frank Brewer house?"

"Haha. Yes, although just between you and me, it was a gift from Jack."

"So Honey Chai isn't making it up. You *are* Jack Bing's mistress!"

"I'm not his mistress, I'm his *girlfriend*. Jack has been a wonderful friend to me. He has bought me many lovely things, and he has rescued me and my daughter from the hellhole that was Mar Vista. Funny that the neighborhood was called that—it means 'view of the sea,' but the only view we ever had was of that damn 405 freeway."

Corinna sighed. "I guess I can't blame you for escaping from there. How is Gisele doing?"

"She's as happy as any little girl can be. She's in the garden playing on the swing with her grandmother. And she's been discovering wonderful things, like pineapple tarts and Barbie dolls."

"Well, I hope you won't come to regret your actions," Corinna said worriedly.

"Higher, I think. Sorry, what were you saying, Corinna?" Kitty asked, momentarily distracted.

"I said . . . oh never mind. I hope you can work things out with Bernard amicably."

"What does 'amicably' mean?"

"Friendly, peacefully."

"I don't want a war with Bernard. I just want him to be able to share Gisele with me, that's all."

"That's the spirit. Anyway, good luck, and be sure to call me the next time you're in Hong Kong."

"We'll take Gisele for high tea at the Four Seasons!"

"No, the Mandarin. Always the Mandarin. And don't say 'high tea'—high tea is only for factory workers. It's 'afternoon tea.'"

"Of course. Whatever you say, Corinna."

Kitty hung up the phone and took a few steps back. "You know, Oliver, you were right. It didn't need to be higher. Let's move it all back to where you had it originally."

Oliver T'sien winked at her. "I was right when I told you to buy this house, and I was right when I told you to buy the painting, wasn't I? I always imagined it looking utterly exquisite against this wall. It's all about how the light filters in through those old lead-glass windows."

"You're right, it's all going to be utterly exquisite," Kitty said, gazing out the window as the workmen began rehanging *The Palace of Eighteen Perfections* on her drawing-room wall.

## ACKNOWLEDGMENTS

I could not have written this book without the help, inspiration, expertise, patience, support, genius, and general good humor of these remarkable people:

Alan Bienstock
Ryan Matthew Chan
Lacy Crawford
Cleo Davis-Urman
David Elliott
Simone Gers
Aaron Goldberg
Jeffrey Hang
Daniel K. Isaac
Jenny Jackson
Jeanne Lawrence
Baptiste Lignel
Wah Guan Lim
Carmen Loke
Alexandra Machinist
Pang Lee Ting
David Sangalli
Jeannette Watson Sanger
Sandi Tan
Jackie Zirkman